The Ex Factor

Debbie Viggiano

The Ex Factor © Debbie Viggiano 2013

Kindle Edition published worldwide 2013 © Debbie Viggiano

All rights reserved in all media. No part of this book may be reproduced or transmitted in any form by any means, electronic or mechanical (including but not limited to: the Internet, photocopying, recording or by any information storage and retrieval system), without prior permission in writing from the author.

The moral right of Debbie Viggiano as the author of the work has been asserted by her in accordance with the Copyright, Designs and Patents Act 1988.

This book is licensed for your personal enjoyment only. This e-book may not be re-sold or given away to other people. If you would like to share this book with another person, please purchase an additional copy for each recipient. Thank you for respecting the hard work of this author.

ISBN: 978-1494750275

www.debbieviggiano.com

http://debbieviggiano.blogspot.com/

Cover by Robert Coveney

Formatting by Rebecca Emin

www.rebeccaemin.co.uk

Annie picked up her mobile and tapped out a message to her ex-husband.

Remember this Sam. As you sow, so shall you reap...

This book is dedicated to Annie.

Foreward

If you have liked my previous novels and are expecting more of the same, please pause before buying this book. My website headlines Addictive Madcap Romance. This novel is anything but. So if you are expecting a romantic romp with a few giggles, this isn't the book for you.

However, if you are a step-parent, or about to become one, or dating somebody with children and finding the whole thing rather challenging, then go ahead and read it.

Two of my previous novels feature a blended family where everybody is happy and life is sweet. In reality, many second-time-around relationships with children from previous partnerships are a minefield.

I spent time researching on step-parent forums. Many people told of huge difficulties which have pushed a high proportion of second marriages to breaking point.

This novel is a work of fiction. The dramas within are not. The overriding message from this particular forum was a plea to ex partners: please stop and think. Do not allow personal grievances to impact upon others, least of all your children. Point scoring bears no winners.

Otherwise just look what can happen...

Prologue

Josie scrubbed the saucepan viciously. The gunge within had long been removed. But Josie couldn't stop scrubbing. She was aware that the frenzied scouring was odd behaviour. Manic even. But it made her feel better. As if the harder she mashed the wire wool against the saucepan, the greater release from the angst in her heart. The scrubbing action was almost akin to emotional self-cleansing. It was cleaning away all her buried pain, upset and tears. And there'd been plenty of tears. Not just hers either. Her husband Sam had broken down more times than she could recall. At least she and Sam were adults. Adults had to get on with it. Deal with whatever life threw at them. But coping with the tears from her child had been hard. Very hard. At fifteen years of age, Lucy might believe she was worldly wise. But she wasn't. She was still a child. Well, a child-woman. It was hard enough for a teenager to get to grips with all the normal changes that went on – hormones, spots, greasy hair, puppy fat. But add family problems into the mix, and most teenagers would be likely to explode. Except Lucy hadn't exploded. Rather she'd imploded.

How had Josie's precious relationship come to this? Stretched to breaking point with everybody at loggerheads? Well she didn't need a crystal ball to work that one out. The answer was obvious. Sam's ex. Annie had been a thorn in the side from the start. But in the last twelve months, Sam's daughter – previously so sweet – had morphed into her mother. Between the pair of them they'd nearly destroyed Sam. And Lucy. Indeed Josie felt as though her own sanity was questionable. Especially right now, scrubbing uncontrollably. She wondered if there was a manual for people like her and Sam. People who'd married for a second time, and had ex-partners and step-children to deal with. Perhaps she'd Google it. Either that or give in to the tears that were once again threatening to take over. And to think that little more than a decade ago, it had all been so different.

Chapter One
Eleven years previously – September

Josie Payne shouldered the College's exit door and stepped out into September sunlight. Close behind her came the sound of hundreds of hurrying footsteps. Students were pounding down staircases or along the corridors, flooding into the lobby and gushing out of the brick building like a human tidal wave. They spilled into the paved square and flowed past her, splitting into different directions. The majority headed towards the bus stop or the train station. A smaller number towards the College's car park. As a mature student, she was definitely one of the drivers. Josie slung her College bag over her shoulder and patted her coat pockets for the car keys.

'Hey Josie!' a voice called. 'Wait up!'

Josie turned to see Kerry hastening towards her. Like her, Kerry was a mature student on the same access course for teacher training. They'd only known each other three days, but Josie sensed she might have made a new friend.

'Want a lift?' Josie asked.

'Yes please. Just to the main road. I won't take you out of your way.' The two women fell companionably into step. 'So, what did you make of that last chemistry lesson?'

Josie rolled her eyes. 'I didn't understand chemistry at secondary school, and I don't think I'm going to fare any better all these years later.'

'It doesn't help that the tutor is a prat,' Kerry pointed out. 'I mean for God's sake, I was nearly asleep on my text book. Why can't the man speak with some enthusiasm? This is his chosen subject – where is his passion?'

'At the bottom of a Bunsen burner,' Josie laughed. 'Let's hope we don't end up being teachers who talk in a dreary monotone. They should record that tutor's voice and use it as a sleep inducer for insomniacs.'

'At least Environmental Studies is fun.'

'You can't be serious,' Josie snorted. 'That water assignment is enough to try the patience of a saint. Oh I see!' Josie observed

Kerry's shift in body language – the girlish twirling of hair around one finger. 'You've got a crush on the tutor.'

'Don't be daft,' Kerry said, but her blushes gave her away. 'I just think Mr Clark is rather good looking.'

'If you like hairy hands.'

'He hasn't got hairy hands! Simon has very nice hands.'

'Ooh, it's *Simon* now is it!' Josie teased. 'Anyway, you'll be a great teacher. Although at this rate I'm wondering if I'll even succeed in completing this access course.'

Josie wasn't exaggerating. Combining intense studies with being a mum to a four-year-old was hard work. She was juggling an awful lot of balls right now. At least she didn't have a husband to worry about. Although in some respects it might have been easier if she had. There would have been shared childcare. Shopping rotas. Chores would have been divided up. Well, not things like housework. Nick had never been very good at pushing a vacuum cleaner about or tackling a pile of ironing. But he'd mown the lawn, washed the car, and occasionally cooked the odd meal. Some help was better than no help.

For the last seven months there had definitely been no help. Back in February, Nick had died in a car crash whilst driving to work. Josie had been numb with shock. Her brain had been unable to take in all the details. Black ice. A lorry. Instant death. For Josie the details were unimportant. It didn't change the fact that the outcome remained the same. At thirty-five years of age, Josie was a widow.

Nick's life insurance had yielded a decent lump sum. Josie had paid off the mortgage and the car loan. She was left with enough money to cushion her for about three years. When the initial raw grief had subsided into a permanent dull ache, Josie realised she needed to think about the future. At present she might have a bit of money, but it wasn't going to last indefinitely. From now on, she was the sole provider. And she needed a job. But doing what?

Before Lucy had come along, Josie had been a secretary. But commuting to London and being tied to a stressed boss wasn't ideal. Nor could she afford a childminder. And anyway, even if she did have the money for child care, it wasn't what Lucy would want. Her little girl had lost one parent. She needed

Mummy more than ever. Apart from anything else, Josie wanted to be the one greeting her daughter at the school gates. Not a stranger. And what about all those school holidays? Most employers only gave their staff three or four weeks per annum. And then a light bulb moment had flashed through Josie's brain. Re-train. As a teacher. It was a career that would fit in perfectly with her child.

Nervously, Josie had telephoned the local College. Forms had been posted. And before she could say *Are you sure about this?* she'd been accepted on an access course for mature students. It dovetailed perfectly with Lucy starting at the nearby church school. On their respective first days, Josie had walked Lucy into the infants' block and watched her pig-tailed baby skip off, eager to make new friends. Josie hadn't driven to her new place of education with quite the same gung-ho enthusiasm. Once in the College car park, she'd waited a good five minutes simply taking deep breaths. Eventually, on rubber legs, she'd crossed the paved courtyard and disappeared into the bowels of the College. What if she was the *only* mature student? What if her classmates were only in their early twenties? What if she didn't make friends?

Fortunately Josie's fears were unfounded. She'd found herself congregating with fifty other adults of similar age, all hugging cups of machine coffee and wearing terrified expressions. Kerry had been one of them.

Josie popped the central locking system on the car. After a pause of sorting out where to shove bulky book bags and buckling up seatbelts, Josie started the car and put it into reverse.

'Good-bye, College,' said Kerry, 'see you tomorrow.' She sank back into the passenger seat with a sigh. 'Forget this teaching lark for a moment. I need to de-stress. What about we round up a few classmates and go out for a knees-up this Saturday night?'

Josie edged out of the car parking space, but braked momentarily to let another car go. 'Sounds great. But unfortunately you'll have to count me out.'

'Why? Oh God, is it–' Kerry clapped one hand over her mouth.

'No, no,' Josie assured.

'I'm so sorry.'

'Really, it's not that–'

'I quite forgot you're a widow. Me and my stupid mouth. You're still grieving. Trying to get your life back together. And here I am being a totally insensitive moron and suggesting you come out on the pull.'

Josie nosed the car out onto Miskin Road. 'You didn't say anything about pulling,' she gave Kerry a sideways look, 'you simply mentioned a knees-up. And really, it's fine. *I'm* fine. You don't have to pussyfoot around me. I'd be perfectly up for a night out if–'

'Really? You're not just saying that?'

'Yes. I mean no I'm not just saying that, but yes I'd be up for the night out if I had a babysitter. But I don't. And I won't be able to find one at short notice.' Josie didn't want to ask her parents if they'd be willing to help out. Much as they adored their only grandchild, Lucy was too much of a livewire and exhausted them.

'That's no problem! Our Toyah can do it. She's always after earning some pocket money.'

'Oh I don't know about–'

'She won't mind.'

'Yes, but Lucy doesn't know Toyah. And don't take this the wrong way, Kerry, but I don't know Toyah either.'

'Then drop me all the way home and meet her now. Come on. She's lovely. And absolutely adores kids. Your Lucy will be enthralled with her. Promise.'

Josie glanced at the car's digital clock. One minute to three. She had half an hour before Lucy came out of school. And it was true; she was perfectly up for a night out with her new friends. But not the pulling bit. That was the last thing she needed. It wasn't that the idea of meeting a man made her feel disloyal to Nick. Because it didn't. Not really. Nick was dead. No, the reason she didn't want a man in her life ever again was because of Lucy. Josie had already decided that should she ever date in the dim and distant future, the man in question would be kept at arm's length. He would never meet her daughter. Because at the end of the day Lucy's father couldn't be replaced.

'Well I–' Josie could feel herself weakening.

'Swing a left down here,' Kerry nodded. 'That's my house. First on the left.'

'Okay.' Josie decided it would be easier to give in. And perhaps it wouldn't hurt to befriend Toyah. If not this time, there might be other moments in the future where she'd appreciate a babysitter.

Josie parked up. Kerry was instantly out of the car and striding purposefully up to her front door. Josie's fingers pressed the car's key fob. The central locking clunked. Josie took a deep breath and followed her friend into the house.

'Toyah? Oh there you are!' Kerry beamed. 'I want you to meet my friend who has a little girl. She needs a regular babysitter. Josie, this is my daughter. Toyah, meet Josie.'

Josie could feel her jaw being overcome by gravity. 'Hi!' she smiled hastily. Never in a million years was this girl looking after her daughter. Josie stared at the vision before her. Purple backcombed hair framed a chalk white face punctuated with a series of metal studs. A part of Josie's brain wondered why a pretty girl would want to mar her looks with so many piercings. No doubt the girl smoked pot too.

Toyah extended a tattooed hand. 'How do you do, Josie?'

The cut-glass accent took Josie by surprise. 'Er, very well thank you. And you?'

'I'm good thanks. Would you like a cup of tea and you can tell me all about your daughter.'

'Oh, thanks, but I'm going to have to fly. Lucy will be coming out of school shortly. Um, listen. It's really nice of your mum to volunteer your services but–'

'But you're horrified by the way I look and don't want your kiddie anywhere near me,' Toyah laughed good-naturedly.

Josie could feel her face reddening. Had her thoughts been so transparent?

Kerry let out a guffaw. 'I told you not to pierce your face, Toyah. It puts people off.' Kerry turned to Josie. 'My daughter wants to be a criminal lawyer one day. Can you imagine her in court looking like this? The judge will be thinking she's the offender.'

'It's just a phase Mum,' Toyah assured. 'All us students look the same. I'd stick out like a sore thumb if I turned up at my College wearing a pinstripe suit with my hair in a chignon.' Toyah leant against the doorframe and folded her arms against her chest. Josie's eyes were immediately drawn to Toyah's tattooed hand. Toyah followed Josie's gaze. 'And this is a wash-off tattoo. I was just having a bit of fun.'

'Ah,' said Josie. She mentally slapped herself for allowing Toyah's style to intimidate her. With every passing second it was quite apparent that Kerry's daughter was a *nice* girl. 'Do you mind me asking a question?'

'Fire away,' Toyah unfolded her arms and moved over to the kitchen table. Leaning forward, she swiped an apple from the fruit bowl.

'Do you smoke?' Josie omitted the word *pot*.

Toyah bit into the apple with a crunch. For a second her jaw rotated. She then shook her head and swallowed. 'No. Never even tried it. My nan was a chain-smoker and died of cancer. It was the most awful, lingering death.' For a moment Toyah's eyes misted. She blinked. 'Smoking isn't for me. Nor, before you ask, am I interested in drugs or drink. Although,' she paused, 'I quite like a lager shandy if I'm out with my mates, but that's about it.'

Now it was Josie's turn to smile. 'Well, if you're still up for it, would you like to meet Lucy?'

Needless to say, Lucy had adored Toyah.

Saturday dawned. Josie had spent much of the day knocking out the water assignment for the Environmental Studies tutor. Lucy had been an angel playing with her dollies and watching Bear in the Big Blue House on the television. But there was only so long a mother could expect a four-year-old to entertain herself.

'Can we go the park, Mummy?' asked Lucy.

Josie hole-punctured the A4 written work and slid it into a ring-binder. 'I don't see why not.' She glanced out of the study window. The sky was a perfect blue, but Josie wasn't fooled. The boughs of the apple tree were blowing backwards and forwards. Leaves floated down to the damp lawn. Josie gave an involuntary shiver. Autumn was just around the corner. 'A trip to the park would be perfect. But only if you wear a coat.'

'Deal,' Lucy dimpled, and scampered off to her wardrobe.

Mother and daughter spent a good hour in the park. Lucy wobbled around on her bicycle stabilisers, whizzed down the slide and got a little giddy on the roundabout. By late afternoon grey clouds were huddling together. Josie felt the spit of rain against her forehead.

'Come on, darling,' she called to Lucy. 'Time to go home.'

By the time Josie had fed Lucy and herself, cleared up, shared a bath with her daughter and rushed Lucy into her pyjamas, there was little time left to dolly up for her night out with Kerry and the girls. Josie hastily applied party make-up and slid into an ancient black dress covered in sequins. It hung off her. She hadn't realised how much weight she'd lost since Nick's death. But the dress would have to do. She hadn't a clue what people wore to nightclubs, other than celebrities like Katie Price who were regularly photographed stumbling out of London clubs. Well she was hardly like Katie Price, more the pity. And *Passé* was no London nightclub. Josie sprayed her wrists with some perfume Nick had bought her last Christmas.

'Mumm-*eee*,' Lucy called up the stairs. 'There's a taxi outside. And Toyah and Kerry are getting out of it.'

'I'm coming.' Josie grabbed her clutch bag, rammed her feet into some strappy high heels and clattered down the stairs. She opened the front door.

'Ooooh you look nice,' Kerry and Toyah chorused.

Josie wrinkled her nose. 'I feel horribly self-conscious.'

'You won't when I get a couple of gins in you,' said Kerry. 'Come on. Our chariot awaits.' Kerry inclined her head at the waiting minicab.

'Okay, just a tick.' Josie turned to Lucy and scooped her up. 'Whoa. You're getting heavy, little lady. Give Mummy a kiss goodnight.' Small arms entwined her neck.

'Love you, Mummy.'

'I love you too. Be good for Toyah.' Josie allowed Toyah to disentangle Lucy from her. 'And bed no later than eight.'

Now Toyah was shooing Kerry and Josie out of the house. Josie opened the minicab's rear door and sank down into the upholstery. Synthetic material scratched her bare legs which were now covered in goosebumps. Kerry squashed herself in next to Josie. The minicab's doors slammed shut on the chill evening air.

'Where to, ladies?' asked the driver.

'Boogles,' said Kerry.

'I thought we were going to Passé,' said Josie in alarm.

'We are. Later. It's only half seven. We'll get a few drinks in us first. Boogles is a really trendy bar. You'll like it.'

'What about the others?'

'We're meeting them in the club at nine. I thought it would be nice for me and you to have a bit of a natter beforehand.'

Josie raised her eyebrows but didn't comment. Privately she thought it odd to exclude the rest of the girls from a bit of chitchat. Josie dismissed the matter and stared out of the window. It was dark now and the roads were busy. Saturday night going-out traffic. The rest of the girls in their group were either divorced or separated. Josie turned her attention back to Kerry. 'You're the only married woman in our group. Doesn't your husband mind you going out on the razzle?'

Kerry looked a bit shifty. 'Ah. That's what I want to talk to you about.'

Chapter Two

'Two gin and tonics please,' Kerry hoisted herself up on a tall stool before turning to Josie. 'You can get the next round.'

'No problem.' The drinks arrived, brimming with ice and a slice. 'Cheers!' The women clinked glasses.

Josie took a sip and looked around. Boogles was full. Women stood around in cliques. Some were eyeing up City guys who were sharing sports anecdotes or bragging about who they'd sacked from work that week. The chatter was loud and interspersed with laughter.

Kerry fidgeted on her stool. A regrouping gesture. Josie took another sip of her drink. Her eyes met Kerry's over the rim. She put the drink down. 'So what did you want to tell me that isn't for the rest of the girls' ears?'

Kerry fiddled with her drink, twirling it round on its paper doily mat. 'You asked if my husband minded me being out tonight. Well, he does. Enormously. But even more, he hates me going to College. In fact, he's giving me a really hard time at the moment. I've had the week from hell.'

'I'm sorry to hear that.' Josie had only known Kerry a few days. She wasn't sure whether her new friend would welcome being questioned. But then again, might it be interpreted as rude not to ask? 'Tell me it's none of my business, but can I ask what's happened?'

Kerry sighed. 'Adam is insisting I give up College.'

'But you've only just started.'

'Yeah, I know. But he's so controlling. He wasn't happy about me enrolling on this course. He wants me back home, pinny on, slave to his every whim. The other thing is,' Kerry hesitated, 'don't tell the girls, I'm embarrassed. But Adam has a drink problem. I think he's an alcoholic. He's always been a heavy drinker, but in the last year or so he's crossed the line. Somehow he's holding his job down. But come the evening, he just sits there drinking whisky until bed time. And come the morning he's like a bear with a sore head. I've tried talking to him, but he bites my head off. It's like living with a volcano and I can't take much more. So I've been quietly assessing my future. Plotting and planning. I can't leave Adam just yet. I lack the skills to have the sort of job that pays enough to support myself and Toyah. But as soon as I'm qualified, I'll be off. Bye-bye, Adam. Go drink yourself stupid.'

Josie leant forward and gave her friend's arm a squeeze. 'Good luck with it all. And talking of drink, are you ready for another?'

Five minutes later the women were once again sipping from refreshed glasses. 'The thing is,' Kerry shifted on her stool, 'there's something else I need to tell you.'

Josie crunched on an ice-cube that had found its way into her mouth. 'Mmm hmm?' She swallowed. 'I'm all ears.'

'Please don't be cross with me, Josie.'

Josie laughed. 'Now you're being daft. What's up?'

Kerry took a deep breath. 'I'm not coming to Passé with you and the girls.'

'What?' Josie stiffened.

'I'm really sorry but, oh please don't look at me like that, Josie. I knew you'd be cross,' Kerry wailed.

'But you were the one who instigated this girls night out!' Josie exclaimed. 'So why the heck are you ducking out?'

'Because I'm meeting Simon Clark.'

Josie blinked. She knew that name. 'Our *tutor*?'

'Yes.'

A mixture of emotions played through Josie. She felt sorry for Kerry's marriage troubles. But starting an affair – especially with one of the tutors – wasn't the smartest thing to do.

'So why rope me into a night out with you and the girls?'

Kerry looked faintly ashamed. 'I need an alibi.'

'I don't understand. Why not just lie to your husband about going out with your girlfriends. Why actually go to such elaborate lengths to arrange a night out that you had no intention of attending?'

'Because Adam wouldn't have let me go out. It's only because Toyah is babysitting for you and came out with me, that he even relented.'

'So you've used not just me and the girls, but your daughter too?' Josie pursed her lips.

'Yes.' Kerry hung her head.

'Does Toyah know about this?'

'No! Absolutely not,' Kerry assured. Her eyes welled. 'I'm really sorry, Josie. But you don't know what my life is like. It's awful. And Simon is so sweet and romantic and–'

Josie sighed. 'Spare me the details, Kerry. Look, I'm sorry I jumped down your throat. But I'm not comfortable being an alibi for a married woman going out with another man. It doesn't make me feel good.'

Kerry nodded. 'Yes, I can see that.'

Irked, Josie took a swig of her drink. 'If you want to go out canoodling with Simon Clark, that's your business. But I think I'd rather give the nightclub a miss if you're not going to be there.'

'Please don't do that!' Josie implored.

'But why? It doesn't affect your evening?'

'Of course it does! If you go home without me, Toyah will ask where I am. She's meant to be sharing a minicab home with me later on.'

'She can have my minicab.'

'No! Don't you see? If Toyah gets back to ours without me, Adam will ask where I am. And then Toyah will say I didn't come home with you. All sorts of questions will be asked. Adam will–'

'There's a saying,' Josie interrupted. *What a tangled web we weave when those around us we deceive.* So in order for you to have your evening of rumpy-pumpy with Simon Clark, I have to tootle off to this nightclub on my Jack Jones. Terrific.'

'But the girls will be there,' Kerry added lamely. 'And the nightclub is only across the road. I'd walk over with you, but I'd rather they didn't see me. Can you tell them I felt poorly but might be in later?'

'And will you?'

'Will I what?'

Josie gave a sigh of exasperation. 'Be in later?'

'Well it seems a bit daft to pay the entry money for just half an hour. I'll text you at about midnight to say I'm outside in a minicab. Is that all right?'

Josie drained her drink and picked up her handbag. 'I guess it'll have to be, won't it.'

By the time Josie had fought her way through the packed club and found the rest of her College girlfriends, she was feeling extremely put out. Fancy Kerry using Josie to her own advantage! Josie hated manipulative people. She hadn't thought Kerry to be someone like that. Ah well. You lived and learned. The music was loud. It drowned out all attempts of prolonged conversation with the girls. Josie didn't know any of the club anthems that were being played. She felt old and out of touch. The evening dragged on. A couple of women staggered past her.

'Where's the bar, Nell?' screeched a blonde woman, clearly the worse for wear. 'Nell? Can you hear me? Where's the–?'

The blonde woman promptly fell off her heels and nose-dived into her friend's shoulder. A guy who had been heading their way, shot her a look of distaste and went off in search of fresh talent. Josie's girlfriends were now indicating she should follow them. They pushed their way through the throng until they were gathered on a large sticky circle passing itself off as the dance floor. The girls began to gyrate sexily. Josie tried to imitate them. And failed. In the end she did her *wedding disco* moves. It was all she knew. As Josie listened to *I've Got So Much Love to Give* now in its fifth full minute with no change to the lyrics or tempo, she began to wonder if the record had got stuck. Around her people were nodding their heads up and down and jerking as though in a trance. Josie put her left foot forward, then back and wiggled her hands about. She looked like she was doing the Okie Cokie. The girls had attracted attention. A group of guys were coming over. Moments later they'd linked arms with her friends and melted off into dark corners. Oh marvellous. So now Josie was well and truly on her tod. She glanced at her watch. How much longer of this interminable evening did she have to suffer?

As she stood there doing her Okie Cokie moves to a club anthem, Josie had a horrible urge to sink down to her knees and crawl off. Preferably somewhere quiet. If she heard one more repetition of *I've Got So Much Love to Give* she might just scream. Please God let Kerry pick her up on time. It wouldn't be a moment too soon.

And then Josie saw him.

Chapter Three

Josie's Okie Cokie went to pot. Dancing towards her was the hottest man she'd ever clapped eyes on. He surely couldn't be interested in her? She instantly dismissed the idea and tried to concentrate on dancing. She looked down. Right foot, in, out. Left foot, forward, back. She looked up. The guy was closer now, still moving to the beat through the crowd. Josie's heart began to pound. Her eyes flicked nervously left and right. Around her, couples were moving together. There was no other single woman dancing all by herself. She looked back at the man. His eyes locked on hers. Josie felt foolish, gyrating woodenly all by herself. The man was now four paces away from her. Three. Two. One.

'Hello,' he said and smiled.

'Hello,' Josie nodded. She felt tongue-tied and ridiculous. The man was staring at her intently. She found it both thrilling and unnerving. Her heart was still leaping about in the depths of her ribcage. How bizarre. No man had ever had this effect on her. Not even Nick.

'I noticed you the moment you came into the club,' said the man. He placed his hands on her waist, guiding her body to move in time with his. Josie stared at him. She couldn't think of a single thing to say. The man smiled encouragingly. 'Well it was your eyes I noticed actually. They are extraordinary. And you have a beautiful smile.'

Josie knew for a fact that she hadn't smiled once since entering the club. She'd stalked in, hump up to her eyeballs due to Kerry abandoning her, before finding the girls and lying about Kerry being unwell, and seethed silently ever since. A light bulb went off in Josie's head. The man was chatting her up. Sweet words of crap. Josie threw her head back and laughed. The man looked bemused.

'Sorry,' Josie apologised. 'I'm very happy to dance with you, but you really don't have to do a number on me.'

'Number?'

'Yes. The chat up. The beautiful eyes and smile thing. Honestly, it's not necessary.'

The man's hands tightened on her waist. 'I'm paying you a compliment. A compliment that happens to be true. You're gorgeous.' He nodded his head in the direction of a voluptuous woman falling out of an ill-fitting leather dress and said, 'You're not one of those girls. You're different. You have *special* stamped all over you.'

Josie smiled. The guy was probably in here every week picking up women. No doubt he bandied those words about every single time he oh-so-smoothly danced his way over to his prey. She couldn't care less. All that mattered to her right now was getting through the remainder of the evening until Kerry was outside in her minicab. If some Adonis with a honey tongue wanted to lavish her with compliments, so what? He could help her get through the evening pleasantly.

So Josie danced. Not the Okie Cokie, but sexy fluid movements, meshed against the man's body. Time passed. And in that time she felt every part of his chest, stomach, groin and thighs against hers. And something in her dared to rise to the surface. Not Josie the widow or Josie the mother. It was the real Josie. The girl she'd been at eighteen. Bold. Beautiful. Even sexy.

Josie couldn't remember the last time she'd felt attractive to the opposite sex. Long before Nick had died. They'd been together for twelve years. Made a child. He'd come to know every stretchmark of her body. The places where her cellulite gathered. They'd been so familiar with each other's bodies. Their relationship had been like putting on a comfortable pair of pyjamas. And no matter how comfortable the pyjamas, at the end of the day PJs weren't sexy. And thus it was with her marriage to Nick. Predictable. Safe. Comfortable. But not remotely sexy. After she'd been widowed, it had bothered Josie that she couldn't remember the last time she and Nick had made love. She'd wanted to find the memory, draw upon it, wrap it around her and take comfort in it. But all she could remember was the exhaustion as they'd shared Lucy's broken nights, and later – when Lucy was sleeping through the night – relishing a good book, or curling up on the sofa in front of the telly.

Josie came back to the present. The music had changed long ago. All the numbers were now slow and languid. Somehow her arms had ended up wrapped around the man's neck, her face resting against his chest. His lips brushed her hair. Josie looked up. And then his mouth found hers. It seemed the most natural thing in the world. He kissed her gently. She kissed him back. The tip of his tongue pushed against her lips. She greeted it with her own. Her eyes closed and her arms tightened around his neck. All she could think about was mouths making love. And suddenly Josie was consumed with desire. She felt a wild, reckless abandonment. Here she was, thirty-five years old, in a nightclub, snogging a stranger.

At that moment the music's volume dimmed and the DJ began to speak.

'Sorry to interrupt folks, but I have an urgent message for Josie Payne. Josie, if you are in the club this evening, could you immediately make your way to the foyer. Josie Payne to the foyer.'

Josie abruptly pulled away from the man. 'That's me. Sorry, I have to go.' She glanced at her watch. Half past midnight. Where had the time gone? Bugger, it must have been Kerry who instigated the DJ interruption.

'Wait,' the man called.

'Sorry, but I'm really very late. I have to go.'

Josie began working her way through the smooching couples. The man was trailing along in her wake. Out in the foyer, she squinted against harsh fluorescent lighting.

'Josie,' the man said. He knew her name now. 'I was hoping to see you again.' He caught hold of her left hand. Raised it to his mouth and kissed her fingers. His lips touched her wedding ring. He stared at it, his expression unreadable. 'You're married?'

'Widowed.'

'God, I'm sorry.'

'It's okay.'

'Look, I know you're in a hurry. But I don't want you rushing out of my life. Is there any chance...would you mind terribly...I mean being a widow and everything—'

Josie stopped dead in her tracks. Was this suave, sophisticated man by any chance making a complete hash of asking for her number?

'Do you want to see me again?'

'Yes!'

'Fine. That's fine,' she nodded. She reached into her clutch bag, found a biro and scribbled her mobile number out on her club entry ticket. 'Here.' She pressed the piece of paper into his palm. 'Thanks for a lovely evening. And now I really must fly.'

It was only when she was sitting in the minicab next to a scowling Kerry, that Josie realised she didn't know the man's name.

Chapter Four

Sam Worthington had been out with the lads, reluctantly celebrating his thirtieth birthday. He'd desperately tried to duck out of the occasion, but Stu had been adamant.

'A birthday needs celebrating,' Stu had insisted. 'And this is a big one after all. It has a zero on it.'

'Oh okay.' Sam had given in. 'I'm up for a pizza and beer.'

'Good idea,' Stu had said. 'And afterwards we'll go to that club. You know. The one where nobody under thirty is allowed in. Passé. You're eligible now. You won't have to get your fake ID out,' Stu had teased.

The last thing Sam had wanted was a night out with the boys. Especially at a club. He'd had a major row with Annie earlier on which had pressed all his buttons and left him with the headache from hell. But right now Sam shoved all thoughts of the lads and Annie from his mind. He didn't want to think about anybody other than the woman he'd been dancing with.

Sam watched Josie hasten out of the nightclub. Through the glass panes of the entry doors, he saw her disappear into the depths of a waiting minicab. Somebody else had been in the car. From this distance he couldn't tell if Josie's travelling companion was male or female. He looked at the piece of paper in his hand. He didn't want to lose this number. He withdrew his wallet from his back pocket. Opening it up, he carefully placed the number between two twenties before tucking the wallet back into his trouser pocket. He glanced at his watch. A little past half midnight. The club shut at two. Suddenly Sam didn't want to be in Passé. He wanted to be in bed. Preferably with Josie next to him. He had a feeling it would happen. But not with the usual speed Sam bedded women. And fancy her being a widow. That had rocked him. He wondered what had happened to her husband. Poor sod.

Sam went back into the nightclub. A woman blocked his entrance.

'Hello, darling. Now that you've seen your mother home, why don't you come and dance with me.'

'You're very sweet,' Sam said, thinking the woman was anything but. 'However, I'm off home.'

'I'll come with you,' the woman winked and stuck out her chest. It was impressive. And maybe a few hours ago, Sam would have taken her up on the offer.

'Babe, I'd love you to come with me. However, I have a wife and child at home. And I don't think my missus would be as appreciative about your charms as me.'

'You fucking bastard,' the girl instantly turned on him.

'That's me,' Sam grinned and pushed past her. He was looking for his mates. They'd disappeared earlier with Josie's friends. He'd told them to steer clear of Josie. He hadn't been lying when he'd told Josie that he'd spotted her walking into the club. And he *had* noticed her beautiful eyes. They had been flashing with anger. But he'd fed her soft soap about the smile. Her mouth had been set in a grim line. He hadn't got to the bottom of why.

'Stu,' Sam clapped the back of a man welded to a woman's mouth. 'I'm off, mate. I don't know where the others are but tell them I said cheerio.'

Stu put up a hand in farewell, and then returned to the object of his desire. Sam gave the woman a cursory once over. God Stu, what are you doing? Rough or what? Sam knew Stu didn't give a stuff about a woman's looks. All he was interested in was the hemline. How far it could be raised. And preferably removed altogether. Well good luck to him. Since his wife Carol had buggered off with her boss, Stu had been drowning his sorrows in women's cleavages ever since. He didn't have the happiest of lives at the moment. None of them did. What a motley bunch they were.

Sam made his way out of the nightclub. It was only a short walk down the road to the Pay and Display. Sam had only drunk one JD and coke this evening. And that had been hours ago. He was good to drive.

Ten paces from his vehicle he popped the central locking. The Mercedes M-Class flashed its lights. Sam always got a vicarious thrill getting into it. The Merc was his pride and joy. He'd bought it brand spanking new just over a year ago. And his little daughter loved it. Ruby said she felt like a princess looking down on other drivers from the elevated seating position. Sam had laughed. The last time they'd been together, he'd taken Ruby shopping. They'd ventured into The Disney Store where Sam had bought the little girl a silver plastic tiara covered in fake rubies.

'Here you are, sweetheart,' he'd smiled and gently placed the tiara on his daughter's head. 'Now you really are Princess Ruby.'

His daughter had squealed with delight. And naturally he'd had to get his wallet out and buy lots of other regal clothes to go with the tiara. But Sam hadn't minded. In his eyes Ruby was indeed a princess. *His* princess. He hadn't known what love was until his daughter had been born. He'd been blown away by the fierceness of wanting to protect the tiny squalling infant. Sam had been a hands-on dad. He'd relished his turn of getting up in the night. Dirty nappies hadn't fazed him. Nor colic. Or teething. More often than not it had been Sam bathing Ruby in the evening while Annie watched Coronation Street or EastEnders.

Sam had been a bit unsure about being a father. It had been Annie wanting to do the parent thing. Sam had hesitated about chucking the condoms away. It had been the same when they were seeing each other. He'd been quite happy just doing the dating thing. But Annie had wanted to live together.

'We've been a couple in everybody's eyes for a good six months,' she'd said. 'All my friends are paired off and looking for properties together. I want to do the same.'

Sam realised that his own friends were in the process of property hunting too. So he'd agreed to Annie's wishes. They'd only been living together for three months when Annie had dropped hints about getting engaged.

'When are you going to buy me a ring?' she'd bleated at every God-given opportunity – usually when they were passing jewellers while out shopping. 'At work everybody's getting engaged. Apart from me.' So a ring had been purchased. 'When shall we get married?' had been Annie's next question. And before he'd known it, Sam had been dressed in a morning suit standing next to Annie who was swathed in a meringue dress. It was only when he was signing the register, that he realised he'd never actually proposed. And he'd barely brushed off the confetti when Annie wanted to get down to the business of making a baby.

'Can't we just enjoy being a couple for two or three years,' Sam had protested.

'No! I want to be a *young* mum,' Annie had said.

Annie had sulked for weeks on end until Sam had caved in. He'd been given a brief respite from impending parenthood because it had taken Annie six months to get pregnant. At one point she'd dashed off to get checked out by a gynaecologist. Nothing had been wrong. Annie simply needed to be patient.

Once pregnant, his wife had milked every day of gestation for all it was worth. Clearly nobody in England had suffered morning sickness the way Annie had. No other woman had endured such an aching back. Such swollen ankles. Such rollercoaster emotions. Every tweak, every twinge, had put Sam on red alert. Their love life had ceased within the first six weeks of the pregnancy. Annie had been terrified sex would hurt the baby. And Sam hadn't pushed the matter because a part of him had fallen into the bracket of males that didn't find a pregnant woman particularly arousing.

When Ruby had been born, Sam had been by Annie's side. Holding her hand. Spurring her on. She'd called him every name under the sun. Dared him to lay a finger on her ever again. Afterwards Sam had looked at Annie's stretchmarked saggy tummy and privately found himself thinking that was fine by him. He'd despised himself for that, and not dared tell anybody. Not even Stu, who was his closest pal.

In time Annie had shed her baby weight. But their sex life had never quite reignited. The pair of them would go weeks at a time without any intimacy. Sam didn't particularly miss it. He had a new person to lavish his love on. Ruby. To begin with, Annie had been pleased. Especially in the first year when her hormones were all over the place and she'd sat and cried without really knowing why.

In Ruby's second year, Annie's sisters had told her she needed a good girls' night out to put her back on feel-good tracks. Soon Annie had been regularly going out Friday and Saturday nights, leaving Sam literally holding the baby. But he hadn't minded. It had been great fun doing finger painting with his toddler. And besides, Annie had cheered up. Which made for a quiet life.

In Ruby's third year, there was a shift in the Worthington household. Sam had come home from work on a Friday evening. As was always the case, he'd greeted his little daughter with a hug and big kiss.

'How's my girl?' he'd beamed. 'How's Daddy's little princess?'

Annie had watched. She'd had a strange look on her face. Then she'd put her hands on her hips and snapped, 'You love our daughter more than you love me.'

Sam's smile had faded. He'd instantly put Ruby down and put an arm around his wife's shoulders. 'Don't be silly, Annie,' he'd said. 'She's our daughter. You're my wife. I love both of you.'

But Annie had pushed him away. Stared at him coldly. 'I don't think so,' she'd spat. 'The only person who matters to you is Ruby.'

And then she'd stormed off upstairs. Moments later the bathroom door had slammed. Sam had been aghast. Surely his wife wasn't jealous of the love he had for their daughter?

Rather than get into a row, he'd topped and tailed Ruby and put her into her Teletubby pyjamas. Then they'd curled up together on the sofa and watched some football. Sam had tried to teach Ruby the offside rule, but she was more interested in pulling the hairs on his arm. Shortly afterwards, she'd fallen asleep tucked into his side. Sam had looked down at his sleeping daughter's face – the exquisite symmetry of her eyebrows, the long dark eyelashes sweeping the pillows of her cheeks – and felt as though the stuffing had been knocked out of him. This beautiful child was *his* daughter! He felt a surge of protective love swell his heart and burst forth with fatherly pride. He'd move mountains for Ruby. Slay dragons for her. And then Annie's bitter words came back to him. *You love our daughter more than you love me.* And Sam realised, horribly, that Annie's words were true. Would he move mountains for his wife? Slay dragons for Annie? Sam had mentally hung his head in shame. What had gone wrong between them? But then again, what had ever been right? What sort of man allowed himself to be coerced into the path their relationship had taken? A weak man, that's what. He'd berated himself. He should have just stuck to dating Annie. He'd only gone out with her because she had a big pair of tits for God's sake. What a prat. What a stupid, idiotic, moronic–

His thoughts had been interrupted by Annie coming down the stairs. She was dressed to go out. Her favourite perfume hung in the air.

Sam had mustered up a smile. 'You look nice, sweetheart. Off out with your sisters again?'

'No.' His wife had glared at him. 'I'm going out with another man. A man who gives a fig.'

And before Sam had been able to properly understand the words his ears had just heard, Annie had turned on her heel and left. And she hadn't come back until Sunday evening.

The Merc's engine roared into life. The vehicle was an automatic. Sam put the gear into drive. The wheels rolled forward and the car purred its way towards the main road. Sam signalled right and pulled out. The streets were pretty much empty now. It only took him ten minutes to drive home. He yawned. Late to bed. Again. He needed to get some early nights under his belt. At least it was Sunday tomorrow. He could have a lie in. It had been a hectic week at his dental practice. Next week several implant surgeries were booked. He enjoyed doing those. Changing gaps into teeth. Transforming people who had previously hated smiling into the sort of folk who couldn't stop beaming twenty-four-seven. It made his patients happy. And when his patients were happy, he was happy. And it also made his Bank Manager happy. Which was just as well, because Annie made sure she milked him of every available penny.

Sam let himself into his flat. The functional space had been his address ever since the marital home had been sold and Annie had moved in with Nigel. It had taken him months to think of this place as home. When Annie had dropped the bombshell about Nigel, Sam had panicked. He wasn't bothered about losing Annie. Not one little bit. But the thought of Annie taking Ruby away had reduced him to a gibbering wreck. He'd done everything in his power to make Annie change her mind.

Suddenly he wouldn't just move mountains and slay dragons for Annie, he would also shift the sun, the moon and a billion stars.

'It's too late,' Annie had told him.

The house had been put on the market. Sam had refused to sign the papers. So Annie had forged his signature. The divorce petition had come next. Annie hadn't quite dared forge the signature on that. She'd pressed a pen into his hands and screamed, 'SIGN IT, SAM. Just *sign* the fucking thing.' Sam had obliged. With a flourish he'd scrawled *Mickey Mouse*.

'I'll make you pay for this,' Annie had hissed.

'I'll pay you any money you like,' Sam had said. 'You can have it all. Every penny.'

'Not money, Sam,' Annie's mouth had twisted. 'I'm talking about you paying *emotionally*. That little bit of nonsense has just cost you dearly. You can forget about seeing Ruby until I say otherwise.'

Sam had gone into meltdown. Annie had been as good as her word. For weeks he hadn't known where she or his daughter were. He'd rung her mobile repeatedly, to no avail. In desperation he'd telephoned Annie's mother.

'If you'd loved and cherished my daughter, Sam, you wouldn't be in this pickle,' his mother-in-law had shouted. 'So I'm not telling you where Annie is. And if you come here and hassle me, you'll have the police to deal with.'

Sam had barely been able to function. He'd cancelled all his appointments at the clinic. Told the receptionist to take some holiday. And then Stu had come to his rescue. Good old Stu. Back then he'd yet to go through his own heartbreak with Carol.

'You've got to do things properly, mate,' Stu had said. 'Get the divorce out the way. Get your access sorted out. And then get yourself a decent place instead of living in this rented shithole.' Stu had wrinkled his nose at the pigsty Sam was living in. Takeaway cartons littered the lounge. A stinking bin was overflowing in the kitchen. 'When you've got a decent gaff you can have Ruby over. Quality time and all that.'

And somewhere in Sam's head, a light had gone on. Hope. He'd dumped the takeaway cartons, cleaned up the rented shithole, shaved off his stubble and driven to the estate agent. Within half an hour he had six back-to-back viewing appointments. By half past seven that evening he'd had an offer accepted on an apartment.

And now Sam stood in that same apartment's hallway. He flicked on the light. The place was very quiet. A nurse lived upstairs. Downstairs resided a widower. There was rarely any noise here. Sam felt mildly guilty about the racket Ruby made when she came to stay on Tuesdays and every other weekend. On those days her feet would thumpity-thump across the floor as she played chase or hide and seek with Sam. Her shrieks and happy screams would fill the air. Occasionally the widower downstairs would get his walking stick and bang on the ceiling. Sometimes Sam wished he'd bought a house. But he'd deliberately shied away from houses when viewing properties. In his mind, houses were for families. They weren't bachelor pads. Maybe he'd have a house again one day. When he was feeling braver emotionally.

He moved down the hall. The answering machine light was flashing. Sam tensed. Who would have called him on a Saturday night? Not the lads – he'd been out with them. Not his parents. They were currently on holiday abroad. Not Corinne, his ex-girlfriend. He'd dumped her the moment she'd started hinting at wedding bells. He wasn't ever going down that path again. All the women he'd been seeing recently were literally one-night stands. None of them had his number. Which left Annie. Sam braced himself. What vitriolic message would his ex-wife have left for him this time?

Annie had made it her business to be foul ever since Sam had moved into this apartment. Apart from one blip of an occasion. Not long after he'd moved in, she'd turned up unexpectedly. She'd been dressed in a skirt practically split to the crotch. Her chest had been ramped to the rafters and showcased by a plunging neckline.

'Sam,' she'd said, standing on the communal hallway's landing. 'We need to talk.'

'Is Ruby all right? Where is she?'

Annie had momentarily pursed her lips. 'Ruby's fine. She's with my mother. Can I come in?' She'd not waited for a reply and simply brushed past Sam. 'Nice place.' She'd nodded her approval.

'Thanks,' Sam had said. 'What do you want to talk about?'

Annie had moved into the lounge. She'd sunk down on his brand new black leather sofa. Crossed one leg. Shown off plenty of thigh. 'Us,' she'd said simply. 'I want to talk about us.'

Sam had been baffled. 'Us? What about us?'

'I want us to get back together, Sam.'

Sam had stared at Annie uncomprehendingly. 'But you're with Nigel.'

'Was, Sam. Was with Nigel. We've split up. I made a mistake. A big mistake. And now I want to put things right again. I want you back.'

For a moment Sam was speechless. He couldn't believe his ears. Annie wanted him back? 'I can't take this in, Annie. I can't get my head around it.'

'I understand,' Annie had nodded. 'But just think, Sam. If we got back together, you'd see Ruby every day. Every...single...day. It would be like old times.' Annie had stood up. Walked slowly towards him. Her perfume had shot up his nostrils. She'd picked up his hand and put it against her breasts. 'We'd be a family again.'

Sam had stared at her. Her words had echoed around his brain. *You'd see Ruby every day...you'd see Ruby every day*. His heart had leapt with joy. It was what he'd wanted more than anything else. But at the same time he'd instantly known he didn't want Annie. That part of his life was over. Gently, he'd reclaimed his hand. Looked his ex-wife in the eye.

'Let's leave things the way they are, Annie.'

Annie's eyes had widened. Her nostrils had flared. She'd been so sure. This wasn't the outcome she'd envisaged.

'You're going to regret those words, Sam. Understand one thing. And one thing only. I'm going to use Ruby to destroy you.'

And now Sam found himself looking up at the ceiling as if offering a silent prayer to God. He looked back at the answering machine. His finger touched the play button. There was a beep followed by a pause. He waited for Annie's sneering voice to begin. But instead it was the breathy voice of Ruby. 'Hello, Daddy,' she said. Sam instantly smiled. He was so sorry to have missed his daughter's call. He'd tried telephoning her earlier but only succeeded in speaking to Annie's answering machine. He'd wanted to tell Ruby it was his birthday and hear her excitedly wish him a lovely day. Annie hadn't even bought a birthday card on behalf of their daughter. Maybe his ex-wife's conscience had pricked her after all. How lovely. Sam waited with anticipation for the magic words. There was some background mumbling. Whispering. As if Ruby was being instructed on what to say. 'Happy birthday, Daddy,' said Ruby eventually. Sam's heart expanded and his eyes misted over. Another pause. More whispering. 'I have a birthday message for you.' Pause. Whisper. 'Stop dating... TROLLOPS!' Pause. Whisper. 'Bye-bye, Daddy.' There followed a clattering noise as the phone clumsily disconnected.

Sam stared at the answering machine, unable to quite believe what he'd just heard.

Chapter Five

Annie could feel little fingers tapping her eyelids.

'Wake up, Mummy. Can you wake up now? Mummy? Mummy? Mum-*eeee*?'

Reluctantly, Annie opened her eyes. The clock radio showed the time as fifteen minutes past six – on a Sunday morning.

'Go back to bed, Ruby,' Annie groaned.

'But I'm not tired.'

'Well I am.'

'But I'm bored.'

'Read a book.'

'I can't read.'

'Well look at the pictures in the book.'

'I have.'

'Then do some colouring.'

'Done that too.'

'Then do some more.'

'Okay. I'll draw Daddy a picture. It was his birthday wasn't it? I'll make him a card.'

Annie instantly swung her legs out of bed. 'No need. I'm getting up. You can watch some television while I make breakfast.'

Annie settled Ruby in front of cartoons before going into the galley kitchen. She put the kettle on, reached into the fridge for some bread, slotted it into the toaster and then shoved some laundry into the washing machine. To complete all these tasks she'd only had to move a distance of two feet. The kitchen was tiny. Just like the house she lived in with Ruby. Two up, two down. And she hated it. She yearned for the semi-detached she'd shared with Sam. They would have moved eventually. A detached would have been the next step. Indeed, for a while she had lived in a detached. Nigel's house. Four bedrooms. Two en-suites. Fab kitchen with granite worktops and all mod cons. Very nice. But then he could more than afford it on his doctor's salary.

Annie had met Nigel at the practice she worked for. He was still there. These days they side-stepped around each other.

When she'd lived in his house, she'd loved his bricks and mortar far more than she'd loved him. Unfortunately, having been stung by his ex-wife, Nigel had absolutely no intention of putting Annie's name on the deeds. Nor would he marry Annie. She'd felt very resentful about that. Ultimately the children had undone her relationship with Nigel. His two boys. Aiden and Ben. Horrible brats. Although Nigel had blamed Ruby. He'd called *her* a brat. They'd ended up screaming at each other in front of all three children whose child was the biggest brat of all. She could still see the kids' faces now. Pinched and white as they'd huddled by the television – which had been the cause of the argument in the first place. Aiden and Ben had wanted to watch one thing, and Ruby had wanted to watch another. And Nigel's boys always got their way because it was Nigel's house and Nigel's television. In the end Annie had told Nigel to shove his forty-two inch screen where the sun didn't shine. Then she'd gathered up her belongings and hauled Ruby off to her mother's house. And there she'd stayed. Until she'd hatched a plan to seduce Sam and win him back. That had been a spectacular fail.

Annie experienced a flare of resentment at the twin memories of Nigel's horrible children coupled with Sam's rejection. Although these days Annie felt resentful about pretty much everything. Sometimes she even felt resentful of Ruby. After all, if Annie had never had a baby, then Sam wouldn't have lavished all his love on their child and they'd still be together.

To begin with Annie hadn't minded Sam's attention being so focussed on Ruby. After all, it had helped smooth over the fact that she'd struggled to bond with her daughter. Not that she'd shared that information. That was her secret. And she'd take it to the grave. Annie had been puzzled by her emotions after giving birth. She'd carried a tiny person within her for nine long months. Why had she felt so detached from Ruby afterwards? Instead it had been Sam who had instantly fallen in love with the baby. Within seconds of Ruby plopping onto the hospital bed, he'd burst into noisy tears of joy. She guessed their different reactions would remain one of life's mysteries. At first she hadn't minded Sam's attention on the baby. It had permitted her freedom. Like shopping for groceries without a screaming baby in tow. Or a bit of much needed retail therapy. And lunch with her mum. Or a night out with her sisters. It had been great. Eventually she'd grown to love Ruby. But it had taken months. And yes, she had been and still was jealous that Ruby only had to bat her beautiful long eyelashes at Daddy to have him come running.

Annie suspected Sam's rejection of reconciliation was because he was playing the field with other women. No doubt he had a little black book listing all his fuck buddies. She could think of no other logical explanation for Sam's rebuff. Well she'd soon see his women off. Each and every one. If Sam didn't want her, fine. But she'd make sure nobody else wanted him either. She'd picked up a message from Sam yesterday asking to speak to Ruby. He'd asked Annie to call him back as soon as possible as he was going out with the lads to celebrate his birthday. Annie had had no intention of returning Sam's call. His rejection of her was an ongoing punishable offence. So she and she alone would decide when he could speak to Ruby. And for how long. She might even screw up his access plans. To hell with what the Court Order said. She was in the driving seat now. Nobody was messing with her emotions again. Not Nigel. And definitely not Sam.

Annie had then had a little daydream. She'd imagined Sam going out to that crap club where all the divorced or dumped plebs went. The place was frequented by men looking for crumpet and women looking for a leg-over. Sam would have pulled a tart and taken her back to his place. Once inside his flat, he'd have seen the flashing light on the answering machine. He'd have caught hold of his tart's hand and said, 'Just a minute, Angie, it might be a message from my little girl. She's so cute. Want to have a listen?' And then – da da! – Ruby's voice would have rung out asking if he was with a trollop. And Angie would have said, 'You pig. Are you in the habit of flaunting women in front of your poor little girl? You're not fit to be a father.' And then the fictional Angie would have slapped Sam hard across the face before flouncing out. And Sam's jolly birthday bedtime would have turned to ashes. Which was only what Sam deserved. He'd rejected Annie. Now women would reject him. It was called karma.

By nine o'clock Annie had completed her chores. The single perk of having a small house was that cleaning didn't take long. She'd bought the house only when she'd been sure Sam wasn't going to back-peddle about a reconciliation. The Victorian terrace hugged a narrow pavement. Residents' cars jostled for off-road parking. It wasn't her dream home, but it was all she'd been able to afford with the settlement money Sam had given her following the divorce. And at least she was back on the property ladder. She could make ends meet comfortably enough between his maintenance payments and her salary as Practice Manager at Pilkington Medical Practice – the very surgery Nigel worked at.

'Come on, Ruby, we're going to Nanny's.'

Ruby tore her eyes away from Cartoon Land. 'But we saw Nanny yesterday. Can I see Daddy?'

'Not today. He doesn't want to see you.'

Ruby's face fell. 'Why not?'

'Because he's busy seeing a trollop.'

'What's a trollop, Mummy?'

'Another woman, Ruby. A woman that wants your Daddy all to herself.'

'Oh.'

Annie didn't feel remotely guilty about the line she was spinning Ruby. As far as Annie was concerned, it was the truth.

A quarter of an hour later, Annie parked outside her childhood home. She let herself in. She still had a house key, as did her three sisters.

'Mum?' Annie called from the hallway.

Lou Adams lived by herself now. She had done for the last two years. Ever since Eric had died. Annie missed her father, but was so glad her mother was still around. At the end of the day Annie was Mummy's girl. Lou was a feisty eighty-year-old with a good fifteen plus years left on her ticker. She had ruled Eric and their daughters with an iron rod. Even now she had a habit of sticking her nose in her other three daughters' marriages and majorly pissing off their husbands. If ever one of Annie's sisters were having a domestic, you could bet your last pound that Lou was somewhere behind it.

But right now Annie's sisters were in their own homes with their own husbands. For the moment Lou was leaving them all in peace.

'I'm in the kitchen,' Lou called back.

Annie walked down the hallway and stood in the kitchen doorway. Her mother was extracting a rack of scones from the oven. Annie went over and pecked her mother on the cheek.

'Hello, Mum.' Annie turned and flopped down at the kitchen table. She pulled Ruby onto her lap. 'The baking smells good.'

Lou grinned. 'Indeed. Fresh out of the oven and begging for butter and jam. Want one, Ruby?'

'Yes please, Nanny,' Ruby slid off her mother's lap and began hopping from one leg to the other in excitement.

'How are you today, love?' Lou turned to her daughter.

Annie pulled a face. 'A bit down actually. I feel so lonely.'

Lou clicked her tongue. 'I've a good mind to get on the phone to that Nigel and give him a ticking off. He should have treated you better.' She pulled some plates out of a cupboard and set some scones before Annie and Ruby. 'Here, take the butter and jam.' She set a carton of Lurpak on the table and a jar of homemade strawberry preserve.

'Oh it wasn't so much Nigel's fault, more Sam's I think.' Annie sighed. 'If he'd loved me properly then I'd never have gone looking for adoration elsewhere.'

'I know, dear,' Lou chucked some teabags in a vast teapot. 'He's the real culprit in all of this.' She filled the pot up with boiling water. 'Don't worry, I'm on your side, love. I always have been. Your life would be very different if he'd looked after you the way he should have. May he never darken this door, or I'll tell him exactly where his fortune lies. Horrible man.'

'Don't you like Daddy?' Ruby piped up.

'No,' said Lou.

'Why?' Ruby asked timidly.

'Because of the way he treated your poor mother,' Lou grimaced.

'What did he do?' Ruby whispered.

'He stopped loving your mummy. And he broke her heart.'

Chapter Six

Ruby had been looking forward to Nanny's scone. It had smelt yummy. And when Mummy had spread thick butter and lashings of jam over the warm cake, her tummy had even done a few rumbles. But now she felt sad. Really sad. Sad enough to cry. And whenever she felt sad enough to cry, for some reason it made swallowing difficult. Ruby had taken one bite of the scone, but the mixture had clogged her throat. So Ruby pushed the scone around her plate. Bits of it broke off. Some dropped into her lap. Butter and jam adhered to her clean pinafore dress. She didn't really like the dress but Mummy did. Whenever Mummy took her shopping for clothes, Ruby loved all the frilly blouses and lacy dresses in shops like Next. But Mummy always made her wear plain clothes in dark colours.

'It's more serviceable,' Mummy had said. 'I don't have time to wash and iron clothes every five minutes. You'll wear this and do as you're told.'

'Yes, Mummy,' Ruby had said.

Now Nanny and Mummy were talking about Daddy. Again. It seemed to be their favourite conversation. She didn't know why the two women didn't like Daddy. Nor could she understand it. Her Daddy was wonderful. He was patient and kind. He played all sorts of games with her. Mummy rarely played with her. She was either working, or doing chores, or tired. If she had any free time, she liked to shop. Ruby found shopping boring. Unless it was toy shopping. But Mummy seldom allowed toy shopping. She said it was a waste of money. Daddy liked toy shopping though. He loved buying her dolls, and dolly clothes. She had a bedroom at Daddy's flat and it was all pink and pretty. It had a Barbie quilt and matching curtains. Her pyjama top featured a grinning Barbie with a blonde ponytail. Ruby even had a pair of little slippers with *Barbie* embroidered on the heels. And recently Daddy had bought her a Barbie bicycle. It had a pink basket at the front and rear stabilisers. If it wasn't raining, Daddy would put the bicycle in the boot of his car and they'd go to Greenwich Park. Ruby would cycle as fast as her legs would go, and Daddy would run after her pretending he couldn't keep up. And then he'd laugh and laugh and laugh. Whenever Ruby visited, he always laughed. He was such a happy person. Ruby couldn't understand why Mummy said Daddy was miserable and rude. As far as Ruby could tell, Daddy was always cheerful and polite. Especially to Mummy. Even when Mummy tried to make arguments about anything and everything, he never shouted back. Not even when Mummy screamed at Daddy and called him a fucking bastard.

The last time Mummy had shouted at Daddy, Ruby had asked what a fucking bastard was. Mummy had said it was a person who wasn't very nice. Ruby had made a point of remembering that piece of information. She'd recently started infant school. One of the boys in her class wasn't nice. His name was Alex. He was always punching boys. Sometimes he'd punch girls too. One day he'd got into an argument with Ruby. She'd been playing on the mat with a toy car and Alex had tried to snatch it from her. Ruby had told him his fortune.

'Stay away from me, you fucking bastard.'

Alex had stopped dead in his tracks. And so had Miss Watling, the teacher.

'Ruby Worthington,' her teacher had boomed, 'I don't know where you have heard such disgusting language, but you do not use it in my classroom. Is that clear?'

Ruby had gone bright red and burst into tears.

Later, when Mummy had picked her up from school, Miss Watling had asked for a private word.

'I am *so* sorry, Miss Watling,' her mother had gushed.

'Is Ruby watching unsuitable television?' her teacher had asked.

'Good heavens no. I'm afraid this is her father's fault.' Ruby had been about to protest when Mummy had shot her a warning look. And then her mother had turned back to the teacher. 'Ruby's father and I are no longer together. He has a mouth like a sewer. I believe his use of foul language in front of Ruby is his way of getting back at me.'

Miss Watling had arranged her features into one of understanding. 'It happens,' she'd nodded. 'Well if I ever meet your ex-husband, Mrs Worthington, I'm afraid I will let him know my displeasure.'

'That's absolutely fine by me,' Mummy had smiled.

Ruby stared at the mess before her. Suddenly Nanny whipped the plate away.

'I can't bear it when children play with food. That really is very naughty, Ruby,' her grandmother scolded. 'Look at that waste. If you'd lived through a war, you'd have gobbled that up. That's the trouble with children today. They're spoilt. Go and wash your hands in the downstairs toilet.'

As Ruby stood up, what seemed like a thousand scone currants fell from her lap to the floor.

'Oh, Ruby,' her mother chided, 'look at the mess you've made on Nanny's kitchen floor.' And then her mother noticed Ruby's pinafore dress. Butter and jam were smeared over the pinafore's bib and skirt. 'For God's sake, Ruby,' her mother leapt up, face contorted with anger. 'You're not a baby anymore, so why are you covered in mess? Do you want me to put a bib on you? Is that it? Are you attention seeking?' Her mother pursed her lips. 'Well we know who you get that from, don't we?'

Ruby's bottom lip jutted out. She was going to cry. She could feel it. Her lip always jutted out when tears were imminent. Her left eye was the first to release a big drop of water. It rolled down her cheek, curled around her lip and dropped off her chin. Then the right eye started. Moments later twin snot trails shot out of her nose. Ruby picked up the bottom of her pinafore dress and wiped her streaming nose.

'Don't do that!' Her mother grabbed her wrist and marched her off down the hallway. 'There are times when you really are a disgusting child. Do you know that?' Her mother yanked her into Nanny's downstairs toilet. A stream of toilet paper found its way into Ruby's hand. 'Blow,' her mother ordered. 'Now wash those hands. And when you've finished, get back in that kitchen and apologise to Nanny for ruining a perfectly good scone.' Her mother stalked off.

It was at times like this that Ruby wished she were with Daddy. He never told her off for spilling food down her clothes.

Once she'd accidentally tipped an entire bowl of ice-cream into her lap. Daddy had guffawed with laughter.

'Hold it right there, princess,' he'd said. 'This is one for the photo album.'

And then he'd produced a digital camera and taken a picture of a grinning Ruby with a chocolate ice-cream mouth and a lap full of goo.

Later, Daddy had uploaded onto the computer all the pictures he'd taken that weekend of them together. She'd sat on his lap while Daddy had shown her how to click the mouse. Together they'd gone through the digital images. Ruby on the roundabout. Ruby on the slide. Ruby peddling her Barbie bike. Ruby feeding ducks. Ruby in McDonalds. Ruby covered in ice-cream.

'Why do you like taking so many pictures of me, Daddy?' she'd asked him.

'Because they are happy memories, darling,' he'd explained.

'Do you have any pictures of me when you used to live with Mummy?'

'No, darling.'

'Not any?'

'Not any.'

'Mummy has lots,' Ruby had said. 'I'll ask her to give you some.'

Ruby could still remember Mummy's terrible reaction that her innocent request had caused.

'No. Your father is not having any baby pictures of you, Ruby.'

'But why?'

'Because he left you, Ruby, so he doesn't deserve any.'

'Oh.'

Ruby struggled to understand the Daddy that her mother talked about. It was as if Daddy was two different people – the horrible Daddy who'd made her mother apparently suffer so much unhappiness, and the nice Daddy who made Ruby feel like she was the most important person in the world.

Ruby rubbed her hands on the hand towel. Then she swiped the towel around her face to dry her wet cheeks. For a moment, Ruby allowed herself to think about her secret wish. She didn't dare tell Mummy what it was. Mummy would go berserk if she knew. But Ruby often told her teddy bear the secret. And her teddy would look back at her with his sewn on brown eyes, and understand entirely.

Ruby's secret wish was that she had a Mummy and Daddy who lived together.

Chapter Seven

Lucy could hear Mummy on the phone. She was talking to a man. Lucy was intrigued. Mummy liked chatting on the phone. Indeed, she made telephone calls every day. As soon as Mummy came home from College, she would invariably pick up the phone to Grandma or her sister or any of her numerous friends. But all of them were female. Not male. With the exception of Grandad of course. But usually Mummy's conversations with Grandad were short. Grandad was simply the bridge to Mummy chatting to Grandma. Lucy turned the television's volume down so she could hear what Mummy was saying.

'Yes, it was nice to meet you too. Ah. Sam. I wondered what your name was.' Polite laughter. 'Lunch?' A small pause. 'That would be lovely but,' another pause, 'I'd need to arrange a babysitter. You see, I have a little girl.'

Lucy jumped down from the sofa. She hovered, unseen, between the lounge and hallway. Mummy was sitting on the stairs, handset tucked between shoulder and chin.

'There might be somebody who can help me out, but I'd have to make a telephone call. Okay. I'll do that. Give me your number and I'll call you back in a few minutes. Let me grab a pen.'

Lucy ducked back into the lounge. She scampered over to the sofa and took a running jump at it. Mummy told her not to do that in case she missed and hurt herself. A couple of times that had happened, but the thrill of briefly flying through the air was too great to resist.

A few minutes later Mummy sat down next to her.

'Would you mind if I went out for a couple of hours this afternoon?'

Lucy shrugged. 'No. But who will look after me?'

'Toyah.'

'I like Toyah. She's funny.'

'Good. Are you sure you don't mind?'

'Sure.'

'Okay. I'll give her a ring and see if she's up for earning some pocket money. Won't be long.'

Lucy wondered where her Mummy was going, and who with. She'd hurried off to phone Toyah without giving Lucy a chance to ask. And now Mummy was once again talking to the person who'd invited her out. Lucy turned her attention back to the television. When Mummy next appeared, she had a big smile on her face. It was a different smile to her normal one. Sort of...goofy.

'That's all sorted. Toyah's dad is going to give her a lift here. She'll be over in an hour. I'd better get myself ready.'

Lucy bounced off the sofa again, and followed her mother up the stairs. 'Who are you going out with, Mummy?'

Her mother's back was to her, otherwise Lucy would have seen hesitation.

'A friend.'

'Kerry?'

'No, darling. Not Kerry. Not today.'

'Who then?'

Her mother walked into her bedroom. 'I told you. A friend.'

'What's your friend's name?'

Mummy pulled on her sliding wardrobe door. It whooshed sideways. 'Ooh, look at all these pretty dresses. Which one shall I wear? Are you going to help me decide?'

Lucy peered inside the wardrobe. She loved looking at her mother's clothes. Sometimes Mummy allowed her to dress up in some of them. And then she'd clip-clop across the bedroom in matching high heels, her wrists jangling with bangles and beads.

'I think this one,' said Lucy pouncing on her own personal favourite. Mummy pulled the silky floral dress from the wardrobe and pretended to consider.

'It's a very good choice – but possibly better suited for a wedding. I'm going out for a meal, so perhaps something a little more casual?'

'What sort of meal?' asked Lucy. 'McDonalds?'

Her mother saw the look of longing on Lucy's face and laughed. 'No. I'm having a lunchtime curry. All you can eat for ten pounds!'

Lucy wrinkled her nose. 'Oh yuck. I hate spicy food.'

'When you're a grown-up, you'll love it. Promise.'

'I think a dress might be the wrong thing to wear, Mummy. Toyah was telling me she goes to Indian restaurants with her College friends, and apparently they always wear jeans.'

'You know, I think jeans might be the perfect thing. What a smart little lady you are,' said Mummy.

Lucy beamed. Mummy was always telling her she was clever. Lucy didn't know if she really was super-intelligent or whether Mummy just said these things because she loved her. Lucy had only just started school so she had heaps to learn. Time would tell if she was bright. And anyway, she was still trying to work out if she even liked school. Some of it was fun. Like playing on the mat. Other parts were harder. Like learning numbers and remembering the alphabet. But Miss Watling always smiled at her encouragingly, and Lucy did her best to please. Unlike some of the children. Take Alex. All he wanted to do was fight the boys. Although recently he'd picked on a girl. Ruby Worthington. Lucy wasn't sure if she liked Ruby. She didn't giggle or chat like Lucy and her friends. Ruby was the silent type. Her Mummy would have described Ruby as *withdrawn*. Although Ruby hadn't been withdrawn when Alex had started on her. Ruby had shouted at Alex and called him something bad. What was it? Lucy furrowed her brow. Oh yes. Mucky mustard. Ruby had got into loads of trouble. Lucy didn't understand why mucky mustard was so awful. Perhaps it tasted so revolting that nobody wanted to be reminded of it. And talking of horrible food, what top should Mummy wear for this curry meal? Lucy tried to remember the advice her mother had given her when eating her own food. Like tucking a napkin into her neck if she was wearing a pale top and eating chocolate pudding.

'I think you should wear this sweater, Mummy,' said Lucy as she tugged at the sleeve of a drab brown jumper. 'And then if you spill your food, it won't show up.'

'Good idea,' Mummy nodded. 'Although I could wear this floaty blouse if I remember to use my napkin.' Mummy pointed to a very dressy top.

'That's beautiful, Mummy. You'll look really pretty. Are you going to get changed right now?'

'Give me two minutes,' her mother said. 'First, I want to have a super quick shower. Are you going to come and talk to me in the bathroom?'

'Only if you let me play with your make-up.'

Mummy smiled. 'What about I have that shower and then, when I'm putting on my make-up, you can pretend you're doing your make-up too. You can copy me.'

Lucy's face lit up. Messing about with her mother's make-up was almost as much fun as messing about with paints and brushes. 'Yeah!' she gave a wide grin.

Forty-five minutes later Mummy had fed her a boiled egg and soldiers and was now grabbing her handbag and car keys. Toyah had arrived and exclaimed how beautiful Lucy's make-up was. Lucy had been delighted. Her lipstick-coated mouth and surrounding skin had turned upwards, so that her smile was clown-like.

'I shouldn't be more than a couple of hours,' Mummy said to Toyah.

'You take as long as you like, Josie,' Toyah assured. 'Lucy and I will be busy playing Kerplunk and Frustration.'

Mummy leant down and enfolded Lucy into a big squeezy hug. Her mother smelt lovely. A mixture of shower gel, toothpaste and perfume all rolled into one.

It was only after her mother had left that Lucy realised she still didn't know who Mummy was having lunch with. Briefly, Lucy looked sad. The clown mouth turned down. She so wished her daddy was still alive. If he was still alive, he'd be able to take Mummy out to lunch every single day.

Lucy's eyes welled. Hastily she swiped at the unshed tears. For a moment, Lucy allowed herself to think about her secret wish. She didn't dare tell Mummy what it was. Mummy might weep otherwise. And Lucy couldn't bear it when Mummy cried. But Lucy often told her dollies the secret. And her dollies would look back at her with their plastic eyes, and understand entirely.

Lucy's secret wish was that she had a Mummy *and* a Daddy.

Chapter Eight

Josie started the car up. As she edged out of the driveway, she paused briefly to wave at Toyah and Lucy. The two of them were framed in the hall window. They waved back, and Josie accelerated off.

She was heading for Sidcup. It was only about seven miles away. Sam had an apartment there. He also had the South-East's best Indian restaurant just around the corner. Sam had originally suggested meeting at his apartment. Josie had hesitated for a second too long. But Sam had instantly recognised her caution and hastily suggested heading straight to the restaurant instead. She knew the place. There was a car park a stone's throw away. She'd never been to the restaurant, but she'd visited the car park two or three times. It was just up the road from the undertaker that had taken care of Nick's funeral.

Josie parked up. Fishing in her purse, she found the necessary coins for the Pay and Display. Locking the car, she walked smartly across the road and into the Star of India. Josie pushed the door open and Sidcup High Street disappeared in a cloud of incense and spices. Sarouk rugs hung on the walls and a sitar strummed softly in the background. At a nearby table, a family were tucking into sizzling chicken tikka. Josie's stomach growled with hunger.

'Yes, madam?' a waiter materialised in front of her.

'I'm meeting Mr Sam Worthington for lunch.'

'This way please.'

The waiter led Josie into the depths of the restaurant. Tucked into an alcove and sitting at a table for two, Sam was studying the menu.

'Hi,' Josie smiled. The waiter pulled out her seat. There was an awkward moment where Sam jumped up to greet her, and Josie sat down to oblige the waiter. She then stood up as Sam sat back down. They both laughed. Josie allowed the waiter to tuck her in, thanked him for the menu and then breathed a sigh of relief at being left alone.

'It's so good to see you again, Josie,' Sam caught her fingers across the table.

Josie felt a little thrill as his fingers curled around hers. 'And you,' she said. And she meant it. She was quite surprised at her reaction. But then again, it wasn't every day a man with the looks of a film star invited you out to lunch. And boy, Sam Worthington was good looking. He was gazing at her intensely. She found it slightly unsettling.

'You're even more beautiful than I remember,' he said.

Josie opened her mouth to say something, but closed it again. She wasn't used to compliments. Especially compliments that were, in her opinion, over the top. Nick had once told her she was pretty. But that was a lifetime ago. And despite thinking Sam was a sensational looker, she certainly wasn't going to tell him that. He might get the wrong idea – think she wanted to be taken to bed or something. And then Josie had a horrible realisation. Sam was probably paying her compliments hoping she'd allow herself to be walked back to his apartment and shagged senseless. Quite apart from the fact that she was sorely out of practice, she wasn't that sort of woman. She'd better drop a hint about that straight away. She didn't want the guy wasting his time on her. Although, with those looks, he probably had no shortage of female companions.

'I'll have to go home straight after lunch. The babysitter–' Josie shrugged.

'That's okay. I'm meeting somebody after dinner,' Sam said. 'But I want you to know Josie, that I really like you and hope to see you again.'

'That would be lovely,' Josie smiled.

'I also think it's important we're honest with each other.'

Josie nodded. Gosh. This sounded a bit serious. What was Sam going to say? 'Of course.'

'So I'm going to tell you that after I've kissed you good-bye, I'll be kissing another lady hello.'

Josie inwardly sighed. There you go! She'd known it. He had women coming out of his ears. Clearly he was a champion at open relationships. Well she wouldn't waste her time. She wasn't interested. She'd have lunch, thank him politely, and go back home.

The waiter appeared. 'Can I get you a drink, sir? Madam?'

Sam looked at Josie. 'House wine?'

'Lovely. But I'm driving, so you'll be drinking the lion's share of the bottle.'

'No worries,' Sam grinned. 'I only live around the corner, so I'll be walking.' He turned his attention briefly to the waiter. 'That's fine, thank you.'

'Are you ready to order, sir? Madam?' asked the waiter. 'You can choose from the buffet lunch, or the menu.'

'Give us a couple of minutes,' said Sam.

The waiter melted away leaving Sam and Josie to cogitate over the menu. Josie's eyes flitted over the printed dishes. She couldn't concentrate. Who was the lady Sam would be greeting – no, kissing! – after saying good-bye to her? Well she wasn't going to ask. She just wasn't.

'You were saying,' Josie peered over her menu.

Sam frowned. 'Saying what?'

Bugger. 'About the lady you'll be kissing hello. After me.' She flushed slightly.

'Ah yes. Ruby.'

Josie nodded. Gosh, he was even telling her the woman's name. Honesty was one thing. Details were something else. She arranged her features into one of nonchalance. 'Have you been seeing Ruby long?'

'A little over four years.'

Blimey. Was the woman so dotty about Sam that she was prepared to wave him off to nightclubs, turn a blind eye to him snogging other women, and dining in dimly lit restaurants? This female clearly had staying power. 'And, er, Ruby doesn't object to you having lunch with me?'

'She doesn't know,' Sam grinned mischievously.

'Hang on a minute.' Josie put the menu down. 'Look, I'm sorry. But if you're in a relationship with this lady, then I really don't feel comfortable sitting here having lunch with you.'

'Who said anything about a relationship?' Sam feigned innocence.

'You did. One that's lasted a little over four years?' Josie arched an eyebrow.

Sam caught her hand again and squeezed it. 'I'm being a bit naughty and teasing you. Ruby is my daughter.'

Josie stared blankly at Sam. 'You have a daughter?' That shook her. He didn't look like a father to her. Where were the Daddsy corduroys, or bobbly sweater? Sam was dressed in jeans and a tee, both by Armani. She'd seen the little labels when he'd stood up to greet her.

'Yes, I have a daughter,' Sam repeated. 'Like you. Although I have to say you don't look like a mother.'

'What do you mean?'

'You're far too glamorous.'

Josie snorted with laughter. 'I was just thinking the same about you.'

The waiter returned with the house wine. There was a pause while glasses were filled. 'Ready to order now, sir? Madam?'

'The buffet?' Sam inclined his head.

Josie put down the menu. 'Why not!' After all, she hadn't a clue what was on the menu.

'Very good, sir, madam,' said the waiter. 'Please help yourselves.' He indicated a central island where tureens were set out and then left them to it.

Sam touched his wine glass against Josie's. 'A toast to glamorous parents.'

Josie smiled and clinked back. 'Indeed.' Her heart suddenly felt much lighter. She took a sip of wine. But then paused. A thought occurred to her. 'So, talking of honesty–' Josie stared at her wine glass, suddenly feeling awkward.

'Yes?'

'Sorry, but I need to ask this question. I'm not treading on anybody's corns having lunch with you?'

'Absolutely not,' Sam assured.

'Ruby's mum?' Josie looked up at Sam.

'Divorced. All done and dusted. Got the certificate to prove it.'

Josie nodded. 'Good.' Then Josie caught herself, appalled. 'God, I'm so sorry. That sounded really insensitive. I mean, I'm sorry you split up and everything. But I'm glad you're not married.' Now she was coming across as if dead keen on him. 'As in,' she hurried on, 'that I'm not doing anything wrong.' Josie slung some wine down her neck.

'A lady with morals. I like that. Come on,' he stood up, 'let's eat.'

Over dinner they talked. And talked, and talked. Josie couldn't believe how easy it was to chat with Sam. He asked about her being a widow, and she told him all about Nick. He squeezed her hand and said she was very brave. Josie felt slightly guilty. She'd loved Nick, and yes she missed him. But there was no denying that before his death their relationship had changed. They'd been like brother and sister. And whilst she'd been flattened by grief, she hadn't felt as though she'd had a limb amputated – like some people did when they were widowed. Was that wrong? Was it acceptable not to think of your dead husband as a lost soulmate? She didn't know, nor did she like to voice the question. And hadn't. Not to anyone. Not even Julie, her sister, to whom she usually told everything. She was worried that people would think she was lacking a sensitivity chip in the emotions department. In turn, Sam told her all about his ex-wife. Annie. Josie expressed sympathy. The woman sounded a nightmare.

'Have you tried mediation?' Josie asked.

'Funny you should say that. We have our first mediation appointment tomorrow. I hope it proves fruitful,' Sam sighed. 'I'm trying to sort out holiday access. I'd love to be able to take Ruby to Walt Disney World. But Annie is having none of it. She carries on as if I'm some sort of potential abductor. Like I'll get on a plane with our daughter and never be seen again.'

'Well,' Josie forked up some rice, 'you do read about these things in the national newspapers.'

'I'd never do that to Annie,' Sam shook his head. 'Or Ruby. Apart from anything else, I have a dental practice here. I'm not going to throw my work away. And then there are my parents. Family. I love them all too much to do a disappearing act.'

'Do you have any holiday time at all with Ruby?'

'Yes, but only in England. This summer we did one week at Camber Sands. It was a wash out. Literally. Nothing but torrential rain. Typically, as soon as we were home again, the thunderclouds packed their bags, the sun came out and temperatures soared. That's the trouble with England. The weather is so unpredictable. Still,' Sam broke off a piece of naan, 'maybe tomorrow's mediation will result in a breakthrough.' He popped the bread into his mouth.

'I'll keep my fingers crossed for you,' Josie said. At least, being a widow, she didn't have a sparring ex-partner to deal with.

'So tell me about your little girl,' said Sam.

Josie grinned. She couldn't help it. Talking about Lucy always made her heart soar. Before long she and Sam were trading funny stories about their daughters, and the classic comments kids had a tendency to come out with.

'How did Lucy feel about you coming out for lunch with me?'

Josie's smile faltered. 'I didn't tell her I was having lunch with a man, as such. I used the word *friend*. I was vague. Do you tell Ruby when you're keeping female company?'

Sam put his fork down. He gave Josie a frank look. 'No. I keep Ruby very separate from my private life. With an ex-wife like Annie, I have to. No girlfriend has ever met Ruby. But then again, no previous girlfriend has ever been a mother,' he smiled at Josie.

'I see,' said Josie. Although she didn't see at all. Did that mean that Sam wasn't averse to her meeting Ruby at some point because she, Josie, was a mother? Or simply that none of his previous girlfriends had met Ruby because they weren't mothers and not particularly keen on kids? Another thought occurred to her. 'Were your previous girlfriends career ladies?'

'No, just very young,' Sam grinned.

'Right.' Well that had told her! Served her right for being nosy. There was a pause while they both cleared their plates. 'Can I ask how old you are, Sam?' Josie eventually said.

'Thirty. You?'

'A bit older. Quite a bit older actually. Thirty-five.'

'You look ten years younger,' Sam teased. 'Annie was older than me too. I've clearly got a thing for cougars,' he winked.

The waiter appeared and cleared the table.

'Coffee?' asked Sam.

Josie glanced at her watch. 'I'd love one, but I'm going to have to pass. I promised Lucy I wouldn't be gone long.'

'No problem.' Sam looked up at the waiter. 'Can I have the bill please?'

'Of course, sir.'

Sam shifted on his seat and dug out his wallet. Josie foraged in her handbag for her purse.

'Put your money away, Josie,' Sam said.

'No really, I insist.' Josie produced a twenty-pound note.

Sam put a hand on hers. 'I mean it. I invited you to lunch. It's my tab.'

Josie hesitated. 'Well, in that case thank you very much. I just don't want you being out of pocket.'

'I'll be a cheapskate next time. You can have dinner at my place.' Josie laughed by way of response. Sam moved so that he was leaning in close to Josie. 'That is if you'll see me again,' he said, suddenly serious.

Josie's stomach did a flip. She found herself suddenly short of breath. 'I'd love that,' she croaked.

'Good. I'll call you.'

Outside the restaurant, they linked arms. Sam walked her back to her car. Before Josie got in, he put his arms around her and drew her close. And then he kissed her. Softly. Beautifully.

Chapter Nine

Annie sat in the waiting room of the Family Mediation Association's offices. She'd agreed to attend mediation more out of curiosity than any sincere reason to resolve issues with Sam. She knew why Sam wanted this meeting. He wanted to change the holiday access currently in place. At the present time Sam's holiday access permitted him one week with Ruby in England only. Apparently this was no longer satisfactory. He wanted to take Ruby out of the country. No chance. She didn't think for one moment that Sam would do a disappearing act with their daughter. The real reason for her refusal to agree to Sam's wishes was because she assumed a girlfriend would be included in a foreign holiday. And she wasn't having Ruby being cared for by another woman.

Annie gazed around the waiting room. What a place. Drab. Dull. Once white walls were now channelling grey. A spider plant trailed listlessly over the edge of the windowsill. From her seat, Annie could see through the window. It had started to drizzle. A minute or two later and the light rain became a downpour. It beat a loud tattoo against the windowpane. At that moment an internal door opened. A pleasant looking woman, about the same age as Annie, greeted her.

'Hello. I'm Linda Grant. Are you Mrs Worthington?'

'Well I was once,' Annie grimaced.

'Do you prefer to be called by another name?'

'Mrs Worthington will suffice.'

Linda checked her watch. 'We have a few minutes before starting our appointment. Can I get you a cup of tea?'

Suddenly the entrance door whooshed open. Sam hastened in bringing the cold with him. He was drenched.

'Hello,' he nodded at Annie before turning to Linda. 'Sorry for dripping all over your carpet. There's a bit of a cloudburst going on out there.'

Linda smiled sympathetically. 'Don't worry about the floor. I was just offering Mrs Worthington a cup of tea. Can I get you one?'

'That would be lovely,' Sam rubbed his hands together, 'two sugars please.'

'Mrs Worthington?'

'No. I'm not here for a tea party. And I want you to know I've had to take time out of work for this appointment. So if it's all the same to you, I'd like to crack on.'

'Certainly,' said Linda. 'But I'll be making myself and Mr Worthington a cup of tea first. Won't be a moment.'

Annie's mouth set in a thin line. Oh bloody marvellous. The simpering cow probably fancied Sam. No doubt she'd be back in a minute asking him if he wanted Tetley, Earl Gray or Jasmine. Her ex-husband sat down next to her.

'Do you have to be so rude?'

'Don't you bloody start on me,' Annie snarled.

'The woman was only being courteous.'

'I suppose you fancy her.'

Sam sighed. 'Annie, do me a favour. Can we just be civil please? If nothing else, then for Ruby's sake?'

Linda reappeared with two steaming mugs. She handed one to Sam. 'Okay. Now both of you should be in receipt of a letter from the Association outlining what happens during this mediation session. I will see you first, Mrs Worthington. Then you, Mr Worthington. This is an assessment meeting. It will give me an opportunity to look at your case and hear the opinions of both sides. Afterwards, the three of us will talk together. There will be a charge of seventy-eight pounds each. I appreciate that sounds quite a lot of money, but it's much cheaper than involving solicitors. Any questions?'

'That's fine,' Sam gave a nod of his head.

'Not with me it isn't,' said Annie. She turned to Sam. 'You wanted this mediation. So you can pay for it.'

'Mrs Worthington, I–'

Sam put up a hand to halt Linda. 'No problem. I'll pay.'

Annie stood up. 'Right. Let's get on with it, eh?'

Annie followed Linda into her office. There was a desk in one corner. To the side were some easy chairs. Linda indicated Annie take one of the comfortable seats. Annie sat down opposite the mediator.

Linda smiled encouragingly. 'It would be helpful if you could tell me the background facts and why you're here today.'

'Sure. Sam and I were married. Together we had a daughter – Ruby. Everything was fine until Ruby was born. Sam wanted nothing to do with me following her birth. He totally ignored me. The only time he interacted with me was to insult me about my post-pregnancy body. He reduced my self-esteem to zero. In due course I returned to work as a practice manager at my local medical centre. One of the doctors saw how distressed I was. He was very supportive. I might add that I wasn't his patient,' Annie said defensively. 'If Sam had been a loving husband, I'd never have started an affair with Nigel.'

'Is Nigel your current partner?'

'No. We split up after three months. I did ask Sam if he wanted reconciliation – for Ruby's sake you understand. But he was busy getting his end away with a string of women.'

'Does Sam have a current partner?'

'Good heavens no! He's a tart. He's not going to tie himself down to one woman. And that's why I don't want him changing Ruby's holiday access. I'm not having Ruby confused by a continually shifting parade of women.'

'But am I right in thinking there are access issues?'

'Sam wants to take Ruby abroad. He talks about going to Walt Disney World – America. It's too far away. What if Ruby were homesick? Or fell ill? Or simply wanted Mummy? I wouldn't exactly be just around the corner would I? Apart from anything else, he's obsessed with our daughter. Unhealthily so.'

Linda looked concerned. 'What do you mean by *unhealthily so*?'

'He's not a pervert if that's what you're implying,' Annie snapped.

'I'm not implying anything, Mrs Worthington. You are the one who indicated there was an unhealthy obsession. I merely asked you to explain what that was.'

'Well I'll tell you,' Annie pursed her mouth. 'I wouldn't put it past Sam to disappear abroad with my daughter. And I'm not going to end up being one of those women you read about in the newspapers, not knowing where in the world your kid is. So the answer is no. Not now. Not ever.'

'I understand. Well hopefully we can find a compromise before you leave this office. Okay, Mrs Worthington. Thank you. I'll see your ex-husband now.'

Sam sat down opposite Linda.
'So, Mr Worthington–'
'Do call me Sam. Mr Worthington sounds so formal.'
'Sam,' Linda smiled. 'Your ex-wife has given me some background details. But I'd be very grateful if you could take me through them yourself.'
'Sure. Right. Well, Annie and I were married. Together we have a beautiful little girl – Ruby. She's four and absolutely gorgeous.' Linda nodded. 'After Ruby was born...well in hindsight I wonder if Annie had the baby blues. Following the birth – and for quite a period of time – Annie was very distant with Ruby. She wanted a break after being with a baby all day. So I'd make sure I was home from work in plenty of time to take over with Ruby. Feeding, bath time, bed time. Annie's mood improved as a result. She perked up. She'd go out with her sisters a lot. That sort of thing. Then she went back to work. Next thing I know, she's having an affair with a colleague and wanting a divorce.' Sam paused. He studied the floor. Focussed hard on his shoelaces. 'So we divorced. It was a very difficult period for me. For several weeks Annie withheld access to Ruby. When Annie's new relationship finally broke down, she suggested we reconcile. And I was tempted. Sorely tempted.' Sam's voice caught. He coughed. Struggled for composure. Then carried on. 'But I'll be honest with you, Linda. After the way Annie had treated me, I didn't love her anymore. Aside from trust issues, she'd put me through hell over Ruby. Also I'd got myself settled in my new apartment and life was back on a fairly even keel. Did I want to rock the boat and change it all again? Ultimately the answer was no. Annie didn't take the news well. She told me she'd use Ruby–' Sam's voice caught again. He paused. Swallowed. 'She told me she'd use Ruby to destroy me.' He looked up at Linda. 'And she's been on a mission to do that ever since. I'd dearly love to take Ruby on holiday to Walt Disney World. But Annie won't entertain the idea.'

Linda nodded. 'America is a very long way away. What about being a little less ambitious and considering, say, Disneyland Paris? If Ruby fell ill or missed her mother, it's a lot easier to jump on a train and whizz through the Channel Tunnel.'

'Sure. I'd be happy with that.'

'Good,' Linda smiled. 'Mrs Worthington also mentioned that, regarding holidays abroad, you would want to take a girlfriend along. She isn't keen that another woman be in the mothering role.'

'I'm looking at a holiday purely for Ruby and myself. My private life is kept firmly away from our daughter,' Sam assured.

Linda nodded. She then took a deep breath. 'Sam, obviously at mediation it helps enormously if both parties are honest. Mrs Worthington has an additional anxiety. She said that if she agreed to Ruby going abroad with you, she feared you'd abduct Ruby.'

Sam momentarily closed his eyes. He rubbed the bridge of his nose before letting his hand drop down onto his lap. 'Look, Linda, if Annie is so concerned about that, I'd be happy to go away as a family. For Ruby's sake obviously,' Sam added.

'Really? Well that *is* good to know.' Linda looked pleased. 'Okay. Let me ask Mrs Worthington to join us. From what you've told me, I'm very hopeful a compromise can successfully be achieved today.' Linda stood up and walked to the door. Sam watched her open it. And then noted her look of surprise.

'Is something wrong, Linda?'

The mediator turned back to Sam. 'I'm ever so sorry, Sam. But Mrs Worthington has gone.'

Chapter Ten

Sam started the Mercedes up. He waited for the Bluetooth to connect, then pressed Annie's name on the car's touch screen. Putting the gear into reverse, he eased out of the car park before heading along the Sidcup By-Pass towards his dental practice. The ringtone to his ex-wife's mobile continued. Eventually it went to voicemail. Sam clicked off and rang Annie's landline. It went to answering machine. He didn't know if she would have gone straight back to work or briefly returned home. Once again he rang the mobile. Again it went unanswered. This time Sam left a message.

'Hi, Annie. It's me. Linda and I were surprised you left the mediation session before it had finished. I was hoping we might have reached an agreement over my holiday access with Ruby. Can you give me a call later? Please?'

Sam gripped the steering wheel. His mood veered between anger and frustration. But it was vitally important not to display these emotions to Annie. If he did, his ex-wife would use it as a weapon against him. It would be a punishable offence. The most obvious punishment would be Annie withholding access to Ruby. So Sam swallowed the irritation and told himself that patience was a virtue, common sense would prevail, and a compromise would be reached. Eventually.

Annie drew up outside Pilkington Medical Practice. Her mobile had rung twice in the last five minutes. She reached into her handbag. Pulling out the handset, Annie checked the caller display. Sam. Obviously. She felt a vicarious thrill ripple through her regarding her exit from the mediator's office before the meeting was over. Good. That would teach Sam to waste her time. And she was absolutely delighted that he'd incurred a combined fee of one hundred and fifty-six pounds for his troubles. Sam needed to understand that she, Annie, was in the driving seat regarding Ruby. Not him. Nor his simpering mediator. Feeling incredibly chipper, she chucked the mobile phone back into her handbag, and went back to work.

Josie was not enjoying her morning at College. So far she'd sat through a challenging chemistry lesson and was now labouring with a physics lecture. She checked her watch. Another forty-five minutes before lunch. She hadn't the faintest idea what the physics tutor was prattling on about. Why didn't the lecturer speak up? How was she meant to pass an exam next summer and gain access into university when she (a) couldn't hear the tutor and (b) therefore didn't understand the lecture? Her hand shot up.

'Excuse me, Mr Finn,' she asserted.

The tutor looked affronted at being interrupted. 'Madam, I think you're old enough to surreptitiously excuse yourself to the Ladies without putting your hand up.'

One or two students tittered with laughter.

'I don't want the toilet, Mr Finn. What I want is for you to speak up. I've been sitting in this classroom for a quarter of an hour and have absolutely no idea what you're talking about.'

'If you have a hearing problem, perhaps you should sit at the front,' said Mr Finn irritably.

'My hearing is one hundred per cent. Unlike your teaching. And as you're not being co-operative, please excuse me.' Josie stood up. 'I'll take this matter to the Principal instead.'

Whereupon a female student sitting three metres from the tutor also stood up. 'I'll second that. I'm sitting at the front and can just about hear you, but you're a diabolical teacher.'

'I'll third that,' said a man. Josie vaguely knew him as Dave. He also stood up.

Suddenly the entire class were on their feet and chuntering angrily. Shocked at what she'd started, Josie walked smartly to the classroom door. The other students were hot on her heels.

'Come back here!' Mr Finn shouted. 'This is outrageous.'

Josie felt a tugging at her sleeve. 'Wait for me.' It was Kerry. The women squeezed their way out into the corridor. 'Mr Finn's making himself heard now,' Kerry grinned. 'Are you really going to the Principal?'

'Yes,' said Josie.

Kerry stuck to Josie like glue. It was the first time the women had spoken since Saturday night. Kerry was anxious to put things right between her and Josie. 'When you've finished complaining to the Principal, do you fancy having some lunch together?' Kerry puffed after Josie. 'Only I'd like to have a chat. You know, say sorry and...stuff.' Kerry trailed off.

Josie hastened up a concrete staircase to the Principal's office. A stream of classmates followed her. Well at least she wasn't alone in this matter – thank God. She glanced sideways at Kerry's anxious face. 'Yes, okay. Lunch would be lovely. And as you're so sorry about Saturday, you can buy me a cup of tea.'

Kerry smiled gratefully. 'Done.'

Half an hour later, the two women sat together in the canteen. They weren't alone. A large percentage of the physics class had joined them. Dave had pushed a bunch of trestle tables together, much to the chagrin of the younger students. Every now and again their younger counterparts shot them dark looks. Josie took no notice. They should be grateful for the service she and her classmates had done them. The Principal had assured future physics lectures would be taken by him until a replacement tutor was found, and that they weren't the first to complain – there just hadn't been quite so many aggrieved students standing in his office before. Josie and her classmates felt sorry for the hapless lecturer, but not so sorry when it came to everybody's future success being jeopardised. Consequently a lot of class bonding had taken place. But now, the chattering had splintered off into groups. Dave was talking with some of the men about getting a five-aside football team together. Some of the women were moaning about their kids. Others were complaining bitterly about the intense workload which ate into family evenings.

Kerry took a few sips of her tea, then set the plastic vending cup down on the table. 'Tell me more about this guy you met at Passé. He must be dead keen to have asked you out the following day. What's his name?'

'Sam,' Josie smiled as she said his name. If the truth be told, Sam kept invading her thoughts. At unexpected moments, his face would pop into her mind. 'He's very nice actually.'

'Married?'

'Divorced.'

'Kids?'

'One. A young daughter.'

'Ooooh,' Kerry rolled her eyes and grinned. 'Same as you. You *have* got lots in common haven't you!' she teased. 'And what does he do for a living?'

'He's a dentist,' said Josie.

'They earn a few bob,' Kerry nodded her head sagely. 'Play your cards right girl, and you could be on to a good thing.'

'Thanks Kerry, but I'm not looking for a meal ticket, or a husband. However, a bit of male company now and again would be...pleasant.'

'Well you only live once, Josie, so don't deprive yourself. Sometimes a bit of,' Kerry posted quotation marks in the air, '*male company*, is just what the doctor ordered.'

Now it was Josie's turn to roll her eyes. 'I don't need sex to survive. And anyway, you're a fine one to talk. What's going on with you and,' she dropped her voice, 'Simon Clark?'

Kerry propped her chin in the palm of her hand and assumed a dreamy look. 'He's divine, Josie. Bloody divine. He makes me feel so damn good. And get this! When we were at his place, he asked me if I'd like a drink and he made me a cup of tea!'

'What's so exciting about that?' Josie asked, perplexed.

'Because in my house, if I asked my husband what he'd like to drink he'd expect me to produce a bottle of whisky, gin or vodka. I asked Simon what his tipple was. What do you think he said?'

'Gosh, I don't know. Sherry?'

'Freshly squeezed orange juice!' Kerry took her chin out of her palm and leant forward, her voice conspiratorial. 'I'm falling for him, Josie. Falling for him hook, line and sinker.'

'Well just be careful you don't get hurt,' Josie cautioned. At that moment her mobile phone began playing a tune in the depths of her handbag. 'I wonder who that can be. I hope Lucy's all right.' Anxious, Josie foraged for the handset. 'Hello?'

Kerry picked up the now empty plastic cups, stacked them and then waggled them back and forth in one hand. Josie gave her the thumbs up. Kerry stood up and headed off to the vending machine for refills.

'Josie?'

'Sam!' Josie could feel herself smiling into the handset. 'How lovely to hear from you.'

'I did get the timing of my call right, didn't I? You're not in the middle of maths or cooking up a chemical storm in the science lab?'

Josie laughed. 'Not at all. I've just eaten a cardboard sandwich in the canteen and about to have a second cup of tea. In half an hour I'll be heading off to Environmental Studies. I hope the tutor is pleased with my water assignment.'

Kerry sat back down with the tea. Josie could see her ears flapping.

'I hope so too,' said Sam. 'And if you've suffered the likes of the College's dismal sandwich offerings, what about I cook you something delectable at my place tonight?'

'Gosh, that would have been wonderful,' Josie sighed. 'Unfortunately I have a heap of assignments that I absolutely have to tackle tonight. But tomorrow would be good.'

'Ah. Tomorrow is earmarked for time with my daughter. She stays overnight.'

'Oh, okay. Maybe the weekend?'

'Definitely,' said Sam. 'Shall I call you Friday night?'

'That would be great.' Josie caught Kerry's eye and grinned.

'I'll call you nearer the time. Oh, and Josie–'

'Yes?'

'I just want to say...I really enjoyed seeing you yesterday. I want you to know that you're very special.'

For a moment Josie felt flustered. She didn't know how to reply. She didn't feel able to say *and you're special too*. After all, she'd only met the guy five minutes ago. 'Thank you,' she said instead.

'Enjoy the rest of your day. Bye for now.'

'Bye.' Josie disconnected the call.

'Well somebody has gone all dewy-eyed,' said Kerry.

'Don't be silly.' Josie chucked the phone in her bag.

'I take it that was lover boy.'

'Sam.'

'So why was he ringing?'

'He was offering to cook for me this evening. A meal at his place.'

'Oh that old chestnut,' Kerry snorted. 'Wants to show you his red onions and what he can do with a ten inch aubergine.'

Josie smiled. 'I've turned him down. Too much homework. However, do you think your Toyah might be available for some babysitting this weekend?'

'If money is involved, then the answer will be yes,' Kerry assured.

'Good,' Josie nodded. 'Meanwhile, Environmental Studies next. How did you get on with the water assignment?'

'Ah,' said Kerry. 'I was a bit too busy to do it. I was going to ask a favour actually.'

'Oh?' Josie knew the question before Kerry had asked it.

'Can I photocopy yours? Just this once,' Kerry added hastily.

Josie sighed. 'Look Kerry, don't put me in this position.'

'Please?' Kerry wheedled.

'Do you know how long it took me to produce this assignment?'

'A good hour I would think.'

'No,' Josie shook her head. 'It took me the best part of Saturday. Not to mention having a four-year-old bored out of her brains while I laboured over different websites and research. Anyway, Simon Clark will take one look at it and know it's not your own work.'

'I know. But at least I'll have something to hand in, and a mark towards my overall scoring. Please, Josie. I'll never ask again. And I'll do whatever favour you want in exchange. Promise.'

Josie sighed with exasperation. 'Just this once. I mean it, Kerry. And you're damn right I'll be calling in a favour at some point. And you'd better deliver, that's all I can say.'

When Josie drew up outside the school gates, all the available off-road spaces were taken. She had to park in the next road and walk back to the school. As she strode along the pavement, she found herself falling in step with another woman. The woman had a mobile phone clamped to one ear.

'I had to laugh, Mum,' the woman was saying. 'Oh to have been a fly on the wall and seen his expression when he walked out of that room.' The woman chortled with laughter. Clearly something was tickling her. 'Just imagine spending one hundred and fifty-six pounds for no reason whatsoever, ha ha ha! Oh definitely. Nobody will get the better of me, Mum, you can be sure of that. Especially that prick. And boy is he going to get a surprise tonight,' the woman laughed again, although there was no mirth to the sound. 'I've been in touch with BT and–'

Josie hastened past the woman. Fancy talking to your mother about a person like that! If Josie had referred to somebody as a *prick* whilst talking to her mum, her mother would have told her to wash her mouth out with soap – regardless of the fact that Josie was thirty-five years old. Moments later Josie had forgotten about the woman. Her attention was now on her little daughter. Lucy erupted through the school gate clutching a damp painting.

'Look what I did for you, Mummy!' Lucy's eyes were shining. 'That's you, and that's me, and we're in the park.'

Josie stared at the colourful blobs. 'It's gorgeous,' she smiled. 'In fact it's so good I'm going to frame it.'

Sam dumped his house keys on the apartment's hall table. What a day. An unsuccessful mediation meeting incurring a waste of both time and money, followed by an afternoon of patients complaining. Mrs Burgess wanted dental implants *immediately* and refused to grasp the concept of her jawbone needing six months to fuse with a titanium rod. Mr Paul had also wanted dental implants but didn't want to pay Sam's prices and had called him a robbing bastard. And the after school appointments had brought forth a flurry of children who'd screamed long and loud the moment Sam had asked them to open their mouths.

He wandered into the kitchen and filled the kettle. At least he'd been successful in speaking to Josie at lunchtime. He was really looking forward to seeing her again. What a shame it wouldn't be until the weekend. He flipped the kettle's lid down and flicked the switch. He liked Josie. *Really* liked her. Speaking to her at lunchtime had been balm. Utter balm. In fact, the only other person who soothed him when a day was challenging, was Ruby. Smiling to himself, he decided to give Ruby a call while waiting for the kettle to boil.

Sam picked up the handset and punched out Annie's number. There was a small pause before an automated message kicked in. *The number you are calling does not accept calls from this number.* Sam hung up and tried again. The automated voice kicked in for a second time. He hung up. He dug around in the pocket of his suit jacket for his mobile phone and rang Annie's landline number. *The number you are calling does not accept calls from this number.* Sam hung up and instead called Annie's mobile. It rang unanswered before finally going to voicemail.

Out in the kitchen, the kettle switch popped. Sam ignored it. Nor did he bother leaving a message on Annie's voicemail. He knew exactly what game she was playing. It was called The Control Game. Well he wasn't having any of it. Ruby was his daughter too. He had every right to make a telephone call to his child and speak to her – without the mother interfering or instructing BT to block his calls. Snatching up his keys, Sam strode out of the apartment. Enough was enough.

Chapter Eleven

Annie scraped the remnants of dinner from Ruby's plate before stacking it next to hers in the dishwasher. She went to the fridge and selected a chocolate mousse for her daughter's dessert.

'Pudding!' Annie called. She grabbed a teaspoon from the kitchen drawer. 'Come and fetch it.'

The doorbell rang.

'I'll get it, Mummy,' Ruby called from the lounge. She'd taken great delight in answering the front door ever since a recent growth spurt had propelled her upwards and within striking distance of the latch. 'Dadd-ee!'

Annie slammed the chocolate mousse and teaspoon down on the worktop. Bugger. She should have foreseen Sam turning up on the doorstep. Ruby was clearly in a state of excitement at seeing her father on an unscheduled day. She could hear her daughter chattering away.

'I did a painting at school, Daddy, look!'

'That's amazing, princess. I'd love to put that on my kitchen wall. Can Daddy have it?'

Annie appeared in the hallway just in time to see Sam holding the painting up and exclaiming over it. 'No you can't have the painting, Sam,' Annie reached for it, 'because it's mine.' She snatched at the sugar paper in Sam's grasp. The painting ripped in two. 'Now look what you've done,' Annie hissed. Ruby promptly burst into tears. 'Well done. Now you've made Ruby cry.'

Sam looked mortified. 'I'm so sorry, princess.' Clumsily he reached for Ruby. 'Daddy will get some sellotape. I'll stick the painting back together and it will be as good as new.'

'Get your hands off her,' Annie pulled Ruby away from Sam. 'Go in the lounge, Ruby.'

'But I want to see Dad–'

'I said GO IN THE LOUNGE,' Annie bellowed. Ruby shrunk away from Sam. 'And CLOSE THE DOOR,' Annie roared again. The door clicked quietly shut. Annie turned to Sam, eyes blazing. 'What the fuck are you doing here?'

'Was there any need to behave like that in front of–'

'FUCK OFF!' Annie screeched.

'What's the matter with you, Annie?'

'You've got a damned cheek, Sam.'

'What the devil are you talking about?'

'You've put me through hell today. And on top of all that, you're now here on my doorstep creating havoc.'

'I'm doing no such thing. Earlier on today I simply wanted to talk to you, but you never answered my calls.'

'That's because I don't want to talk to *you,* Sam. I have nothing to say. Absolutely nothing.'

Sam's cheeks flushed red. Annie knew this was nothing to do with embarrassment and everything to do with anger. When they'd been married, Sam had always turned the colour of beetroot when he was seriously wound up. 'I'm sorry if you feel I've put you through a day of hell,' he said quietly. 'It hasn't been a stroll in the park for me either. But it would have helped if you'd stuck around and concluded the mediation meeting. That's the whole point of mediation – trying to avoid a row. And if you don't want to talk to me, fine. You can talk to me through a solicitor instead. You leave me no choice now, Annie, nor can you stop me talking to my daughter.'

'Oh yes I can,' Annie hissed.

'Is that why you've blocked my landline and mobile? To score cheap points?'

'You don't get it, Sam. You still don't get it.'

'Get what?' Sam asked, struggling to keep fury from his voice.

'I've told you before. But as you're thicker than shit, I'll tell you one last time. I am the one who decides when you see Ruby. *Me.*'

'I only wanted to talk to her on the telephone!' Sam cried.

'And I am the one,' Annie enunciated, 'who decides when you can *talk* to Ruby too.'

'Was there really a need to block my numbers? What happens if she's with me and taken ill? How can I contact you?'

'Then – and only then – you can call me on my mobile, Sam. *Just* the mobile. And I will only answer my mobile when Ruby is staying with you. The rest of the time, if you call me, I will not answer my mobile. Do you understand, Sam? Am I

70

FINALLY GETTING THROUGH TO YOU, SAM?' Annie had so much anger and adrenalin coursing through her body, her heart rate had picked up. It was now banging away at an uncomfortable speed. She clutched the door frame, chest heaving, and her own cheeks now pink from shouting.

For a moment the ex-husband and ex-wife stood there exchanging glares, faces puce from their war with each other.

'This is ridiculous,' Sam eventually said. 'Why can't you get along with me, Annie?'

'Because I hate you,' Annie snarled. 'If you were the last man on this planet, and I was the last woman, and it was down to us to re-populate Earth...then humankind would die out. That's how much I hate you.'

'Fine. So you detest me. But do you have to let your feelings impact upon Ruby? This isn't good for her. You'll screw her up.'

Annie cocked her head to one side, as if considering. When she spoke again, her voice was unnaturally calm. 'You leave Ruby's welfare to me, Sam. Now go home. Go back to your trollops.'

'Annie, please. Stop speaking to me like this. Anybody would think I was the one who cheated on you and walked out.'

'You might as well have done. And for all I know, you probably did. It's your fault we split up. Now piss off.'

And with that Annie slammed the door in her ex-husband's face.

The doorbell immediately rang.

'Annie? Annie can I say good-bye to Ruby please?'

The doorbell rang again. Ruby crept out into the hall. 'Can I answer the door, Mummy?'

'No, Ruby. Go back into the lounge.'

'Ruby?' Sam called from the other side of the door.

'Why won't you let Daddy in?'

'Because he was horrible to Mummy.'

'Ruby?' Sam called again. 'I have to go home now, princess, but I love you.'

'I love you too, Daddy,' Ruby called out tremulously, bottom lip wobbling.

'I'll see you tomorrow,' Sam called again.

But his last words fell on deaf ears. Annie had taken Ruby back into the lounge and shut the hallway door.

Chapter Twelve

When Sam walked into his dental surgery on Tuesday morning, his receptionist could see at a glance that her boss wasn't in the sunniest of moods.

'Morning, Sam,' said Judith.

'Morning,' Sam replied curtly.

'You have time for a coffee. Your nine o'clock appointment has cancelled. It was only a check up.'

Sam stopped in front of the reception desk and checked his watch. Eight forty-five.

'So the next appointment will be nine fifteen. What's happening on that one?'

Judith consulted her computer. 'Mr Dandy. Root canal.'

'Thanks, Judith. I need to make a call. Other than bringing in that coffee, please don't disturb me until Mr Dandy arrives.'

Sam pushed open the door to his consulting room. Seconds later he had his briefcase open, divorce and Court paperwork in front of him, and his mobile clamped to one ear.

'Graham Burnley Solicitors,' said a female voice.

'Hello. My name's Sam Worthington. Is Mr Burnley available please?'

'One moment.'

Judith came in with the coffee. Sam nodded his thanks. Moments later he was bringing his solicitor up to date about Annie's refusal to attend mediation, the unresolved holiday access abroad and finally Annie blocking her BT line so that Sam was unable to speak to Ruby.

'I'm sorry about this,' said Sam, 'it must sound so incredibly petty to you.'

Graham Burnley chuckled. 'No worries, Sam. It's the petty that pays my pennies. But rather than waste your money instructing me to write a series of costly letters to your ex-wife, can I suggest we swiftly move forward. Let's make an application to the Court and revise all access – both home and abroad – including telephone access. Let's get it all in writing. Signed, sealed and delivered. Any nonsense and Annie will be in contempt of Court. And judges don't take too kindly to that.'

'Let's do it.'

'On it. Take care, Sam.'

Sam put the phone down. He took a deep breath, and then slowly exhaled. For the first time since yesterday's up-in-the-air mediation appointment and subsequent problems with Annie, he felt himself relax. Good. Things would be resolved in due course. He just had to be patient for a little bit longer. He chucked the paperwork back in his briefcase, and took a sip of coffee.

By five thirty, Sam had finished for the day. He stripped off his white medical coat and slid into his suit jacket. The best bit about leaving work on a Tuesday was the drive to Annie's house. Not that there was any pleasure in seeing his ex-wife. Rather the joy was knowing that Ruby would be climbing into the big Mercedes and heading home with him. He wondered what his daughter would like to eat this evening. She was passionate about McDonalds, but recently Sam had introduced Ruby to the joys of Pizza Express. Sam's mouth began to water in anticipation of a huge pizza layered in cheese, tomatoes, red onions and green peppers.

When Sam arrived at Annie's house, the place was in darkness. He parked up and waited a couple of minutes. No lights shone from within. Levering open the Mercedes' door, he glanced up and down the street. Annie's car was nowhere to be seen. Nonetheless he went through the gate, up the short path and rang the doorbell. The minutes ticked by. A gust of wind blew some dried leaves into the gutter. Sam shivered and felt in his jacket pocket for his mobile. He rang Annie. It went to voicemail.

'Hi, Annie. It's Sam. I'm outside your house but you're not home. I've come for Ruby. Can you call me please?'

Sam walked back to the Mercedes. Getting in, he slotted the key into the ignition and put the radio on. The minutes ticked by. He listened to Capital Radio's latest hits. Then the news. More music. Then the traffic report. After forty-five minutes he rang Annie's mobile again.

'Hi, Annie. I know you said you wouldn't answer my calls unless Ruby was with me, but in case you've forgotten, it's

Tuesday. It's my access time. And I'm waiting for my daughter. I hope everything is okay – that there isn't a problem. Can you call me please? I'm getting a bit worried about the two of you.'

Another half hour trickled by. Where was his ex-wife? Sam decided to telephone his ex-mother-in-law. Lou answered on the fourth ring.

'Hello?'

'Hi, Lou. It's Sam. Sorry to trouble you but–'

The phone went down. Sam could feel his chest tightening. This wasn't fair. Now his stomach was contracting. He could feel his guts literally screwing up with tension. Sam made a decision. Starting the engine up, he pulled out, drove to the top of the road and swung a right. Annie's mother lived just a few streets away. Was it possible Annie and Ruby were with Lou?

Within minutes the Mercedes was cruising slowly down Bower Road. Cars littered the road on both sides, parked bumper to bumper. Sam prayed he wouldn't meet another vehicle travelling in the opposite direction. There would be no room to pass, and he didn't fancy reversing all the way back to the junction. And then he hit the brakes. There was Annie's car. Right outside Lou's house. Sam looked around. There was nowhere to park. He accelerated forward and took a left into the next road. The place was like a rabbit warren. All the residential roads linked up. Another car-infested road greeted him. This time he turned right. More cars. Finally, four roads away, he found somewhere to park.

Sam jumped out of the Mercedes and pressed the key fob. The lights flashed as he walked away. As he strode towards Bower Road, a wind whipped up. Seconds later a fine drizzle started. Sam hunched down into his suit jacket. It wasn't the best thing to wear in the cold and wet. Pushing through Lou's gate, he took the half dozen steps to the front door two at a time. The drizzle had now turned to steady rain. Sam rang the doorbell. The hall light went on. Suddenly Ruby was standing in front of him.

'Dadd-ee!' she squealed.

'Roo-bee,' Sam laughed. Scooping his daughter into his arms, he closed his eyes and hugged her tight.

And then Ruby was yanked from his embrace.

'What the fuck are you doing here?' said Annie. Ruby crept silently behind her mother's legs.

Sam met his ex-wife's eyes. He gazed at her calmly. 'It's Tuesday. I've come to collect my daughter.'

'Well you're not having her.'

'Don't be silly, Annie. I have a Court Order permitting me access every Tuesday evening to Wednesday morning, and alternate weekends.'

'I don't care if you've got a Court Order to fly Ruby to the moon. It's not happening.'

'Annie, enough of this nonsense. Get out of the way please. I'm taking Ruby with me. Come on Ruby.' Sam extended his hand to his daughter.

'Don't you dare!' Annie rounded on Ruby. The child instantly shrank back.

'Annie, I'm not leaving until I have Ruby.'

'What's going on here?' said a shrill voice. Lou came into the hallway. She looked down her nose at Sam. 'Oh. It's you. What do you want?'

'Good evening, Lou,' said Sam politely. 'The only thing I want is my daughter.'

'And you're not having her,' Annie repeated.

'If Annie says you're not having Ruby, you're not having her. Go home,' said Lou. 'You're not welcome here.'

'Sorry, Lou, but this is nothing to do with you. And I repeat, I'm not leaving until I have Ruby.'

'Enough!' said Lou. 'Get out the way, Annie,' she shoved her daughter to one side and stood before her ex-son-in-law. 'This is *my* house, Sam, and I'm telling you to clear off.' With that Lou went to shut the door on Sam. But he was too quick. He stuck his foot in the door and pushed hard against the panels with his hands. Lou staggered backwards. Annie screamed loudly, and Ruby burst into tears. 'How dare you!' Lou grabbed hold of her daughter's arm to steady herself. She stared at Sam, visibly shaken. Sam put out a hand to reassure her. 'Don't you touch me,' she spat, 'or I'll have you for assault.'

'Look, Lou, I have no argument with you,' Sam raked his hair, 'and no harm has been done.'

'That,' hissed Annie, 'is a matter of opinion, you *cunt*. I'm calling the police.'

'For God's sake, Annie!' Sam put both his hands to his temples. 'Why are doing this to me?'

'Call the police, Mum,' Annie shouted, 'and hurry up. Ruby, go with Nanny. GO!'

'Stop it!' Sam howled. 'You're behaving as if I'm some sort of dangerous lunatic.'

'That's because you are,' screamed Annie. 'How *dare* you attack my mother?' She lunged forward, palms outstretched, and shoved Sam as hard as she could. Sam stumbled backwards as the front door slammed shut. His left heel rocked over the edge of Lou's top step, while his right foot encountered air. And suddenly Sam was tumbling.

He landed in a painful heap. For a while Sam just lay there, upside down on Lou's steps. The rain beat against his cheeks and formed rivulets which ran into his hairline. He felt water seep under his collar and roll down his back. Sam realised he was winded. It was lucky he hadn't cracked his head open, but his back was killing him. In the distance a police siren wailed. He was still sprawled on Lou's steps when the police car turned into Bower Road and screeched to a halt. The blue light flickered and blinked repeatedly across Sam's face. From his topsy-turvy perspective on the world, Sam watched Lou's gate open and a pair of size tens walk up the path.

Lou's front door sprang open. Annie jumped over Sam and rushed to the policeman's side.

'Oh thank God you're here, officer.'

'What's happened to him?' the policeman asked.

'He's my ex-husband.' Annie paused. Lou was now standing in the doorway with Ruby. 'He assaulted my mother, threatened me and terrified my daughter. Arrest him, officer.'

The policeman looked from Annie to Lou to Ruby. His gaze fell on Annie again. 'Just a moment, madam.' He crouched down next to Sam. 'Are you all right, sir?'

'My back,' Sam gasped.

'Arrest him,' Annie repeated. 'I want to press charges.'

The policeman looked up at Annie. 'Madam, right now the only person who appears injured is your ex-husband.' He turned back to Sam. 'How did you end up like this?'

'He's faking,' Annie interrupted.

'I was pushed,' said Sam.

'Do you think, if I helped, you could stand up?' asked the policeman.

'Maybe.'

'Shall we try, sir? Otherwise I'll have to call an ambulance.'

Sam did his best to nod and groaned. The policeman gently rolled Sam sideways, and as he did so Sam's gaze met Ruby's. Her eyes were like saucers, cheeks pale and streaked with tears. 'Don't let my daughter see. Please,' he whispered.

'Madam,' the policeman called to Lou. 'Take your granddaughter inside and shut the door.'

Seconds later the front door closed. Annie remained outside, standing in the rain. The policeman helped Sam fold his legs so that his heels gained purchase on one step. Sam stuck out his hands and pushed against another step. The policeman put both his arms in a loop under Sam's armpits. Bit by bit, Sam eased himself upright and into a sitting position on one of Lou's steps. He ached from head to toe.

'See. Nothing broken,' Annie sneered. '*Now* are you going to arrest him, officer?'

'Is this a domestic argument?' the policeman asked.

'Officer, I'm here to collect my daughter,' said Sam. 'But my ex-wife is withholding access.'

'He has access when I say he can have access,' Annie countered.

'I have a Court Order,' Sam asserted. 'It's in my briefcase. In my car. But I'm parked a few streets away. I'm happy to show it to you, officer.'

The policeman took a deep breath. 'Sir I'm sorry, but I can't get involved.'

'What do you mean?' Sam cried. 'My ex-wife is stopping me from seeing my child. I have every right to see my daughter! I have the documentation to prove it!'

'I'm sure you do, sir,' the policeman replied carefully. 'Unfortunately I have no more power than you against your ex-wife. You'll have to go back to Court. Tell them the problems you've been having.' The policeman looked at Annie squarely. 'I do believe though that a Court takes a pretty dim view of such things.'

Annie stood there, dripping wet now, but defiant.

'And what about me, officer?' she demanded. 'What about arresting my ex-husband for assaulting my mother?'

'I was called to check out a disturbance, madam,' said the policeman. 'As far as I'm concerned, this is a domestic. And your husband is coming with me now, so your problems are over.'

'You're arresting him?' Annie's face lit up.

'No, madam,' said the policeman curtly. 'I'm giving him a lift to his car.'

'You bloody men all stick together,' Annie snarled.

'I'm cautioning you to be careful what you say, madam. Off the record, I'm a father too. Thankfully my ex-wife is nothing like you. I strongly urge you to think upon your actions. You wouldn't want to end up on the wrong side of the law.'

And with that the policeman led Sam down the path leaving Annie inwardly raging.

Chapter Thirteen

Sam let himself into the apartment. His body ached all over. He had an overwhelming urge to break down and cry. What a bloody evening. Why was his ex so vile? What had he ever done to deserve this? He was a loving dad and made sure he was honourable to Annie. Every month hundreds of pounds were electronically transferred from his bank account to hers. He'd never missed a payment. More often than not he gave Annie extra money in her hand. Only last week she'd demanded additional funds for Ruby's swimming lessons. Sam hadn't hesitated and pressed a fifty-pound note into her palm. He would understand his ex-wife having an axe to grind if he was the sort of father who skipped payments, or bunked off seeing his kid, or shirked his responsibilities. But he wasn't. Being denied access to his daughter was the swiftest way to hurting Sam. And his ex knew it.

Sam suddenly longed to hear a friendly voice. He picked up the phone and rang Josie. She answered almost immediately.

'Hello?' she whispered.

'Hi, darling,' Sam said softly. 'I haven't disturbed you have I?'

A few miles away, Josie smiled into the handset. Sam had called her *darling*. That was a first. It was such a loving endearment, and Josie's heart sang. 'Not at all,' she assured. 'But Lucy is asleep and I didn't want the phone waking her. Hence me pouncing on it.'

'Gosh I'm sorry – I hope I haven't woken her.'

'You haven't. Promise.'

'How are you?'

'I'm good. Totally up to date with all my studies and assignments. Consequently I'm feeling very smug! And you? Have you had a lovely evening with Ruby?' There was a pause. Josie's smile faded. 'Sam? Are you still there?'

'Yes. Sorry. I just...for a moment...in all truth, I've had better evenings.' And then, like a dam bursting, Sam found himself telling Josie everything that had happened. Josie was appalled.

'So you're injured? I'm coming over.'

'No, don't, Josie–'

'Give me thirty minutes.' She hung up before Sam could argue. Seconds later she was on the phone to Kerry. 'You know that favour you owe me over the water assignment? Well I'm calling it in. Get your butt over here now.'

Ten minutes later, Kerry stood in Josie's hallway. 'Him indoors is moaning like billy-ho about me being here. He thinks I'm having an affair.'

'Well you are,' said Josie as she buttoned her coat up.

'Not with you I'm bloody not. Gawd, if I'm going to have a row with my husband, it would have been good to actually be getting my leg over instead of sitting in your house babysitting.'

'Well you can plot your next bit of adultery while watching my telly.' Josie picked up her car keys. 'And no ringing Simon Clark and having him here while I'm out.'

'Spoilsport.'

'I won't be long.'

'Take as long as you like,' Kerry waved one hand airily. 'I'm in no hurry to get home to Adam. Another hour and he'll be drunk and fast asleep in his armchair.'

'Is Toyah okay?'

'Yeah. She's sleeping over at her boyfriend's tonight.'

Josie hadn't been to Sam's apartment before, but she knew where it was. She parked in the private car park of Saddlers Court, and then let herself into the block's rear entrance. Crossing the communal gardens, she buzzed the entry phone. Seconds later she was standing outside Sam's front door. He pulled her into the hallway and held her tight. She melted into his chest. Her arms snaked around his neck. It was only when Josie tightened her grip that she realised Sam was wincing. She released him instantly.

'Let me see your back.'

'I'm fine. It's nothing. I just need a hot soak in the bath.'

'I'll be the judge of that.' It was only then that Josie took in the dirty suit jacket and soiled shirt. She gave Sam an even look. Wordlessly she slid his jacket off. Moving behind him, she pulled shirttails out of belted trousers. The breath caught in her throat. Sam's back was hard and muscular. It was also covered in bruises that seemed to be blooming before her very eyes. An angry scrape, like a carpet burn, scorched across one shoulder blade. 'Your ex did a good job on you,' Josie said quietly.

'I'll mend.' Sam attempted to laugh it off, but the sound was hollow.

'Have you eaten?'

'No. Look, don't worry about me, Josie. You shouldn't have come over–'

But Josie had spotted an open doorway to the kitchen. Moving down the hallway, she located the fridge. Rootling inside, she withdrew bread, eggs and a packet of grated cheese. A few minutes later Sam was tucking into hot buttery toast and a vast cheese omelette. Josie left him to it and went off to the bathroom. Soon the taps were blasting forth hot water. Josie tipped in some bubble bath. Kneeling down, she put her hands in the water, whooshing them backwards and forwards. Frothy towers leapt upwards. Sam appeared in the bathroom doorway.

'That was a superb omelette.'

Josie rocked back on her heels. 'Good.'

'I was hoping you'd come to my apartment one day. But I never dreamt it would be in these circumstances.' He grinned ruefully. 'Not very romantic is it, helping your battered boyfriend into the bath.'

Josie froze. She stared up at him. 'Are you?'

'Am I what?'

'My boyfriend?'

Sam gazed at Josie. She was nothing like Annie. Everything about the woman before him was soft, warm, pliable, and wonderful. He knew he was falling for her. Sam swallowed. 'Well I...hope so.' And then Josie smiled. Sam noticed how her whole face lit up.

'Then...yes. You are.' Josie stood up and walked into his arms. She inclined her head as his lips came down on hers. She kissed him hesitantly at first, and then with more urgency as their passion built. Suddenly they were tugging at each other's clothes. Josie's hands found the buttons of Sam's shirt. With shaking fingers she undid them. Sam's palms were cupping the curves of her bottom, now moving round to the zipper on her jeans and up to her top. She shrugged her way out of her blouse.

Garments began to litter the floor as they stumbled about, still joined at the mouth. Sam pulled Josie against him, wrapping his arms around her naked back, savouring her scent. It was only when the bath threatened to overflow, that they pulled apart. Josie lunged for the taps.

'That can wait,' said Sam, 'but I can't.' He held out his hand. Josie took it, and allowed him to lead her to his bedroom.

And one by one, the bath's bubbles silently popped.

Chapter Fourteen
Three months later – December

Josie was in love, and she didn't care who knew it. Her parents had half-guessed a man was responsible for their daughter's emotional transition. Almost overnight Josie had gone from coping on auto-pilot to full-blown elation. Josie's parents were happy their daughter was happy, and had dropped hints about meeting Sam. Likewise her sister, Julia. However, Nick's parents hadn't been so chuffed when Josie had mentioned she was dating.

'My son – your husband,' Marjorie Payne had exhorted, 'hasn't been dead a year. It's disrespectful.'

Alf Payne had puffed out his cheeks. 'Quite frankly I'm shocked. It doesn't seem right.'

'I'm sorry you both feel that way,' Josie had said quietly. 'But life goes on. If it had been me in that car crash and Nick surviving, I wouldn't have wanted him mourning me forever. And anyway,' Josie had quavered whilst gazing at their stony faces, 'it's not as if I'm engaged to be married. It's just a few dates!'

A few dates wasn't strictly true. Josie had crammed Sam into every available moment between looking after Lucy and studying flat out for the first lot of college exams. She'd lived and breathed Sam. During the day his face invaded her thoughts. At night she dreamt about him. When they were together, her hands constantly touched him. When they made love, she floated into another dimension. Josie had never known anything like it. And amazingly Sam felt the same way about her. She couldn't believe how lucky she was to feel so loved and cherished. It was intoxicating.

Throughout this, Josie and Sam had kept their daughters firmly out of their blossoming romance. But a shift had occurred in their relationship. Last week, as Josie had lain in Sam's arms, he'd said something that had made Josie's heart beat a little faster.

'You do realise,' Sam had paused to kiss her forehead, 'that I'm deeply in love with you. So much so, I think of you as my partner. My life partner.'

Josie had manoeuvred her body so she'd been able to properly look at him. The tenderness in Sam's eyes had hit her like a ten-ton truck, and she'd known in that moment she felt the same way too. The talk had turned to their daughters.

'Don't you think it's time I met Lucy and you met Ruby?' Sam had smiled. Josie had hesitated. This was big stuff. Josie was up to speed about Sam's ex-wife and the difficulties Annie created over seeing Ruby. A Court case loomed in the New Year. Therefore Josie knew Sam wouldn't entertain introducing a woman to his daughter unless he was one-hundred per cent certain she was going to remain firmly in his life. Likewise, the last thing Josie wanted for her own daughter was to have a succession of 'uncles' coming and going. Deep in her heart, Josie had hoped that Lucy would one day have a father figure in her life. She just hadn't counted on it happening so soon. Certainly she couldn't think of a nicer or more suitable man than Sam Worthington. And Josie had a feeling that Lucy would absolutely adore Sam.

'Okay,' she'd grinned and nodded her head. 'We could certainly have a casual get-together. See how things go. What had you in mind?'

'Christmas isn't far away.' Sam had sat up, excitement illuminating his face. 'What about a pantomime?'

'Won't everywhere be booked?'

'Leave it to me!'

Sure enough, Sam had secured four tickets to see Cinderella at The Churchill Theatre. Josie didn't know how he'd managed it. Lucy was so excited at the prospect of going to her first panto.

And now, as Josie chivvied Lucy into her duffle coat and ushered her out the front door, she wondered how the afternoon would pan out. For neither Lucy nor Ruby had a clue they were about to meet each other or the other's parent. Josie and Sam had decided to stage friendship. The plan was to pretend not to know each other, jostle together in the entrance, make polite small talk, and then exclaim at sitting together in the auditorium. Then, in the interval, Sam would politely suggest having an ice-cream all together followed by...well...just seeing how their daughters took to both each other and Josie and Sam. Caution was the key word. And if there were any problems, they'd pull back. Review the situation. Their children, they agreed, had to come first.

Josie started the car. Her stomach was leaping with both nerves and excitement. She reversed out of the driveway and headed off towards Bromley. She only hoped their grand plan would go well. But as everybody knows, even the best laid plans can turn on their head.

Sam hung around the theatre entrance. People were milling about, shuffling through the door, splitting up and breaking off to queue for sweets or programmes. Cheerful usherettes mingled among the crowd, their strapped on boxes piled high with flashing headbands and glo-rings. Children stared, enthralled, at the goodies. Parents dug deep in pockets. Ruby tugged at Sam's sleeve.

'Daddy, please can I have a flashing headband?'

'Of course, sweetheart.'

Sam moved towards one of the usherettes just as Josie swung through the theatre doors. He caught her eye. Josie instantly bent her head to talk to the little girl holding her hand. Sam saw the two of them confer. Lucy was now pulling her mother towards the same usherette.

'Can I wear the headband now, Mummy?' Sam heard Lucy ask.

'I don't see why not,' Josie was saying. And now she was standing right next to him.

'Excuse me, are you in the queue?' she asked Sam.

'Yes. But please – after you.'

Whereupon Ruby and Lucy had started giggling at each other. Sam and Josie had been flummoxed. It simply hadn't come up in conversation where their respective daughters went to school.

'Well how lovely that Ruby has a friend here,' said Sam. He stuck out a hand. 'I'm Sam Worthington by the way.'

Josie took it. 'Josie Payne. And this is my daughter, Lucy.'

'Hello,' Lucy smiled shyly.

'Ruby, say hello to Josie,' Sam prompted.

Ruby stared up at Josie. 'Hello. Are you friends with my Daddy?'

'I guess I am now,' Josie gave a brief shoulder shrug and laughed.

Ruby's gaze was unflinching. 'Does that mean you're a trollop?'

There was a stunned pause only broken by Lucy. 'What's a trollop?'

'Are you buying?' asked the usherette.

Josie jumped. 'Um, yes. I'll have a flashing headband please.' She delved into her purse and removed a tenner.

Seconds later the public address system asked everybody to take their seats in the auditorium.

'Where are you sitting?' Ruby asked Lucy.

'Mummy?' Lucy turned to Josie.

'Er,' Josie pretended to consult a piece of paper in her bag. In reality Sam had the tickets.

'What a coincidence,' said Sam peering into the depths of Josie's handbag. 'You're sitting next to us. Everybody follow me.'

The girls squealed with laughter and skipped down the aisle, headbands flashing away. They wanted to sit next to both their parents and each other. So Josie and Sam ended up sitting apart. Not that it mattered. They were both too relieved their daughters were getting on like the proverbial house on fire.

In the interval Sam bought ice-creams. And when Cinderella finally married her prince and the curtain came crashing down to rapturous applause, Sam suggested they all go for a pizza.

Outside it was dark. The High Street was ablaze with Christmas lights. Carols blared out of a distant loudspeaker. Shoppers, arms loaded with Christmas purchases, hurried this way and that, their breath misting the early evening air. Sam led the way to an Italian restaurant along North Street.

'This is nice,' Sam murmured in Josie's ear. He was finally sitting next to her. 'Here's to a very successful afternoon.' He picked up his glass of chilled white wine and clinked it against Josie's.

'Indeed,' she whispered back. 'I'm so happy the girls are enjoying each other's company.'

Sam took Josie's hand under the table. 'You know, I've got Ruby for Christmas Day. What about we all get together?'

'Is that an invitation for me to do the cooking, Mr Worthington?'

'Ah, I guess I didn't word that very well.'

'Actually, we'll probably be sharing the day with my parents and in-laws, but we could get together later. Christmas tea perhaps?'

'Sounds like a plan.' And Sam gave her hand a squeeze.

The following morning Ruby awoke in her bedroom at Daddy's apartment. She couldn't tell the time yet, but fingers of light filtered through spaces in the curtains. Outside she could hear birdsong. If the birds were awake, it must be time to get up.

Ruby flung back her Barbie cover and padded over to her wardrobe. She had her own clothes at Daddy's because Mummy wouldn't let Ruby bring clothes she'd paid for herself to Daddy's flat. Daddy had to buy extra clothes for Ruby's to wear here. Invariably the clothes Daddy bought ended up at Mummy's house. Mummy never returned the clothes to Daddy. But Daddy didn't mind, saying he was happy to buy Ruby more.

Ruby reached into the wardrobe and pulled out her dressing gown, then went to find Daddy. His bedroom door was open. So was Daddy's mouth. He was in bed, lying on his back and snoring loudly. Ruby giggled. Daddy opened one eye.

'Good morning, princess,' her father yawned.

Ruby scampered over to the other side of Daddy's bed and clambered under the duvet. She wriggled close to her father. He put an arm around her and for a little while they both drifted.

'You are a fidget,' Daddy finally declared. 'So much so, I think I'm going to get out of bed.'

'What are we going to do today?' Ruby asked as she followed her father into the kitchen.

'Unfortunately I have to get you home to Mummy fairly soon.' Daddy lifted her onto a stool at the kitchen table. It's your Nanny's birthday. I think Mummy is doing a little party for her.'

'Oh,' said Ruby. 'I don't really want to go to Nanny's birthday party. It will be boring. And full of old people. Can't we see Josie and Lucy instead? I really like Josie. She's pretty. Do you think Josie's pretty, Daddy?'

'Yes,' her father nodded, 'I think she's very pretty.' He put a cereal bowl on the table and shook some Coco Pops into it. 'I thought I might ask her out actually. Do you think she'd like me to take her out?'

'Maybe,' Ruby added some milk to her cereal. Some slopped on the table. Daddy didn't tell her off. He never minded if she made a mess. 'If she agrees to go out with you, does that mean she'll be your trollop?'

Daddy pulled a chair out and sat down opposite. 'No, princess. And actually, that isn't a very good word to use. It's best not to say it anymore.'

'But Mummy says it.'

'I know. But she's...mistaken. The correct word is *girlfriend*. So if Josie agrees to go out with me, that's what she'll be. A girlfriend.'

Ruby munched her cereal. 'I think Mummy would like a boyfriend.'

'It would be nice if Mummy had a boyfriend,' her father said carefully. 'I'd like Mummy to be happy again.'

Ruby slurped chocolate milk from her bowl. 'I think Nigel might have asked Mummy out again.'

'Really?'

'Yes. He rang the other day. Mummy got very angry with him. She said she wouldn't go out with him ever again because he was a fucking bastard.'

Daddy flinched. 'Don't use words like that, Ruby. They're bad words.'

'Mummy uses them.'

Daddy blew out his cheeks and wiped a hand across his forehead. 'Tell you what, princess, would you like an early Christmas present?'

'Yes!'

'Come on. It's in the lounge.'

Ruby jumped down from the table. How exciting! She wondered what it could be. She hastened into the adjacent room.

On the sideboard was a small package. Ruby's brow puckered. Whatever it was, it wasn't a Barbie doll. She attacked the ribbon and bow with gusto before shredding the wrapping paper. On the box was a picture of a mobile phone. Ruby couldn't believe her eyes. How grown up was that!

'Shall I help you open it?' Daddy asked.

'I'll be able to ring all my friends up!' Ruby chattered excitedly. And then her face fell. 'Oh. None of my friends have mobile phones.'

'Never mind,' said Daddy. 'You can ring me instead. And I'll be able to ring you.'

Ruby beamed with pleasure. 'I won't have to ask Mummy if I can speak to you anymore. Or have her snatch the phone out of my hand.'

'That's right,' said Daddy. 'We can talk to each other whenever we want. Let me show you how to charge the battery and how to work it.'

Annie opened her front door. Sam stood on the doorstep with Ruby.

'You're late,' Annie snapped.

Sam looked at his watch. 'It's not yet ten o'clock.'

'I told you to have Ruby home at half nine.'

'I could have sworn you said ten–'

'Are you calling me a liar?'

'No! I just...look...I'm sorry if I misunderstood. No harm done eh? Lou's birthday party isn't until this afternoon.'

'That's not the point. It's the principle of the matter.' Annie froze. 'What's that in your hand, Ruby?'

'It's an early Christmas present,' Ruby beamed. 'Look! Daddy bought me my very own mobile–'

The phone was snatched from Ruby's hand. Annie stared at it. Her lip curled back. 'You fucking bastard, Sam.'

'Look, Annie, could you please stop using bad language in front of Ruby. She swore in my presence earlier on and if–'

'Shut the fuck up. Don't you *dare* presume to talk to Ruby on a phone without my permission?' Annie slotted the mobile into the back pocket of her jeans. She saw Ruby's lip wobble. Damn her ex-husband for doing this! It was *his* fault their daughter was now upset. 'I've told you before, Sam, and I'll tell you again. I'm the one who decides when you see Ruby. And I'm the one who decides when you can talk to her on the telephone. You really shouldn't have done that. You've made things difficult for yourself now. Very difficult.'

'What do you mean?'

'That's for me to know and you to find out. Come on, Ruby.' Annie jerked her head. 'Indoors. Now.'

'Can I give Ruby a kiss good–'

The door slammed in his face. Sam knew better than to ring the doorbell or argue. Roll on the New Year and the Court case. He just hoped his solicitor and the presiding judge would give it to Annie with both barrels.

When Sam saw Ruby again, two days prior to Christmas, she had the mobile phone in her little rucksack. Sam checked it. The battery was charged. He scrolled through the numbers. Annie had deleted Sam's mobile and landline numbers. Instead she'd programmed in her own landline and mobile numbers, and also Lou's contact numbers. Sam felt his stomach constrict into the familiar knot. Why did Annie do this? He was worried about his ex-wife's bitterness impacting on Ruby. The fact that his daughter was repeating bad language made his heart twist. He programmed his numbers back into the phone before replacing the mobile into the rucksack. Sam wandered into the lounge. Ruby was munching her way through a packet of crisps whilst watching a Walt Disney DVD. On the screen Peter Pan was flying through the air with Wendy.

'Fancy doing some cooking when the film has finished?'

Ruby pressed the pause button. 'Ooooh yes. I love playing with flour and butter. Can we do it now? I'll watch the rest of this later.' She put the crisps down and stood up. 'What shall we cook?'

'What about mince pies?' Sam walked into the kitchen. 'I've invited Josie and Lucy over for Christmas tea, so we'll need to make at least twelve.'

'Yay!' Ruby hollered while jumping up and down.

As father and daughter set about cooking up a festive storm, little did Sam realise that a very different storm was about to break. That in forty-eight hours time his Christmas would be wrecked. And Ruby would be halfway across the world.

Chapter Fifteen

'Happy Christmas, Josie,' Sam cupped the phone into his shoulder as he lifted a china mug from the kitchen cupboard. On the worktop, the kettle began to boil. 'I hope you have a lovely day with your family. I can't wait to see you later darling. Ruby has made a stack of mince pies, so I hope you and Lucy like them.'

Josie grinned into the handset. 'We certainly do. Can I bring anything?'

'Just yourselves,' Sam chucked a teabag into the mug and poured boiling water over it. 'We can play charades later and watch a movie. I've got Miracle on 34th Street.'

'Sounds good.' Josie lowered her voice. 'I'm looking forward to seeing you.'

'Me too. I have a present for you. Just something little.'

'Only small?' Josie teased. 'I was hoping for a big one.'

Sam chuckled. 'You can have the big one when it's just the two of us. See you later, gorgeous.'

Sam then tried ringing Ruby's mobile, but it was off. He sighed. It had been switched off last night too, when he'd telephoned to say goodnight. He'd only succeeded in ringing Ruby once on the mobile he'd bought her. And as soon as Annie had realised their daughter was talking to him, she'd snatched the mobile from Ruby and switched it off. Sam told himself it didn't matter. That he'd see Ruby soon anyway.

Sam then spent the rest of the morning cooking a chicken roast dinner for Ruby and himself. While he tended to the vegetables, he telephoned his two sisters, nephews and parents, all of whom lived in Leicestershire. He assured his mother he would see them all tomorrow, and yes he would stay a few days, yes he'd drive carefully on the upward journey, yes it was cold but as far as he was aware there was no snow or black ice on the roads, and no he wouldn't forget to wrap up warmly.

The timer on the oven went off. Sam covered everything in foil and turned the oven to low. The Christmas pudding was Tesco's own and would only take a few minutes in the microwave. In the fridge was a carton of cream, and in the freezer he had Ruby's favourite ice-cream. There was a stack of cold meats, salad and sausage rolls for later when Josie and Lucy joined them.

Checking the time, Sam saw he it was nearly mid-day. His seasonal access this year was Christmas Day from noon until Boxing Day noon. Next year it would be Annie's turn leaving Sam's access to be Christmas Eve until Christmas Day morning. Sam grabbed his car keys and did a quick check around the room. The Christmas tree's fairy lights twinkled. There was a lovely stack of presents, and Father Christmas had kindly visited not just Annie's house but Sam's apartment too. Ruby's stocking lay under the tree. Whistling merrily, Sam let himself out of the apartment.

When the Mercedes purred into Annie's road, the parking was more chaotic than ever. Sam decided to pull up alongside Annie's house and beep the horn. With a bit of luck she'd hear and Ruby could jump straight in the car. He braked and put the Mercedes' hazard lights on. Nothing was coming in either direction. Sam gave the horn a couple of toots. Annie's door remained shut. The front bay window looked rather gloomy. No Christmas lights shone from within.

A horrible churning began to play in Sam's stomach. He had an uneasy sense of déjà vu. He tooted the horn again. Net curtains twitched in the neighbour's house to the left. Sam glanced up and down the road. No traffic. He decided to risk blocking the road for a couple of minutes and jumped out of the car. As he walked through Annie's garden gate, the door to the neighbour's house opened.

'She's not in,' said the old lady, 'so you might as well stop beeping that horn of yours.'

'Sorry if I disturbed you,' Sam apologised. 'I expect Annie's at her mother's. I'll be off. Happy Christmas,' he put up a hand and walked back to the car.

'Does her mother live a long way away?' the old lady called after him.

Sam stopped and turned round. 'About five minutes from here. Why?'

'I don't think she'll be at her mother's then. She took suitcases. Big suitcases. Looked like she was planning on being away for quite a few days.'

Sam opened his mouth to say something, but nothing came out. He stood there, a look of bewilderment on his face. Wordlessly he turned on his heel. Throwing himself into the Mercedes, he roared off to Bower Road.

When Sam screeched to a halt outside Lou's house, he didn't give a hoot if his vehicle was blocking the road. He raced up the steps, rang the doorbell and then stood to one side. Nobody was pushing him down these steps again! Sam could hear merriment coming from inside the house. Christmas hits were belting out of tinny speakers. There was the sound of children running around. Annie's nephews and nieces no doubt. Sam rang the bell a second time and took to the door knocker for good measure. Out of his peripheral vision, Sam saw a van had entered Bower Road. He rattled the door knocker again. The van had now ground to a halt in front of Sam's Mercedes. And now a window was buzzing down. A man with a pissed off expression stuck his head out.

'Oi mate, move yer bleedin' car.'

Sam put up a hand up by way of apology. 'Just give me a minute please,' he called. His guts were really starting to knot up now. Why was it always like this? Why did Annie make things so difficult for him? The van driver tooted impatiently. Sam resorted to leaning on the doorbell with one hand and rapping the door knocker continuously with the other. The van driver was now aping Sam and sounding one long note of his van's horn. Sam's head began to throb.

Suddenly the door flew open and Sam nearly fell into the hallway.

'Get out of my house.' Lou pulled herself up to her full five feet two inches. 'If you've come to make trouble on Christmas Day I'll have the police after you, and this time they'll lock you up.'

'Where's Ruby?' Sam demanded.

'What's going on, Mum?' Stella, Annie's oldest sister, had appeared in the hallway. Her eyes met Sam's. 'Ah.' There was a sudden rumpus as Stella's two boys shot into the hallway, thoroughly over-excited. They had paper party streamers in their mouths which they repeatedly blew. The duck-like sound merged with the horn of the van driver out in the road.

'Where's my daughter?' Sam asked Stella.

'Sorry, Sam, it's nothing to do with me. But I think what Annie's done is bang out of order. She's behaved like a right cow.'

'Don't you talk about your sister like that,' Lou turned on Stella.

'Well it's true,' Stella said. 'Right you two,' she grabbed hold of her young sons, 'get back in the lounge. Dave!' she called to her feckless husband. 'Sort these kids out. Mum, you go and see to the dinner. Leave me to speak to Sam.'

Lou looked from Stella to Sam, lips pursed. 'Any trouble,' she jabbed a finger at Sam, 'and you'll go down. Understand?'

'I've done nothing wrong!' Sam raised his voice.

'There you go!' Lou spat, 'Shouting the place down and behaving in a threatening manner. I'm calling the police.'

'MOVE YOUR FUCKING CAR,' bellowed the van driver.

'Look, Sam,' Stella put a placatory hand on Sam's forearm. 'Just do yourself a favour and go home.'

'I want to see my daughter,' Sam's voice cracked. 'Ruby is spending Christmas Day and tonight with me.'

'No she's not, Sam. Ruby's in America. Annie's taken her to Florida. Walt Disney World. They went yesterday. With Nigel and his boys. Annie and Nigel are back on again.'

Sam stared at his ex sister-in-law. He shook his head. 'No. That's not true.'

'Yes it is, Sam. I'm sorry.' Stella withdrew her hand and took a step back into the hallway. 'Go home. For what it's worth...Happy Christmas.'

'Happy Christmas?' Sam stared at the front door as it closed in his face. His daughter was in America. Happy Christmas? He went down the steps on auto-pilot. Ruby was in Florida. Walt Disney World no less. The very place he'd hoped to take her himself. Happy Christmas? He wondered how long Ruby would be gone. It wasn't worth going all that way for one week. More likely a fortnight. Happy Christmas?

'YOU FUCKING PLEB!' yelled the van driver as Sam climbed into the Mercedes. 'Happy fucking Christmas you DICKHEAD!'

Sam revved the engine. Through the windscreen he stared at the apoplectic van driver. He could see the guy's mouth working overtime. No doubt he was letting rip with another stream of invective. Sam's eyes misted. The guy's face blurred and for a moment it morphed into Annie's. Her mouth was always working overtime. Twisting this way and that. Lips pinched, pursed, or stretched right back as she opened her jaw to spew forth a tirade of filth. For one heart-stopping moment Sam had an overwhelming desire to press down on the accelerator, crash into the van and shove it, backwards, all the way down Bower Road and out onto the High Street, preferably into the path of an oncoming steamroller. The van driver must have caught a flash of momentary madness in Sam's eyes, for he suddenly ceased leaning on his horn and his mouth stopped working. Sam's head was full of the roar of the Mercedes' engine. His heart was banging away somewhere in the region of his temples. And then Sam took his foot off the accelerator. The engine note dropped. With his left hand shaking slightly, he put the gear into reverse and carefully backed up to the T-junction at the other end of Bower Road.

A quarter of an hour later he was back at his apartment. As he walked into his hallway, the delicious smell of chicken roast dinner assaulted his nostrils. The smell seemed to mock him. He went into the kitchen and turned the oven off. For a moment he leant against the warm oven door. And then his face crumpled.

Four and a half thousand miles away, Annie peered out of the hotel window. Balmy breezes and swaying palms might not be everyone's idea of a typical Christmas, but right now she had no complaints.

Up until two weeks ago, Annie and Nigel had hardly spoken to each other. At the Pilkington Medical Practice they'd skirted neatly around each other ever since their split. Then out of the blue Nigel had telephoned Annie at home. He'd wanted to talk, but she'd told him in no uncertain terms she wasn't interested. And that, Annie had thought, was that. But at work one morning, two of Nigel's patients had consecutively cancelled within minutes of each other. It was a busy practice with six GPs in total and as many admin girls behind the reception desk. So when Nigel had filled the patient gap by requesting Annie to step into his consulting room, she'd known it was personal.

'I'm not going to beat around the bush,' Nigel had said. 'But for what it's worth I miss you. A lot. I'd like us to try again.'

'I can't deal with your boys, Nigel,' Annie had said.

'I could say the same thing about Ruby,' Nigel had shrugged. 'It's never going to be easy when we have kids by other partners. But I'm sure, in time, things will get better.'

'I don't know.'

'I'm going to Florida for Christmas. Aiden and Ben are coming with me.'

Annie had folded her arms across her chest. 'I hope you all have a nice time.'

'Hear me out. We're doing Walt Disney World for the first week, Clearwater for the last. I took a chance Annie. A chance on us. I've booked you and Ruby to come too. Let's start again. We don't have to rush back into living together – just do things slowly. For now, separate houses with our respective kids. But shared holidays. And perhaps you can stay over on the weekends Ruby is with her father and my boys are with their mother?'

For a moment Annie had been speechless. And then the cogs of her brain had started whirring. She hadn't been able to afford a holiday this year. The thought of jetting off for some winter sun was appealing. Plus it would be nice to be one half of a couple again. And how great would it be to take Ruby to Walt Disney World! And how nice to pre-empt Sam's plans to do the same thing. There was the small matter of a Court Order decreeing that Sam had access for twenty-four hours over Christmas. But she didn't give a toss about that. Any judge worth his salt would agree there was no comparison between twenty-four hours with one parent cooped up in a flat, or two weeks with the other parent in Florida. It was a no-brainer.

'In that case,' Annie had undulated over to Nigel and plonked herself down on his lap, 'I'd better get the suitcases down from the loft.'

Annie helped herself to a breakfast muffin. Nigel and his boys were tucking into a full English. Ruby was nibbling a chocolate croissant. The children had, thankfully, all been getting on like a house on fire. Aiden, at the age of seven, was the one who had the most rapport with Ruby. Ben, ten years old, was hoping to pal up with some older children at the hotel.

In the dining room was a vast Christmas tree. It looked surreal against the bright blue sky outside. A second mega tree graced the lobby. Its fake snow and umpteen fairy lights provided an incongruous backdrop against tourists in shorts and flip-flops.

'Well Happy Christmas everybody,' said Nigel putting his knife and fork together. 'What an amazing Christmas this is eh?' he smiled around the table. 'Who's looking forward to seeing Mickey Mouse?'

'Me!' the children chorused.

'Well before we go see him, somebody in Reception told me that Father Christmas had visited our rooms while we were having our breakfast. There are three stockings in our suite addressed to Aiden, Ben and Ruby.'

The children suddenly lost interest in food. 'What are we waiting for?' Ben whooped in excitement.

'Hold on a minute, guys,' Nigel put up a hand. 'We're going to have a great day. But before we kick off I want you two,' he nodded at Aiden and Ben, 'to give your Mum a call and wish her Happy Christmas. Deal?'

'Deal,' they agreed.

Ruby looked timidly at her mother. 'Can I ring Daddy?'

Annie smiled indulgently. 'Of course. He'll be over the moon to hear from you.' She turned to Nigel. 'You go on up. We'll be right behind you.' Annie waited for Nigel and the boys to leave the table, then rootled through her handbag. She pulled out Ruby's mobile phone. Switching it on, she waited for the network to kick in. A minute later the display registered half a dozen missed calls from Sam. The phone tinkled. Ah, a voicemail too. She ignored it and rang Sam's mobile. He answered on the first ring. Wordlessly, Annie passed the mobile to Ruby.

'Hello, Daddy!' Ruby chirruped. 'Happy Christmas. Are you having a nice day?'

Back in the UK, Sam listened to his daughter's disembodied voice and felt his heart twist with both love and pain. 'Hello, princess.' His voice caught. He coughed and wiped the cuff of his sleeve across his eyes. 'I'm having a lovely Christmas, darling. But I'll bet it's not as wonderful as yours. What are you up to?'

'I'm going to see Mickey Mouse,' Ruby gabbled, 'and Snow White and Cinderella and there's going to be massive rides and fireworks and–'

Annie took the phone from Ruby. 'That's enough now. It's costing too much money to speak to Daddy for more than a minute. Finish your croissant and let me quickly talk to him.' Annie stood up and turned away from Ruby. 'Happy Christmas, Sam.'

For a moment Sam was overwhelmed with an emotion he didn't want to acknowledge. Regrettably, the feeling was becoming more and more familiar. Hatred. He didn't think he'd ever truly hated anybody in his entire life. Until now. 'You do realise, Annie, that I'm going to see you in Court over this don't you?'

'Oh please. Don't deny your daughter some fun. How selfish are you?'

'I'm not selfish. I was going to take Ruby to Walt Disney World myself. But this isn't about Florida. It's about you going behind my back. Taking off with no warning. You didn't even have the decency to tell me about your plans.'

'What, and have you stop me? More turning up on my doorstep and creating a scene?'

'Annie, all I want is what's right and fair – seeing my daughter without hassle. Sticking to access as decreed by a Court of Law. Just being allowed to be a father to my daughter without you constantly twisting words...or causing trouble...or making scenes...or just generally making my life a misery. Why, Annie? Why?'

'Don't speak to me like that, Sam, or you'll make things even more difficult for yourself. I'm seriously thinking about not returning to England.' Annie paused, allowing her words to sink into Sam's head. 'It's beautiful out here. A lovely place to raise a child. I'm looking into emigrating, Sam. Do you understand? So stop whinging about not seeing Ruby. Up until now you don't know how lucky you've been seeing your daughter.'

Sam thought he was going to have a coronary. His heart was now physically hurting. 'Emigrating? I don't think so! Now you listen to me, you witch. You bloody bitch. You aren't taking my daughter to live abroad. Not now. Not ever. Not...hello?' But Sam was talking to thin air. Seconds later his mobile tinkled the arrival of a text. With shaking hands, he clicked on the message.

I can do anything I want, Sam. And don't you forget it. And because you verbally abused me, you will be punished. There will be no further telephone contact with Ruby until I deem otherwise. Don't bother texting back. This mobile will be switched off.

Sam stared at his mobile phone in disbelief. He had no idea of his daughter's exact whereabouts, or even if he'd ever see his daughter again.

Chapter Sixteen

Sam didn't realise he'd fallen asleep on the sofa until the flat's entry phone buzzed. He hauled himself upright and squinted at the clock on the lounge wall. Oh God. It would be Josie. With Lucy. They were meant to be having tea and Ruby's mince pies. Exchanging presents. Playing charades. Watching *Miracle on 34th Street*. Sam couldn't do it. He just couldn't. He'd break down. And that was the last thing he wanted to do in front of them both. The entry phone buzzed again. He picked up the handset.

'Hello.'

'Hi, darling!'

'Come up.'

Sam pressed the door release button. Lucy's head was the first to appear bobbing up the stairwell. As she turned on the half landing, he caught her face. It was alight with excitement. He wondered if Ruby had a similar expression on her face at this moment. And now Josie was bringing up the rear. She was carrying Christmas gift bags and puffing slightly. Her eyes met Sam's and a wide grin split her face in two. And then the smile faltered. Now she stood uncertainly outside his door.

'Are you all right?'

'Yeah, yeah. I'm good.'

'You don't look it. In fact you look dreadful.'

There was a pause. Lucy broke the silence. 'Can we come in? I want to see Ruby.'

'Yes, of course. Sorry. I'm not thinking properly.' Sam stood to one side. 'Happy Christmas.'

'Happy Christmas,' Lucy sang as she brushed past Sam. She skipped off down the hallway.

Josie remained on the landing. 'What's wrong, Sam?'

Sam looked up at the ceiling and blinked hard several times. 'Um, I guess everything. For me anyway. I haven't seen my daughter today and...' Sam's voice cracked. His eyes returned to the ceiling. More rapid blinking. He regained his composure. 'Look, Josie. I'm really sorry. But would you mind terribly if I cancelled. I'm feeling pretty lousy right now. I'm not the best of company and I don't want to spoil the rest of your day.'

Lucy reappeared and ducked under Sam's arm. 'Where's Ruby?'

Sam looked at her. 'Unfortunately she's not here. Her Mummy took her to Walt Disney World.'

'Oh wow,' Lucy's jaw dropped, 'what a brilliant Christmas present.'

Josie looked astonished. 'America?'

'Yes. And apparently Annie likes it over there so much, she might not come back.' Sam wrestled with his emotions. 'I need to be alone,' he whispered.

'Yes of course. How dreadful for you. I'm so sorry. That's just–' Josie paused. No matter what words of comfort she offered, nothing was going to help. She turned to Lucy and took her hand. 'Come along, sweetheart. Unfortunately Sam's not well. We'll have to do this another time.' And then, before she forgot, she turned back and thrust the Christmas bags at Sam. 'I...we...this is from us.'

Sam took them. Stared at the red foil carriers covered in snowflakes. 'Thanks. I have something for you too. And Lucy. Let me just–'

'It's fine. Another time.'

'No, really. Wait.'

Josie didn't want to follow Sam into the apartment. She could feel the cloud of gloom within. Even now it was spilling out of the flat. Spiralling around her ankles. Making her feel depressed. She remained resolutely on the landing. Josie had a horrible urge to cry. The day had been difficult enough. The first Christmas without Nick. Fortunately Lucy hadn't been too sad. But lunch with Alf and Marjorie had been tricky. Marjorie had grabbed hold of a napkin covered in galloping reindeer and trumpeted into it several times over the turkey. Her own parents had made sure the in-laws' sherry glasses were constantly topped to the brim. It was only when they'd gone home after the Queen's Speech that Ted and Miriam had dared to get the champagne out.

'Are you up to a bit of celebrating, darling?' Ted had tentatively asked his daughter.

'Of course, Dad,' Josie had assured. 'Although I'll just have half a glass. I'll be driving in a couple of hours.'

It was the thought of seeing Sam that had kept Josie going through the day. Perhaps, if she hadn't met Sam, she would have sat around moping for the loss of her usual Christmas. Nick eating too much. Sitting down and falling asleep in front of the television. Patting her bottom and saying, 'That was a nice bit of turkey, love.' Certainly there wouldn't have been any exchange of mushy sentiments. No romance. Which was why Josie had so been looking forward to today. Because with Sam it was most definitely romance. Well it had been. Up until now.

Sam reappeared and thrust a large badly wrapped package at Lucy and a smaller, professionally wrapped and beribboned gift at Josie.

'Forgive me, Josie.'

'There's nothing to forgive.' Josie's voice wobbled. 'When will I see you?'

'I'll be at my parents' for the next few days. I haven't seen them for months. So I'll stay with them until New Year's Day. I'll call you when I'm back.'

And then he took Josie in his arms and held her tight for a moment. Dropping a kiss on the top of her head, he released her, tweaked Lucy's ponytail, and then stepped back inside the apartment. Josie took hold of Lucy's hand again and together, they made their way down the stairs and back to the car. What a wash out. Happy Christmas, Josie. Happy chuffing Christmas. And in the back of her mind, a small doubt about Sam began to form. He was a lovely guy. Gorgeous. Open and honest. Loving and decent. So many good qualities. But... Josie started the car up. Why was there always a *but?* She tried to bat the doubts away. Well, just the one doubt. But it was a big doubt. She'd known pretty much all along that Sam's ex caused him a lot of problems. And all over Ruby. Josie's worry was – if she hooked up permanently with Sam – would Sam's ex impact upon her and Lucy? What if, right now, Josie was living with Sam? Married to him? Then today would have been absolutely horrendous. Even more unbearable than this moment. Right now Josie could step out of Sam's misery and go home to her own space. She could put on some music, or watch a bit of telly – a comedy maybe. Something to make her laugh and forget the gloom for a little while. But if she was living with Sam, there would be no escape from misery moments caused by his ex. And for the first time, Josie began to worry whether falling in love with Sam would involve more heartache than happiness.

Sam put the phone down. He'd been talking to his mother. Joyce Worthington had been disgusted upon hearing about Annie's latest treatment of her son.

'And to think she dares to call any woman friend a *trollop* when she is the one who has behaved like a tart,' Joyce had sniffed. 'Annie is the ruddy trollop – dropping her drawers for a doctor at the practice where she worked.'

Sam had placated his mother. He felt too weary to listen to a rant. 'I'm more concerned about the impact on Ruby. I don't want her being a tug-of-love child.'

His father had been less vocal. Nonetheless he'd detected Stan Worthington's quiet fury across the one-hundred and fifty mile distance.

Sam pulled out a suitcase and began chucking things into it, including Josie's Christmas present. A long drive in the dark to Leicestershire was just what he needed. Nothing for company, except a motorway stretching on and on. And maybe the radio. He reckoned if he left now he'd be at his parents' place just before midnight. It would be a brief hello, hug and goodnight before tumbling into his old childhood bed. And then he could draw a line under today. Forget about all its upset.

Ten minutes later Sam was in the Mercedes. Another ten and he was on the M25. As he drove, his mind turned to all the other single fathers out there. Men like him. Some were successfully seeing their children. A great many more weren't. He knew he wasn't the only father who had access problems. You only had to pick up a newspaper and read the awful headlines. Never a month went by without some tragic story being splashed across the broadsheets. And the on-line comments from the public never ceased to amaze Sam. 'Fathers like this are despicable and wicked.' Sam didn't condone some of these men's terrible actions. But a very small part of him recognised they'd been pushed into madness. That they'd crossed a line and fallen into the blackest depression. The worst desperation. What sort of women had pushed them? But Sam knew. They were women like Annie.

And it didn't matter who you were. Whether you were rich, poor, a dustman or a celebrity. Why, only recently an actress's ex had hit the headlines. A brawl had taken place between him and the actress's fiancé. And why? Because the actress wanted to move to a different country. And the fiancé had had the cheek to tell the ex that he needed to move on. Move on! Ha! The day Nigel took over the parenting reins and told him to move on so Ruby could live in America, would be over Sam's dead body. Sam shuddered. Nobody was going to stop him seeing his daughter. And nobody was going to drive him mad in the process. Sam switched the radio on and let the Mercedes eat up the miles.

Josie snuggled down under her duvet. It was nearly midnight. She hadn't yet opened Sam's present. She'd delayed the moment. Held on to the package. Savoured it. As if by stringing out the unwrapping, she could salvage some of the sweetness they should have shared together today. The present was by the bed. She propped herself up on one elbow and stared at the pretty paper and gold ribbon. Lucy had adored the enormous plush teddy Sam had given her. She hoped Ruby would enjoy the doll she'd bought her. If Ruby ever came back to the UK of course.

Josie sighed and reached for the gift. She pulled off a tiny envelope taped to the paper and set it to one side. Upon tearing the wrap, a swanky jeweller's box was revealed. Inside that box was another one. Opening it up, she gasped. Earrings. Diamonds in the shape of hearts. She ripped open the message card. Sam's handwriting. *Diamonds are forever. And you are my forever girl.*

Sam lay in his old bedroom. Posters of Ferraris and bosomy female pop stars had long been taken down. But the furniture was the same. He reached for Josie's Christmas present on the bedside table. There was a large Snowman tag attached to it. He flipped it over. Josie's round handwriting greeted him. To my darling Sam. You've made my Christmas a very happy one. I hope I can do the same for you. Always. Love Josie xxx

Sam rubbed a hand over his eyes. He definitely hadn't made her Christmas happy. And suddenly Sam felt appalled. He'd spent the entire day pitying his lot, when Josie had bravely endured the first Christmas without her husband and been turned away by her boyfriend.

His finger tugged at the paper. Glamorous packaging peeked through. His favourite aftershave. He reached for his mobile phone and began to tap out a message.

I'm in bed and thinking of you. So very sorry for today. Please forgive me. I love you more than words can say. And then Sam turned the light out.

Chapter Seventeen
Four months later – Spring

Needless to say, Annie did return to the UK with Ruby. Her taunting comments about emigration had been nothing more than a spiteful desire to put Sam into a fearful depression. Annie snorted with suppressed laughter as she thought back to Sam's over-reaction. Stupid man. As if she'd have done a thing like that. Annie was a home bird. She would never leave her Mum. And despite frequently falling out with her sisters over various issues, bottom line was she couldn't leave her siblings either.

Annie twitched the net curtains and searched the road for Sam's Mercedes. He was late to pick up Ruby. Annie would have something to say to Sam about that. But more importantly, she wanted to talk to her ex-husband about his trollop. This Josie woman. From what Annie could gather, this particular trollop had been on the scene for a while. Annie had been hearing Ruby chatting about a girl called Lucy for some time – apparently her latest best friend at school. Annie hadn't given the name a second thought, until Ruby had started mentioning Lucy's Mum. And how Daddy was friends with her. How they'd been bumping into each other here, there and everywhere. From what Annie could gather, the first fluky meeting had occurred at The Churchill Theatre for the last Christmas panto. But since then their paths had crossed at the local swimming baths, Tesco's cafeteria, shopping in Sidcup High Street, and queuing to see the same film at Bluewater's cinema. One could be forgiven for saying it was an extraordinary coincidence locally. But Godstone Farm? Hever Castle? And the weekend before last, Brighton Pier? Yeah, right.

Annie had interrogated Ruby periodically. Had Ruby ever seen Daddy hold Josie's hand? Or kiss Josie? Had Ruby been to Josie's house? Had they ever all travelled in the same car together? The answer to all these questions had been no. Ruby was positive that all meetings had just been a happy accident. But Annie wasn't. The fact that this Lucy girl was in Ruby's class meant it was quite incredible Annie and Josie hadn't met, considering the odds of things like Parents' Evening and nativity plays or a special assembly for an award of gold stars. But then again, Annie's hours at Pilkington Medical Practice didn't afford the luxury of taking time out for such events. Annie reasoned she wouldn't even bump into Josie at the school gates because it was her own mother, Lou, who took Ruby to school in the morning and then collected her at half past three.

Sam's Mercedes pulled up outside and Annie dropped the curtain. She crossed into the hallway to answer the front door. Ruby was still upstairs, playing in her bedroom. For now Annie refrained from calling Ruby downstairs. First she wanted to arm herself with some facts. She opened the front door before Sam could ring the bell.

'Hello,' Sam said. His expression was guarded. 'Is Ruby ready?'

Annie noted Sam's anxiety. Ruby wasn't in the hallway with her shoes on and ready to go. Sam was instantly misreading the scenario, inwardly panicking that Annie was about to withhold access. She wasn't. Not this time. But only because she had big plans for the weekend. She was spending it with Nigel. This afternoon they were taking in a show in London's West End followed by dinner at The Oxo Tower. Sunday morning would be spent lazing in bed with newspapers, coffee and croissants. However, it wouldn't hurt to make Sam sweat for a bit. She dispensed with pleasantries and came straight to the point.

'Who is Josie?' Annie watched Sam's eyes widen. The intake of breath. The way he shifted very slightly from one foot to the other. It was as if somebody had given him the tiniest of electric shocks. He recovered quickly, but not before Annie had noted these reactions.

'She's a school mum. The mother of Ruby's best friend,' Sam said casually.

'Yes. I know that. But what is she to you?'

'Josie is a friend.'

'You mean a trollop.'

'Annie, do you have to keep–'

'I thought so. Rumbled. She's your fuck buddy.' Annie noted the anger flare in Sam's eyes. 'Oh hang on a minute. Did I get that wrong? Don't tell me. Jesus. You're in love with her!'

'Annie, my personal life is no business of yours.'

'It is where my daughter is concerned.'

'Our daughter.'

'It might be your name on the birth certificate, Sam, but Ruby is *my* daughter. She lives with me. Your access time is meant to be about seeing Ruby. Just Ruby. Not gallivanting off on jollies around the country with another woman.'

Sam took a deep breath. 'I could say the same to you, Annie.'

Annie's eyes narrowed. 'What do you mean?'

'You do the same with Nigel.'

'No I don't. I see Nigel when Ruby is with you.'

'Course you do. And he wasn't in Florida with my daughter last Christmas. That's just a figment of my imagination, eh?'

'I have Ruby's best interests at heart, Sam. Christmas in Florida was simply a case of putting Ruby first. Her pleasure. Her education. Widening her horizons.'

'Annie, I'm not interested in pursuing this conversation. Can I see Ruby now please?'

'But I *am* interested in pursuing this conversation. So I'll ask again Sam. What is this woman to you?'

Sam took a deep breath. He might as well tell her. After all, sooner or later she'd find out. 'Josie is my fiancée.'

Now it was Annie's turn to visibly jerk. She felt as though somebody had pulled the hall carpet from under her feet. 'Does Ruby know about this?'

'I only proposed last night.'

'How touching,' Annie sneered.

Sam ignored her. 'I'll be telling Ruby this weekend.'

'I want to meet this woman Sam. Check her out. I'm not having one of your trollops being a step-mother to my daughter without having a word with her first.'

'I'm sure Josie would be very happy to meet you and have a chat.'

'I'm not interested in making conversation. The only thing I'll be telling your trollop is to keep her hands off Ruby. I,' Annie pointed an index finger to her chest, 'am Ruby's mother. Nobody else. Ever. So you tell your trollop before I do that under no circumstances is she to touch my daughter. No hugging. No kissing. Nothing.'

'Annie, Josie is a mother herself. She's tremendously fond of Ruby.'

'Rubbish. She's just making out she is.'

'Don't be silly.'

'I'm not. I should know. Nigel has two boys and I don't give a stuff about them.'

'Well maybe you just need to try and get on their wavelength, and let a bond develop.'

Annie looked horrified. 'I don't *want* to bond with them, thank you very much. I'm not interested in anybody else's child apart from my own.'

At that moment Ruby appeared at the top of the stairs. 'Daddy!' She skipped down the steps, ponytail swinging. 'I didn't know you'd arrived.'

Annie swung round to face Ruby. 'Daddy has something to tell you.'

Sam gave his ex-wife a warning look. 'Leave it Annie,' he muttered.

'Daddy's getting married.'

'I said–'

'To a trollop.'

'Jesus, Annie, I'm insisting you pack it in and–'

Ruby's lip wobbled. 'A trollop? Isn't that somebody who will take you away from me Daddy?'

'No!' Sam cried. 'Nobody is going to take me away from you. Mummy's got it wrong.'

'No I haven't,' said Annie coldly. 'Daddy is marrying Josie.' She noted the way her daughter's eyes lit up. That wouldn't do. 'And he's going to live with Josie and Lucy. And then Daddy won't love you anymore, because he'll love Lucy instead.'

Ruby promptly burst into tears. Sam looked appalled. Annie enfolded her daughter into her arms.

'I want to stay with you this weekend, Mummy,' Ruby sniffed.

Now it was Annie's turn to look horrified. 'Sweetheart, I think the best thing is for you to go with Daddy right now and have a chat with him about all this. You need to point out that you, Ruby, must come first. Always.' She gave Ruby a gentle prod. The little girl walked, reluctantly, to her father. Sam bit his tongue. He didn't want a slanging match with Annie in front of Ruby. His ex was wreaking enough emotional damage without him potentially adding to it by calling Annie vile names in front of his daughter. Although God only knew how much he'd like to stoop to her level right now. The bitch.

Sam took Ruby's hand. Wordlessly he turned and walked his daughter to the car.

Josie sat with Lucy in the cafeteria of British Home Stores. She was nursing a cappuccino while Lucy sucked up a strawberry milkshake.

Josie had been in a blissful haze ever since the start of the New Year. The Christmas upset was over and done with. Following the festive blip, her relationship with Sam had gone from strength to strength. He was the most amazing lover. A sensitive partner. Importantly, he was kind to Lucy too. Romance was abundant. Every moment with this man was like a honeymoon. And the icing on the cake was that their daughters got along so famously too. The girls were delighted to share time together, particularly Ruby. The last time they'd been all together, in Brighton, Ruby had skipped along the pier holding hands with Lucy. She'd later said something that had totally taken Josie and Sam by surprise.

'I wish we were a family.'

'Yeah,' Lucy had echoed. 'How cool would that be – you'd be my sister!'

'I'd love you to be my sister,' Ruby had sighed wistfully.

And then, to cap it all, last night Sam had proposed. He'd taken her out to the most exquisite restaurant. There had been candlelight, roses on the table, champagne, the works. And then Sam had taken Josie's hands in his and looked deep into her eyes. 'Josie,' he'd murmured, 'my beautiful Josie. I love you so much. Would you do me the honour of becoming Mrs Josie Worthington?'

Josie had promptly burst into tears. 'Yes,' she'd replied.

And now there was the delicious anticipation of so many wonderful things yet to come. They'd talked about engagement rings, buying a house together, and planning a summer holiday with both Ruby and Lucy. Not necessarily in that order. Josie hugged herself with excitement. But first, there was the small matter of Sam meeting Annie in Court to review access. Josie's brow puckered at the thought of Sam going head to head with Annie. It wasn't just about access. He was taking no chances after Annie's taunts about emigrating. Sam's solicitor wanted a Prohibitive Steps Order put in place, specific access rights in black and white, including permission for Sam to take Ruby out of the country for two weeks every summer. And it was all kicking off after this weekend. Monday morning to be precise. Ten o'clock, Bexley Magistrates Court – Family Division.

'Oh wow, look who's here!' said Josie.

Lucy looked up and spotted Ruby and Sam coming towards their table. She grinned and waved. Josie smiled too. However, Ruby wasn't smiling back. And then Josie noticed Sam looking a little strained.

'Hi,' said Sam. He pulled out a chair. 'We'll have to stop meeting like this.' The attempt at jocularity sounded forced.

'Hey Ruby,' Josie smiled at the little girl. 'How are you today?'

Ruby fixed Josie with her big eyes, but made no response.

'Do you want some of my milkshake?' Lucy offered.

'That's sweet of you to offer your drink, Lucy,' Sam said, 'but I'll buy Ruby one. Do you want another?'

'Yes please,' Lucy swung her heels backward and forward in delight.

'Another cappuccino?' Sam asked Josie. 'And perhaps you could give me a hand with the tray?'

Josie caught Sam's look. 'Of course.'

They walked the few steps to the service area and left Lucy and Ruby at the table together.

'I'm so sorry, Josie, but Annie gave me the third degree about you. I would imagine she rumbled us as an item by interrogating Ruby.'

'Well, Annie would have found out sooner or later. No harm done.'

'On the contrary. She demanded to know what you were to me, so I told her you were my fiancée. And with that, the bloody bitch told Ruby.'

Josie helped herself to another cappuccino from the self-serve machine. 'Okay, so Annie has pre-empted the news. But we were going to tell the children this weekend, so try not to fret.'

'You don't understand. It was the way she told Ruby. It was just—'

Sam broke off as a blood-curdling yell filled the restaurant. Josie spun round in alarm. Lucy was sitting at the table bawling her eyes out. Next to her sat Ruby, looking as if butter wouldn't melt in her mouth. Josie instantly abandoned the self-serve machine and rushed over.

'Whatever's the matter Lucy? Oh!'

Lucy had a bright red handprint across one cheek.

'What's happened?' Sam was now by Josie's side.

'Ruby s-slapped me,' Lucy sobbed.

'Didn't,' said Ruby in a flat voice.

'Yes you did!'

'Well somebody did,' said Josie, 'because Lucy has a mark on her face.'

'Excuse me,' said a little old lady at the table to the left. 'But your daughter,' she nodded at Ruby, 'slapped her sister. Hard. I saw it.'

Ruby jumped up. 'She's not my mummy,' she stamped her foot, 'and that's not my sister!'

And with that Ruby dodged around the tables and ran out of the restaurant.

Chapter Eighteen

Sam caught Ruby in a matter of seconds, but not before crashing into an elderly man who was holding a loaded tray aloft. There was a horrible noise of china and cutlery smashing down on stone tiles. The racket momentarily brought the cafeteria to a halt.

'Stay there,' said Josie to Lucy, before springing up and hastening over to help the pensioner. 'Are you all right?' She took his arm to steady him. The old boy looked both shocked and furious. A pot of tea had emptied down his coat. Thank God he'd been wearing it, Josie thought. Otherwise he could have been badly scalded.

'Bloody hooligan,' the man spluttered as Sam re-appeared, hanging grimly on to Ruby. She was screaming the cafeteria down.

'I'm so sorry,' said Josie. 'Our daughter is having a bit of a paddy.' It was easier to say *our daughter* rather than *my boyfriend's little girl*. It made Josie offering the apology on Sam and Ruby's behalf more appropriate. 'Can I replace everything on your tray and pay for the dry cleaning of your coat?'

Forty minutes later, they were in Sam's living room. Both girls had stopped bawling. They were sitting side by side on the sofa. Sam and Josie were sprawled on the floor at their feet. Lucy's red slap mark had faded. Ruby's face was white and tear-streaked. Josie inwardly felt very angry at Ruby's behaviour. The protective mother instinct was always so close to the surface. However, listening to Ruby talking to her now, Josie realised it was hardly the child's fault she'd behaved aggressively.

'My Mummy said you're marrying my Daddy.'

Lucy's jaw dropped open.

'And that you're a trollop, which means you'll take Daddy away from me. And my Mummy also said,' she turned to look at Lucy, 'that my Daddy only loves you now.' Ruby's lip wobbled and a fresh tear plopped into her lap.

'Oh my goodness,' Josie muttered.

'Girls,' Sam looked from Lucy to Ruby, 'I think we all need to have a chat. A proper chat. And sort out this pickle we've found ourselves in. But first of all, Lucy, Ruby is going to apologise for slapping you. Aren't you, princess?'

'Sorry,' Ruby mumbled.

'And I want to assure you, Ruby, that I love you. And always will. Mummy has said some things that just...aren't...true.'

'Are you saying she's telling fibs,' Ruby demanded, 'because mummies don't do that.'

'I'm saying that Mummy is mistaken. That she's muddled things up.'

Josie could see Sam picking his words carefully, ever anxious not to bad-mouth Annie to Ruby. Desperate not to add to the emotional carnage his ex-wife seemed happy to cause, irrespective of the effect on her daughter.

'First of all girls,' Sam leant across the floor towards Josie and took her hand, 'we wanted to tell you some exciting news this weekend. We've all been having such a lovely time bumping into each other and enjoying family days out. And you, Ruby, recently said how you wished Lucy was your sister. So we thought it would be wonderful to make that happen. And it can happen.'

'How?' asked Lucy.

'It can happen if your Mummy and I get married. We love each other. And we both love you. And when we're married, you two girls will be step-sisters – which means we'll be a family. Would you like that?'

Josie held her breath. If there were any negative shakes of the head, or any more tears, she and Sam wouldn't get married. They'd already decided that.

'Yes,' said Ruby in a small voice. 'I'd like that a lot. I'd like Lucy to be my sister. She's my best friend.'

'I'd like you to be my sister too,' said Lucy timidly, 'but only if you don't slap me again.'

'I won't,' Ruby's eyes once more welled. 'I was just scared.'

'Well there's no need to be scared,' said Sam. 'It was all just a silly misunderstanding.'

Ruby nodded. 'When you get married, can I be a bridesmaid?'

Lucy gasped. 'Oh, and me too. Can I? Please?'

Josie didn't realise she'd been holding her breath until she exhaled with relief. 'Of course.' She squeezed Sam's hand as she looked at the two little girls before her. 'You will *both* be bridesmaids. And you'll wear the most beautiful frilly and flouncy dresses in the whole wide world!'

'But where will we live?' Lucy asked. 'Here?' She looked uncertainly around Sam's living room.

'We're going to go house shopping,' said Sam, 'and buy the best place we can find. Are you both up for checking out which bedroom you want?'

For the first time since leaving the cafeteria, Ruby's face lit up with happiness. 'Yes, Daddy! Yes, yes, yes!'

That night, as Lucy lay in her own bed, she felt extraordinarily happy. Mummy was getting married to Sam. He was so nice. And Ruby would be her sister! Which surely meant that Sam would be her Daddy? How wonderful! Sam was so kind. And he never seemed to shout. Lucy had a hazy memory of her dead Daddy once bawling her out for spilling orange juice all over his white jeans. She couldn't wait to talk about *my Daddy* at school. Everybody had a Daddy apart from her. Sometimes Lucy felt left out because of the circumstances of her father's early demise. It would be so good to fit in with everybody else. And she'd be able to boast that she had not just a Daddy, but a sister too. Ruby. When Lucy finally drifted off, her head was full of church bells and frothy bridesmaid dresses.

That night, as Ruby lay in her bed at Daddy's, she felt anxious. So Daddy was definitely getting married to Josie. She was so nice. And Lucy would be her sister! Which surely meant that Josie would be her mummy? But that couldn't be right. Ruby already had a mummy. She'd have to ask Daddy about that. Best not ask Mummy – it might upset her. When Ruby finally drifted off, her head was full of church bells and frothy bridesmaid dresses. And Mummy turning up at Daddy's wedding shouting that Ruby couldn't be Josie's bridesmaid.

By Sunday late afternoon, the new family unit had viewed three properties. This was actually a short list of houses that Josie and Sam had spent hours looking at on a website. Lucy and Ruby were ecstatic with the bedrooms in all three houses. Sam and Josie were particularly enamoured with a four bedroom detached in leafy Chislehurst. It had a larger than average garden, so perfect for swings and a trampoline.

'We can have a bedroom each,' Ruby had said in delight.

Sam had laughed. 'When Josie and I are married, we'll be sharing a bedroom. And then we can have a spare room for when all the nannies and grandads come to stay.

'Ruby had looked disconcerted. 'Will Mummy's mummy come and stay?'

'If she wants to,' Josie had smiled.

'But unlikely,' Sam had quickly added. 'After all, Grandma Lou only lives a short distance away.' Sam knew that Lou wouldn't put her big toe over the threshold, never mind stay the night. 'So, now that we've found a house we like, Josie and I had better sort out selling our places so we can buy 2 Sycamore Drive.

And now, as they were driving to the local carvery for a late afternoon Sunday roast, Ruby's mobile phone chirruped a text message. Sam tensed. He checked his rear view mirror. Behind him, Ruby was opening the message.

'Who's the text from, princess?' Sam asked. Although he knew it could only be Annie or Lou.

'Mummy. But I can't read it properly.'

'Would you like me to help?' Josie asked from the passenger seat.

'Please.' Ruby handed over the mobile.

'Tell Daddy I'd like to meet his...um...Josie...this evening.' The message had in fact read: *Tell Daddy I'd like to meet his trollop this evening.*

Sam gave a forced jolly laugh as he drove into the carvery's car park. 'I'm sure that's not a problem. Now then, who's hungry?'

As Sam turned the Mercedes into Annie's road, it seemed as though a thousand butterflies took off in Josie's stomach. She told herself not to be ridiculous. This was just a meeting between two women. Adults. Annie had no reason to hate Josie. She simply wanted to be sure her little girl was being looked after when in Josie's company. Her reference to Josie as a trollop would cease once they'd met. Annie would be reassured. Everything would be fine.

Sam rang the doorbell. Ruby was holding his hand. Behind him stood Josie with Lucy hugging one of her mother's jeaned legs. Apprehension was etched on Lucy's face. The front door opened.

'Hello,' said Sam.

'Hello,' said Annie coolly. 'Baby!' She turned her attention to Ruby, gathering up her daughter, even though Ruby was now too big to comfortably sit on her hip. Annie peered around Sam. 'Hello. You must be Josie. Come in. Get out the way Sam. Show some manners.'

Sam felt taken aback. He couldn't recall a single time where Annie had ever cordially replied to his greetings, much less been polite to a girlfriend. Not that she'd ever met a girlfriend before, but still. It was a first. Was a civilised Annie about to emerge? Sam sincerely hoped so. He was acutely aware of Lucy's presence. Ruby was familiar with her mother bad-mouthing him, but Lucy was a different kettle of fish. Sam doubted Lucy had ever heard a grown-up being foul to another grown-up. He prayed she wasn't about to have her first taster. And now Josie was moving past him. Sam felt queasy as he watched his fiancée shake Annie's hand, wipe her feet on the mat and go the short distance down the hallway and into the living room.

Annie put Ruby down. The child was a weight now and made her back ache. But she'd wanted to show Josie to whom Ruby belonged. She watched Sam hasten after his fiancée and shut the front door.

'I won't keep you too long,' said Annie as she came into the lounge. She sat down on the only available sofa. She beckoned Ruby to sit next to her. Annie had phrased her opening gambit carefully. She wanted Josie to know there were no cups of tea on offer. This wasn't an *aren't-we-going-to-be-good-friends* meeting. She didn't ask them to sit, instead taking pleasure at the threesome standing awkwardly in her small front room. Josie's daughter was looking like a rabbit caught in headlights. Good. 'I hear congratulations are in order,' Annie smiled pleasantly.

'They are indeed,' Josie smiled back.

'It's hard second time around. I know that from personal experience. So I wish you all the luck in the world.'

'That's very generous of you.'

'And I want you to know, contrary to whatever *he's* told you,' Annie nodded her head at Sam, 'I don't have a problem with you. All my problems are with him.'

Josie resisted an urge to snort. Annie's words certainly didn't stack up with the earlier text message to Ruby. Instead she just nodded politely. She was acutely aware of Ruby's body language. The child might be sitting quietly next to her mother, but she wasn't relaxed. Her back was ramrod straight, and her face tense.

'You're a mother, Josie. I'm sure you know where I'm coming from.'

'Of course,' Josie nodded. She thought it might be wise to support Annie at this juncture. 'Like you, my daughter means everything to me. If she was in the care of anybody else, I'd want to meet them too and be reassured. But I promise you needn't have any worries when Ruby is with me. I love her to bits. And I'd just like to add that she's a real credit to you.'

Annie arched an eyebrow. Josie loved Ruby. *Loved her to bits.* What a load of shite. Ruby wasn't Josie's flesh and blood. She couldn't possibly love her. And nor did Annie particularly want her to.

'But Ruby's not in your care.'

'Sorry?'

'You said that if your daughter was in the care of anybody else, you'd want to meet them too and be reassured. But I'm saying Ruby's not in your care. She's in Sam's care.'

Josie back-peddled. 'Yes, yes of course. What I meant is, when Sam and I are married. And living together. And when Ruby stays with us.'

'Well we'll have to see about that.' Annie arched an eyebrow. 'Sam and I are in Court tomorrow sorting out access issues. It's just as well I've heard your happy news before our solicitors go head to head.'

Josie's brow furrowed. Time to take the bull by the horns. Politely of course. Try not to aggravate the woman. 'Annie, you just said you didn't have a problem with me. So why should there be a problem about Ruby staying with us?'

'No problem for me,' Annie said.

'Oh good, good,' Josie gabbled. She could feel the tension in the room building.

'But it will be a major problem for Sam.'

'I...I don't understand,' said Josie. This woman was a mass of contradictions.

Annie gave Josie a level look. 'Ruby's access is with her father. Yes?'

'Yes.'

'Therefore Ruby's access is not with you.'

'Well, no, I suppose not right now because we're not living togeth–'

'Not ever,' Annie interrupted. She glared at Josie, all pretence at politeness abandoned. 'My daughter is absolutely nothing to do with you.'

Josie swallowed. 'Annie, when Sam and I are married, I will be Ruby's step-mother. Surely you would want to encourage a good relationship between the two of us?'

'Why?'

'For the emotional well-being of your daughter, especially when she visits us in our family home.'

'Are you thick?' Annie's voice was like a whip. 'My daughter will not be staying in your,' she posted quotation marks in the air, *'family home*. Not now. Not ever. Why would Ruby want a step-mother when she has a mother already? I tell you now, Josie, I do not condone you forming a relationship with my daughter. In fact I forbid it. And I will be telling the Court words to that effect tomorrow.'

Josie was incredulous. But she bit her tongue. It wouldn't do to sound off in front of the girls. But inwardly she burned with anger. What sort of a mother carried on like this in front of their child? And she certainly didn't want her own daughter listening to any more of this woman's unreasonable diatribe. God only knew how Sam coped with his ex. He clearly had the patience of a saint. She glanced at him briefly. His face mirrored Ruby's. Stone.

'I'd like to think that we could be friends,' Josie murmured, 'if only for our daughters' sakes.'

'Then you'll be disappointed,' Annie snapped. 'And as for you,' she turned to Sam, 'if you want to continue a relationship with your daughter, I strongly suggest you think twice before you sell your flat and hook up with this trollop.'

Josie gasped. Annie had gone too far now. Lucy's eyes were currently the size of saucers. Josie took Lucy's hand and turned her back on Annie. 'I'll see you outside, darling,' she said to Sam. Walking past Ruby, she gave a brief wave. 'Bye-bye, sweetheart. See you soon.'

'No you won't,' Annie snarled.

Josie ignored Annie and let herself out of the house. As she walked down the path to the car, she was surprised to find her legs had turned to jelly. Lucy looked up at her.

'Are you all right, Mummy?' she whispered.

'Never better, darling,' Josie forced a grin. She tucked a bit of stray hair behind one ear, and was taken aback to find her hand shaking too.

'What a horrible Mummy Ruby has,' Lucy whispered.

'Yes. She is a bit of an ogre,' Josie agreed. 'Best not tell Ruby though, eh?'

They both jumped as the front door slammed after Sam. He came down the path towards them. 'I'm so sorry, girls.' He put his arms around their shoulders and gave them both a quick squeeze. 'Come on. Let's get in the car.' He pointed the key fob at the Mercedes.

'Is Ruby still going to be my sister?' Lucy asked tremulously.

'Absolutely,' Sam assured. 'Your Mummy and I are going to get married. And we're all going to live happily ever after. And nobody's going to stop us.'

As the Mercedes pulled away, they didn't see Annie behind the net curtain, staring after them. Nobody was playing happy families with her daughter. She couldn't wait to get to Court tomorrow.

'Bring it on, Sam,' she murmured. 'Bring it on.'

Chapter Nineteen

Annie was sitting in her car at Sainsbury's car park. The place was fairly busy for a Monday morning. Women were trolleying to and from the supermarket. She watched the progress of a pensioner, head bowed against a keen breeze, shopping trolley skittering noisily over the car park's potholes. Annie would have liked to go into Sainsbury's herself. Food shopping would be quite relaxing compared to what lay ahead. Instead she was utilising the supermarket's parking facilities. Her destination was across the road. Bexley Magistrates Court, Family Division. She took a deep breath and let herself out of the car.

Inside the building, Annie passed through Security and was directed to a female Court usher. After telling the usher the name of the case and number, Annie was signed in and shown to a private corner to await her lawyer. Minutes later Annie observed Sam's arrival. He was with his solicitor, Graham Burnley. Annie disliked Graham Burnley on sight. He had a puffed out chest and a smug expression. Moments later her own solicitor came in, a woman by the name of Anita Scott. Annie stood up.

'Good morning,' Anita trilled. She shook Annie's hand perfunctorily before dumping a hefty briefcase on the floor. 'Right, we've got half a day set aside for this. In a minute we'll meet up with Mr Burnley and Mr Worthington. We'll find out what the other party are thinking and try to reach an agreement before we go into Court. This will help the judge with his decision. Hopefully both parties will be of the same mind beforehand. That way there will be a draft Consent Order. Then, when we go into Court, the judge should agree to make that into an Order. Any questions?'

'There have been some developments over the weekend. Consequently I'm not agreeing to anything previously drafted.'

Anita blinked. 'I see. I'm aware you're against Mr Worthington having your daughter for holiday access abroad. But surely you're not indicating weekend access is now in dispute?'

'Yes I am.'

'Can I ask why?'

'Because Mr Worthington has embarked on a whirlwind romance resulting in a fiancée. I don't know this woman from Adam. And neither does my daughter. Ruby's access is about time with her father. Not time with another woman who means absolutely nothing to her.'

'That's certainly something that will need to be discussed,' said Anita. 'Meanwhile, let me run through this document and make some margin notes.'

Annie and Anita conferred for a few minutes before the usher signalled everybody to come over. They were shown into a side room to discuss the previously drafted Consent Order and make any necessary amendments. Everybody sat around a functional table. Graham Burnley and Anita Scott shook hands. Sam smiled politely at Anita. Annie ignored Sam and glared at Graham Burnley.

'I've had a talk with my client,' Anita Scott began. 'Mrs Worthington has advised me of some developments that occurred this most recent weekend which have caused her immense concern. Regrettably the whole access situation needs rethinking. Mr Burnley, can I suggest we start with your client putting forward his case for what he wants.'

'Certainly,' said Graham Burnley. 'Before doing so, I'd ask your client to take on board that by the parties changing previously agreed arrangements – the existing Court Order in this case – the Court expects both parents to have used the help of a mediator to assist before getting to this point. My client tells me Mrs Worthington attended mediation, but walked out before any middle ground had been negotiated. I would urge Mrs Worthington to now think about a compromise prior to this case going before the judge.'

'I'm not agreeing to anything your client wants,' Annie spoke out.

'Mrs Worthington,' said Graham Burnley, 'it is the Court's duty to put the welfare of your child first. I understand it can be hard to accept some things happening, especially if – in your opinion – you don't believe it to be best for your child. But if you cannot agree on anything at all, the judge will make a decision instead. That decision will be based on what he and he alone thinks is in the best interests of your child. So please bear this in mind.'

An expression passed over Sam's face. He was appalled to think it might come to a stranger deciding what was best for Ruby.

'Do you have children, Mr Burnley?' asked Annie.

'I do.'

'And how would you feel seeing your precious child going off into the sunset with a person who is nothing to do with them?'

'That isn't what we're in Court to discuss, Mrs Worthington. We are in Court to discuss Mr Worthington's rightful access to his daughter. The previous Order included fortnightly access, and holiday access covering Christmas, New Year, Easter, Bank Holidays and an unspecified number of days over the summer period. Mr Worthington would like to now enforce this Order, which I understand has not been adhered to. You have repeatedly withheld Mr Worthington's access where you have deemed fit, including the Christmas period. Mr Worthington was denied any access at all over the festive season due to you taking Ruby to America for two weeks. At the same time you informed my client you were emigrating, indeed that you might not even return to the UK. Therefore my client is seeking a Prohibitive Steps Order blocking you from taking Ruby out of the country other than for an agreed specified period.'

Annie's mouth disappeared into a thin line. 'This is outrageous.'

'Mr Worthington will also be seeking,' Graham Burnley continued, 'a two week vacation in the school summer period to include travelling abroad. And finally my client wants daily telephone access with his daughter on the mobile phone he bought her.'

'Thank you, Mr Burnley,' said Anita Scott. 'Mrs Worthington will happily agree to fortnightly access but this is limited to Mr Worthington only. The access must not include any other person or persons without Mrs Worthington's express permission. Holiday access, likewise, with the exception of the summer period. Mrs Worthington will agree to one week's summer vacation in the UK only and, again, this is subject to

Ruby being solely with her father. Mrs Worthington has also assured me she has no plans to emigrate and says Mr Worthington was mistaken for thinking otherwise. Regarding daily telephone access, this is agreed only if Ruby wishes to speak to her father. Mr Worthington needs to understand that sometimes when he calls his daughter she is tired, or having her tea, or in the bath, or even in bed.'

'Then let us agree a set time to avoid that from happening,' Sam said.

Anita Scott ignored Sam. Instead Graham Burnley spoke. 'My client is engaged to be married to a woman who is the mother of Ruby's best school friend. It is in Ruby's best interests to build a relationship with her future step-mother. Just as it was in Ruby's best interests to build a relationship with the man Mrs Worthington left my client for.'

'I'm not agreeing to your client's trollop having access to my daughter,' Annie spat.

'You didn't afford my client the same courtesy when you set up home with another man.'

'I'm not living with that man anymore.'

'But you are partners.'

Annie gazed stonily at Graham Burnley. 'I'm not having this. Nigel is a doctor. An eminent and honourable man. Sam's fiancée is nothing. A nobody. I don't even know her.'

'You met Josie yesterday,' Sam spoke up. 'She tried to befriend you. Reassure you. Instead you were absolutely foul to her.'

'I don't want introductions to your trollops, Sam.'

'Mrs Worthington, this isn't about you. It's about your daughter. Try and remember that.'

'My client is fully aware who this is about,' Anita Scott interrupted. 'She has her daughter's best interests at heart. And it is because of having Ruby's best interests at heart that my client is guarded about a woman she doesn't know having contact with her daughter.' Anita looked at Sam. 'Ruby's mother cannot make a judgement after one brief meeting Mr Worthington.'

'Thank you, Miss Scott,' Annie inclined her head.

Graham Burnley let out a small sigh. 'Based on what I've just heard, it would seem the judge will have to decide the outcome of this case.' He raised a questioning eyebrow at Annie.

'I'm not agreeing to that trollop having care of my daughter. End of.'

Anita Scott cleared her throat. 'I would urge Mr Worthington to think about my client's decision. Future access will not be denied. Mrs Worthington has assured me of that. But only if access is just between father and daughter.'

'Miss Scott,' said Sam, 'I'm getting married. My future wife will be my daughter's step-mother. My future step-daughter will be Ruby's step-sister. I want us to be a family. I will ensure there are moments when Ruby has time just with me. But essentially we will be all together. And I want Ruby to enjoy that too.'

Anita Scott shuffled her papers together. 'Thank you Mr Worthington. But it will be the judge who decides whether that is going to happen.'

Inside the Court room, Annie sat next to Anita Scott. The judge was a dour looking fifty-something with pince-nez spectacles. He gave Annie a stern look. Was she meant to be intimidated by that? She gave him a cool look in return. She wasn't going to be bullied by anybody, least of all him. Fuck's sake. She should have stayed in Florida. To hell with all this crap Sam was putting her through.

Annie's attention shifted to Graham Burnley. He was now introducing the case. Seconds later he'd launched into a smooth summary of the basic facts. The judge had some papers in front of him. He made reference to them as Graham Burnley spoke, periodically nodding. Suddenly it was Anita Scott's turn to speak. Annie's solicitor was half way through her summary when the judge interrupted.

'Mrs Worthington, why do you object to your ex-husband taking Ruby abroad?'

'My client does not wish Mr Worthington's fiancée to have–'

'Thank you, Miss Scott. I'm asking Mrs Worthington the question. I would like her to answer.'

Annie cleared her throat. 'I do not want a woman my daughter barely knows participating in Ruby's care.'

'Your initial objection to Mr Worthington taking Ruby abroad was prior to him meeting his fiancée. Could you please tell me the reason for that objection?'

Annie swallowed. 'Ruby is five years old. She's far too young to be travelling abroad. Mr Worthington wanted to take Ruby to America. Walt Disney World.'

'But despite Ruby being so young, you took her away yourself?'

'Well yes, but Ruby had me with her.'

'Are you saying Ruby cannot travel abroad with Mr Worthington because she would miss you?'

'Partly. But also I had concerns about Mr Worthington abducting Ruby.'

'Even though you yourself took Ruby to America without her father's permission, and during Mr Worthington's access period, and allegedly informed him you would not be returning to the United Kingdom?'

'Mr Worthington was mistaken. It was a misunderstanding.'

'Why didn't you conclude the mediation meeting with Linda Grant?'

Annie was starting to feel flustered. 'As far as I'm concerned, I did conclude the meeting. There was nothing else to discuss. I didn't think matters were progressing. I've tried to sort things out with Mr Worthington properly. But he's not an easy man to deal with.'

'I have a Statement from Linda Grant. You left before mediation had concluded. Regarding Mr Worthington taking Ruby abroad, Linda Grant states you voiced fears over Ruby being abducted.'

Annie nodded vigorously. She was back on firmer ground now. 'Absolutely.'

'If you had concluded the mediation meeting, you would have heard Linda Grant suggesting two compromises that Mr Worthington supported. The first addressed your anxieties about Ruby being taken so far away – Walt Disney World America. Mr Worthington was prepared to change this to Disneyland Paris. If Ruby needed you, she would only be a train ride away.

Secondly, regarding abduction fears, Linda Grant states Mr Worthington was prepared to have you come away with him and Ruby if need be, in order to reassure you.'

Annie's mouth had gone dry. Bugger Linda Grant. And bugger mediation. Annie didn't know what else to say. So she did the only other thing she could think of, and burst into tears. Her hands shook as they fluttered to her eyes to wipe away the tears. She gave it her all. The distressed woman. The victim.

The judge made no comment or showed any sympathy. He did, however, give Annie a moment to compose herself. 'I want both parties to understand the seriousness of this situation. Both parties should make every effort not to let hostilities between themselves impact upon their daughter. Both parents should encourage the child to have a good relationship with the other parent. It is best for the child to spend time with both parents and, in this case, that includes Mr Worthington's future wife and step-daughter. The welfare of the child comes first. Now I shall tell you my decision.'

Annie sat and listened in disbelief as the judge agreed to everything in Sam's draft Consent Order.

Chapter Twenty
Summer

Josie dumped the last empty crate in the garage and brushed off her hands. They'd done it! Number 2 Sycamore Drive was theirs. And she had the *New Address* cards to prove it.

Josie straightened up. God her back ached. With the exception of nipping out for a bit of shopping earlier, she and Sam had worked like Trojans all weekend. The girls were over the moon with their rooms. Both of them had definite ideas on how they were to be decorated. Lucy wanted pink everything. Ruby was going to be adventurous and try lilac and white. Josie had brought up a furniture website on her laptop and shown the girls how to scroll through the displayed items. She'd left them oohing and aahing over raised beds with inbuilt playhouses that resembled castles. Josie was just so relieved that the move had gone smoothly, and that access arrangements with Ruby were running like clockwork. Not that Annie had changed. She was as vitriolic as ever. Still jack-booting around and rapping Sam's knuckles for minor misdemeanours whenever the opportunity arose. Two weeks ago, due to a bit of traffic, they'd been precisely eight minutes late returning from a day out in Whitstable. Annie had stood outside her house screeching at Sam like a fishwife. Josie couldn't understand the woman's attitude. At times she wondered if Annie was mentally ill. She'd pondered it over lunch in the College canteen with Kerry.

'Nah,' Kerry had dismissed the notion. 'Take it from me, that Annie is just a bitter old bag.'

'But why does she behave like that in front of Ruby? Doesn't she care about the emotional damage she's doing to her daughter?'

Kerry had shrugged. 'Evidently not. Some women are like that. So determined to cause pain to their exes, they don't care what casualties are incurred along the way.'

Josie had tried hard to see things from Annie's perspective. To feel a modicum of sympathy and understand why Ruby's mother was so bitter. From Josie's perspective she saw a woman with a good job, running a medical practice, partnered up with a doctor – okay not living with him, but certainly she was the doctor's *significant other* – and a beautiful daughter. So why give Sam such a hard time? Why couldn't the woman move on? And despite Josie's best efforts to befriend Annie, she'd drawn a blank. Annie's reaction to Josie was usually to morph into a Rottweiler – lip curled, teeth bared.

Josie locked the garage. She took the paved path down the side of the house and into the rear garden. The door to the conservatory was open and a warm breeze lifted the blinds. As Josie went through the conservatory door, she stooped to pick up some photographs that had fluttered to the floor in the downdraft. Earlier on, whilst she'd been packing shopping at Asda's checkout, Lucy had spotted the passport booth.

'Can we take our pictures while you're packing the shopping, Mummy? Please? Oh pretty please?' Lucy had begged.

It had been easier to give in than say no. Josie had given the girls some change and they'd had a marvellous time sticking their tongues out and pulling faces behind the privacy curtain. She peered at the images. There were even a couple of them on their own looking like butter wouldn't melt. She smiled and took the photographs into the kitchen, propping them up against the toaster.

Josie looked around the kitchen. The units and worktops were okay'ish. Apart from the disgusting canary yellow paint on the walls. In time, they'd decorate the house. Put their own stamp on it. For now, the next priority on Josie's list was the impending summer holiday to Spain. Lucy had shot up and needed new everything for the holiday. Sam had recently spent quality time with Ruby and taken her shopping for sundresses, but Annie had gone potty when Ruby had told her about it.

'I will pack Ruby's holiday suitcase,' she'd remonstrated with Sam, 'do you understand? You haven't the first idea what a little girl needs to go abroad.'

'Of course I do,' Sam had protested, 'and anyway, Josie will point me in the right direction if I forget anything.'

'Don't you mention that trollop's name to me,' Annie had roared.

So Josie had stepped out of it. She now kept a low profile where Annie was concerned. Josie's only wish was that whilst Ruby was in her care, she be happy and relaxed and regard 2 Sycamore Drive as her home too.

Annie was absolutely livid that a judge – a man who knew nothing about her daughter – had taken Sam's side in Court. Her solicitor had presented her with a copy of the new Court Order. Annie had snatched it from her and promptly ripped it into pieces.

'Call yourself a solicitor?' she'd shrieked. 'And don't look to me with your invoice. Send it to Mr Worthington. If it wasn't for him I wouldn't have incurred expense in the first place.'

When the solicitor's bill had turned up on her doormat, Annie had flung it at Sam.

'This is for you,' she'd whacked his face with the envelope. 'It's the least you can do after trying to take my daughter away and putting me through hell.'

'Annie, please,' Sam had taken the envelope and tried to placate her. 'Why does it always have to be like this? Why can't we just get along? The judge told us to make an effort with each other – if only for our daughter's sake.'

'Don't you preach to me, Sam Worthington. Of course I think about Ruby. I think about her welfare all the time. And do you know what Ruby needs, Sam? *Really* needs? Well I'll tell you. She needs you out of her life. Permanently.'

'Absolutely no chance.'

'All you do is stress her out. Confuse her.'

'Don't be ridiculous.'

'It's true. Her home is here. With me. Her mother. She doesn't need a part-time father living with a trollop and replacement daughter.'

'Josie and Lucy are neither of those things. Why do you talk like this? You'll give Ruby a complex.'

'Oh she already has one, Sam. Thanks to you.'

Needless to say, Sam had paid Anita Scott's bill. Not that Annie was grateful. In her eyes it was only right and proper. As for that outdated judge, he could go jump. No way on this earth would Annie pretend to Ruby that she was happy to wave her daughter off at the airport with Sam and his trollop and the trollop's kid. She didn't condone them playing happy families. Nor did Annie want Josie helping her daughter get bathed, or rubbing sun cream on Ruby's skin, or blowing up her water wings. None of it. And by God, Sam had better be grateful for his fortnight in Spain with Ruby because he wouldn't have the pleasure of repeating it next year. She, Annie, would see to that.

Annie went to the living room window and lifted the net curtain. Sam was due back with Ruby in ten minutes. The only power Annie had at the moment was berating Sam if he was a minute late. That and the telephone contact. Annie always answered Ruby's mobile when Sam rang. Sometimes she looked at Ruby beforehand and put an index finger to her lips. Then she'd take the call and say that Ruby wasn't available. She was having tea at a friend's. Or had fallen asleep. Or was at the park with her grandmother. It was important to let Sam know that he couldn't have control in everything. Annie never failed to remind Ruby that her father was a control freak.

Sam's Mercedes appeared outside her house. Annie glanced at her watch. Six minutes early. She squinted myopically at the Mercedes. No sign of the trollop and her daughter. Sam was now unfastening Ruby's seat belt. Annie hastily dropped the net curtain and stood back. She wasn't going to rush to open the door. Let Sam ring the bell.

Thirty seconds later the doorbell shrilled into life. Annie looked at her watch again. Sam officially had another minute and a half of access time. Well he was the one who wanted a Court Order set in stone. So he could play by the rules. Annie waited, watching the second hand rotate. The doorbell rang again, this time with the letterbox clattering. Suddenly a pair of eyes met Annie's. Ruby.

'What are you doing, Mummy?'

'Coming to answer the door of course,' said Annie.

The front door swung open and Ruby came into the hall. 'You took ages, Mummy!'

'Hey, princess,' Sam called playfully after her. 'Come back here and give your Daddy a kiss good-bye.'

Ruby made to go back, but Annie caught her by the arm. 'Go into the lounge, Ruby.'

'But I was going to give Daddy a kiss.'

'If giving Daddy a kiss was important to you, you'd have done it without prompting. So go into the lounge. Now please.' Annie gave her daughter a look that defied argument. Ruby's face immediately went blank. Annie noticed that Ruby had developed a way of masking her emotions. The child's face was now totally expressionless. Ruby turned away from her parents and walked into the lounge. 'And shut the door after you,' Annie called. Seconds later the door closed.

Sam looked at Annie in amazement. 'You really are something else aren't you,' he said softly.

'Are you going to start an argument, Sam?'

Sam gave a bitter laugh. 'No, Annie. If you want to stop my daughter giving me a kiss good-bye, then so be it. I'm not playing your point-scoring games.'

'No games, Sam. Just remember this is about Ruby. And what Ruby wants. And if she wants to give you a kiss good-bye then she will.'

'But she did!'

'Only when you asked her. Try and understand, Sam, that you don't mean an awful lot to her. She knows she's second best.'

'I'm not interested in pursuing this line of conversation, Annie. Before I go, could I have Ruby's passport please?'

'What for?'

Sam felt his guts begin to tense. Was this another of Annie's silly mind games? He kept his voice calm and indifferent. 'We're going on holiday next Saturday.'

'Well when it's Saturday I'll give you the passport.'

Sam stood his ground. 'There's some information to fill in on the flight website.'

'What information?'

'Passport numbers, dates of birth, that sort of thing. I'm not exactly sure why the information is asked for. Josie took care of the booking and is dealing with it.'

At the mention of Josie's name, Annie's lip curled. 'Too bad.'

'Is it really so much of a big deal to give me the passport now?'

Annie put her head on one side and considered. 'I don't have it,' she said eventually.

Sam's guts were really starting to hurt now. 'Well who *does* have it?'

'I'm not sure,' Annie frowned theatrically. 'It might be at Nigel's house. Or it might be lost.'

'Lost?'

'Yes. Lost.'

'Can you ask Nigel if he has it?'

'Yes, I'm seeing him Friday evening. I'll let you know.' Annie went to shut the door.

'But, Annie,' Sam put a hand out to stop the door from closing, 'I need to know where the passport is now!'

'Get your hand off my door, Sam,' Annie's voice rose an octave. 'If you start behaving aggressively I'll call the police.'

'Annie, I'm not being aggressive, I just need to know where the passport is.'

'I said get...your...hands...OFF!'

'No, listen, I–'

Suddenly Annie let out a blood-curdling scream. 'RUBY,' she yelled, 'DADDY'S THREATENING ME. CALL THE POLICE.'

Ruby erupted out of the lounge. Her face was pale. 'Stop it, Daddy,' she cried, 'stop hurting Mummy.'

Sam gazed at his daughter, appalled. 'I'm not hurting Mummy. She's fine. See? I was just asking Mummy for your passport,' he gabbled, 'for the holiday.' Ruby stared at him, eyes wide. Sam felt his heart lurch. His daughter didn't believe him. He could tell. Ruby thought he'd hit her mother. Sam realised it was imperative to do urgent damage limitation. He needed to leave. Now. 'It's not a problem though. I'll ring tomorrow, Ruby, and you can let me know if Mummy has found the passport.'

He turned and made his way back to the Mercedes. Behind him Annie's front door banged shut.

Josie heard the front door open.

'Yoo hoo,' she called out. 'I'm in the kitchen – just putting the finishing touches to...oh! What's the matter?' Josie abandoned decorating a macaroni cheese with tomato slices and looked at her fiancé. His face was grey.

'She's going to fuck up the holiday,' Sam said through clenched teeth.

Josie frowned and shut the kitchen door. She'd never heard Sam swear before, but she didn't want Lucy hearing.

'By *she* I presume you mean Annie?'

Sam chucked his car keys on the kitchen table and pulled out a chair. 'Yes. Annie. She's having the last laugh.' He pulled out a chair and sat down heavily. 'It doesn't matter what I do – mediation, solicitor's letters, a judge's Court Order – that woman manages to turn it all upside down.'

Josie reached for the kettle and turned on the cold water tap. 'Cup of tea?'

Sam nodded. 'Please.'

'So what's happened?'

'We have a serious problem. Annie says she doesn't know where Ruby's passport is.'

Josie froze. Water overflowed from the kettle and sprayed against her sweater. She jumped back, as if scalded, and hit the tap. 'As in lost?' Reaching for the tea towel, Josie mopped her top and then plugged the kettle in. 'Or won't hand it over?'

Sam raked a hand through his hair. 'What do you think?'

'Maybe,' said Josie sitting down, 'you should give Annie the benefit of the doubt for twenty-four hours.'

'Are you kidding? We fly out next Saturday. What if she doesn't hand over the passport?'

'Get in touch with the Passport Office first thing tomorrow morning. Explain the situation. Make an appointment with them for Tuesday morning. And then, if Annie hasn't found the passport by Monday evening, you'll just have to spend Tuesday at Peterborough.'

'Josie, it's not that simple. I need passport photographs of Ruby. Can you see Annie playing ball over this? She's doing this deliberately. I know it.'

Josie stood up and walked over to the passport pictures propped up against the toaster.

'I don't know how good these are,' she showed them to Sam, 'but with a bit of luck they might be acceptable in an emergency.'

Sam heaved a sigh. 'Oh my God. Oh Josie. I don't believe it. What a stroke of luck.'

Josie gave a grim smile. 'Well, I wouldn't call it luck. But let's be grateful for small mercies.'

The kettle switch popped. Josie pulled two mugs down from the cupboard. As she tossed in the teabags, Josie found herself wondering just how far Annie would go to stop Ruby coming away with them. Her hand shook slightly as she poured water into the mugs. Josie decided that where Annie was concerned, it might pay to be one step ahead. She wouldn't tell Sam. He had enough on his plate worrying about an emergency passport and cancelling Tuesday's patients at the surgery. She had a feeling about what Annie would try next. And Josie would be ready.

Chapter Twenty-One

Annie pulled the passport from its hiding place in her handbag. Flipping it open, she regarded the picture of Ruby. Her daughter's face gazed solemnly back at her. Earlier, Ruby had been full of chatter about her *new home*. Annie had instantly put a stop to that.

'You only have one home, Ruby. And that's here. With me. In this house.'

'But Daddy said he wants me to think of 2 Sycamore Drive as my home too.'

'He's just trying to get into your good books.'

'What do you mean?'

'Well look at it this way. Who's living with him all the time?'

Ruby had frowned. 'Josie. And Lucy.'

'Exactly. Lucy. Daddy thinks of Lucy as his daughter now.'

'No he doesn't. He told me. We had a chat.'

'He's lying, Ruby. If he loved you the way I loved you, he wouldn't live with anybody else. And he definitely wouldn't live with another little girl.'

Ruby had gone quiet after that, her features arranged in the blank expression that was growing increasingly familiar. Annie shut the passport and tapped it against her chin while she thought about what to do. It hadn't entered her head to withhold the passport until Sam had asked for it. If she didn't give Sam the passport, would the judge find out? Without a doubt, Sam would rush off to Court to tell tales. But nobody could prove anything could they? Just as long as Annie kept shtum and didn't tell a soul. Not even her mother.

Annie sighed. Did she really want to wreck Sam's holiday? Did she really hate him that much? The answers were yes and yes. She loathed Sam for making her share Ruby. She despised him for winning in Court. And she detested him for finding happiness with another woman. Annie slid the passport back into her handbag. Ruby was not going to Spain. She was staying in the UK with her.

When Sam arrived home Tuesday evening he felt as though he'd been put through a mangle. What a day. What a God-awful horrible day. He'd arrived at the Peterborough Passport Office, first in the queue. Instantly there had been problems. First off, the passport photograph of Ruby didn't meet the exact criteria. Her head was slightly turned to the left. There had been an exchange of words between him and the man behind the desk, which – on Sam's behalf – had gradually become very heated.

'What are you talking about?' he'd eventually cried. 'She's looking at the camera.'

'Her head isn't straight.'

'But what's the problem? You can see what she looks like. Two eyes, a nose and a mouth.' Sam could feel his guts twisting with tension. Just like when Annie was giving him difficulties. Was this bloke in league with his ex-wife?

'Where are you taking your daughter?'

'Spain.'

'And your wife has lost your daughter's passport. Do you have your wife's passport?'

'No. She's my ex-wife.'

'And your ex-wife knows you are taking your daughter out of the country?'

'Yes. Of course.'

'Is there documentation proving this. A Court Order?'

'Yes.'

'Can I see it please?'

Sam had stared at the uniform in front of him. 'Excuse me?' A stalling tactic. And they'd both known it. Sam had spent so much time running around like a headless chicken, re-scheduling patients, and dashing over to Ruby's school to get the headmistress to countersign the back of the passport photographs, he'd hardly been able to think straight. Persuading the headmistress to countersign had been a mini nightmare. Mrs Chalmers had quite rightly pointed out she'd not known Ruby for two years. Thankfully she'd noted the desperation on Sam's face and listened patiently while he had explained about the fraught relationship with his ex-wife. Eventually Mrs Chalmers had relented and countersigned. But it had taken time and added to the overall hassle. He'd thought of everything. Apart from remembering to bring the wretched Court Order.

The uniform had looked Sam in the eye. 'I can't do anything without that document.'

Sam had been on the verge of meltdown. A security guard had sensed it and made his presence known. Sam had put up his hands. 'I'm sorry,' he'd said to the security guard. 'I don't mean to shout. I'm not a violent person.' In fact, at that precise moment, Sam had wanted to punch everybody in his immediate path. He'd closed his eyes and willed himself to be calm. 'It's just that you don't know what I've been through to get this far...to take my daughter away with me. And my ex-wife says she's lost the passport. Although truly I don't believe her. But I can't prove a thing. And the holiday is this weekend.' His stomach was in such a knot Sam thought he might vomit. And then his eyes had suddenly welled. Frantically he'd willed himself not to cry. Mentally he began chanting: *please God don't let me break down, please God don't let me break down.*

'I'm going to suggest something that is not strictly acceptable,' the uniform had said, 'we're only meant to accept original documents. But if you can get your solicitor to fax me a copy of the Court Order and certify it as a true copy, I'll give you a passport.'

'Yes. Thank you. Thank you very much. I'll do it. Now. Thank you.' Sam had been a gibbering wreck.

By the time he'd tracked down Graham Burnley – enjoying a day off and on a golf course – and liaised with Graham's PA, five painful hours had elapsed. When Sam finally left clutching Ruby's new passport, he'd been at the Passport Office for ten hours with not so much as a coffee passing his lips.

Sam let himself into number 2 Sycamore Drive. Josie came into the hallway and greeted him. He fell into her arms. 'I can't take much more of this,' he whispered into her hair.

Josie clung to him. She loved this man so much. For a moment, Josie found herself wishing Sam didn't come with such horrendous baggage. Then she felt guilty and shoved the thought away. Josie's thoughts didn't relate to Ruby. On the contrary. It was Annie. The woman was like a ghost in their relationship. Not there but...always there.

Josie shifted her weight and pulled back from Sam. She looked up at him. 'The hard part is done, darling. All we have to do now is go on holiday. A few more days and we'll be sipping Sangria in Spain, and all our troubles will be behind us.'

'I hope you're right.'

'I know I'm right,' Josie smiled.

'Sorry to have left all the packing to you.'

'That's okay. Just so long as you don't blame me for forgetting anything,' she teased.

'Swimming trunks and sun cream. That's all I need.'

'Nothing else?' Josie pretended to pout.

'And you. Only you.' And Sam squeezed her tightly.

When Saturday dawned, Sam turned up on Annie's doorstep at ten o'clock on the dot. He rang the doorbell. As Sam waited, he found his eyes scanning the parked vehicles in the road. There was Annie's car. Thank God. He'd half expected Annie not to be in – to have taken Ruby somewhere and lead Sam a merry dance finding her.

The door opened. Ruby stood there in a lilac tracksuit. 'Hello, Daddy.'

'Hello, princess!' Sam beamed at his daughter. 'You look a picture in that colour. It really suits you.'

Annie suddenly appeared behind Ruby. 'What are you doing here?'

Sam's smile faded. Was she serious? 'I'm here to collect Ruby. We're going to Spain for two weeks.'

'Oh, sorry, Sam. I meant to call you,' Annie slapped her forehead theatrically. 'Ruby, go into the lounge please. I need to talk to your father.' Ruby melted away, her face unreadable. Annie turned back to Sam. 'I've turned the house upside down. And Nigel's place too. Ruby's passport is nowhere to be found.'

Sam smiled thinly. 'Never mind.' For a moment he felt like Cinderella with the missing glass slipper. 'I have another one here.' He patted his top pocket and watched Annie's expression change from smug to gobsmacked. 'Now if you don't mind, would you give me Ruby's suitcase? There's a plane to catch.'

Annie's eyes narrowed dangerously. 'She's not going with you, Sam.'

'Oh yes she is. And if you give me any trouble, Annie, then rest assured that this time it will be me calling the police. I have the Court Order in my pocket and will show it to anybody who attempts blocking me. So give me the suitcase please.'

'You fucking bastard.'

'Call me what you like. I really don't care. Just give me Ruby's suitcase.'

'I haven't packed anything. Nor am I going to.'

Sam closed his eyes. Here we go. 'Fine. I'll buy clothes for Ruby in Spain. Now move out of the way please, I want my daughter.'

'Piss off.'

'RUBY?' Sam bellowed. Ruby peered uncertainly around the lounge door. 'Come on, princess. We're off to Spain. Say good-bye to Mummy.'

'I don't have any clothes,' Ruby said timidly.

'But that's fantastic,' Sam grinned, 'we can go shopping!'

Ruby crept over to her father. She took his hand and looked uncertainly at her mother.

'HOW DARE YOU!' Annie roared at Sam.

'Bye, Annie.' But as he turned to walk to the car with Ruby, Annie launched herself at their daughter. Sam initially thought Annie was attempting to drag Ruby back into the house. Instead he was shocked to find Annie pulling the lilac tracksuit off their daughter. 'What the hell are you doing?

'You might be taking my daughter to Spain,' Annie snarled, 'but you're not taking her clothes.'

'For Christ's sake, woman, have you taken leave of your senses?' Sam attempted to bat Annie's hands away. Their daughter was already naked to the waist. Ruby made no attempt to stop her mother undressing her, even obliging and lifting her legs as Annie hauled the trainers from her feet. 'Pack it in!' Sam howled as Ruby's socks were pulled off. Next Annie grabbed at the lilac tracksuit bottoms. 'For God's sake, Annie, this is despicable.' Ruby was now standing on the pathway in just her underpants. Although it was summer, it was a typically British one. Goosebumps flecked the little girl's skin. 'This isn't going to stop Ruby coming with me, Annie.' Sam shrugged his jacket off and wrapped it around the little girl's shoulders. Scooping the child up, he strode off to his car.

'You're a CUNT Sam Worthington,' Annie shrieked after him. 'Nothing but a FUCKING CUNT.'

As Sam drove off, he looked across at Ruby. She was staring impassively ahead. Dear God. What was going through his daughter's head? The child was showing no emotion whatsoever. Not a tear. Not a catchy breath. Nothing. She wouldn't see her mother for two whole weeks. A normal parent would have hugged their child good-bye, wished them a lovely time, made sure they had their suitcase with a favourite doll or teddy, asked the other parent for telephone contact every day, and waved their child off with a smile. Even if that parent's heart was breaking. A normal parent would make that effort for their child. But then again, Sam pondered, it had been a long time since he'd seen Annie behave normally.

When Sam arrived at 2 Sycamore Road, he told Ruby to wait in the car for a few seconds. Inside the house he quickly brought Josie and Lucy up to speed.

'I need you to be very grown-up for me, Lucy,' Sam explained, 'and pretend you don't notice Ruby is only wearing a pair of knickers.'

Lucy regarded Sam in astonishment. 'Yes. Yes of course. And anyway, Ruby can share my clothes.'

'You are such a sweet girl. Thank you, angel.'

'Don't panic,' Josie said, 'I've shopped for Ruby. There's a packed suitcase for her upstairs.' She dropped her voice. 'I half expected something like this to happen.'

Sam closed his eyes in relief. 'Thank you, darling. Now let me get Ruby.'

As Sam disappeared back to the car, Lucy turned to her mother wide eyed. 'Why does Ruby's Mummy behave so badly?'

'I don't know,' Josie sighed, 'but I suspect it's because she's not a happy lady.'

Annie wasn't so much unhappy as absolutely livid. Sam had outwitted her! And in her anger to get back at him, she had omitted saying good-bye to her daughter. It was all Sam's fault.

The bastard. She'd make him pay for that. All in good time of course. She picked up her mobile and tapped out a message to her ex-husband. *I will never forgive you for not giving me the chance to say good-bye to Ruby. Remember this Sam. As you sow, so shall you reap.* Annie hit the send icon, and then began a second text, this time to Ruby. *Hello my little dolly, I'm sorry Daddy didn't let you say good-bye to me. So I'm sending you a big kiss and a hug. Mummy loves you very, very much and will miss you every single day xxxxxxx* Finally Annie sent a third text, this time to Nigel. *I'm on my own for the next two weeks. Can I stay over?* Five minutes later her mobile chirruped the arrival of a text. She clicked on the touch screen. Nigel. *Of course. I haven't got the boys until next weekend. Pack a bag.*

Annie went upstairs and pulled a suitcase from her wardrobe. At least not having Ruby around meant she could concentrate on her next plan of action. The Child Support Agency. Sam's new abode – 2 Sycamore Drive – was in Chislehurst. Very posh. You had to be earning big money to have an address like that. So Annie reckoned Sam could afford to quadruple her maintenance. As soon as Sam and his family had left for the airport, Annie would drive to Nigel's via 2 Sycamore Drive.

She had a property to check out.

Chapter Twenty-Two

Josie poured liquid bubbles into the bath and watched as the water instantly frothed and foamed. They were one week into their Spanish holiday. There had been some very fraught moments. And after today's antics, Josie was starting to feel as if she were permanently walking a tightrope.

'Girls,' she called a few minutes later. 'The bath is ready.'

Lucy and Ruby appeared. At six years of age they had no inhibitions about stripping off and jumping into a tub together. Josie emptied a net of alphabet letters into the water. The girls enjoyed playing with them, making words on the bathroom tiles with their own version of Hangman. Josie encouraged it. She was pro education and believed all children were clever, they just needed inspiration and encouragement in realising their potential.

The girls set about making words while Josie bent down and picked up discarded wet swimsuits and sandy flip-flops. The villa they were renting was superb. Two bedrooms, two bathrooms, and a private swimming pool. The pool wasn't much bigger than a postage stamp, but that hardly mattered when it was only four of them using it, although they spent most of their time on the golden beach across the road. It was the perfect location. And it would be the perfect holiday if Ruby wasn't displaying such....Josie frowned. What was the right word? Troubles? Insecurities?

Ruby was either laughing and happy or withdrawn and unreachable. It was the unreachable bit that bothered Josie. All kids had moments of being sullen or stroppy. Lucy was champion at having a tantrum when the mood took her. The bottom lip would jut out, her foot would stamp, and she'd toss her hair back before generally giving Josie a full-on outburst. But not Ruby. Instead, Ruby went quiet. Majorly so. And then she'd lash out. Physically. But there would be no display of emotion. Her face would be a mask. Unreadable. Devoid of expression. And Ruby's target was Lucy. So far, Ruby had hurt Lucy three times.

Josie sighed. She suspected the trigger had been Lucy calling Sam *Daddy*. Her mind went over their arrival at Gatwick Airport. Ruby had been very quiet to begin with. Hardly surprising after her mother had publicly stripped her without a care for Ruby being embarrassed or humiliated. The little girl had perked up seeing a suitcase of pretty clothes just for her. By the time they were seated in the Departure Lounge, nobody would have known what Ruby had endured earlier that morning.

'I'm so happy,' Lucy had trilled, her legs swinging backwards and forwards on the plastic seat. 'We're all going away as a family. Mummy, Ruby my sister, and Sam my Daddy.' Nobody had seen anything, but five minutes later Lucy had shrieked with pain. 'You pulled my hair!' she'd cried at Ruby. 'Why did you hurt me?'

Ruby's face had been deadpan, her body language still. She didn't admit or deny what she'd done. Sam had looked bewildered. Josie had read his face like a book. Anxiety. He clearly didn't know what to do, no doubt terrified of repercussions from Annie if he dared to correct their daughter. In the end, Josie had quickly jumped in.

'I think it was an accident. Don't you, Ruby?' Josie had given the child a tight smile. And a look that said she knew otherwise, and not to do it again.

Lucy had rubbed her head and, for a moment, regarded Ruby warily. But Lucy was a big-hearted child. Within minutes the girls had been back to giggling and gossiping as if nothing had happened. Until that night when, at the villa, Sam and Josie had tucked the girls into bed with a hug and a kiss.

'Goodnight, Mummy.' Lucy had thrown her arms around Josie's neck and squeezed tight. And then it had been Sam's turn. 'Goodnight, Daddy.'

Sam and Josie had retreated to the lounge for a nightcap. Fifteen minutes later, a cry had gone up. Lucy. Josie had flown into the girls' bedroom. Lucy was sitting up in bed, sobbing. Ruby – in a single bed just inches away – had apparently been asleep.

'Did Lucy have a nightmare?' Sam had appeared in the doorway.

'I'm not sure,' Josie had looked across at the sleeping Ruby. 'I think maybe I'll have Lucy in with me tonight, Sam. Just while we're settling in.'

'Sure.' Sam hadn't argued.

All Josie had managed to ascertain was that both girls had been tired and fallen asleep quickly, but Lucy had woken up with her arm being pinched. Josie had examined it, but there was nothing to see. Then things had settled down again. Until earlier today. This time Josie had caught Ruby out. She'd been watching them as they paddled in the sea with their water wings on. Neither child could swim. And although Josie was clasping a book, she was certainly not reading it. Her eyes were on the girls and their being safe. One minute they'd been splashing cold seawater at each other and squealing, the next Ruby had slapped Lucy hard across her upper arm. Her wet hand had added to the pain factor. Lucy had instantly burst into tears.

Livid, Josie had tossed her book down on the sand and rushed over. 'How DARE you hurt Lucy,' she'd bellowed at Ruby. The child had looked up at her with no expression whatsoever. No guilt. No embarrassment at being caught out. No tears. No remorse. Zero reaction. Josie had been shocked. There was a saying. What was it? Ah yes. The lights were on, but nobody was home.

'Why are you shouting at Ruby?' Sam had appeared by Josie's side, clearly affronted.

'Because your daughter,' Josie had cringed at the accusation in her voice, but fury had driven her on, 'has just belted Lucy for absolutely no reason whatsoever.'

'I see,' Sam's lips had disappeared into a thin line. 'Well if you don't mind, Josie, I'll be the one to discipline Ruby. Not you. Okay?' Whereupon Sam had taken Ruby by the hand, and the two of them had walked off together along the beach. She'd not seen either of them for two hours. When they'd returned, Ruby had been licking an ice-cream. The pair of them had acted as if nothing had happened. Sam had been laughing and joking with Ruby. Josie had been incredulous.

'Hi, darling,' Sam had trilled. 'Having a good time?'

'I've had better. And so has Lucy,' she'd replied pointedly.

'Would you both like an ice-cream?' he'd asked.

And that had been that. No mention of what had happened earlier. Josie wanted to talk about it with Sam. But not in front of the children. And as the girls had stuck to them like glue for the rest of the day, Josie had told herself she'd have to be patient. Wait for a convenient moment.

Now Josie stood in the bathroom clutching the wet towels and sandy flip-flops, uncertain what to do next. She wanted to chuck the towels in the dryer and put the flip-flops by the front door, but daren't leave the girls unattended in the tub. A small voice in her head expressed anxiety, not over a drowning incident, but rather what Ruby might do to Lucy if Josie's back was turned. In the end Josie peered round the bathroom doorway and hollered.

'Sam? Can you hear me? A hand please!'

Sam appeared seconds later. He came into the hallway, towelling himself off. The breath caught in Josie's throat. Christ but the man was gorgeous. The sun had turned Sam the colour of mahogany. His tan showcased the washboard stomach, broad shoulders and nicely muscled arms. And to think this vision was all hers. Well, he was all hers when Lucy and Ruby were asleep. Sam and Josie had ended up keeping the sleeping arrangements as they'd started off. Lucy next to Josie. Ruby next to Sam. So far Sam and Josie's sex life had been confined to one of the bathrooms with the door locked and Josie bending over the side of the bath. It wasn't ideal.

'Sorry, darling,' Sam rubbed the towel over his hair, 'I was just enjoying a last swim. Do you want to go in the pool? I don't mind keeping an eye on the girls.'

'No, that's okay. I'll just sort these wet towels and swimsuits out and grab a quick shower if that's all right.'

'Of course. But before you go,' Sam pulled Josie towards him, 'have this.' He tilted Josie's chin up and planted a kiss on her lips. Josie closed her eyes and relished Sam's warm mouth briefly grazing against hers.

Pulling away, Josie grinned. 'Won't be long.' As she disappeared through the bathroom doorway, she didn't see Ruby staring after her. This time there *was* expression on Ruby's face. It was spite.

'Sam, I really do think we should talk about what's been going on.' Josie was standing next to her fiancé, holding his hand as they watched the girls on a carousel. It was dark now. The mobile fairground was full of fun rides, screeching klaxons, and flashing coloured lights. The night was hot and Josie welcomed the breeze ruffling her hair.

For a moment Sam was silent. He stared ahead at their two happy girls on garishly painted horses as the ride went round and round, up and down. 'I'm aware Ruby is troubled, Josie,' he eventually said. 'Thanks to her mother.' Sam took a deep breath. When he exhaled it came out as a sigh. 'I know Lucy has lost her real dad. And it's been hard for her, dealing with grief at such a tender age. But Ruby is dealing with grief too.'

'How do you mean?'

'Ruby doesn't have her father living with her permanently.'

'Not quite the same thing, Sam. After all, you're not dead!'

'No. Of course not. What I'm trying to say is that I think Ruby is possessive about me. She doesn't want to share me. Where I'm concerned, her mother has made Ruby insecure.'

'Yes, I can understand that.'

'So I hope you'll also understand that it would be best if Lucy stopped calling me Daddy.'

Josie bit her lip. 'That's a bit tough, Sam.'

'Yeah. I know. And I'm going to say something else too. Something you also won't like. But I'm confident it will be a temporary thing. Just until we've all settled into the new house and Ruby has adjusted.'

Despite the balmy night air, Josie felt as though a piece of ice had settled in her stomach. 'And what is that?'

'I want – for a few weeks – to keep Lucy at arm's length from me in front of Ruby. No hugging. No climbing on my knee. No kisses good-night.'

'Are you kidding?'

'I want my daughter to know her Daddy is *her* Daddy.'

'But Ruby *does* know that!'

'No she doesn't. She's had a mother telling her I don't love her. A mother who has told Ruby that I only love you and Lucy. If Annie is capable of voicing such things in front of me, you can only begin to imagine what lies she spouts when I'm not around.' Sam saw the pain on Josie's face. 'I'm sorry, darling. Truly I am. I don't want to hurt you.'

'Bugger hurting me,' Josie blurted, 'it's *my* daughter I'm concerned for. What about Lucy's feelings? She's six years old, Sam. Don't you think *she'll* feel hurt?'

'Not if I explain to her. There's a way of dealing with this. If it's done properly...carefully...it will be fine. It will work out. You'll see.'

Josie chewed her lip again. Bloody Annie. Josie felt tremendously sorry for Ruby being caught up in her mother's poison. But now the wretched woman was impacting on her own daughter. It wasn't fair. 'I don't know. I'm not sure.'

'Josie, we're a second-time-around family. It was never going to be a bed of roses. Not with children from previous relationships.' Sam squeezed her hand. 'But we can work through this. Yes?'

The merry-go-round was slowing down. Josie turned troubled eyes to Sam. She'd invested her future in this man. Lucy's future too. All her hopes and dreams were bound up with Sam. She'd bought a house with this man. Tied up every last penny of her equity in bricks and mortar. A home. A family home. She took a deep breath. Sam was right. Things would work out. Together she and Sam would *make* it work out. Josie looked into Sam's eyes. Kind eyes. Loving. Finally she nodded.

'Yes. We'll work through this.'

Lucy was sitting on the edge of the swimming pool. Her bottom was immersed in a shallow puddle of chlorinated water, while her legs dangled below the waterline. The sun was hot on her shoulders. Lucy longed to belly flop into the pool. But she wouldn't. Couldn't. She was sitting on the outside looking in. In front of her Sam and Ruby played in the water together. It was the last day of their Spanish holiday. Almost a week since Sam had told her not to call him Daddy. His voice had been gentle and kind. So how come his words had cut like a knife?

The little girl hadn't grasped all of Sam's speech. Her ears had developed invisible shutters that had clanged down, like those metal roller blinds that folded over the front of shop windows. She'd got as far as hearing that Sam must be called

Sam, and that she mustn't hug or kiss him in front of Ruby. But the whys and wherefores had evaded her thanks to those invisible ear muffs. All Lucy knew was that Sam was suddenly out of bounds.

Inside the villa, Mummy was packing suitcases and emptying cupboards. Lucy had wanted to help her, but Mummy had insisted it would be quicker to do it by herself.

'You go outside and make the most of this beautiful weather. It's raining in England. Go and have a nice swim with Ruby and Sam.'

Lucy had started off swimming with them, but Ruby had clung to Sam like a limpet. Finally Ruby had released her father but only in order to play water chase. And then throw and catch. And then who could float the longest. And then who could jump the farthest off the side of the pool. Lucy had drifted away ages ago. She'd hauled herself up onto the edge. The little girl gazed down at her toes in the water. The constant movement of the pool's water shifted and distorted the image of her toes. They rippled from big to small, from wavy to crooked. Lucy knew what her toes looked like, even though the image in front of her was distorted. She had a feeling that what Sam had told her was like the image in front of her. All muddled up. Sam had said he loved her. But she didn't believe him. If you loved somebody you showed it. You didn't tell them to stay away.

Lucy began splashing her legs. Something inside her had died. She'd lost her real father. And just when she thought she had another Daddy to love, he'd been snatched away too. But confusingly, he was still here. She kicked her legs faster. Sam was right in front of her. There...but not there. She kicked harder. Water sprayed over Sam and Ruby.

'Stop it, Lucy,' Ruby protested.
'But it's fun.'
'Not for me it isn't.'
'That's enough, Lucy,' said Sam.
'No.'
'Daddy, tell her to stop. I don't like it.'

Lucy abruptly ceased splashing. She withdrew her legs from the pool and tucked them under her bottom. Pushing her palms against the ground, she stood up and looked down at Ruby.

She'd had enough of being excluded all afternoon. Lucy gave Ruby a dark look. A look that said I don't like you.

Ruby watched Lucy go inside the villa. She was secretly pleased to have kept Daddy all to herself this afternoon. Last week, quite by chance, Ruby had overheard Daddy talking to Lucy. Explaining that from now on she must call him by his name. Sam. Ruby hadn't heard Lucy's reply, it had all been mumbles. But Ruby had gathered Lucy was upset. Good. Much as Ruby liked Lucy, she didn't want to share Daddy with her. In the beginning it hadn't entered Ruby's head that another little girl would vie for the attention of Daddy. But thanks to Mummy, she had learned differently. Mummy's words had worried her. Mummy had told her that Daddy didn't love her any more. To begin with, Ruby hadn't believed Mummy. But then a tiny gnawing doubt had settled in. Like a worm. Right in her brain. It had wriggled and niggled. Especially in bed at night, when everything was quiet. That was when the little worm had turned into a big fat nagging snake. What if Daddy really didn't love her anymore? What if he only loved Lucy? And so Ruby had exacted her revenge wherever she'd been able. Pulling Lucy's hair. Pinching. Slapping. She hadn't felt guilty. Why should she? After Josie had told her off, Ruby had been more careful about punishing Lucy. Like hiding one of Lucy's flip-flops so that Josie told Lucy off for carelessness. Lucy didn't yet know that a souvenir she'd bought earlier in the holiday was now resting in the garden of the unoccupied villa next door. Lucy had lingered by the arts and crafts stall, finally buying herself a little fabric frog. The cloth was in all the colours of the rainbow and the finished product filled with beans. Lucy had loved it. And in a flash of insight, Ruby had seen a different way to hurt Lucy. Take away the thing she loved. Just like Daddy had been taken away from her and transported into this new, now unwanted family arrangement. Because it was unwanted. All the excitement about having her own bedroom at 2 Sycamore Drive had vanished when Mummy had stripped her down to her pants in the front garden. Mummy was clearly very unhappy. And Ruby didn't want that. Ruby was too young to handle divided loyalties, so it was easier to be loyal to just one person. Her Mummy. And anybody who upset Mummy, or threatened to take Daddy away would be punished. Starting with Lucy. Ruby had palmed Lucy's frog and dispatched it in the space of a minute. It had been easy. Confusingly, Ruby was starting to feel angry with Daddy too. But she didn't want to punish him the way she'd punished Lucy. Instead she had a plan forming in her head. A plan to get Mummy and Daddy back together again. That way Ruby could push away the anger she had started to feel at Daddy, and be assured her parents would love just her and nobody else. Ruby didn't want Nigel and his boys in her life. Nor did she want Josie and Lucy on alternative weekends. Ruby gave a little smile. Daddy was always telling her she was a princess. And everybody knew princesses always got what they wanted. Ruby's smile turned into a banana grin. Mummy and Daddy would get back together. She, Princess Ruby, would make it happen.

The wipers on the Mercedes were working overtime. It was chucking down. When Sam's Mercedes turned into Sycamore Drive, there was a surprise waiting at Number 2. A car was parked on their driveway. Seconds later the driver's door opened and Annie erupted out. Within seconds the rain plastered her hair to her face. Annie gave Josie a filthy look, ignored Lucy and Sam, and hauled open the rear passenger door of the idling Mercedes. Leaning in, she unstrapped Ruby and manhandled the child out.

'For God's sake, Annie,' Sam unclipped his seat belt, 'what the hell are you doing?'

'Time's up, Sam.' Annie yanked Ruby towards her car. 'You've had your two weeks in the sun. Now it's time for Ruby to come home with me.'

'But you didn't have to drive out.' Sam followed Annie over to her car. The rain was darkening his shirt. It began to stick to his body. 'I'd have taken her home to you shortly.'

'Sure,' Annie buckled Ruby into the front seat, 'when it suited you. After you'd all had tea together and played Happy Families for a little bit longer. Sorry to spoil your fun.'

'Why does it always have to be like this?'

'You made it like this, Sam.'

'No I didn't.'

'Bullshit. Oh, nice house by the way. Enjoy living in it. While you can.'

'Annie stop this. Please. This isn't doing Ruby any good.' Sam moved round to the passenger side of Annie's car. Raindrops bounced off the end of his nose. He brushed them away. 'Hey, princess, let me give you a kiss good-bye.' He crouched down and pecked Ruby's rigid cheek. The child was staring straight ahead, face expressionless. 'Ruby?' The little girl continued looking at the windscreen. 'I love you, sweetheart.'

'Love?' Annie slid behind the steering wheel. She stared across at Sam. 'You don't know the meaning of the word. Now piss off back to your family.'

Sam gave Annie a dark look before turning his attention to Ruby. 'See you soon, darling.' He straightened up. He'd barely shut the car door when Annie hit the accelerator. Leaping back, he watched Annie speed away with his daughter.

'Welcome home, Sam,' he said quietly to himself.

Josie had kept herself busy while Annie exchanged her barbed words with Sam. Silently she had helped Lucy out of the Mercedes and taken her daughter indoors. Stepping over piles of post on the doormat, Josie had led Lucy into the lounge and flicked the television on.

'Won't be a mo,' she'd said brightly. 'I'll just get the suitcases and then make us all a nice hot chocolate. Good old England. Cold and pouring with rain.'

Josie had been aware of jabbering, but she'd wanted to distract Lucy from the kerfuffle taking place on the driveway. She was aware Annie didn't give two hoots about screaming and shouting in front of her own neighbours, but Josie really wished she wouldn't do it in front of theirs. They'd only moved in recently. The last thing Josie wanted was the residents of Sycamore Drive thinking they were the neighbours from hell.

Removing the suitcases from the boot, Josie had lugged them through the driving rain and into the hallway. Shaking herself off, she'd then trolleyed them into the utility room. And now she was busy unzipping them all and attending to dirty laundry. She might as well get a wash on immediately. Seconds later the front door shut. Josie turned. From where she was standing she could see Sam crouching over the doormat.

'Sorry about that,' said Sam as he scooped up all the mail.

'Hey,' Josie said softly, 'not your fault.'

Sam peeled off his wet shirt and went into the utility room. Balling up the sodden fabric, he chucked it in the direction of the washing machine before going out to the kitchen where he dumped the mail on the worktop. Then he paused. Sifted through the envelopes. Stopped at the big brown one. That looked ominous. Josie was now chattering on about a hot drink. He was only half listening. His finger found the edge of the envelope's seal. He ripped it open.

'You bitch,' he said softly.

'Sam?' Josie looked shocked.

'Sorry, darling. Sorry.' He raked his damp hair. 'Not you. Never you.'

'What's wrong?'

'This.' He smacked the papers down on the worktop. 'Annie's been busy while we've been away. It's a demand. From the Child Support Agency.'

Chapter Twenty-Three
The following year, close to Easter.

'If you could bite down hard on this articulating paper, Mr Forbes,' said Sam. 'Perfect. Now open wide. Excellent. The filling hasn't altered your bite. All done. I'll see you in six months time.'

Mr Forbes was the last patient of the day. As the man went off to Reception to settle his account, Sam removed his mask and latex gloves. It had been a long day and he couldn't wait to get home and relax. Although going home wasn't always the stress buster Sam hoped for. These days Sam was never quite sure what would be awaiting him when he put his key in the front door. The last twelve months had been fraught with correspondence from The Child Support Agency and demands for ridiculous amounts of money. Josie had had the screaming heebie-jeebies that their house – a house she had personally invested well over two hundred thousand pounds in – would have to be sold to placate the battleaxe at the CSA who was working on Annie's behalf. In the end it had gone to Court. Sam had appointed Graham Burnley at considerable expense. And what had Annie achieved? Instead of quadrupling her maintenance payments, Sam's monthly payments had actually been reduced by two hundred pounds. But it was a hollow victory. Annie had immediately poured more verbal poison into Ruby's ears.

'Daddy's reducing his payments to Mummy because he's spending all his money on Lucy and Josie. He can't afford to spend money on you.'

So despite the Court outcome, Sam made sure his payments to Annie stayed at the previous rate in order to disprove Annie's words to Ruby. He also started an ISA account for Ruby and told the little girl too.

'I'll tell you how precious you are to me, princess,' he'd told Ruby, 'Daddy has a special savings account just for you. Nobody else. Not even Mummy. Look. I'll show you.' And Sam had put the papers in front of his seven-year-old daughter and tried to explain how money earned interest and that if Ruby wanted to go to university one day, or get married, or buy a flat, there would be lots of money to do so. Just for her.

But it was exhausting trying to constantly prove himself to his daughter. To endlessly demonstrate loyalty to Ruby. To smash down the wall Annie tirelessly strove to erect between him and his child. A wall of bitter words and rebuke. Sam didn't know how much Ruby believed of the venom that Annie fed her. All he knew was he never stopped worrying about Annie succeeding in severing the relationship with his daughter. It haunted him. Sometimes he awoke at night panicking that Ruby didn't want to see him ever again.

The receptionist stuck her head round Sam's consulting room door. 'I'm off.'

'Cheerio, Judith. See you tomorrow.'

Half an hour later Sam was home. As he opened the front door, the delicious aroma of boeuf bourguignon welcomed him. Josie was a wonderful cook. Lucy wandered out of the television room and greeted him.

'Hi, Sam.'

'Hey, Miss. Good day at school?'

'Yes thanks.'

It had been a long time since he'd asked Lucy to stop calling him Daddy "for just a few weeks". The weeks had turned into months. And now he was simply Sam. Lucy hadn't attempted to call him Daddy again. Sam felt a mixture of guilt and relief. Guilt at denying Lucy. Relief at appeasing Ruby. Although ever since last year's summer holiday, the girls weren't as close as they had been. At school they no longer hung out together. Worryingly, Ruby didn't seem to have any friends. From what Sam could gather, she had a skipping rope that went to school with her. But instead of playing skipping games with other children, Ruby skipped around the playground singing songs to herself. He'd asked Lucy to play with Ruby at school, but the child's reply had surprised him.

'Ruby doesn't want to play with me, Sam. She doesn't like sharing her skipping rope.'

'Well what about you ask her to join in your games? Or just ask her to hang out with you at playtime?'

'She doesn't want to. Ruby likes her own company best. She's not into sharing.'

Those words had troubled Sam. Still, hopefully Ruby and Lucy would forge fresh bonds when they went on this year's summer holiday. He'd already paid the deposit on the same villa as last year.

Sam kicked off his shoes, tweaked Lucy's ponytail and went off to find Josie. She was dishing up the boeuf bourguignon.

'Hi, darling,' he kissed the top of her head. 'Good day at uni?'

Josie wrinkled her nose. College days were over. She and Kerry were now at Greenwich University, sharing the driving as they commuted in and out of South London. 'I have a massive assignment to tackle after dinner, so try and keep the television down later.'

'Sure. Any mail?'

Josie gave him a wary look. 'Yes. Over there. On the table.'

Sam caught Josie's expression. Instinctively his chest tightened. He moved over to the table and picked up a large A4 envelope. It looked official. He tore back the sticky strip and removed the documents within.

'What the fucking hell is this?'

'Sam,' Josie frowned, 'language.'

'I don't bloody believe this.'

Josie put the plates down on the table. She gave a sigh of resignation. 'What now?'

'More shit,' Sam waggled the papers at Josie, 'instigated by that bitch. This is from Cafcass. And in case you don't know what that stands for–'

'Children and Family Court Advisory and Support Service. I know what it means.'

'Well isn't this just fabulous,' Sam ground his teeth together.

Josie decided against feeding Lucy with them at the table. She ladled a serving into a bowl and briefly disappeared into the television room. Thirty seconds later she was back. Pulling out a chair, she sat down. 'Let's have dinner, Sam.'

'Dinner? I can't eat. The food would stick in my throat. That bloody cow has involved an organisation independent of the Court to – listen to this – *safeguard and promote the welfare of*

Ruby. What the bloody hell does that mean, eh?' Josie opened her mouth to speak but Sam cut across her. 'I'll tell you what it means. It means that some unknown person is going to visit me, you and Lucy here in our house. They will interview us. Assess our parenting skills. Dissect our family unit. Ultimately that stranger will deem whether we're fit enough parents to take Ruby on holiday with us or even allow her to stay here. I tell you, this organisation will ask every question under the sun. They'll want to know everything about us. Right down to the colour of the toilet paper we use.'

'Now you're being ridiculous.'

'No I'm not.' Sam stared at the papers before him. 'Oh, and get this! Cafcass will talk to Ruby and get to the bottom of what *she* really wants – not what *I* want. Because apparently it's all about Ruby. Not me, her father. Never mind my wishes about being allowed to see my daughter. Can you Adam and Eve it? They're going to interview a seven-year-old. A seven-year-old who will have been primed and prepped to word perfection by the biggest scheming bitch of the century.'

'Sam, everything will be fine–'

'You think?'

'Yes.'

'How do you know, Josie? How do you *really* know?'

'Because I do. We have albums full of family photographs. Pictures of our kids playing – both together and with us. On holiday. Days out. Riding bicycles. In the park. The garden. Making cakes. Being a family.'

'Except things have changed in the last few months, Josie. Haven't you noticed the number of weekends that Ruby hasn't been over this year? Because she's had a tummy ache? Or a cold? Or been invited to a sleepover at a cousin's? I think, in hindsight, those were excuses. Perhaps my daughter doesn't want to stay here. Perhaps she doesn't want to see me anymore.'

'Now you're being paranoid.'

'I can't deal with this, Josie,' Sam's voice cracked. 'All the time,' he raked his hair, 'it haunts me. Terrifies me. Sometimes I can't sleep at night for worrying–'

'Stop it.' Josie reached out and put one hand over Sam's.

'I can't help it. What if Ruby doesn't really want to come on holiday with us? What if my daughter doesn't want to stay at this house anymore? Don't you understand how I feel, Josie? I feel like a failure. Like a useless father.'

Josie gave up trying to eat and put her knife and fork together. 'You're not a useless father, and I won't have you talking like that. Now pack it in, Sam.' The words came out harsher than she meant. But she needed to snap Sam out of the spiral of anxiety the Cafcass documentation had put him in. 'We will talk to whoever comes here. We will put their mind at rest. And if necessary we will go to Court. Again. Nothing is going to jeopardise your relationship with Ruby. Not Annie. Not Cafcass.'

Sam gripped Josie's hand. He stared at her face. It was calm. Reassuring. He took a deep breath. Exhaled shakily. Then nodded. 'Yes,' he whispered. 'Yes. You're right.' He picked up his knife and fork and began to eat. Of course his daughter wanted to see him. Josie was right. He was being paranoid. He swallowed some meat and vegetables without really tasting it. Roll on the weekend. Ruby would be with them. Thank God. He couldn't wait to hug his child.

The Cafcass wheels had been set in motion. Annie was tremendously pleased. Fuck Sam. He should have played ball with her over quadrupling the monthly maintenance payments. A social worker had been in touch. A woman called Janet Marsden. In a fortnight Janet was going to *pop round* and chat to Ruby. Get to the bottom of what Ruby wanted. And Annie knew what Ruby wanted. Her daughter wanted to just be with her mum. She didn't want a part-time dad. And she definitely didn't want anything to do with Josie or Lucy. Ruby hated spending alternate weekends at 2 Sycamore Drive. She felt homesick and missed her mother. Annie knew this because Ruby had told her so. Excellent. Put that in your pipe and smoke it, Sam. Meanwhile Annie had a holiday to pack for. She and Ruby were going to Turkey this Saturday. Nigel was paying. Nigel's boys would be joining them too. Nigel was beginning to make noises about them being *a family*. Interesting. She wondered if Nigel might finally be about to propose.

Meanwhile, first things first. Passports. Annie went to the sideboard in the lounge. Crouching down she removed a file. Flipping it open, she found her passport. Putting the file away, she then went upstairs to her bedroom. Reaching to the back of her wardrobe, she pulled out an old handbag. Tucked inside was Ruby's passport. The passport she'd hidden away from Sam last year prior to his Spanish holiday. She smirked at the thought of Sam having to dash off to Peterborough and endure a day of hassle. Putting Ruby's passport together with her own, she chucked them both on the bed. Suitcases next.

Ruby flopped down on her bed. Her legs were aching. She'd skipped hundreds of times around the playground at school today. Well, maybe not hundreds. But not far off!

She could hear her mother next door pulling clothes from the wardrobe for their holiday. Ruby wasn't bothered about going. She didn't know why Mummy made her spend time with Nigel, a man who wasn't her father. Especially when Mummy didn't want her spending time with her real father. It didn't really make sense to Ruby. When it came to her Mummy, all Ruby knew was that the words *Daddy* and *Sam* were like a red rag to a bull. Mummy would flip out. Mummy had already had a big chat to Ruby about Daddy. Asked her lots of questions.

'You don't really love Daddy, do you, darling?'

Ruby had gazed at Mummy in amazement. Well of course she loved Daddy. He was her Daddy! All children loved their daddies. Didn't they? Ruby had blinked. Looked at her mother carefully. Mummy had had an expression on her face. An expression that Ruby clearly understood. Mummy had been hoping that Ruby would answer in the negative. So to please her, and keep her from flipping out, Ruby had given her mother the answer she wanted.

'Not really.'

'I knew it. It's hard loving somebody who isn't around, isn't it baby?'

Ruby had shrugged. 'I suppose.'

'And you don't like Josie do you?'

Ruby had frowned, about to protest. But then she discarded the expression and the objection died on her lips. She didn't want to antagonise Mummy. Ruby knew Mummy loathed Josie. Ruby had nothing against Josie. She just wished it was Mummy living with Daddy, rather than Josie living with Daddy. Ruby shrugged again. 'No. I don't like Josie.'

'Ah, my poor baby. Has she ever been horrible to you?'

Ruby tried to think of an occasion. 'She once told me to eat all my carrots up.'

'That's outrageous. Fancy making you eat something you don't like.' Mummy had tutted in disgust. 'And you don't like going over to Daddy's house every other weekend, do you, poppet?'

Ruby regarded her mother solemnly. 'No. I'd rather be here. With you.'

'Of course you would. It's unsettling being constantly bounced between two houses, isn't it?'

'Yes.'

'Would you like to go to Spain with Daddy this year?'

'Only if you come too.'

Mummy had let out a tinkle of laughter. 'My poor baby. Did you miss Mummy last year?'

'Yes.' In fact Ruby hadn't so much missed her mother as been worried about Annie being lonely while she was away.

'I think it's best that you give Spain a miss. Don't you?'

'Yes.'

'After all, it's not like you're going without a holiday, is it? We're off to Turkey!'

'Yes.'

'And Turkey is much nicer than Spain.'

'Yes.' Ruby hadn't a clue whether Turkey was more preferable than Spain. All she knew was that every time she said *yes* Mummy smiled and smiled and smiled. And that made Ruby happy. Because it meant that Mummy was happy. And more than anything, Ruby wanted her Mummy to be happy.

When Sam pulled back the curtains on Saturday morning, he felt his spirits lift. The sun was already up and shining bravely. It was a perfect day for a trip to the local park. Sam smiled and rubbed his hands together. He'd get the girls' bikes out of the garage after breakfast. One of the bike's wheels had looked flat.

He'd pump them up before driving over to Annie's to collect Ruby. He turned back to Josie who was propped up on one elbow in bed.

Josie gave him a coy look. 'Why are you smiling so secretively, Mr Worthington?'

Sam joined her back in bed. 'No reason, Ms Payne, other than I'm very happy. Want to know why?'

'Go on.'

'Because of you. You make me happy, sweetheart.'

'I should think so.' Josie feigned indignation.

'You're the love of my life.' Sam folded her into his chest. 'You keep me sane and calm. And you put up with a hell of a lot. I do know that. And I can't tell you how grateful I am. I couldn't get by without you, Josie.'

Josie smiled and mentally sighed. She spent so much time worrying about Sam and his well-being. Sometimes she wondered how the heck he coped with a busy dental practice whilst dealing with the merry dance Annie constantly led him. Josie snuggled against Sam's chest and relished the moment. Right now she was in a lovely bubble. Peaceful. Quiet. No boisterous daughters. No aggro from Annie. Just calm. With Sam. And it was bliss.

Annie lugged the suitcases into the hall. Nigel would be along in ten minutes or so. She went into the lounge to make sure windows were closed. Ruby was sitting in front of the television.

'Have you got everything you want to take on holiday, Ruby?'

'Yes.'

'Sure? I don't want any last minute panics because you've forgotten Rosie the rabbit.'

'Rosie is in my bag.' Ruby patted the small rucksack next to her.

The doorbell rang. 'That will be Nigel. Come on. Turn the telly off and pick up your rucksack.' Annie hastened out to the hall. But instead of Nigel, it was Sam standing on the doorstep. Annie grimaced. 'What do you want?'

Sam looked at his ex-wife. The usual words. He was about to reply when he noticed the suitcases in the hallway.

'Going somewhere?'

'Yes. Turkey. In about,' Annie glanced at her wristwatch, 'five minutes.'

'Have a lovely holiday.' Sam spotted Ruby peering out of the lounge. 'Hey, princess. Looks like you're with me for a few extra days.'

'Don't be ridiculous,' Annie snorted. 'Ruby is coming with me. We're holidaying with Nigel and his boys. This time it's *my* turn to play happy families.'

'You can do what you like, Annie, but Ruby is coming with me.'

'Piss off, Sam. I'd call the police for harassment except I'd be gone by the time they arrived.'

'I'm not harassing you,' Sam said mildly. 'And no need for the police, because I'm leaving. With Ruby.' He held out a hand towards his daughter. But Ruby remained where she was, her expression frozen.

Annie put her hands on her hips. 'You don't get it do you, Sam? Well let me spell it out to you. Ruby doesn't want to stay at your place. Not now. Not ever. And don't go booking her on your Spanish holiday this year, because it won't be happening.'

Sam ignored his ex-wife. 'Ruby.' His voice came out as a croak. He coughed and cleared his throat. 'Ruby, come on, darling. It's a lovely day. I've pumped up the wheels on your bicycle. Josie's making a picnic and we're going to spend the day at the park.'

'I said piss off,' Annie snarled. 'Ruby is coming on holiday with me. It's all booked.' She looked at her wristwatch again. Where the fuck was Nigel?

'I have a Court Order, Annie. It says that neither of us takes Ruby out of the country without the other's consent. There's also a Prohibitive Steps Order in place. Do you want to be in contempt of Court?'

'You can take all your Court Orders and shove them where the sun doesn't shine. Cafcass are involved now, Sam. Your precious documents aren't worth the paper they're written on.' Annie turned to Ruby. 'You don't like staying at Daddy's, do you, sweetie?'

Ruby stared from one parent to the other. Sam could feel his chest tightening. So much so, he was struggling to breathe. This was his worst nightmare. He didn't want to hear his daughter telling him any such thing.

'Pack it in, Annie,' he gasped, 'you're trying to put words in Ruby's mouth.'

'No I'm not. Tell him, Ruby. Tell Daddy what you've told me.'

Sam spun on his heel. He couldn't...wouldn't...wait around to listen to Ruby confirm what he most definitely didn't want to hear. To hell with it. Let Annie have her holiday in Turkey with their daughter – and the man she'd left him for.

Suddenly Sam was moving towards his Mercedes like an Olympic sprinter. He wanted to put as much distance between himself and his daughter's potential words as possible. If he didn't hear Ruby say the words, then they didn't exist, and everything would be as it was before. Fine. *Everything's fine Sam.* He popped the central locking. *Everything's just fine.* Leaping into the car he started the engine. *Take no notice of Annie. Everything is fine.* Sam screeched away from the kerb, narrowly avoiding a car coming in the other direction.

Josie heard the front door crash back on its hinges. Alarmed, she abandoned the bread she was buttering and rushed into the hallway. Sam stood there, tears pouring down his cheeks. Cheeks that were the colour of putty.

'Whatever's happened?' Josie took hold of Sam's elbow and steered him into the lounge. Hearing commotion, Lucy came out of the television room opposite. The little girl caught sight of Sam's face before glancing at her mother. Josie gave a small shake of her head. Lucy instantly retreated. Josie shut the lounge door. She didn't want Lucy hearing Sam when he was like this. It wasn't good for her. And as Sam didn't have Ruby with him, no prizes for guessing that access wasn't taking place this weekend.

'I-It's true,' Sam gasped.

'What's true?'

'Ruby, she doesn't want... oh God, Annie said–' Sam's gibbering was lost in a torrent of fresh tears.

Josie pushed him down on the sofa. She stood over him. Wrapped her arms around him. Pulling his head into her midriff, she rocked him backwards and forwards like a child.

'It's all right, Sam,' she murmured. 'Hush. There, there.' Josie found herself slipping into the sort of speak she reserved for Lucy when she'd scraped a knee. For the next two or three minutes the only noise was Sam sobbing his heart out. Eventually his shoulders stopped heaving. He leant away from Josie.

'Sorry. Oh God. You shouldn't see me like this. I'm meant to be a man.'

'It's all right for men to cry.'

'No. It's not.' Sam rubbed his hands across his face. 'I need to grow a pair of balls.'

'You've got balls,' Josie replied. 'It's just that your ex keeps kicking you in them. What's the wretched woman done this time?'

'She's on her way to the airport. With Ruby.' Sam pulled a Kleenex from his pocket and blew his nose. 'She's off to Turkey for a week. With Ruby obviously. And Nigel and his boys.'

Josie's mind whirled. Annie wasn't going to get very far without Ruby's passport. It was residing in the study's filing cabinet. Surely to goodness Annie wasn't so daft as to overlook a small matter of needing it. Unless...her eyes widened. Annie *did* have a passport – Ruby's old passport. A passport she'd been emphatic about losing. So clearly Annie had told a pack of lies about the whereabouts of the original passport.

Josie glanced down at the man before her. Her darling Sam. Reduced to an emotional mess. And all because of that blasted woman. Month in, month out, nothing but abuse. Upset. Stress. Josie cast her mind back to last summer. The terrible anxiety Sam had endured at The Passport Office. All because of that woman. Josie wasn't a spiteful person, but in that moment something in her heart hardened. She wanted revenge. Just a small balancing out on the scales of retribution. In any other circumstances, Josie would have voiced aloud that Annie didn't have the right passport. She wasn't one-hundred per cent sure, but might Ruby's old passport now be invalid? Ideally, Sam should telephone Ruby's mobile and tell his daughter to warn

Mummy about a potential passport problem. Otherwise the holiday to Turkey could be jeopardised. Josie chewed her lip and wrestled with her conscience. If she mentioned it to Sam, he'd try and get hold of Annie like a shot. He was too honourable. It wasn't that he cared about Annie missing her holiday, but he would care about his daughter missing hers. Josie came to a decision. To hell with scruples.

'Darling, I want you to take Lucy to the park. She's been looking forward to it.'

Sam nodded. 'Sure. We'll still have our picnic. I need to get some fresh air. It's no use sitting around here. I'll only mope.'

'Good. The thing is I need to go over that assignment one more time. Would you mind terribly if I didn't come. Apart from anything else, I think it would do Lucy good to have some quality time with you. She hasn't really had that for while you know.'

Sam bowed his head. 'I know,' he whispered. 'I'll just go to the bathroom and wash my face.' He stood up. 'Is the picnic ready?'

'Almost.' Josie pulled away from Sam. 'You sort yourself out. I'll get the picnic.'

As soon as Sam was upstairs, Josie palmed his forgotten mobile phone lying on the sofa. Switching it off, she chucked it in her handbag. Ten minutes later Sam and Lucy were out on the driveway astride their bicycles.

'Oh,' Sam paused. Patted his pockets. 'My mobile phone. Could you pass it to me?'

'Where is it?'

'Um...did I leave it in the lounge?'

Josie pretended to look. 'It's not there. It's probably upstairs somewhere. Do you really need it? You're only cycling to the park.'

'You're right.' Sam mustered up a smile. 'Well, see you later then.'

'Bye,' Josie smiled as she waved Lucy and Sam off.

'Have fun with your assignment!' Sam called over his shoulder.

'I won't. Enjoy your bike ride and picnic.' She gave a final wave to Lucy as her daughter wobbled off behind Sam. Heaving a sigh, Josie shut the front door. She hurried into the study. Rummaging in the cabinet, she removed the file that contained birth certificates and passports. She peered inside the manila wallet. Three passports. Josie palmed the one with Ruby's iffy photograph and slid it into the back pocket of her jeans.

All she had to do now was wait.

Chapter Twenty-Four

Annie was standing in the check-in queue. She couldn't wait to get rid of the suitcases and grab a coffee. Nigel was in front of her, refereeing his boys who were attempting to punch each other's lights out. Thank God she'd never had a son. Boys were nothing but trouble. She glanced down at her daughter standing quietly next to her.

'All right, poppet?'

Ruby nodded. Rosie rabbit had been pulled from the rucksack and was now being tightly hugged. If Rosie had been real, her ribcage would now be crushed. Annie frowned. She hoped Ruby wasn't coming down with something. She'd not said two words since Sam had rushed off. Annie shuffled forward a few paces as her mind cast back to Sam's exit. He'd been in quite a state. So much so that he'd nearly crashed into Nigel coming in the opposite direction. Not that Sam had realised who it was. The queue moved forward again. Nigel was next.

'Get your passports ready,' said Nigel.

'I already have.' Annie flapped them at her boyfriend.

'Good. You're after me.'

He moved forward with his boys. Nigel lifted the first suitcase onto the conveyor. Annie could see the female clerk greeting him and asking for the flight tickets and passports. Now the little machine was spewing forth boarding passes. Nigel's suitcase disappeared through the plastic curtain. Two minutes later the boys' suitcases followed. The female clerk wished Nigel a pleasant holiday. Now it was Annie's turn.

'Good afternoon,' the female clerk smiled. 'Passports and tickets please.'

'Hello,' Annie replied. She slapped the documents down on the counter.

The clerk checked Annie's passport. Her eyes scanned the details. Then she picked up Ruby's passport. The clerk's eyebrows knitted together.

'There's a problem with this passport.'

Annie froze. Did this woman somehow know that she'd withheld this passport from Sam? Surely not! And even if she did, so what? Unless...Annie's blood ran cold...unless you weren't allowed to have two passports and this woman knew Sam also had a passport?

'What's wrong with it?'

'It's out of date.'

'Don't be ridiculous,' Annie spluttered, 'of course it's not out of date.'

'I'm afraid it is.'

'Where?' Annie snatched the passport back. 'You're wrong. See?' She stabbed the back page with her index finger. 'It has a whole month before it expires.'

'You're travelling to Turkey. Your daughter's passport must have at least six months unexpired time at the date of entry into Turkey. And upon exit from Turkey there must be at least three months unexpired time on your passport.'

'I'll make sure it's renewed as soon as I get back from my holiday,' said Annie. 'In the meantime, could you just hurry up and put our luggage through.'

'I'm very sorry, but your daughter isn't going to Turkey.'

'This is outrageous. I want to speak to your Manager. I will personally make sure you are sacked. Do you understand? This is discrimination.'

Nigel appeared at Annie's side. 'What's the matter?'

'This bloody woman is saying that Ruby's passport is invalid. Even though it doesn't expire for another four weeks.'

'Do you mean to tell me you didn't know Ruby's passport was due for renewal?' Nigel asked incredulously.

'It's not due for renewal for another four weeks,' Annie protested. 'It's a perfectly valid passport. It's this stupid bitch causing problems.'

'You're the stupid bitch, Annie,' Nigel hissed, 'so stop creating a scene and just for once shut your mouth.' He turned to the female clerk. 'Is there absolutely no way we can use this passport? Not even in an emergency like now?'

'I'm sorry, sir, but the answer is no.'

'Fine,' Nigel pursed his lips. 'Follow me, Annie.'

'No, I'm not leaving this queue until I've seen this woman's boss and—'

'For Christ's sake, Annie, shut up and come with me.' He grabbed hold of Annie's and Ruby's suitcases and shoved them away from the now chuntering queue. Wheeling the cases over to a row of plastic seats, he spun round to face Annie. 'Your ex took Ruby to Spain last summer. Didn't you notice the date on the passport back then?'

'Sam didn't use this passport.'

'What do you mean?'

'I couldn't find Ruby's passport,' Annie felt herself reddening, 'so he had to get another passport.'

'Hang on a minute,' Nigel frowned, 'you're telling me that right now Ruby has two passports?'

Annie shrugged. 'I suppose.'

'You stupid bloody cow,' Nigel blew out his cheeks.

'Don't you talk to me like that,' Annie glowered.

'I bloody well will. Don't you realise, even if Ruby's passport hadn't been about to expire, you shouldn't be using it anyway if a second one has been issued. What's the matter with you?'

'Well I didn't know,' Annie huffed.

'I suggest you get on the phone to your ex and ask him very nicely to drive, at great speed, to Gatwick Airport with Ruby's passport.'

Annie glared at Nigel. Well this was a great start to their holiday wasn't it? And Nigel wanted her to phone Sam and ask – ha! – *nicely* if she could have Ruby's other passport? She'd rather pull her fingernails out.

'No. You phone him.'

'He's *your* ex-husband Annie. Not mine. So you do it. Meanwhile I have a plane to catch.'

Annie's mouth dropped open. 'You'd go off without us?'

'Well there's no point in me and my boys missing a holiday just because of your stupidity. Sort it out, Annie. And get a move on. Because our flight leaves,' Nigel glanced at his wristwatch, 'in exactly one hundred minutes.' And with that he turned on his heel and walked off to Security Control.

Annie stood staring after him, impotent with fury. Another five minutes and Nigel and his boys would be in the Departure Lounge – without her and Ruby. Suddenly there was a tugging at her sleeve.

'Mummy?' Ruby quavered.

Annie looked down at her daughter. 'Yes?' She could feel the start of a throbbing headache. She rubbed her temples viciously.

'Why don't you go on holiday with Nigel? I can always stay at Daddy's.'

Something stirred within Annie. Let Ruby stay at Sam's? Allow Sam to enjoy additional access that he wasn't entitled to? Never! 'Leave this to Mummy.' Annie's mouth set in a grim line. 'Come hell or high water, we're going to Turkey.'

Josie was seated at the kitchen table with her assignment papers spread around her. She was only three pages into revision when the phone began to ring. She tapped her pen against her teeth and leant back in her chair. The phone continued to ring. Josie had no intention of answering it. Instead she let the answering machine take the call. There was a pause followed by a beep, and then Annie's squawks filled the kitchen.

'Sam? Sam, are you there? This is an emergency. Can you pick up?' There was a pause. 'SAM! Can you hear me? Call me. On Ruby's mobile. As soon as possible.'

The phone went dead. Josie continued tapping her teeth with the pencil. Not even a please or a thank you. Just an angry demand. Josie put the pencil down. Bugger Annie. She could go f–

The phone began to ring again. Once again the answering machine clicked in. 'SAM,' Annie yelled. 'I bloody well know you're there. And why is your mobile switched off you bastard? Fucking pick up. Do you hear me? If you don't pick up this phone, I'll make sure you never see Ruby again. Do you understand? You will NEVER see Ruby–'

Josie leant across and picked up the phone. 'Hello, Annie,' she said coolly.

'Put me on to Sam,' Annie demanded.

'Pardon?'

'I said put me on to Sam?'

'Pardon?'

'Are you fucking deaf?' Annie snarled. 'I said PUT ME ON TO SAM.'

'I'm terribly sorry, Annie. This is the most appalling line.' And with that Josie put the phone down. She was surprised to see her hand shaking slightly. Her heart rate was certainly up. It was banging away under her ribcage. She couldn't believe she was doing this. She felt like she was going head to head with a heavyweight boxer. Deflecting punches. Dodging blows. The phone rang again. Josie steadied herself and picked it up on the third ring.

'Hello?'

'PUT ME ON TO SAM YOU FUCKING BITCH.'

Josie forced herself to talk calmly. 'Listen to me, Annie, and listen carefully because I'm in no mood to repeat myself. Sam isn't here. And his mobile phone is switched off and languishing in my handbag. So you've got me. And if you keep shouting and swearing, you're going to get absolutely nowhere. Do I make myself perfectly clear?'

'You're only making things more difficult for Sam, you do realise that don't you? I'll make his life hell for this.'

'Don't threaten me, Annie.'

'I'm not threatening you. I'm stating a fact.'

'In which case, you won't mind me stating facts too. Like the fact that I happen to know you need a passport. Like the fact that I have the passport you need in my pocket. Like the fact that I'm not going to give it to you, and you can go to hell. Good-bye, Annie.'

Carefully, Josie replaced the handset. Almost instantly the phone began to ring. Josie took a deep breath. This was making her feel quite ill. Adrenalin was whooshing round her body. Her armpits had broken out into a gushing mess. The answering machine clicked in.

'PICK UP THE PHONE, JOSIE,' Annie shouted. 'I know you can hear me. Will you just pick up the phone? Please?'

Josie picked up the handset. 'Ah. At last. The magic word. *Please*.'

'Oh bugger off.'

Josie instantly hung up. The phone began to ring.

'Hello?'

Annie's voice was suddenly sugar sweet. 'Hello, Josie. It's Annie here. I have a problem. Ruby's old passport is invalid. I need the passport Sam has.'

'I see. So you now have Ruby's old passport?'

'Yes.'

'Have you any idea the terrible time you put him through at The Passport Office by refusing to hand over Ruby's passport?'

'At the time it was lost.'

'It wasn't lost, Annie. You know it. I know it. So now I want you to apologise for lying and to say sorry for taking my fiancé to hell and back in his efforts to get another passport – the passport you now want.'

There was a pause at the other end of the phone. 'Josie, my plane goes in eighty-five minutes.'

'Then you'd better get a move on with your apology.'

'I am sorry. I am very, very sorry.'

'Apology accepted. Which brings me to Cafcass.'

'Don't push your luck, Josie.'

Josie instantly put the phone down. Two seconds later it was ringing again.

'We can do this all afternoon, Annie,' Josie said amiably. 'I'm not the one with a plane to catch.'

'What do you want from me?' Annie howled.

'Okay. Now you're on my wavelength. In exchange for me giving you Ruby's passport, you will tell Cafcass you were mistaken at requesting their involvement. You will make it clear you had a misunderstanding with Sam, but that everything has now been sorted.'

There was a silence. In the background Josie heard a flight being called and for passengers to make their way to Gate 6. The seconds ticked by. Finally there was the sound of Annie exhaling. 'Okay.'

'You promise?'

'I promise.'

'You may come and collect the passport.'

'I don't have time to get the passport!' Annie's voice rose an octave. Panic had well and truly set in now. 'I need you to drive to Gatwick Airport and deliver the passport to me!'

Josie raised her eyebrows. 'You want me to run around after you as well?'

Annie took a deep breath. Right now she was completely at Josie's mercy. 'Yes. Yes, if you don't mind. I will pay you petrol money. I won't see you out of pocket.'

'This isn't about expense, Annie. It's about emotional bankruptcy. I will bring the passport to Gatwick Airport for you. But only if you stop giving Sam a horrendous time. Is that a deal?'

Annie looked at her wristwatch. Shit. Seventy minutes until her flight. 'Yes. Yes, it's a deal. Just get here.'

'Pardon?'

'*Please.*'

'Which Terminal are you at?'

'North.'

'I'm on my way.'

Josie hung up. She scribbled a hasty note to Sam and taped it to the front door. Sam didn't have his house keys on him. So Josie rushed around to her neighbours and deposited a spare house key with them. Minutes later, she was rattling along the M25 towards Gatwick Airport.

'Is everything all right now, Mummy?' Ruby asked timidly.

'I don't know,' Annie raked her hair. 'Josie is driving down with your other passport.'

'That's good. Josie's very kind isn't she?'

'No, Ruby. Josie is not kind. She just put me through hell on the phone and wasted fifteen precious minutes arguing with me. There's no guarantee we're going to catch this flight. No guarantee at all.' Annie checked her wristwatch. The big hand seemed to be whizzing around the clock face. And to think when she'd arrived at the airport all she'd craved was a coffee. Now the only thing she yearned for was that passport. Even if Josie drove quickly, Annie still had to check the suitcases in. Then there was Security to contend with. All that messing about taking your shoes off. Having your handbag dissected. Going backwards and forwards through the scanner. Someone patting you all over because your bra straps were metal and the machine didn't like it. God's sake. Annie paced to and fro. She had Ruby's mobile phone in her hand, waiting for Josie to call and say she was here. Annie was just checking her wristwatch again when the mobile burst into life.

'I'm outside. Illegally parked. You'll have to come to me.'

Suddenly Annie was tearing towards the exit, the suitcases bouncing along in her wake. Ruby panted after her. They jostled and pushed and side-stepped people until they were outside. Annie stood panting, gulping cool air into her lungs. She looked about wildly. There was Josie! Seconds later the passport was in her hands. Annie's fingers curled tightly around the document. Only when it was safely within her grasp, did she look Josie in the eye. Annie's face contorted with rage.

'Thanks for nothing, you bitch.'

'Remember we have a deal, Annie.'

'The deal's off.'

Annie spun on her heel. Dragging Ruby and the suitcases after her, she allowed the crowd to swallow her up.

Josie stared after Annie. She'd driven like a lunatic for that woman. And she'd taken a gamble. A gamble for a peaceful future. Except it looked like the gamble wasn't going to pay off.

Chapter Twenty-Five

Annie flung herself into the plane's seat. Ruby slid in beside her. The air stewardess immediately locked the aircraft's door. She was now speaking into the plane's internal phone. Instantly the sound system crackled into life and the Captain began speaking to all the passengers, apologising for the delay and assuring they were ready for takeoff. The plane began slowly reversing. Drop down screens started to play a film of the regulation in-flight safety procedure.

Annie was still terribly out of breath. She sat slumped in her seat while other passengers openly stared at the pink faced woman with the heaving chest. She was sweating like a pig. Even her scalp was wet. Across her forehead, Annie could feel her fringe steadily curling. Clearly Ruby was a lot fitter than her. The little girl was breathing hard, but unlike Annie didn't sound like a hyperventilating lunatic.

Across the aisle, Nigel looked at her with raised eyebrows.

'That was a close shave. How did you pull it off?'

Annie was too out of puff to even speak. She put up a hand and flapped it at Nigel. The arsey gesture was clearly designed to convey *whatever*. Annie allowed her gaze to slide past Ruby to the window. She didn't owe Nigel any explanations. Not after him clearing off without her. Fancy doing such a thing! They were meant to be partners for heaven's sake. Partners were meant to stick together. Through thick and thin. Sam would never have done that. Annie scowled. Don't think about Sam. He's history. But to think she'd left Sam for Nigel! Huh! Fine choice of partner he'd turned out to be. The pair of them were like a light switch. On and off, on and off. Annie was so mad with Nigel she'd already decided to dump him upon their return to England. She'd get her money's worth out of him first though. He'd paid for the holiday, so no point shooting herself in the foot.

Annie's breathing was calming down now. Thank God. She shifted in her seat and leant back. Catching the plane had been a nightmare. She closed her eyes and re-lived hurtling away from Josie, Ruby pounding along behind her. Back inside the airport, the queue to check in had been a mile long. Annie was in such a state she thought she'd been about to faint. By a stroke of good fortune, an airport official had spotted Annie's distress and asked if he could assist in some way. Annie had promptly burst into tears. And then a miracle had occurred. The official had declared it was too late to check in luggage and to carry it on to the plane. From there it could be put down in the cargo hold. Then Annie had found herself fast-tracked to the front of Security and finally on to their departure gate. She and Ruby had run like the clappers, almost tripping over their suitcases in their haste.

And now, as the plane rumbled down the runway and threw itself into the sky, Annie felt a warm hand come down on hers. Her eyes pinged open. Nigel was looking at her.

'Friends again?' he smiled.

Annie glared at him. 'I don't see why.'

'Oh put the scowl away Annie. One day you'll laugh about this.'

'I don't think so,' Annie said coldly.

Nigel squeezed her hand. 'Don't be silly. We're going on holiday. Can we just put this behind us and enjoy our time together? Have some fun? And romance?'

Annie stared at him. *Fun. Romance.* The words sounded foreign. When was the last time she'd even felt in the mood for fun or romance? And then Annie's shoulders drooped. She allowed herself to surrender to the warmth from Nigel's hand and the hopeful look in his eyes.

'I suppose.'

'You only suppose?' Nigel teased. 'Come on Annie. Give me a smile.'

Annie bared her teeth.

'What about – when the air hostesses are ready – we have a nice glass of wine eh?'

Annie shrugged. 'Okay.' Maybe she wouldn't dump Nigel after all. A small voice in her head pointed out that none of this had been his fault. 'And you can make mine two glasses of wine.' She might as well get in the holiday mood.

Two and a half weeks later Sam and Josie were seated at their kitchen table. A social worker by the name of Janet Marsden sat opposite them. Josie had greeted the woman warmly and made everybody a cup of tea. Sam was on edge and had hardly said two words. He kept alternating between fiddling with the handle on his mug, and rubbing his palms against his trousers.

'Try not to look so alarmed, Mr Worthington.'

'Please, call me Sam.'

'Okay, Sam.' The social worker smiled. 'My visit today is to chat to you both about Ruby. Now then,' Janet consulted some paperwork in front of her, 'Annie has been in touch with us because she claims Ruby is unhappy about the existing Court Order and wishes to change her access. It's–'

'Janet, I'm sorry to interrupt,' said Sam.

'Not at all, that's absolutely fine. What's the matter?'

'Before you continue, I want you to be aware of the very fraught relationship I have with my daughter's mother. So much so that I've had to resort to Court time and again just to *see* my child. You know, there are fathers out there,' Sam gestured at the kitchen wall with one hand, 'who just walk away from their kids. Never see them. They leave the mother struggling for funds and the kids wondering what the hell it's all about. Well I'm not like that. I just want you to know that. I *want* to see my child. I *want* my child staying at our family home. I *want* my child enjoying family holidays. I'm a hands-on father. When Ruby was a baby I did my turn changing nappies and getting up at night. When it comes to school, I always attend Parents' Evening. I make sure I'm in the audience for sports day and the nativity play. If Ruby is sick I drop everything and go with her mother to the doctor or the hospital. I regularly pay maintenance and have never missed a payment. Financially I go the extra mile and take care of Ruby's mobile phone contract, school activities like swimming lessons, her uniform, and even have a separate savings account for when she's older. There is absolutely nothing I won't do for my daughter. And yet her mother wants me out of Ruby's life. This isn't about what my daughter wants, Janet. It's about what Annie wants. Make no mistake about it.'

Janet steepled her fingers and looked thoughtful for a moment. 'I hear what you're saying, Sam. However, Annie has started something which we are duty bound to follow through. You do understand that don't you? As far as Cafcass goes, this isn't personal.'

Sam sighed and nodded. 'Yes.'

'But if it helps, my job isn't to sanction what Annie wants. It's to listen to Ruby. To see what *she* wants.'

'The thing is, Janet,' Sam quavered, 'I'm absolutely terrified,' he paused, willing himself to sound matter of fact, 'that Annie will have influenced Ruby. Indoctrinated her. Ruby won't want to see her mother upset. She'll want to keep her happy. And if that means agreeing to her mum's wishes–'

'Let me stop you there, Sam,' Janet touched Sam's forearm. 'Cafcass are trained to listen to the child and get to the bottom of what is best for that child. Rest assured this is what I'm doing.'

Sam closed his eyes and took a deep breath. He was just going to have to sit tight and hope everything came good. 'Okay. Thank you.'

'Now, I have spoken to both Annie and Ruby,' said Janet. She noticed Sam pinch the bridge of his nose, Josie discreetly nudge him, then Sam quickly lower both hands onto the surface of the table. He was now rotating his mug of tea, to the point that Janet was worried it would tip over. She surreptitiously moved her paperwork a couple of inches to the right. 'Ruby spoke to me – both in front of her mother and on her own. Talking to her in front of her mother was challenging. Annie constantly tried to lead Ruby. There were long silences before questions were answered. Ruby's responses were monosyllabic. When the time came for me to speak to Ruby one to one, Annie was both agitated and reluctant about it. I reminded Annie that Cafcass is about the needs of the child and championing the interests of that child. She didn't take kindly to that.' Janet smiled at Sam. 'So don't worry, I've got her covered.' Sam gave a half-smile back. 'Talking to Ruby on her own was...enlightening.' Janet observed Sam stiffening. 'And yes, Ruby does want to,' she hesitated, choosing her words carefully, '*tweak* her access arrangements.'

Sam gasped. 'Oh God. Please don't tell me my daughter doesn't want to see me.'

'Darling,' Josie murmured, 'just listen to Janet.'

'Sam, your daughter is currently very troubled. Now whether this is as a result of the indoctrination you talked about, or whether it's what Ruby sees as needing to,' she posted quotation marks in the air, '*parent* her own mother, what Ruby *did* tell me was that whenever she is here in this house with this family–'

'*Her* family,' Sam automatically corrected.

'Yes,' Janet nodded, 'her family at this house...Ruby spends much of her time worrying about her mother.'

'That's ridiculous,' Sam interrupted. 'Ruby is as happy as anything when she comes here.'

'Actually,' Josie put her hand on Sam's, 'I would like to say that there are also times when I catch Ruby staring blankly into space. She withdraws. One minute she and Lucy will be out on their bicycles, shrieking their heads off with laughter, and suddenly – without any warning – Ruby will abandon her bike and...well...just drop out. Retreat into a shell.'

'What's wrong with that?' Sam snapped. He was aware of being on the defensive.

'Well, I find it rather odd,' Josie said quietly. 'Ruby is either deliriously happy or silent and expressionless.'

'Kids are like that!'

'Lucy isn't.'

'What are you trying to say? That Ruby isn't normal?'

'No, Sam, I'm just pointing out–'

'If I could speak for a moment,' Janet interrupted. 'Your observation, Josie, is a good one. And Sam, Ruby swinging between two types of behaviour isn't anything to worry about, okay? But this backs up what Ruby confided in me. Which is...she comes here, has fun, and then feels massively guilty.'

'For having fun?' Sam looked incredulous.

'Yes. You see in Ruby's mind she envisages her mother at home, all by herself. She believes her mother is incredibly lonely. That the only thing that brightens Annie's day is having Ruby there. Ruby is too young to take on board that when she's with you Annie is probably doing housework, shopping, or seeing the chap she's dating. Ruby doesn't *see* any of that. And if she's not *seeing* it then she's none the wiser to what her mother really does in her absence. When she's with her mother, it's just Ruby and Mum. Occasionally Nan makes an appearance, but I gather even Nan is on her own. Ruby has the weight of the world on her shoulders worrying about her mother when she's away. She told me that when she immerses herself into the things you do in this household – days out at the park, picnics, swimming, the cinema – she gets caught up in the fun of it all. But sometimes – for example a lady sitting alone on a park bench – will bring her up short. Remind her of her own mother. Supposedly on her own at home. Miserable and lonely. And then Ruby instantly goes into guilt mode. Guilt that she's having fun, and her mother isn't.'

'Why didn't you tell Ruby her thoughts were ridiculous? Or get Annie to confirm she's not lonely?'

Janet put up a hand to halt Sam's questions. 'Firstly, it's not for me to confirm or deny what Annie is or isn't doing. What *I'm* doing is listening to Ruby. Hearing what she wants.'

'She's a child!' Sam protested. 'She shouldn't be making these decisions.'

'Hear me out, Sam. Ruby clearly loves her mother very much. But equally she loves *you* very much too. And she may be a child and not particularly able to articulate all the thoughts going on in her head, but she was perfectly able to make me understand she feels extremely pressured into keeping *both* parents happy. That she is trying to juggle both parents' emotions and cleverly come up with a compromise.'

Sam shook his head. 'It's not right that a child of her tender years is in this situation. She shouldn't be trying to pacify both parents.'

Janet took a deep breath. 'Well, quite. But that's where we're at. That's the situation. Taking Ruby's thoughts into account, she's looking to reduce her fortnight's summer holiday to one week–'

'No!'

'And her alternate weekend access–'

'Not that as well?' Sam gasped.

'Weekend access currently spans Saturday morning to Sunday evening. Ruby would like it to be Saturday morning to Sunday morning.'

'I don't believe I'm hearing this,' Sam had gone very pale.

'Like I said, Sam, this is Ruby's suggestion. Her compromise. But – bless her – it's based on a need to protect her mother...look after her mother...*parent* her mother. And it isn't for a child to do those things. Therefore, Ruby's proposals are not in her best interests.'

There was a stunned silence as Sam and Josie digested Janet's words. 'You mean–'

'I will not be recommending Ruby's proposals to the Family Court. My advice is that the current Court Order remains as it is.'

Josie smiled and squeezed Sam's knee. Sam was looking quite overcome with emotion. 'I don't know what to say,' he eventually said. 'It's just...it's such a relief...your decision...it's–' Sam shook his head in bemusement. 'Thank you. Just thank you.'

Janet smiled. 'There's a little bit more to do before we advise the Family Court.'

'Oh?' Sam was rubbing his eyes, clearly struggling to hold it together.

'I've seen Ruby in the home environment with Annie. I'd like to see Ruby here too in due course. No need to let her know I'm coming. I'll pop in on the pretext of having a cup of tea with you both and just observe what goes on in the background with Ruby. Whether she interacts with your daughter and, if so, how. Whether she's relaxed. Treating this place like home. That sort of thing. Would that be okay?'

'Of course,' said Josie.

'No problem,' said Sam. He still sounded dazed.

'Good,' said Janet. 'Ruby's with you this weekend. I'll pop round Saturday morning.'

Annie was pegging some washing out. As she worked, she hummed. Things were going well at the moment. The holiday with Nigel, after the initial passport upset, had been reasonably successful. Although Ruby hadn't played very well with Nigel's boys. Annie had noticed Ruby shooting Aiden and Ben some very dark looks. Nor had Ruby been overly friendly with Nigel. One evening the children had gone to The Crocodile Club leaving Nigel and Annie to enjoy a candlelit dinner. When the children had returned they'd been clutching wet paintings. Ruby had made a big show of giving Annie her painting in front of Nigel and the boys. Annie had looked at it in bemusement. A pin man and a pin woman stood either side of their pin child. Everybody was holding hands and smiling. Underneath, in her childish writing, Ruby had written, Mummy, Daddy and me. Annie reached for another couple of pegs and secured some jeans on the washing line. She wondered what on earth Ruby had been thinking of. Still, at least the Cafcass business was now off the ground. Annie had met Janet Marsden who had listened intently to Annie's complaints about Sam and his trollop, the damaging experience Ruby had suffered over the passport fiasco thanks to Josie's outrageous treatment, and that in Annie's opinion Josie wasn't even fit to be a parent, never mind train to be a teacher. Janet Marsden had noted it all down. Good!

Sam and Annie were once again at Court. Except this time Cafcass were there too. Janet was attempting to be the amicable bridge between the two ex-spouses. Annie was having none of it. She was ignoring Janet and focussing all her attention on Sam.

'At last you're going to get your comeuppance,' Annie crowed.

'You're not stopping me from seeing my daughter, Annie.'

'I've told Janet what sort of a father you are. And I don't want your trollop anywhere near my daughter. Ruby is still having nightmares about running through airport lounges and hanging onto airborne planes by her fingernails. The pair of you need to be kept away from Ruby. And today I'm going to make sure that happens.'

'Annie,' Janet interrupted, 'I need to remind you that today isn't about what you want. 'It's about what your daughter wants. And also what I consider to be in your daughter's best interests.'

'Well any social worker worth their salt will understand that Sam and his trollop aren't fit to be parents. Did I tell you about the time when Josie insisted Ruby eat carrots? I think I missed that out. Ruby detests carrots. What Josie did was wicked. Tantamount to child cruelty and–'

'Don't be ridiculous, Annie,' Sam cut in.

'But it's true. Ruby was force fed carrots.'

'Oh, so you're saying that Josie strapped Ruby's arms to her sides, stuck a funnel in her mouth and tipped a bowl of carrots down her neck? Do you have any idea how ridiculous you sound?'

'Don't you mock me, Sam Worthington,' Annie's eyes narrowed. 'Janet's on my side. She's going to back me up. And you'll be ordered to stay away from Ruby.'

'Annie,' Janet Marsden interrupted, 'I'm very sorry, but you don't seem to have taken on board one word I've said. When you contacted Cafcass and asked for our involvement, it was only ever about Ruby's wishes. Not yours. There is absolutely no reason why Sam should not see his daughter or have her stay with him. And as for Josie, I found her most amicable. It is clear she has great affection for your daughter. Likewise Ruby demonstrated fondness for Josie.'

'That's absolutely not true,' Annie snapped. 'Ruby detests Josie.'

'I visited Sam and Josie at home with Ruby–'

'Ruby's home is with me and only me.'

'Annie, I appreciate this is difficult for you. Clearly you are hearing words you don't want to heed. But I can assure you Sam and Josie consider their home to be Ruby's too. Ruby has her own bedroom there. The room is decorated in colours and soft furnishings that she selected herself. Whilst visiting, I observed Ruby interacting with all three members of the family unit. It was perfectly apparent she was at ease in her surroundings, so much so I found it hard to believe she wasn't Sam and Josie's biological daughter and that Lucy wasn't her biological sister.'

'What is this? Annie hissed. 'Some sort of conspiracy? How dare you. How fucking dare you!'

Janet Marsden wasn't remotely fazed by Annie's outburst. 'Anybody can see what's going on here, Annie. You have an axe to grind. But this isn't the place to do it. And Cafcass isn't an organisation to do it with.'

'I'm going to complain bitterly about you,' Annie waggled a finger at Janet. 'You're a total incompetent. No wonder you bloody social workers end up splashed all over the newspapers when things go wrong for children. You can't see what's right under your nose!'

'Ruby isn't at risk Annie. And you know that.'

'When we go into Court I will tell the judge the truth. The truth, do you hear! And the truth is that Ruby doesn't want to spend time at Sam and Josie's house, or go on holiday with them, or have anything to do with them. In fact, why don't we get Ruby out of school right now and she can tell the judge herself.'

'Unfortunately Annie, that isn't going to happen. The only reason Ruby is saying those things is because she's trying to appease you. She knows it's what you want to hear.'

'I've had enough of this conversation,' Annie glared at Janet. 'When we go into the Court room, I will personally make sure the judge is aware of all the facts. Do you understand? The facts. Not this crock of shit you're flogging. Enjoy the few hours left of your job, Janet. Tomorrow you'll be unemployed.'

Ninety minutes later and it was all over. Sam's access arrangements remained unchanged. The only addendum was that Ruby's wishes should be reviewed annually. Sam wasn't altogether overjoyed at this. It meant going through more of the same next year. Where Ruby and Annie were concerned, it was like constantly walking an emotional tightrope. But for now he had twelve months' grace. Twelve months to enjoy seeing his daughter without any problems. Which showed how little he knew.

Chapter Twenty-Six
Eighteen months later

Josie hastened down one of the many corridors of Greenwich University. She was late to her next lecture. These days life seemed to be so fast-paced. Josie felt as though she were perpetually caught up in some sort of race. She was always checking her wristwatch or clocks on walls. Whatever she did – be it driving, working on her laptop, or even shopping – there was always a digital display or timepiece urging her to go faster.

She brushed past a gaggle of students chatting at the bottom of a stairwell. Grabbing the handrail, she took the steps two at a time. Late, late, late. Like her period. She'd lost track of the days and wasn't entirely sure how overdue it was. The last few weeks had been manic. Huge assignments. Umpteen exams. None of which blended well with family life, not to mention running a home and supporting Sam as he deflected the usual crap from Annie.

Sometimes Josie wondered what on earth she'd got herself into by hooking up with Sam. She loved the man to bits. He was sweet, kind, romantic, caring and loving. He'd wrap her in his arms and make her feel so safe. Protected. Life was almost perfect. Almost, but not quite. The thorn in their relationship was Annie. If Annie metaphorically said *jump*, Sam responded with *how high*? And it rankled Josie.

Josie reached the top of the staircase and briefly paused for breath. She needed to get fitter. Lose a bit of weight. A few pounds had crept on. Not a lot. But enough to make her clothes feel tight. She moved away from the stairs and immediately broke into a trot. She could see Kerry ahead. Thank God, she wouldn't be the only late student.

'Kerry!' she called. 'Wait for me!'

Her friend swung round. 'Good heavens. You're a sight for sore eyes.'

Josie caught up. 'Thanks,' she puffed. 'We can't all look like models. What's your secret?'

Kerry grinned. 'Love.'

'But I *am* in love!' Josie protested.

'Ah, but you're missing out on the glow factor because you're stressed. You have a hot guy, but also a load of shite to cope with.'

'It's not that bad,' Josie lied.

'It's not that good either,' Kerry pointed out. 'Let's face it, when you shacked up with Sam you might as well have invited his fruitcake of an ex to move in with you both.'

'Don't be silly.'

'I'm not. It's a fact. She's there, in your house. All the time. Whenever Sam's mobile rings, I bet you twitch. Will it be her? Is she going to start on Sam? Is it going to impact on me? And will that, in turn, impact on Lucy?'

Josie sighed. 'Well, put like that–'

'Yes! Put like that! I don't have any of that, thank God.'

Kerry had since divorced her husband Adam and was still enjoying a full blown love affair with Simon Clark, the college tutor. They weren't living together, which was probably why they were so loved up. Nothing dented their relationship. Not work. Not kids. And most definitely not exes.

'What are you suggesting then? That Sam and I stop living together? That we just date instead?'

'Bit late for that, sweetie. You've bought a house together and there's a whopping great ring on your finger.' Kerry nodded at the sizeable solitaire that now graced Josie's left hand. 'You've all but tied the knot.'

'I'm happy,' said Josie firmly.

'Glad to hear it, because you don't look it.'

'Oh for goodness sake,' Josie huffed. 'I'm just feeling a bit frazzled, that's all. Tired. And my period is late.'

Kerry's eyes widened. 'Are you pregnant?'

'Don't be ridiculous,' snorted Josie. 'We use–'

'What's the matter?'

'I've just had a horrible thought.' One of Josie's hands fluttered to her mouth.

'What?'

'Oh my God.'

'Josie?' The two women were now standing outside their classroom. Voices drifted from within. The lecture had begun. 'For the love of God will you tell me what's wrong?'

'A few weeks ago. I've just remembered. We were...you know...and just as...well...the condom came off. But we didn't panic. Sam was fairly sure nothing had,' Josie cringed, 'leaked.'

'Cripes,' Kerry paled. 'How late are you?'

'I don't know. Not exactly. Three weeks? Four? Maybe even five.'

'*What?*' Kerry's voice was like a whip. 'How on earth can you not know?'

'Oh, Kerry, don't tell me off. You just don't know what my life is like. It's hectic. Days roll seamlessly into one another. I fall into bed way after midnight, and when my eyes open five or six hours later I hit the ground running.'

'I'm amazed you have the energy for bonking.'

'I don't. Not really. It's terrible. Half the time I'm faking just in order to hurry things up and get to sleep.'

Kerry's jaw dropped open. 'Josie, that's awful.'

'I know. I do love Sam. And I fancy the pants off him. But I'm finding life just so full on. Being a mature student with a little girl – two little girls every other week – combined with uni and,' Josie shrugged, 'washing, ironing, shopping, cooking, cleaning. You know how it is. Hard graft. Not forgetting constant aggravation from that blasted woman who does anything to disrupt our lives. I keep telling myself that once I'm qualified and working, it will be easier. That there will be more time for romance. And if Annie's boyfriend could whisk her down the nearest aisle and put a ring on her finger, I reckon she'd then be out of our hair. Life would be very sweet.' Josie gazed wistfully into the distance.

'Kiddo, life isn't going to be sweet if you've got a baby on the way. It will be turned upside down. If you think you're stressed now, think again in nine months time. Or eight months time in your case. Or even possibly seven.'

Josie looked appalled. 'Kerry, I can't go into this lecture. I won't be able to concentrate. Not for a second. You go. You're late enough as it is.'

'Why? Where are you off to?'

'To the chemist. To buy a pregnancy test.' Josie turned and began to walk away.

'Hold it right there, madam. I'm coming with you.'

'Don't be daft. Get into class. Go on.'

'No.' Kerry grabbed Josie's arm and fell in step with her.

'You really don't have to do this,' Josie protested as they moved towards the staircase and then clattered downwards.

'I want to,' Kerry said firmly, 'and anyway, that's what friends are for.'

When Sam came home from work the house seemed abnormally quiet. No sounds came from the television room. He stuck his head around the door. The room was empty.

'Lucy?' he called out.

'Up here,' Lucy's voice filtered down the stairs, 'in my bedroom. I'm learning spellings.'

'Okay, pet.' Sam wandered down the hallway. Usually Josie was in the kitchen clattering about. And although nice cooking smells hung in the air, there was a lack of background noise. No plates rattling out of the cupboard. No cutlery tinkling against the table top. No saucepans banging against the hob, or squeaking hinges as Josie peered in the fridge for tomato sauce. 'Josie?' Sam pushed the kitchen door open. His fiancée was sitting slumped over the kitchen table. 'Hey, darling.' He caught her expression. 'Oh my God, has somebody died?'

'No,' Josie spoke softly as she shook her head. 'Nobody's died.'

'What's up then? Bad day?' Sam pulled out a chair and sat down next to her. He put a hand over hers.

'I've had better.'

'Do you want to tell me about it?'

'Not really. But unfortunately I have to. Because it affects you, as well as me.'

Sam's brow knitted in puzzlement. 'Really? Well go on. Tell me.'

'I'm pregnant.'

Sam blinked. There was a pause as he stared at Josie incredulously. 'But...but you can't be.'

'I am.'

'But you can't be.'

'I am.'

'But you can't be.'

'Sam, we can sit here repeating ourselves all evening. It won't change a thing. I'm pregnant. At some point we've either had a condom fail or been careless. But the result is the same. Pregnant.' Josie reached into her handbag and removed a clear plastic bag. Inside was a white stick with two blue lines. 'Congratulations, Sam. You're going to be a dad again.'

Sam instantly recoiled. He dropped Josie's hand like a hot coal. 'I...I can't take this in. Are you absolutely sure? These tests,' his eyes flicked to the white stick, 'can they ever be wrong?'

Josie shrugged. 'I don't know. Possibly. But I don't think it's wrong.'

'No?' Sam asked hopefully.

'My period is late. Very late.' Josie saw the hope die in Sam's eyes. 'I know. It's a shock. You're looking how I feel.' She gave the ghost of a smile. 'But we'll get through it.'

'What do you mean *we'll get through it?*' Sam looked perplexed.

'Having a new baby of course,' Josie gave a sigh of exasperation. Sam was behaving like he was a thicko. 'I initially thought it was horrendous timing. But in fact, it's not so bad. Fortunately I'll have achieved my degree just before the baby comes along. Then I'll take a gap year for the first twelve months. After that the baby can go to crèche, and I'll start teaching. It will be a bit full on,' Josie tilted her head to one side as she considered, 'but we'll manage. And just think how nice it will be for the girls having a baby brother or sister. I've already told Lucy and she's over the moon. But I asked her to stay in her room while I talk to you. Just so you can digest it first. I didn't want any negative reaction in front of her.'

'What the hell did you tell Lucy for?'

Josie looked startled. The initial shock on Sam's face had given way to...what was it? Josie stared at him. Fear? Surely not. 'She's a family member, Sam. Why wouldn't I tell Lucy?'

'Josie,' Sam raked his hair, 'you do realise you can't possibly have this baby.'

For a moment Josie thought she'd misheard him. 'Sorry?'

'You can't have this baby.' Sam abruptly stood up and began pacing around the kitchen. 'It's not going to happen.'

'What the heck are you talking about?' Josie looked at Sam in bewilderment.

'I don't want a baby.'

'Well I'm not so chuffed about it myself,' Josie blew out her cheeks, 'but we're both in shock at the moment. We'll get used to the idea. And by the time the baby comes along we'll be like all new parents. Dotty about our newborn.'

'No,' Sam shook his head. 'You're misunderstanding me. I don't want a baby. You'll have to have an abortion.'

Josie found herself grabbing hold of the table edge with both hands. She felt as though the chair had just been pulled out from under her. 'What did you say?'

'An abortion,' Sam repeated. 'You'll have to terminate. Our family is complete. We have two lovely girls. We don't need another child.'

'You're talking as if this baby is little more than a packet of biscuits or a tin of baked beans. It's not about what we need Sam. It's about the situation we've found ourselves in. Children are a gift from God for crissake. And to advocate abortion–' Josie broke off, her throat suddenly thick with tears. She couldn't believe Sam had even suggested such a thing.

'Look,' Sam sat back down. 'I can't take this in, Josie. I'm sorry. I don't want to upset you. That's the last thing I ever want to do. Understand? I'm sorry. That was insensitive of me.'

'Damn right it was.' A tear rolled down Josie's cheek.

'Look, darling,' Sam reached for her hand again. This time Josie allowed him to take it. 'I'm truly sorry.'

'Okay.' Josie wiped the tear away with her other hand. 'The news took me by surprise.'

'Yeah,' Josie's voice was thick with emotion, 'I understand.' She dredged up a watery smile. 'It rocked me too.'

Sam patted his fiancée's hand while his mind rocketed off in a thousand different directions. A baby. Oh my God.

Sam was suddenly transported back in time. Back to being married to Annie. It seemed a million years ago and yet, paradoxically, it also seemed like yesterday. Annie desperate for a baby. Sam most definitely not. The endless sulking until Sam had given in. And then coping with Annie's mood swings for nine long months as she went through morning sickness, backache, puffy ankles, and accusing him of looking at other women because he didn't find the sight of a woman with a huge belly particularly attractive. And what if he and Josie – God forbid – split up one day in the future? That would be another child he'd love and lose to the alternative weekend scenario. He found it hard enough as it was having a part-time daughter. He couldn't go through all that again.

He looked at Josie's confident face. She seemed to think she was going to breeze through the rest of her time at uni without a hitch. She complained of being tired now. How the heck did she think her energy levels were going to be when she couldn't bend down to do up her trainers in six months time? And apart from anything else, how the hell would all this impact on Ruby? Sam could see Annie now. Whispering more poison into Ruby's ear. *Daddy doesn't love you anymore, he has a new baby to love instead.* He gulped. And what would Ruby think? That she'd been replaced? Apart from anything else – and it shamed Sam to admit it – he truly didn't think he could love another child. He was so emotionally bankrupt from years of proving himself exclusive to Ruby, he had nothing left to give. Sam came to a decision. First things first.

'I think the important thing for now, darling,' he said carefully, 'is to get the pregnancy properly confirmed.'

Josie nodded. 'Okay. I'll make an appointment with the GP first thing in the morning.'

'No. Not the GP. Let's see a gynaecologist. We'll go private. Leave it to me to make the appointment. Miss Birch at Queen Mary's is excellent. Annie saw her when she was trying to get pregnant with Ruby. Miss Birch has one of those scanning things in her consulting room. She'll be able to tell us straight away – let us know whether everything is okay.'

'Fantastic!' Josie sat up straighter. For the first time she was looking excited. 'We might even be able to see some tiny arms and legs!'

'It's probably a bit early for that.' Sam tried to smile back. It came out as a grimace. 'But we should be able to hear a heartbeat.'

'You're right!'

Josie was practically squirming in her seat now, joy flooding her features. Sam couldn't bear it. He hoped to goodness the pregnancy test was wrong. And if it wasn't? Sam wasn't a religious man, but he suddenly found himself praying. And his prayer was that Josie would miscarry.

Chapter Twenty-Seven

It was a week before Miss Birch could see Josie and Sam.

'Come in,' the gynaecologist indicated two chairs by her desk. 'How can I help?'

Josie came straight to the point. 'My period is late. I did a test and it was positive.'

'Congratulations,' Miss Birch smiled.

'Thank you,' Josie beamed.

'The thing is,' Sam interrupted, 'we want to be sure that the pregnancy test wasn't wrong.'

'The tests are very accurate, Mr Worthington.'

'Can we have a scan? Just to make sure?' Sam was still holding out that the tester Josie had used was defunct.

'When was your last period?' Miss Birch turned to Josie.

'Er, I'm not really sure. I think it was about six or seven weeks ago. Sorry to sound so vague.'

'Is life a bit fraught?' Miss Birch smiled.

'Yes,' Josie gave an apologetic shrug. 'Plus we use precautions, so I didn't take too much notice when my period didn't arrive. I just thought it was a hormonal blip.'

'Okay,' Miss Birch made some notes and then looked up. 'I'll do an internal vaginal examination. The uterus is deep in your pelvis in the early weeks, so the ultrasound probe permits more detail. I'll also be able to check if there are any cysts in your ovaries, or fibroids in the uterus, and confirm the pregnancy is not ectopic.'

Josie nodded, suddenly nervous. She was thirty-eight years old. Up until now it hadn't dawned on her that – statistically speaking – there was a higher risk of things going wrong. 'Can you tell if everything is okay with the pregnancy?'

'Why don't you come over to the couch,' Miss Birch put down her pen and stood up. She indicated a curtained area. 'Get undressed from the waist down. To answer your question, the later the scan, the more can be seen.'

Moments later, Josie found herself craning her neck and peering at a grainy image on a screen. A lump formed in her throat. That blob was Lucy's brother or sister. And Ruby's of course. She wished the girls could see this and be as excited as she was.

'Well, Mrs Worthington,' Miss Birch raised an eyebrow. Josie didn't like to say her name was Mrs Payne. She had a sudden horrible thought that Miss Birch might otherwise think Sam was having an affair with a married woman. The sooner they sorted out a wedding date the better. 'Your last period was a little further away than you thought. Baby's crown to rump length is twenty millimetres. Here's the head...the body...limbs. It's very nearly fully formed. This is a foetus, not an embryo. You're nine weeks pregnant.'

Josie's smile turned into a banana grin. She glanced at Sam in delight.

'Is...is there a heartbeat?' he asked.

'Absolutely, Mr Worthington. You have no worries there.'

Sam nodded. He was looking very pale. 'Um, Miss Birch. This wasn't a planned pregnancy. There are some questions I'd like to ask.'

'Of course. Ask away.' Miss Birch removed the ultrasound probe and indicated that Josie should get dressed.

'How much would it cost if we were to go down the route of termination?'

Josie's grin disappeared in a trice. 'Sam, I'm not–'

'I'm only enquiring. Just so we have all the options covered.'

Miss Birch blinked. Suddenly there was tension in the air. 'My fee is eight hundred and fifty pounds. On top of that there would be some smaller additional charges like use of theatre and–'

'Thank you, Miss Birch, but that's not necessary.' Josie swung her legs off the couch. She reached over to a nearby chair and grabbed her knickers and tights. Her movements were short and jerky. She was seething with anger. 'Unless something is drastically wrong with the pregnancy, there will be no abortion.'

One week later and Josie was barely on speaking terms with Sam. She dumped some plates in the dishwasher. The china crashed together alarmingly. Sam's relentless pressure for her to have an abortion since seeing the gynaecologist was getting to her. He'd cited every reason under the sun for the pregnancy to be terminated. The cost of a new baby impacting on their income. Disruption to the house. Interference with Josie's teaching plans. Josie's age and the chances of having a disabled baby. Josie had kept dissolving into tears. She didn't know if it was pregnancy hormones making her ultra sensitive, or whether it was because she was so stunned at Sam's reaction. His last reason to terminate had been to do with the girls being jealous and rejecting their sibling. Josie shoved mugs onto the dishwasher's top shelf. Ah yes. The girls. Well she could rule Lucy out of the equation. Lucy was already asking a zillion questions about whether the baby was a boy or a girl and what they should call it. But Ruby? Ruby was an altogether different matter. Ruby didn't even know a little Worthington was on its way. But she would this weekend. Josie would make sure of that. She angrily stacked knives and forks into the plastic basket. Sam was currently out, collecting Ruby from Annie's. He'd asked Josie not to mention the pregnancy and to have a word with Lucy about not doing so either.

'But why ever not?' Josie had asked, cheeks pink, temper flaring.

'Because all sorts of things could go wrong. It's early days. I'd rather not worry Ruby.'

'Oh but it's okay for Lucy to worry?' she'd snapped.

'I didn't say that. I wish you hadn't told Lucy. But I'd just rather not say anything about it while Ruby is here.'

'What, as in, if it's not discussed, it will go away? Brush the subject under the carpet? Is that what you mean, Sam?'

'I just want you to try and understand where I'm coming from.'

'Well I don't know where you're coming from, but at this rate I know where I'll be telling you to go.'

They'd stood there, glaring at each other, Josie with her hands on her hips, open hostility on their faces. Josie couldn't believe the way things were between them. There had been strain in their relationship before. But that had always been caused by Annie, and very different to this. This tension was heated. Angry. Josie couldn't get her head around it. Her lovely, calm, reasonable Sam. Where had he gone? It was as though an imposter had come along and hijacked his body. This Sam kept coming out with things she neither understood nor wanted to hear. Sam adored being a father. He loved it. He revelled in it. So much so he'd gone to Court time and again to fight to see his daughter, because he wanted to be a dad. So why didn't he want to be a dad again? Excuses like expense didn't ring true. He was a dentist for crying out loud. He earned not just well, but very well. And in time Josie would be working too. So what was the problem?

Josie slammed the dishwasher door shut. She wanted her Sam back. The real Sam. And for everything to be all right.

It was Saturday lunchtime, and everybody was tucking into Josie's homemade Shepherd's Pie. Sam was the first to clear his plate. He put his knife and fork together and looked from Lucy to Ruby.

'There's a new Walt Disney out at the cinema. Do you fancy it, girls?'

'Is that the one with the baby giraffe in it?' asked Ruby.

'I think so,' said Lucy.

'Ooh goody,' Ruby wrinkled her nose. 'I love baby things.'

'My Mummy's expecting a baby,' Lucy said shyly.

'We don't know that for sure,' Sam said hastily.

Josie could feel her hackles going up. 'Actually, we do know it for sure, Sam,' she said quietly before turning to Ruby. 'I've had a scan, Ruby. The doctor had a special machine which let me see the baby. I was going to tell you about it after dinner anyway.' Josie gave a bright smile. 'So it's absolutely true. There's a tiny baby growing in my tummy. Isn't that exciting?'

For a brief moment Josie saw an expression cross Ruby's face which conveyed she thought it anything but. And then the shutters came down rendering the child's face an emotionless mask.

'I thought I told you not to say anything,' Sam murmured to Lucy.

'Sorry,' Lucy shrugged. 'I forgot.'

'There's no reason why Ruby shouldn't know,' Josie smiled through gritted teeth.

'I just don't want Ruby worrying about it.'

'Why would Ruby worry?' Lucy asked.

'Because it's very early days,' said Sam, 'and sometimes things go wrong. It's a bit silly getting excited about it so early in the pregnancy. There's no proper baby in Josie's tummy yet. It's just a collection of cells.'

Lucy was starting to look as if she might burst into tears. 'What do you mean about things sometimes going wrong?'

'Anything,' Sam said.

'You couldn't die could you, Mummy?'

'No of course not,' Josie gave a tinkling laugh. If the girls weren't sitting at the table she would have picked up the Shepherd's Pie dish and lobbed it at Sam. Pregnancy hormones were in full swing as far as her fluctuating moods were concerned. 'And as for it being a collection of cells – well it's a little bit more than that. There's a head, and tiny arms and legs and diddy fingers, but they're webbed at the moment like duck feet, and–'

Ruby jumped down from the table.

'Where are you going, princess?' asked Sam.

'To my room,' Ruby mumbled, 'I don't feel very well.'

'I'll come with you,' said Sam. 'Now look what you've done,' he murmured as he brushed past Josie.

Josie stared at her congealing plate of Shepherd's Pie.

'Mummy, I'm worried now. What could go wrong?'

Josie sighed. 'Nothing major, darling. Honest. There are very clever doctors and nurses out there with lots of highly advanced machinery to detect any possible problems.'

'Like what?'

'Oh, you know, like the baby not developing properly. But these things are rare. Promise.'

'Is our baby all right?'

'I think so,' Josie nodded. 'In three weeks I'll have another scan. The baby will have grown quite a bit by then so the doctor will be able to see more detail.'

'What sort of detail?'

The sound of crying filtered down the stairs. Josie tensed. 'Well, like the heart for example. The special doctor just makes sure it's developing properly.'

'And what if it isn't?' Lucy's eyes were like saucers.

'Then...then the doctor will advise an operation.'

'To fix the baby's heart?'

'Er, no, to take the baby away.'

'Away where?'

Oh God. This conversation had got completely out of hand. 'Um, away to a special place in the hospital where another doctor tries to fix the heart.'

'And then they put the baby back in the mummy to carry on growing?'

'Yes,' Josie nodded, 'Yes. That's right.' She was not, absolutely not going to talk about pregnancy termination with her eight-year-old daughter. Footsteps were coming down the stairs. Two seconds later and Sam appeared. He was holding Ruby's hand.

'Ruby's not feeling well. She wants her Mum.'

'Oh dear,' said Josie standing up. 'Are you going home?'

Sam flinched. 'This is Ruby's home, Josie.'

Josie closed her eyes for a second. Home was a taboo word in this house. As far as Sam was concerned, Ruby had two homes. Two bedrooms. Two wardrobes with two sets of clothes. Two shelves full of toys.

'You're going back to Mummy's?' Josie tried again.

'Yes,' Sam answered on his silent daughter's behalf. 'I'll be back in half an hour.'

'Right.' Josie stood up to kiss Ruby good-bye, but Sam had already ushered Ruby out into the hallway towards the front door. 'I hope you're feeling better soon,' Josie called out. But she was talking to thin air.

Josie rolled over in bed. Grey light was filtering through the curtains. She wondered what the time was. She peered blearily at the clock radio next to her side of the bed. A little after six. She closed her eyes again and tried to find a dark, womb-like place to go with her thoughts. She didn't want to wake up. Or face the day. Or cope with Sam. Sam who had blamed her for his weekend access being shot to pieces. Josie snuggled deeper under the duvet and let her mind drift. She was floating in a beautiful lake. The waters were deep and black. Vividly coloured plants and grasses fringed the lagoon, reflecting brightly on the water's surface. Beyond the flowers and greenery was a quaint church nestling in a hilly fold. The church bell was ringing. But the sound was at odds with the tranquil scene. This bell was shrill and sharp. It demanded attention. Josie swam to the surface of wakefulness just in time to hear Sam answering the phone on his side of the bed.

'Hello? Oh, hello. No I wasn't awake. Never mind. It's fine. Is Ruby feeling better?'

Josie lay very still and pretended to be asleep. Clearly it was Annie on the phone.

'She's not? What's wrong with her? Oh. I see. Yes, it's true. Josie is pregnant.'

Josie stiffened.

'I'm sorry to hear you've been up all night with Ruby.'

Josie could feel herself starting to seethe with resentment. It was a Sunday morning. She was knackered and had hoped for a much needed lie-in. Instead she had Sam's ex on the phone at the crack of dawn giving him earache.

'I'm sorry Ruby's upset about the pregnancy. Well that's not really any of your business, Annie, but no, it wasn't planned.'

Josie felt irked. What had her pregnancy – planned or unplanned – got to do with Annie?

'I appreciate it's hard for Ruby. No, of course the baby wouldn't have her room. Yes obviously Ruby is my number one priority. What do you mean? Define hysterical. She won't come over anymore? She truly said that?'

Oh for God's sake.

'No it's not what I want. It's possible.'

What was possible?

'We're talking about it.'

The mattress dipped. Josie sensed Sam carefully leaning across, checking if she was asleep. She made herself do long shallow breaths. In...out...pause...in...out. The mattress flattened out again.

'We've seen a gynaecologist. Miss Birch. Yes, she can do it.'

Do what?

'I don't know when. Soon. It will happen soon.'

And then Josie clicked. They were talking about her having an abortion. And Sam was placating Annie, and telling her it would happen. And then Josie found herself emotionally going to a place she'd never been before. She understood exactly why there was that saying...seeing red. It truly existed. She might be laying here with her eyes shut, but instead of seeing grey mist behind her eyelids, it was all red. Red mist.

'I *am* a good father, Annie. Yes I *do* only want Ruby. *Please* don't tell her otherwise, Annie. I'll make sure it happens. I will. I prom–'

Suddenly Sam found the handset being wrenched from his hand and a pillow battering his head.

'You bastard!' Josie walloped the pillow over his head again before clamping the handset to her ear. 'And as for you, Fanny Annie,' she spat into the phone, 'how dare you ring my house at six in the morning on a Sunday discussing abortion. Yes I do indeed dare to call you Fanny Annie. Oh really? What would you prefer me to call you then? What about Bitch?'

Josie hit the cut off button and lobbed the handset at Sam. It bounced off his shoulder and landed on the floor. Almost instantly the phone began to ring again. Josie dived across the duvet, almost stretching herself flat, and grabbed it.

'Hello? No you can't speak to him. Tough. You'll make things difficult? Ha! When have you ever not made things difficult? Don't you threaten me, you silly cow. No, you listen to me because I'm going to give you some long overdue advice Fanny. And that's to fuck off.'

Josie hit the cut off button before once again flinging the handset at Sam. This time it hit his chest before landing in the crease of the duvet. Almost immediately it began its shrill ringing.

'You do realise that my life isn't going to be worth living after you speaking to Annie like that.'

'Oh man up, Sam. Annie doesn't do polite. I've simply spoken a language she understands. I'm sick of that woman pulling your strings. You're like a puppet. "Jump this way, Sam. Dance that way, Sam. Or I'll make your life hell, Sam." Who does that woman think she is?'

Sam lay propped up in bed, his face stony. The phone rang on. 'Unfortunately that woman is the mother of my child. She has custody of my child. And if I want to see my child, I have no choice but to dance to her tune.'

'Well you go dance, Sam. Dance away.'

'Please, Josie, let's not argue–'

'Don't speak to me, Sam. Just...don't...speak.'

Downstairs in the kitchen the answering machine clicked in. Upstairs in the bedroom Josie was spared from hearing Annie's diatribe. She moved around the bed to the wardrobe. Sliding the door back, she pulled her dressing gown from a hanger. She was shaking from the after effects of so much adrenalin whooshing around her body. That couldn't be good for the baby. Josie's hand automatically fluttered to her stomach. Poor little thing. She hoped all her see-sawing emotions and stress weren't impacting upon it. She shrugged her way into the dressing gown and stalked out of the bedroom.

Down in the kitchen the answering machine light blinked away. Josie ignored it. The phone began to ring again. This time Sam took the call upstairs. She could hear him making placatory noises. Bloody woman. Bloody man. She grabbed the kettle and blasted some water into it.

Josie was just pouring boiling water over a teabag when Sam came into the kitchen. He was fully dressed.

'I'm going over to Annie's.'

'Have fun.'

'Hardly. I'm going to speak to Ruby. She's distressed.'

'Oh, and I'm not.' Josie stirred her tea so vigorously it slopped all over the worktop.

'She's a child, Josie.'

'Yes, I know. And so is my daughter, but I don't see you pandering to Lucy.'

'Lucy isn't distressed.'

'No? I think you said enough at the dinner table yesterday to make her anxious. All that talk of things potentially going wrong. She looked horrified.'

'Josie, there's no reasoning with you at the moment. Lucy isn't the one in floods of tears.'

'And why exactly *is* Ruby in floods of tears? Do you know, Sam?'

'Yes, of course. Hearing that you're pregnant makes her feel threatened. Vulnerable. She thinks I won't love her if I have another child.'

'And whose fault is that, Sam?' Josie rounded on her fiancé.

'Mine, for using a dud condom.'

'That's not what I'm talking about.' Josie's eyes flashed. 'I'm asking you whose fault it is that Ruby is so insecure.' Sam stood there, looking at her, but didn't answer. 'The answer is Annie. It's Annie's fault that Ruby is so insecure. So Annie should stop bellyaching to you. This is her doing, Sam. There are thousands of kids out there whose parents remarry and go on to have more children. It doesn't cause this sort of hoo-ha. My pregnancy should not affect Ruby to the point she's up all night bawling. So you tell Annie from me that if she has a shred of genuine concern about her daughter she'll–'

'I'm going, Josie. My daughter needs me.'

'And I don't?'

Sam didn't bother replying. He swung out the front door leaving Josie shouting after him. He couldn't cope with this situation. It was driving him mad. Having another baby wasn't on the agenda. In any other circumstances, he'd have loved to make a child with the woman he adored. But he knew, he just knew, that if this pregnancy went ahead, Annie would be even more determined to sever his relationship with Ruby. She'd done her damndest to date, and already the damage was showing in his daughter. Josie was right. A child should not be up all night crying her eyes out about it. And yes, of course he knew Annie was the one who'd made Ruby so insecure. Which meant he had to work even harder counteracting his ex-wife's actions and prove to Ruby he was there for her. That he always had been, and that he always would be. Sam resolved that this current situation had to end. There was no choice in the matter. The relationship with his daughter was at stake, and he wasn't going to lose it. Later, he would sit Josie down and calmly put forward his proposal. And ultimatum.

Chapter Twenty-Eight

Josie didn't see Sam for the rest of the day. She kept herself busy with studies, and caught up on chores before being overcome with nausea. The thought of cooking made her involuntarily retch, so she took Lucy out for a McDonalds as a special treat. To hell with junk food on this one occasion. Lucy was in bed and asleep when Josie finally heard Sam's key in the front door.

'Hi.' Sam stood in the doorway to the lounge where Josie was curled into the sofa watching television.

Josie glanced up. 'Hello.' She felt drained and miserable. And tired. Oh so tired.

'Sorry to have been gone all day.'

Josie shrugged. 'How's Ruby?'

'In a state.'

'Still?'

'Yes.'

'I'm sorry to hear that.' In fact Josie was beyond caring.

'Can we talk?'

'We are.'

'No. I mean properly. Without the television on. No distraction.'

Josie pressed the remote control. The television screen went black. 'Fire away.'

Sam came into the lounge. He sat down next to Josie. 'Can I?' He took one of her hands and pulled her towards him. 'Don't resist me, Josie. Come here. No, right here. Get on my lap. I want to hold you.'

Josie looked down at her hand within Sam's. It was warm. Firm. When she looked up again, she saw Sam's eyes were full of love. And tears. She felt her own eyes begin to well. Shifting, she slumped across his lap. His arms went around her, pulling her into his chest. She allowed herself to be cradled for a moment, before wrapping her arms around his neck. And suddenly his mouth was on hers. But they weren't tender romantic kisses. These kisses were fierce. And full of desperation. She matched them one by one, her fingers creeping up and tangling in his hair. Sam's hands were now cupping her face. Josie's heart was hammering. She felt hope soar within her. They were going to get through this. Everything would be all right. Suddenly she was being pushed away. She sat back, slightly breathless, arms still loose around Sam's neck.

'Josie,' Sam whispered, 'my darling Josie. I love you so much. Despite everything that's happened. All the upset. All the cross words we've hurled at each other. I've never stopped loving you.'

'Yes,' Josie murmured. 'I know. Couples do row Sam. It doesn't mean they stop loving each other.'

'I know. But sometimes couples split up. Even though they still love each other.'

'That won't happen to us,' Josie assured. But Sam didn't reply. He just continued to gaze steadily at her. As if memorising every detail of her face. Suddenly Josie was uneasy. 'Are you trying to say something here?'

Slowly, Sam nodded. 'Yes.'

Josie paled. 'And what,' she swallowed, 'is that?'

'I've never loved anybody the way I love you. Understand that Josie. I cannot express just how profound my feelings are for you. You're right here,' he touched his heart, 'all the time. And I want to spend the rest of my life with you.'

Josie was see-sawing between desperate hope and the brink of despair. She couldn't grasp what Sam was saying. One minute he was talking about couples splitting up, the next about spending the rest of his life with her. What was going on? 'Can you just...spit out what you're trying to say.'

Sam took a deep breath. 'I don't want this baby. Seeing Ruby today confirmed what a disastrous decision it would be to go ahead with this pregnancy. I'm not prepared to risk the relationship with my daughter. Much as it grieves me to say this Josie, if you don't agree to an abortion then...I'm leaving you.'

Josie recoiled. She scrambled off Sam's lap. 'You want me to kill a living thing?' Her voice shook with emotion. 'I don't believe I'm hearing this. You've just sat there telling me sweet words of love. That I'm there,' she pointed at Sam's chest, 'in your heart. That you want to spend the rest of your life with me,' tears began to course down her cheeks, 'when all the time,'

Josie's chest began to heave, 'all the time...what you really want–'

Sam was off the sofa in a trice. Suddenly Josie was being held so tight she could hardly breathe. 'I *do* love you, Josie. I *do*. But I don't love this situation. We *have* children. Two *beautiful* little girls.' Sam's voice cracked. 'It's so hard second time around, Josie. There's been so much grief. Lucy has lost her Dad. And Ruby feels as though she's losing *her* Dad. Can't we just concentrate our energies on our girls? Please? *Please?*'

Josie shook her head. 'You're asking too much, Sam.'

'I'm not.'

'Oh yes you are. I wouldn't be able to live with myself. I just wouldn't. I can't. I'm sorry, Sam. If it's come to this...us splitting up...then so be it.'

And with that Josie fled from the room. She couldn't take Sam's words in. So cruel. One minute saying he loved her. The next insisting she kill their child. Well she wasn't going to. Never in a million years. As far as she was concerned, Sam could go to hell.

Lucy gasped and shrank back from her position on the landing. She'd been peering through the banisters listening to a grown-up conversation. But now Mummy was coming. Straightening up, she scampered back to her bedroom. A second later and she was under the duvet. She'd heard every word. And even though they hadn't shouted, she knew they'd been arguing. She knew because Mummy had started to cry. And it was to do with the baby.

Lucy lay very still as Mummy hurried past her bedroom. She waited to hear Mummy go into her bedroom. But instead she heard the door to Ruby's room open. Moments later it shut again. That was strange.

Lucy lay in the gloom, chewing her lip. Her brain was whirring. Mummy must be very upset not to want to sleep in her own bed with Sam. But then again, Lucy understood why her mother was so distressed. It was because Sam didn't want her to have the baby. He'd told her to have an abortion, and that if she didn't do as he'd asked then he'd leave her. Lucy didn't know what an abortion was. But Mummy had been adamant she wasn't going to kill a living thing. Did that mean abortion was some sort of weapon that killed unborn babies? Lucy didn't know. But the thought made her frightened. Why would anybody want to kill a tiny baby? In particular, why did Sam want to kill *his* baby?

Lucy was starting to dislike Sam. First of all he'd told her to stop calling him Daddy. Now he was telling Mummy to kill their baby. And somehow it had something to do with Ruby. Lucy cast her mind back to Saturday. Yesterday. Ruby had listened to Mummy telling her about the baby, but Ruby had abruptly disappeared to her bedroom. Shortly afterwards she'd gone back to her mum's house. Did Ruby not want the baby either? Was that why Sam wanted to kill it?

Lucy suddenly felt very insecure. She knew Ruby had felt threatened by her own relationship with Sam – that was why she'd been told to stop calling Sam *Daddy*. So if Ruby was now feeling threatened by the baby, so much so that Sam wanted it dead, did that mean Lucy's life was at risk too? Lucy felt a frisson of terror run through her. She grabbed hold of her doll and leapt out of bed. Nipping across the landing, she burst into Ruby's bedroom.

'Get out, Sam.'

Mummy's voice was so congested with tears it was little more than a croak.

'It's me,' Lucy clutched the doll to her chest. 'I'm scared.'

'Oh darling,' Josie sat up in bed, 'I'm so sorry. I thought it was...never mind. What's the matter? Have you had a nightmare?'

Lucy bit her lip. She didn't like to tell fibs. It was wrong. But she found herself nodding. 'A little one.'

'Do you want to get into bed with me?'

Lucy didn't need asking twice. She scrambled under the duvet. A single bed didn't afford much room for two people. 'Why are you sleeping in Ruby's room?'

'Because I have a cold, darling, and don't want to give it to Sam.'

Now it was Mummy's turn to tell fibs.

'Mummy,' Lucy whispered urgently, 'can I ask a question?'

'Yes, darling.'

'Does Sam want to kill me?'

There was a stunned silence.

'What...why on earth do you ask such a question, Lucy? Of *course* Sam doesn't want to kill you. Sam *loves* you!'

'I don't think he does, Mummy. I don't think he even likes me.'

'Lucy this is ridiculous.' Josie sat up in bed. Reaching to the side she found the night light on the little cabinet next to Ruby's bed. The room was instantly bathed in a cheerful orange glow which was in stark contrast to the two occupants' emotions. 'Whatever has brought this on?'

Lucy hung her head and regarded Ruby's lilac duvet for a moment. She'd been taught to always be honest. Which wasn't easy. This was one of those times when honesty was necessary, but tremendously difficult. She took a deep breath. 'I heard your conversation with Sam.'

'When? You mean five minutes ago?'

'Yes.'

'What exactly did you hear, Lucy?'

'That...that Sam wants you to kill the baby. And if you don't, he'll leave you.'

'It's...not quite like that, Lucy.' Josie was desperate to undo the damage from her daughter's eavesdropping.

'What do you mean?'

'Well...um...Sam's very worried there is something wrong with the baby. Because of my age. And...er...he wants me to have a special test. And if that test shows there's a problem, then the doctors and nurses can take the baby away.'

'That's where they fix the baby before putting it back, right?'

Josie really didn't like all these lies. 'Yes,' she found herself saying. 'Except sometimes, if things are very badly wrong, unfortunately the baby can't be fixed. So the doctors and nurses make the decision not to put the baby back.'

'So why did Sam say he'll leave you?'

'He didn't really mean that, Lucy.'

'But he sounded like he did.'

'Sam's just anxious. About the baby. And me. He wants me to have this test but I'm against it. Because such a test is a bit risky you see. Risky for the baby's health.'

Lucy nodded. She'd heard about these tests. At school, Chloe's mum was expecting twins and she was having all sorts of tests. Almost every week according to Chloe. 'So what's this all got to do with Ruby?'

'Well, nothing, other than the fact that...I believe Ruby has been worried about the baby too. You know, being unhealthy,' Josie finished lamely.

'Is there a big chance of the baby not being healthy?'

Josie thought for a moment. She needed to explain away everything Lucy had overheard. Just until she could get her head around leaving Sam and going it alone as a pregnant single mother with a young child. One small fib at a time. 'Well, there's a fairly big risk, darling. Which is why Sam was a bit over the top when he was talking to me. He's just nervous. That's all. But I promise you, I don't think there is anything to worry about.'

Lucy bit her lip. 'I think you should have the test Mummy.'

Josie gave a wan smile. 'Okay.'

'And if the baby isn't healthy, don't let the doctor put it back.'

Josie was startled. 'Well, we'll see.'

'No Mummy, it wouldn't be a good idea to put it back. I think there's enough strain in our family as it is, without having a baby that might not be healthy.'

Josie was flabbergasted at her daughter's comment. Firstly Lucy sounded so...horribly grown up! Secondly, her daughter was clearly nobody's fool. She was far more aware of this family's dynamics than she'd given her credit for.

'Can I ask you a question, Lucy?'

'Yes.'

'Are you pleased Mummy's having a baby?'

Lucy began to fiddle with the duvet. 'Well...I was.'

'Was?'

'But now I'm not so sure.'

'Why?'

'Because it seems to be causing a lot of problems. I know you say Sam is worried about the baby's health, but he seems to be very sad too. And Ruby was sad yesterday. And...well I haven't told you this before because...because I didn't want to upset you but–' Lucy trailed off and hung her head.

'Tell me, darling. Please. You can tell me anything.'

'Well, okay. If you must know I'm just really nervous about it all. I'm worried what it will be like when you have the baby. I know you want to be a teacher too, and you'll probably be really tired looking after Sam and me and a baby and sometimes Ruby and then trying to fit in teaching.' Lucy's words were coming out in a jumble and rush. It was as though a dam had burst. 'And this probably sounds really awful, but what time will you have for me? I've already lost my Daddy, and there's a part of me that is really scared I'm going to lose my mummy too – to the baby. I'm a big girl now so I won't get the same attention as a baby. And I've stopped getting much attention from Sam because of Ruby. And soon I'm going to lose all your attention because of the baby. And that makes me feel really miserable, Mummy. Right now I have you all to myself. I know that sounds mean, but I can't help it. I don't want to share you.' And with that Lucy burst into tears.

Josie automatically put an arm around Lucy to comfort her. But mentally she was reeling. She felt as though she'd just been given a huge reality check. Nothing could have prepared her for Lucy's emotional outburst. Sam had given her a string of reasons why this pregnancy should not go ahead. But listening to her own daughter had taken her breath away. Was this what Sam had been contending with regarding Ruby? At least Ruby would have her own mother's undivided attention, regardless of a baby coming along in this household. Whereas Lucy would have to share not just Sam, but her mother too. A mother she clearly clung to following the death of her father. Josie just hadn't realised how needy Lucy was. And suddenly Josie felt ashamed. Guilty that she'd not properly asked Lucy until now about how she felt about the pregnancy. That she'd allowed herself to just assume her daughter was thrilled while she burbled about whether it was a girl or a boy and what name to call it. If Josie had previously felt her world was swinging on its axis, now she felt as though it had been well and truly turned upside down. Nobody wanted this baby. Not Ruby. Not Sam. Not even her own daughter. And *that* was a whole different ball game for Josie.

'Bloody hell, Josie, you look like you've been flattened by a steamroller,' said Kerry as they sat together in the university's cafeteria. 'What's up?'

Josie shrugged. 'Oh you know. This and that.'

'No I don't know. Define *this and that.*'

'A small matter of an unwanted pregnancy. First of all, trouble with Ruby over it. Then last night Sam actually said if I don't abort the baby to end Ruby's distress, he'll leave me. He actually said that, Kerry! Can you believe it?'

'It was emotion talking. Sam wouldn't really leave. He's madly in love with you. Any fool can see that.'

'Oh yes, he loves me all right. So much so that he touched his heart and said I was,' Josie touched her own heart to illustrate, '*right here.* He dressed up an ultimatum in a load of rosy bullshit. The bottom line is, either the baby goes or he does.'

'Sam's bluffing.'

'I don't think so actually. And apart from Sam's little homily, I then had one from my own daughter. She doesn't want the baby either.'

Kerry's eyes widened. 'Eh? Where did that come from? I thought Lucy was over the moon. Hasn't she got a shortlist of names?'

'Yes. But she went through the motions of being enthusiastic. Apparently she can't bear the idea of sharing me. Said she'd lost one parent and it will make her feel as though she's lost the other one too. To put it succinctly, Kerry, nobody wants me to have this baby.'

Kerry contemplated her coffee for a moment. 'Forget everybody else for a moment. What about you, Josie? What do *you* want? Are you eagerly awaiting the birth of this baby?'

Josie rolled her eyes. 'What do you think?'

'Just for one moment block out the pressure you're under from the others. I'm asking you how you feel. Does the thought of a future child thrill you?'

Josie stared at her coffee morosely. 'Not really, no. Even if Ruby, Sam and Lucy were over the moon, a part of me would be...panicky. And a tiny bit resentful. Babies are exhausting at the best of times. To add a newborn into the mix of returning to work full time, running a home, caring for Lucy, dealing with all the stress from Annie over Ruby...' Josie trailed off.

'You'll be cream crackered, chuck,' Kerry gave a sardonic smile. 'So – don't bite my head off for asking this – but...why won't you abort?'

Josie shook her head. 'You're a woman. A mother no less. How on earth can you ask such a question? You've carried life within you!'

'Yep. And bringing a life into this world is a heck of a responsibility. There's never a right time to have a baby, Josie. But there are plenty of wrong times to have one.'

'You're not making sense.'

'It's tough having a baby at the best of times. You need a lot of love and a load of support. Is it fair to bring a child into the world when everybody else doesn't want it? What sort of reaction are you going to get when you get home with your bundle? Love and support? Or festering resentment? Not to mention a potentially absent father if Sam carries out his threat. Is that what you want?'

'I don't have a choice.'

'Of course you have a choice,' Kerry thumped the table so hard Josie visibly jumped. 'Stop being so bloody Victorian.'

'Okay, I have a choice,' Josie glared at Kerry. 'I can book myself into a clinic, have the pregnancy surgically removed, and carry on with my life.'

'Absolutely.'

'But what about here,' Josie banged her heart to illustrate, 'and what about here?' she tapped her head. 'I've got emotions, Kerry. And morals. And unfortunately I can't have *those* surgically removed. That's something I'd have to contend with afterwards. Guilt. And it's a burden I don't wish to cart around for the rest of my life.'

'Why the hell should you feel guilty?'

'I've seen the baby, Kerry! I've seen it on a screen. A tiny rudimentary shape. The start of arms and legs. This isn't a pair of jeans I've bought from Next and then decided I don't like them and will take them back. It's a living thing!'

'I'm going to stop you there,' Kerry held up a hand, 'no, hear me out for a minute, Josie. First of all, this isn't a baby. No it isn't. Listen to me. You just said it yourself. A tiny *rudimentary* shape. It's a foetus. At this stage it's perfectly feasible to abort. I quite agree that it's a different ball game for those who abort at twenty-three weeks given that care for extremely premature babies has improved. But that doesn't apply to you. Nowhere near it. So why the moral dilemma?'

Josie could feel herself getting teary. She took a deep breath and let her eyes wander up to the ceiling, partially to contain the unshed tears. The fluorescent lights met her gaze. They were covered in fly marks and looked quite disgusting. She blinked and concentrated on the brown spots until the tears had shrunk back into their ducts.

'The way you've put it, it all sounds incredibly easy.'

'That's because it *is* easy.' Kerry reached out and squeezed Josie's hand. 'I'll let you into a secret. I had a termination last summer.'

Josie gasped. 'You never said.'

'No, I've never told a soul. Not even Simon knew.'

'Was it his?'

'Of course it was his!'

'Didn't you let him have a say in making such a decision?' Josie felt outraged on Simon's behalf.

'Absolutely not.'

'Why?'

'Because at the end of the day, kiddo, it's my body. Not Simon's. And nobody else tells me what I can or cannot do with my own body. I booked myself in on a Saturday morning, came out Saturday evening, had a few cramps, took it easy and put my feet up, and told Simon I had period pain. A few days later the bleeding stopped, just like a period. And I got on with my life. Do I feel guilty? No. And neither should you.' Kerry drained her coffee. 'So before you dismiss the subject out of hand, just think about it. No harm in weighing things up. Sam might be pro abortion, but he's predominantly thinking about the family dynamics. And personally I think the advantages of having an abortion far outweigh any disadvantages. You've got a great bloke there Josie. An absolute gem. And a lovely home and a beautiful daughter. You want to wreck all that?' Kerry stood up and gathered her files. 'I know what my decision would be, and without a moment's hesitation.'

Josie sat in the car with Lucy. They were on their way home. Josie couldn't wait to get indoors and slip into her comfy old PJs. Her heart felt heavy and she felt about a hundred years old.
  'I saw the doctor today,' Josie said tentatively to Lucy.
  'About having a test?'
  'Yes.' Josie's mouth was suddenly dry.
  'Are you having it done?'
  'Actually,' Josie licked her lips, 'the doctor was able to do the test while I was there.'
  'Oh.' Lucy looked down at her lap. Her hands fiddled with the lunchbox she was holding. 'And what did the doctor say?'
  'He said... he said it's sad news.' Lucy didn't answer. Josie risked a quick sidelong glance. Lucy was staring at the picture of the Power Puff Girls dancing across the lunchbox lid. 'And the doctor thinks it might be better to take the baby away.'
  Lucy nodded. 'That *is* sad Mummy. But,' she paused, 'I think it would be for the best. Don't you?'
  Josie's fingers tightened on the steering wheel as she gazed resolutely through the windscreen. 'Yes,' she agreed, 'I think it would be for the best.'

Sam lay in bed, on his back. The bedroom was in total darkness. Josie was lying, rigid, by his side. He had come home from work not knowing what to expect. He'd delivered a terrible ultimatum to Josie. At the time, he'd meant it. And as his working day had worn on, he'd allowed his mind to drift to Josie. What was she thinking? How was she feeling? He couldn't begin to imagine the terrible duress he'd put her under. The whole situation was difficult. But to have told the woman he loved – correction, the pregnant woman he loved – that she'd be on her Jack Jones if the baby went full term, made him cringe. He felt despicable. His ultimatum had been cowardly and cruel.

As he'd slotted his key in the front door, he'd resolved to take Josie in his arms and apologise. To tell her that, even though he didn't want the baby, he wouldn't leave her. Instead, he'd come into the hallway to find Josie sitting on the stairs waiting for him.

'Can we talk?' she'd asked.

'Of course,' he'd replied.

And then she'd given him a level look and calmly delivered words that had made him inhale sharply.

'I've decided to have an abortion.'

And now, as Sam lay in the dark, he couldn't get his head around it. He'd begged, argued, reasoned and ranted with Josie. Apparently to no avail. Until now.

'Is it,' his words sounded loud in the darkness, 'is it because I threatened to leave you?'

'No.'

'You can be honest with me, Josie. I wouldn't have left you. Not really. I just said that,' his voice caught, 'to force your hand. I'm not proud of it.'

'It's not because of anything you said.'

'You're just saying that.'

'I'm telling you the truth.' Josie turned on her side, her back to Sam. 'Can we just leave it there? I'm tired. I want to go to sleep.'

'Sure.' Sam turned over and faced the other way. Silently the tears began to flow. He didn't know if it was sadness, relief, or a bit of both.

Josie squeezed her eyes shut to stop the tears. She moved a hand down to her abdomen and gently caressed it. And in her mind she began to speak to the tiny life deep within her. *Darling baby. I am so, so sorry. So sorry that I will never know you, or hold you in my arms. I have to give you up. You see, I was talking to your sister. Lucy. She's had a tough time in her short little life. Her dad died a few years ago, and there are...difficulties...in this new family. And because of those difficulties, my little girl needs me more than ever. She needs me one hundred and ten per cent. And much as it pains me to say good-bye to you, I have a parental duty to put the needs of my child already in this world before the needs of a child that isn't actually here. Please forgive me.*

The following morning, Josie telephoned Miss Birch's secretary. By the end of the call, her diary contained a date for termination. Saturday. Which was tomorrow.

Chapter Twenty-Nine

Sam still didn't know why Josie had changed her mind about the termination. One minute she'd been so adamant it was a route she'd never take, she'd tossed his ultimatum back at him and been prepared to go it alone. And then suddenly, a U-turn. He'd tried talking to her, but drawn a blank. She'd shut him out and put the barriers up, which was hardly surprising given his previous behaviour. And now, as Josie stood at the kitchen sink peeling vegetables for dinner, Sam determined to try talking to his fiancée one more time.

'Josie, I...er...just want to say thank you for putting Ruby first.'

'I haven't.'

'Oh. Um, well, for thinking of my feelings then.'

'Don't flatter yourself. My decision has absolutely nothing to do with either you or Ruby.'

'Right.' Sam stuffed his hands in his pockets and contemplated Josie's rigid back. These last few days he'd been treated with utter contempt. Which was understandable and no less than what he deserved. 'So...the operation...when is it?'

'Tomorrow.'

'So soon?'

'Yes. Fortunately Miss Birch had availability.'

'I'm coming with you.'

'Oh please. Don't trouble yourself.'

'Don't be like that.' Sam moved forward until he was standing next to her at the sink. 'I know this isn't easy for you, Josie,' he touched her arm lightly. She instantly flinched away. 'Look, I want to be there. To support you.'

'Support me?' Josie gave a mirthless laugh. 'Bit late for that.'

'You know what I mean. I don't want you in hospital on your own, anxious or frightened. I'll be with you every step of the way.'

'To make sure I go through with it?' Josie spat. For a moment the vegetable peeling was suspended as she turned to him, eyes blazing.

'No, darling, please! I've said I'm sorry a million times. What can I do to make amends?'

Josie gave him a long look. 'Okay,' she finally said. 'In all honesty, I'm apprehensive about the procedure. Having made this decision I just want to get it over and done with. But yes, it would be...reassuring...to know you're there.'

Sam nodded, relief washing over him. 'Good. Can I...can I give you a hug?'

For a moment Josie just stared at him, her face eerily resembling Ruby's expressionless mask. 'I suppose,' she finally shrugged.

In a trice Sam had knocked a half peeled potato and vegetable knife from Josie's hands. A moment later and she was wrapped in his arms. She stood, rigid, in his embrace. But he didn't care. At least she was allowing him to hold her. It was a start to repairing the terrible hurt he'd inflicted. They stood that way for several minutes.

'What about Lucy?' Sam finally said. 'Who is looking after her tomorrow?'

'She's going to her grandparents for the weekend. Just in case I feel like shit afterwards.'

Sam nodded. Of course Josie would feel like shit afterwards. She'd be in floods of tears no doubt. The last thing she wanted was for Lucy to see her like that. Sam kissed the top of Josie's head. 'I'll be with you tomorrow,' he whispered into her hair, 'I won't let you down.'

'Promise?'

'Promise.'

There was just the small matter of telling Annie that he wouldn't be able to have Ruby this weekend.

Annie flicked through the television channels. Nothing much on the box tonight. She'd just come off the phone to Nigel. They'd been getting on really well lately. So much so that Nigel had suggested a jaunt to London to do a bit of shopping. Hatton Garden had been mentioned, and every woman worth her shopping salt knew you didn't go to Hatton Garden for groceries. Annie's head was full of diamond solitaires when Ruby came into the lounge, mobile phone clamped to one ear.

'She's right here, Daddy, just a minute.' Ruby extended the mobile to her mother. 'Daddy wants to talk to you.'

'Tell him I'm busy.'

Ruby put the mobile back to her ear. There was a pause as she listened to Sam and then once again regarded her mother. 'Daddy says it's important.'

'What I'm doing is more important. He'll have to call back.'

'He's asking when it's convenient to call.'

'Tomorrow.'

'He says tomorrow is too late.'

'Too bad.'

Ruby wandered out of the lounge. Annie put her head back against the sofa. Should she hint at Nigel buying a round solitaire or a square diamond? And she didn't want a measly half carat job. Nigel earned well. He could afford something decent. And ideally platinum. That was more expensive than yellow gold. And definitely more classy than white gold. Annie paused in her musings. What did Ruby just say to Sam?

'Yes I understand, Daddy. You want me to tell Mummy that you can't see me this weekend because Josie isn't well. Okay, Daddy. I won't forget, I'll do it right now–'

Suddenly the mobile phone was snatched from Ruby's hand.

'What are you telling Ruby?'

'Annie. Hi. I was just telling Ruby that unfortunately I can't see her this weekend. Would it be okay if we swap weekends and I see her next weekend instead?'

'Absolutely not. You can't just alter access arrangements at the drop of a hat to suit your social life.'

'It's not quite like that, Annie. Josie is terminating the pregnancy. The operation is tomorrow. She needs supporting and I want to be there.'

'I see.' Annie looked at Ruby standing quietly in the hallway listening to the conversation. 'So let me get this straight, Sam. You wish to put Josie before your own daughter.'

'Annie, please don't talk like that. You know I always put Ruby first. I always have done and always will.'

'Doesn't look like that to me, Sam. What sort of father cancels last minute on his little daughter?'

'For God's sake, Annie, can't you have a bit of compassion?'

'Can't you think of your daughter for once instead of yourself?'

'I hope you're not talking like this in front of Ruby.'

'Yes, Ruby can hear every word Sam – that she is way down on your list of priorities. And after last weekend with Ruby in floods of tears over your trollop carrying your bastard child, the least you could do is be there for her this weekend.'

'Annie please stop talking like that. Don't you care what you're doing to our daughter?'

'Unlike you, Sam, I'm here for Ruby. She is my priority.'

'She's my priority too goddammit, so stop talking like that. I'm just asking you to be reasonable on this one occasion. You caused all Ruby's upset over this baby in the first place. Well now that baby is going to be aborted. The least you could do is be charitable and afford me time to be with Josie. This isn't easy for her you know.'

'Go ahead, Sam. Put your trollop first. I'll explain to Ruby that she's not important.'

'Wait! Please, don't hang up Annie. Okay, listen, I can do both. Josie goes into hospital in the morning. The op is scheduled for early afternoon. What about I pick Ruby up straight afterwards?'

'What time would that be?'

'Well, I'm not sure, can I call you tomorrow and–'

'No, Sam, I have my own arrangements tomorrow. You have to fit in with me. I need you to pick up Ruby no later than twelve noon. Is that understood?'

'Yes, yes, I'll be there. Can I speak to Ruby again please?'

'No. I need to comfort her after you letting her think she's not your priority.' Annie instantly hit the disconnect button and turned the mobile off for good measure. She looked at Ruby. 'Your Daddy is a shit. But don't worry, I've put him straight. He'll be here to pick you up at noon.'

Ruby gazed at her mother, blank expression firmly in place.

When Josie awoke at six the following morning she felt sick with apprehension. She'd been told she could have a light breakfast of tea and toast, but absolutely nothing after seven o'clock. Josie padded downstairs and put the kettle on. She needed to be at the hospital by eight. Lucy would be dropped at her grandparents' house en-route to hospital.

Sam wandered into the kitchen.

'Why are you eating? You're meant to be having an anaesthetic.'

'Yes, I am. But not until much later. The hospital said as long as there was a four hour gap between eating and being knocked out, it wouldn't present a problem.'

Sam glanced at the clock on the kitchen wall. 'Do you think you'll be in theatre soon after ten?'

'I don't know what time I'll go down.'

'Didn't Miss Birch tell you?'

'No. We'll know more about the operating list when we get to the hospital.'

'Okay. But I wouldn't eat any more of that toast if I was you. Just in case you're first on the list. In fact, I think I'll have a word with the staff when we get there and ask if you can go to theatre sooner rather than later.'

Josie frowned and put down her toast. 'What's the rush? We've got the whole of today set aside for this. Even if I'm first on the list, I have no idea what time I'll be discharged. At best it will be late afternoon, but more likely the evening.'

Sam paled. 'No, no, that can't be right – it mustn't be right. We need to be out of the hospital by quarter to twelve at the latest.'

Josie stared at Sam. What on earth was he talking about? And why was he suddenly so agitated? She took another bite of her toast and watched Sam begin to pace the kitchen. Swallowing the toast, she picked up her mug of tea. Sam was now raking his hair. 'Is something wrong?'

'Yes. No. Well, not specifically. I just...er...there's a problem with Ruby you see.'

Josie froze. 'A problem? What sort of problem?'

'Um...Annie couldn't...ah...Annie said–'

'You're not trying to tell me that Ruby is still coming over this weekend are you?'

'Er...not exactly...I mean...she is. Coming over that is. But not until noon.'

Josie gaped at Sam. 'Noon *today*?'

'Er, yes, you see...Annie was saying things in front of Ruby about–'

'I don't believe I'm hearing this.'

'And...ah...Annie has a commitment which–'

'What about your commitment to me?'

'Yes...yes that's what I said to Annie but–'

'But she gave you a load of shit, and instead of standing up to her you keeled over and did her bidding,' Josie barked. 'Am I right, or am I right?'

'She was telling Ruby derogatory things. Damaging things. Josie, please don't have a go at me–'

'Have a go?' Josie screeched. She stood up, tea and toast abandoned, and stalked over to Sam. 'HAVE A GO?' she bawled into his face.

'Josie, calm down, please. You don't understand. Annie was saying things in front of Ruby. She was telling Ruby I wasn't putting her first.'

'THAT'S RIGHT,' Josie yelled, 'because on this ONE occasion Sam, you'd agreed to put ME first.'

'Josie, please. Don't shout. Can't you see the invidious position that woman put me in? I was trying to compromise. Compromise between you and Ruby. Trying put you both first. Do you understand? Annie was damaging Ruby with her words. I had to agree to her wishes, Josie. I had to try and undo the harm she was causing,' Sam began to choke up, 'I can't have Ruby thinking I don't care about her,' the tears began to flow, 'or that she's not my priority.'

Josie ignored Sam's tears. What about her tears for once? 'So what are you proposing, Sam?' Her lips, bloodless, were drawn back across her teeth so that she appeared to be almost snarling.

'Well I thought,' Sam gulped, 'I thought you could go to hospital and...er...be first on the list. The procedure is very quick. We know that. And,' he swiped a fist across his eyes, 'that as soon as it was over, I'd help you in the car, and then we could whizz over to Annie's and...well...pick Ruby up,' he shrugged and held both palms wide, 'everybody's happy.'

'Happy?' Josie stared at Sam incredulously. 'You expect me to come straight out of hospital, minutes after an anaesthetic, bleeding and with a belly full of cramps so that you can collect your daughter purely to appease your ex-wife?'

'Well, put like that—'

Josie raised both arms up and shoved Sam as hard as she could. He stumbled backwards, slamming awkwardly against the huge American fridge. 'You said you'd be there for me!' Josie turned and took two strides to her empty breakfast plate. 'You said you'd be with me all the way!' She grabbed the plate and hurled it at Sam. It sailed through the air, missed his head by millimetres, and smashed against the fridge. 'You said you wouldn't let me down!' Josie picked up her mug of half-drunk tea and flung it across the kitchen. Brown liquid splattered across the cabinets before china fragmented and clattered onto the floor. Tugging at her engagement ring, she palmed it before lobbing it at Sam. This time her missile hit target. The ring grazed Sam's right eyelid. His hands automatically clutched at his face. Josie stood there, chest heaving.

'Fuck you, Sam. I rue the day I met you, but thank God I never married you.'

'Mummy?' Lucy stood in the kitchen doorway, face pinched and anxious.

'Lucy!' Josie swung round. Shit, shit and triple shit. This was all that bloody woman's fault. If it wasn't for Fanny Fucking Annie none of them would be taking part in this hideous scenario in their kitchen at the crack of dawn on a Saturday. Regrettably, Lucy had just witnessed a blazing row with her mother in full crockery throwing mode. Josie knew nothing she did or said would undo what Lucy had seen and heard. She'd just have to make the best of it with her daughter and be honest. 'I'm so sorry, Lucy. You've just heard Sam and Mummy having a very big argument but I promise it sounded worse than it really was, okay? Meanwhile, I have to go out. So I need you to go back upstairs, clean your teeth and get dressed as quickly as possible. Mummy is still taking you to Grandma and Grandad. Can you do that for me?'

Lucy nodded. 'Yes,' she said in a small voice.

'Go on then. Quick,' Josie dredged up a reassuring smile for her daughter. Lucy spun round and scampered back upstairs.

For a moment there was silence in the kitchen. Sam was the first to break it.

'Does that mean...as Lucy is going to your parents...that you're still–'

'Still having a termination? No, Sam. No, I'm not having a termination. Not now. Nobody has put me first in this situation. Instead everybody has expected me to think of them. How *they* feel. How this pregnancy impacts on *their* lifestyle, *their* emotions, *their* convenience. Nobody has asked how I'm coping. Nor does anybody seem to care. But you know what? I'm now putting me first, along with the baby in my belly. A baby who doesn't yet have a voice, but if it did it would probably say, "And what about me? I don't want to be killed to suit everybody else." So guess what? This time I'm going to put my baby first too.'

'Josie please–' Sam lunged forward and grabbed Josie's arm. A second later he was clutching his private parts and retching.

'Don't...ever...touch me...again.' Josie's whole body was shaking with emotion. She turned and stalked out of the kitchen.

It was a full five minutes before Sam's breathing had returned to normal. By the time he felt able to let go of his throbbing testicles, Josie and Lucy had gone.

Chapter Thirty

'Is everything okay, Mummy?'

Josie's hands gripped the steering wheel of her car as they headed towards Ted and Miriam Payne's house. Bugger Annie. And bugger Sam. 'Yes, darling. Everything is absolutely fine.'

'But I thought Sam was taking you to hospital?'

'No, no,' Josie shook her head and tried desperately hard to talk normally. 'It's not necessary for Sam to take me now.'

'But,' Lucy's brow furrowed, 'I thought the baby wasn't well, and you had to have it taken away.'

'You'll never guess what,' Josie gave a bright smile, 'it looks like the doctors might have got the test results wrong.'

'Really?'

'I'm just waiting to hear,' Josie's voice cracked slightly, 'and have proper confirmation.'

'Oh.' Lucy stared out the window.

'But one thing at a time, eh? I'll drop you off at Grandma's and Grandad's and wait to hear from the hospital.'

Josie stared resolutely ahead. She wasn't going to get into a discussion with Lucy about the baby. Or her relationship with Sam being in tatters. Nor did she know how she was going to explain to her parents that she wasn't going ahead with the termination. In the end Josie decided not to say anything. She didn't feel up to talking to anybody, least of all her parents. Miriam had made it plain that she thought Josie's decision to terminate was the right thing to do in the circumstances. If Josie told her mother that she had now changed her mind, Miriam would be horrified and start giving Josie a lecture about getting her priorities right. Josie knew her mother meant well, but she wasn't in the right frame of mind to listen to yet another set of opinions on what she should or shouldn't be doing.

When Josie pulled up outside her parents' house, it wasn't quite half past seven. Miriam had evidently been waiting by the window watching out for Josie's car. As Josie walked Lucy up the narrow driveway, the front door opened.

'Are you all right, love?' Miriam looked at Josie's tear stained face with concern. 'I know this isn't easy for you.'

'I'm fine,' Josie gave a brittle smile.

'Mummy's baby might be all right after all,' Lucy informed her grandmother.

'Eh?' Miriam gave her daughter a quizzical look.

'*Pas devant l'enfant* mother.'

'Oh. Right. Well Dad's still in bed. Come in Lucy, darling,' Miriam waved Lucy in under her arm. 'You can help me make Grandad's breakfast, and I expect you'd like some nice scrambled egg and bacon too, eh?'

'Yes please.'

As Lucy's eyes lit up at the prospect of a fry up, Josie's stomach contracted at the very thought.

'Go through to the kitchen love. I'll just say good-bye to Mummy.'

'I'd best be off, Mum.'

'Just a minute,' Miriam watched Lucy disappear into the kitchen, 'where's Sam?'

'Um, he'll be joining me later.'

'Later? But I thought he was going with you?'

'Not now, Mum,' Josie's eyes welled, 'I can't talk–'

'Something's wrong. Have you two had a row?'

Josie shook her head. 'No.' But tears were spurting out of her eyes. 'Got to go, Mum. See you later.'

'Josie?'

But Josie was already halfway down the drive, key fob extended. She popped the central locking and jumped into her car without a backward glance at her mother. Seconds later and she was beetling towards Chislehurst and home, on automatic pilot. Horrified, Josie came to a roundabout and swung around it. Where to go? She headed off in the direction of Farnborough, following signposts willy-nilly. Soon she was bucketing along country lanes. Cudham. Knockholt. Sevenoaks. Otford. Josie's car ate up the miles although she was actually only driving around local outskirts. She drove aimlessly, her brain numb. Every time a thought about Sam, Annie, Ruby or Lucy popped into her head, she distracted herself by glancing fleetingly at sheep in muddy fields, or berries hanging on hedgerows. Anything to stop herself from thinking. At one point she drove with a hand resting on her belly. *Right little baby, it's just you and me. And I'm not going to let anything happen to you.* And then Josie allowed her mind to go blank again, else she tip over the edge and descend into madness.

Back home, Sam was tearing his hair out. He'd called Josie's mobile repeatedly, but it was switched off. Finally, after a moment's hesitation, he called his future mother-in-law.

'Hi Miriam. It's Sam here.'

'Hello dear. Are you at the hospital? Is Josie okay?'

'Er,' Sam closed his eyes for a moment, 'I don't know where Josie is. I was rather hoping she might have been with you.'

'What?' Miriam's voice was sharp. 'I knew something wasn't right when I saw her. I asked her if the pair of you had had a row, but she wouldn't tell me anything.'

Sam took a deep breath. 'Yes, we did have a row.'

'Bad?'

'Enough for her to fling her engagement ring at me and say she wasn't going through with the abortion.'

Sam heard Miriam suck her breath in. 'But why? She was absolutely adamant she was going to go ahead with it. Whatever has happened to change her mind?'

'I...er...it's my fault. I came under pressure from my ex-wife to pick up my daughter at noon today. I was trying to juggle Josie and Ruby together.'

'Are you kidding me, Sam?'

'It's not what you think, Miriam. My ex was doing the usual hatchet job and telling Ruby stuff and nonsense–'

'Sam, your relationship with your ex-wife is none of my business, but when it comes to my daughter, well that is my business. I'm very aware of your ex being a bitter woman and causing problems. But quite frankly it's high time you stood up to her.'

'And what about *my* daughter, Miriam? How am I meant to undo all the damage my ex does?'

'Just keep telling your daughter you love her. That's all you can do. But if you don't start putting your foot down with that ex-wife, you're going to do irrevocable damage to my granddaughter.'

'Lucy's fine, Miriam, she understands.'

'Oh does she? That kid had her world turned upside down losing her father. Now she has another father figure in her life but he's having nowhere near enough input with her.'

'That's not true, I–'

'Yes it is true, Sam. And to top it off my granddaughter heard the two of you arguing this morning. Lucy's been left here, seen her mother go off in a tizzy, and given me some cock and bull story about tests on the baby and possibly having a sibling. Lucy doesn't know whether she's coming or going. And quite frankly I don't think Josie does either. My daughter has enough on her plate, Sam, worrying about her own child and juggling her studies with running a home, without all the upset your ex adds into the mix. You should have been by my daughter's side from the start, and then you wouldn't be ringing up now asking where she is – not to mention worrying me senseless about her. What if Josie does something daft?'

'She won't, Miriam, she's a strong woman, she's–'

'Josie didn't look strong when I last saw her. She looked like a woman about to crack up. So you find her, Sam. And make it soon.'

'Yes, Miriam, I–' but Sam was talking to himself.

Fuck, fuck, *fuck*.

Not for the first time Sam cursed Annie and the mayhem she indirectly caused. A small voice spoke in his head. *It doesn't have to be mayhem. If you'd refused to dance to Annie's tune, none of this would be happening.* Sam grabbed his car keys. He decided to cruise the streets and try and find Josie that way. Perhaps he'd find her holed up in Tesco's cafeteria, reading a paper and having a coffee.

Half an hour later Sam had checked out the two big supermarkets within striking distance of home. Josie's car wasn't in either car park. Nor was she in store. He'd asked Customer Services to do an announcement asking if Josie Payne were shopping to please make her way to the foyer. But Josie hadn't appeared. And then Sam had had a brainwave. What if Josie had only been calling his bluff about not having a termination? What if she might be with Miss Birch right now? Sam pointed his Mercedes towards the Sidcup By-Pass and roared off to the hospital.

One hour later he was none the wiser. Josie wasn't at the hospital. Miss Birch was in theatre operating and unavailable. Sam had spoken to Miss Birch's secretary but nobody had heard from Josie.

'If she eventually shows up, can she still be seen?' Sam had asked.

'Miss Birch is operating until six o'clock. If your partner shows up before then, Miss Birch can still operate.'

Sam had thanked the secretary and raced back to his car. Where next? Sam swung the Mercedes in the direction of Greenwich University. Maybe, just maybe, Josie would be there. To the best of his knowledge, there was no parking on campus. But he knew Josie parked at a pay and display on Avery Hill. Perhaps he'd locate her car there? She had a gaggle of friends, in particular one called Kerry. But he'd never involved himself with Josie's circle of female acquaintances. He'd met Kerry on a handful of occasions, but the woman had barely registered on his radar. He certainly had no idea where she lived. As he drove, Sam once again tried calling Josie's mobile phone.

It was a little after eleven o'clock. Josie felt a wave of tiredness wash over her. She needed to stop driving. A cup of tea would be nice. She was now trundling through Eynsford. This was Kerry's neck of the woods. Josie had no idea if Kerry would be in, but thought it might be worth a try. A few minutes later she was in Kerry's cul-de-sac. Her friend's car was on the drive. Oh, thank God. Josie parked behind it and killed the engine. Grabbing her handbag she reached inside and picked up her mobile phone. She'd been driving around with it switched off. What if Lucy needed to speak to her? Josie fumbled with the tiny button. Seconds later the mobile tinkled out its opening activation tune. She chucked it back in her handbag before getting out of the car.

A twitch of net curtains signalled she'd been spotted. The front door opened.

'What the bloody hell are you doing here?' asked Kerry. 'Shouldn't you be in hospital?'

'Yes,' Josie answered as she went through the front door. Kicking off her shoes she padded into the lounge. 'Are you on your own?'

'For now. Toyah said she might swing by later, but I'm not holding my breath. But never mind that. What's going on?'

'Everything,' Josie sighed. She tugged off her coat and flopped down on the sofa.

'Let me go and put the kettle on. You put your feet up and stay there. You look totally done in.'

'I feel totally done in.' Josie agreed.

Kerry went off to make tea leaving Josie alone. She leant back against the sofa and massaged her temples. Crying might be therapeutic but it gave you one hell of a headache. From inside her handbag, her mobile phone started to ring. Josie foraged in the handbag's depths and located the handset. The caller display announced it was Sam. She switched the phone to silent and chucked it back amongst a detritus of tissues, defunct biros and make-up.

'So,' Kerry appeared carrying a tea tray and biscuit assortment. 'Don't tell me. You've bottled out.'

'No. I just decided that I wasn't going to be bullied anymore.'

Kerry arched an eyebrow. 'I thought you were doing this for Lucy? You can hardly say your *daughter* was bullying you.'

'Actually yes,' Josie took a sip of tea, 'in her own way, she was. Lucy let me know she wasn't happy about the baby. Oh she has her reasons – and very valid ones. But at the end of the day, it's all pressure on me isn't it? And then pressure from Ruby – indirectly – letting us know she was worried about her Daddy being shared and all the usual emotional crap. Ditto Sam.'

'So what was the catalyst for changing your mind.'

'Annie.'

'Sam's ex? What the hell has she got to do with it?'

'Plenty. She expected Sam to drop everything, including me, and pick up Ruby. Berated him – as always – for not being there for his daughter. The usual shit.'

'Well surely Sam explained to her that it wasn't possible, today of all days.'

'Of course. Annie knew I was going to hospital to terminate the pregnancy, but it still didn't stop her being vile and wanting to cause problems. Which she did. Big time.'

'The woman is a head case.'

'Of that I have no doubt. But she's starting to make the rest of us head cases too. The last straw was Sam trying to juggle being with me and picking Ruby up from Annie's. In a nutshell, we're over.'

'I think your phone is ringing.' Kerry nodded at Josie's handbag which was visibly vibrating.

'It will be Sam.'

'Don't you think you should speak to him?'

'And say what?'

'Well, I don't know, he's probably frantic with worry. At least let the guy know you're all right.'

'I really don't want to speak to Sam right now. If I do, invective will spill out of my mouth. And I don't want to sound like Fanny Annie.'

Kerry snorted. 'Is that your nickname for her?'

Josie gave a ghost of a smile. 'Yes. Small amusements keep me sane. Just.'

'Right. Well if you're not going to answer your phone, what about another cup of tea?'

Sam sat in his car. He was now parked up in a Greenwich residential side road drinking cappuccino from a polystyrene cup. He'd lost track of how many times he'd tried ringing Josie. He'd left umpteen voicemails. Suddenly his mobile began to ring. Hope surged within him. But it was Annie.

'Where are you?'

'In my car.'

'How far away are you? You're late.'

'I'm not coming.'

'What the fuck do you mean you're not coming?'

'I should be with Josie right now, holding her hand as she goes into Theatre. Instead, because of you insisting I pick Ruby up at noon, Josie has gone AWOL.'

'I'm not interested in your trollop. Get your backside over here and collect your daughter. She's your priority, not some silly tart that's got herself up the duff.'

'Don't speak about Josie like that.'

'I'll speak how I like. So you're going to let your daughter down? Ruby's right here, Sam. She can hear me talking to you and is looking absolutely devastated that you're not putting her first.'

Sam almost gave in to the wave of panic that threatened to engulf him. Before he even realised what he was doing, one hand was shoving the cappuccino into the cup rest, the other starting the car up ready to dash over to Annie's house. But a little voice in his head spoke up. *Stop dancing to her tune. Hang up and simply text Ruby a message of explanation.*

'Good-bye, Annie.'

Sam then hit the envelope icon on his phone and began to text his daughter.

There is a problem with the baby. I have to be with Josie today. I love you, Daddy xx

Sam wasn't sure if Ruby would be able to read the entire message by herself. But if nothing else she could read *I love you* and understand the kisses. Sam picked up the cappuccino from the cup rest and thought about where to look next for Josie.

Josie was halfway through her fourth cup of tea when she felt an overwhelming need to empty her bladder. Kerry had disappeared into the kitchen to take a call from Simon. Josie could hear Kerry billing and cooing down the phone. She felt a stab of jealousy. Only a couple of years ago, she and Sam had been like that. A part of her yearned for those days. Despite everything, Josie still loved Sam. She couldn't, in all truth, imagine life without him. If only Nigel, Annie's boyfriend, would pop the question. Josie suspected that if Annie were happily married, life would be much easier all round. Annie would want time with her husband, so there would be none of this nonsense over weekend access and holidays.

Out in the kitchen, Kerry was still talking. Josie hauled herself up from the depths of the sofa and took herself off to the downstairs toilet. Just as she lowered herself down, Josie experienced a strange sensation in her stomach. A fluttering. Like a tiny squeezing sensation. Good heavens. Was that the baby moving? Josie had read somewhere that second and third time mothers had sworn they'd felt movement from as early as eleven weeks. Well, how amazing! For a moment, Josie felt almost grateful to Annie for causing a rumpus. But for Annie's furore, Josie would now be in hospital. She'd never have experienced the incredible miracle of feeling life within her. No way on this earth was she aborting now. Not for all the tea in China. Reaching for some loo paper, Josie patted herself. And then she froze. What was that? She scrutinised the damp toilet paper. The smallest trace of blood. Was the blood in her urine? Or...she paled. Trying to quell a sudden rush of fear, she ripped off more loo paper. This time she made sure to press the tissue hard against her vagina. She held it there for almost half a minute before examining the paper a second time. Definitely blood. And then Josie became aware of another tiny squeezing sensation deep within her abdomen. Oh my God. That wasn't the baby moving. It was a tiny contraction. Her body was trying to expel the pregnancy. She was miscarrying.

'KERRY!' Josie screamed.

Chapter Thirty-One

Annie was having the perfect day. She'd given Sam a good bollocking for failing to collect their daughter. Such spats always left her buzzing. Although Ruby had actually been relieved not to be with her father.

'I'd have been bored, Mummy, hanging around a hospital,' Ruby had said.

'That's not the point, Ruby. It's the principle of the matter. Your father didn't put you first. Just remember that.'

Annie was aware that she was a walking contradiction. After all, not so long ago she'd been telling Sam that Ruby wanted nothing more to do with him. That Sam should go away and leave them both in peace. Whereas now Annie was berating Sam for not being available. But at the end of the day, it was all about control. *She* would decide if Sam stayed away, not him! And right now it didn't suit Annie to have Sam staying away. She wanted more time to be with Nigel – without a little girl impacting on her romantic relationship. So Annie had deposited Ruby at her mother's house before driving on to Nigel's. Leaving her car on his drive, they'd walked to the station and caught a train to London. It was only a hop, skip and a jump from Thameslink to Hatton Garden. And now the pair of them were ensconced in a very chic restaurant perusing menus, and drinking champagne!

'What are you going to order?' Nigel asked Annie.

'I can't decide between the Lemon Sole Meunière or the Sautéed Escalope of Calf's Liver.' Annie's eyes roamed over the printed options. They were all delectable. 'What about you?'

'I think I'll have the Lobster Risotto Provençal with Parmesan Tuile.'

'Ooh, that sounds nice. Actually, I'll have the same as you.'

Nigel caught the waiter's eye. After much bowing and scraping and topping up of their glasses, the waiter departed.

'Have you any idea why we came to Hatton Garden today?' Nigel casually asked.

Annie decided to play it cool. 'No. Care to enlighten me?'

'I need to buy a wedding suit, and I'd like your opinion.'

'Oh.' Annie felt an immediate sense of deflation. 'You've been invited to somebody's wedding?' She mentally filed through a list of Nigel's acquaintances she'd heard him talk about. Who was getting married?

'Yeah. It's going to be a posh do and I'm under orders to get it right.'

Annie took a sip of champagne. Was it her imagination or did the drink now taste as flat as she felt? What a disappointment. 'Well I don't know why you want my opinion,' she sniffed, 'it's nothing to do with me.'

'I'm fairly sure you'll be invited too.' Nigel picked up his glass and twiddled with the stem.

'Thrilling,' said Annie, sounding anything but.

'Don't you want to know who is getting married?'

'Not really,' Annie stared around the restaurant at other diners. There was a loved-up couple a few tables to their right. They were holding hands across the linen, gazing rapturously at each other. The woman was all starry eyed and grinning stupidly at her amour. Was he about to pop the question? Or had he already asked and she'd agreed? God, what she'd give for being like them, all loved up and engaged to be married. Dissatisfaction washed over her. Everybody she knew had a ring on their finger. Even Sam's trollop. It wasn't fair.

'God, you're a prickly cow sometimes, Annie.'

Annie took her eyes off the loved-up couple and turned her attention back to Nigel. 'Well that's charming,' she said sulkily. 'If you'll excuse me a minute, I'm going to the Ladies.'

'Hang on a minute,' Nigel grabbed Annie's hand as she made to stand up. 'Stop having a strop. I was having a joke with you, but I can see it's backfired.'

'Joke about what?' Annie frowned.

'The wedding we've been invited to.'

'What about it?' Annie was bored with this conversation.

'It's *our* wedding.'

Annie stared at Nigel. Had she just heard right? 'Ours?'

'Yes. Ours! I'm asking you to marry me, Annie.'

Annie's eyes widened. She'd just been proposed to! Oh my God, Nigel had popped the question. He really had! 'Gosh.

Well. This is all a bit of a surprise.' She instantly reverted back to playing it cool. 'Do I get time to think about it?'

'Of course,' Nigel demurred. 'You can take as long as you like. Although I was rather hoping that we'd buy a ring after lunch, but if you want to mull it over, that's fine.'

Annie instantly back-peddled. 'I've thought about it, and my answer is yes. And I'd like a platinum solitaire.'

'Please.'

'Pretty please.'

'Good,' Nigel winked.

'Does that mean Ruby and I will move into your house?'

'No,' Nigel shook his head. 'I'd like a fresh start. We'll carry on living in separate houses for the meantime, but we can start shopping for a house right away. And I think the kids should come along too. Get them involved. They can do a bit of bonding about being brothers and sister. I suggest we get married after we've all moved in together.'

'Fab.' Annie suddenly found her face wreathed in smiles. She picked up her champagne glass. 'Here's to us.'

Annie wasn't too thrilled at the prospect of living with Nigel's boys every other weekend. But hopefully, with a bit of discreet encouragement from her, they'd reduce their visits to once a month. That was the trouble with boys. So rowdy. Kicking footballs around the front room one minute then fisticuffs the next. At least Nigel couldn't complain about Ruby being a pain. Ruby was so quiet these days. In fact half the time Annie didn't know the child was there.

Josie was discharged from hospital late evening. Sam took her home. On the drive back to Chislehurst, neither of them spoke. It had been an emotionally draining day. Earlier, upon arrival at the hospital, a scan had been carried out. The foetus had been found to have no heartbeat. *The foetus.* Strange how everybody had instantly stopped saying *baby.* An internal examination revealed a slightly dilated cervix. Josie was told she could either go home to let nature take its course or, as she'd been booked in for an abortion anyway, to have the failed pregnancy surgically removed. Josie opted for the latter. She didn't think she could cope with prolonged cramps and bleeding on top of the day she'd had. Upon hearing the foetus had died, Sam had broken down. He'd sobbed to the point where one of the nurses had expressed concern.

'Oh don't worry about him,' Josie had calmly said, 'he's just upset he didn't get to see his daughter today.'

The nurse had given Josie a strange look and not said another word. Josie hadn't shed a single tear upon entering the hospital. She'd known she was miscarrying and just wanted to get it over and done with. A peculiar calmness had descended, as if part of her mind had detached from her body and was watching events play out before her. From a safe place that nobody had been able to penetrate, she'd watched herself be wheeled down to Theatre, and later regain consciousness in Recovery. Then back to her room to find Sam, still slumped, still in bits, sitting on a chair in the corner. Josie had said nothing to him. What was the point? The man was a total failure in her eyes. He might be a successful dentist, run a surgery, and be Mr Magnificent during the day, but in his private life he was weak. The one and only time she'd asked to be put first, he'd let her down. She could taste the bitterness in her mouth. Sam was far more interested in spending every available moment seeing his daughter. Josie could understand that but...in Sam's case...it was almost like an obsession. Was that healthy? Josie didn't think it was. No doubt a counsellor would have all the answers. Say that it was due to Annie's diabolical treatment. But at the end of the day, Josie wished – for once – Sam had told Annie where to get off. But it was all irrelevant now. They were finished. This baby business had completely undone them.

Josie stared out the car window. Outside it was pitch black. She hoped that Lucy wouldn't be too affected by the split. Josie closed her eyes. Oh God. There was so much to sort out. Selling the house that they'd barely lived in for five minutes. A recession had started and house prices were falling every week. And what if they didn't sell quickly? How interminable would it be living under the same roof? How would that affect Lucy? Things were never straightforward when children were involved. Lucy had lost one father, been given a sometime-father – when Sam wasn't placating Annie or fawning over Ruby – and now Lucy wouldn't even have a sometime-father. That was what really upset Josie. It would be bad enough getting through her own heartache over her doomed relationship, but she had to worry about Lucy being upset too. Thank God her daughter was currently tucked up for the night at her grandparents' house. The last thing Josie wanted was Lucy observing a strained atmosphere and prolonged silence.

'We're home,' Sam murmured.

Josie's eyes refocused. She'd been so lost in thought that the street lights of their road hadn't even registered. Sam jumped out of the car, trotted around to the passenger side and opened the door. The tears had stopped, and now he was all concern and contrition. He leant in and took her arm, attempting to assist her out of the car. Josie shook his hand away. She didn't need his help. She didn't need anything from him. Not anymore.

Sam watched Josie go upstairs. She wouldn't talk to him. Wouldn't look at him. Didn't even want to be in the same room as him.

He rubbed the heels of his hands into his eyes in an attempt to eradicate the grittiness. He felt like shit. And thanks to Annie's endless dictating and putting him in a constant red-alert state over access to his daughter, his private relationship was now shit too. Could it be salvaged? Could he possibly persuade Josie to forgive him? To put this all behind them? The ringing of the telephone interrupted his thoughts. He went through to the kitchen.

'Hello?'

'It's me,' said Annie. 'Are you going to be a proper parent and see your daughter tomorrow?'

'I would love to see Ruby on Sunday. But I can't.'

'Still not putting her first?' Annie sneered. 'You should be ashamed of yourself, Sam. Well at least when I'm married to Nigel my daughter will have a man who will be there for her all the time.'

'You're getting married?'

'Yes, Sam. Married. And Nigel will be more of a father to Ruby than you've ever been.'

Sam closed his eyes. The thought of another man having the privilege and pleasure of seeing Ruby every day filled him with both despair and jealousy. 'Congratulations Annie. I hope you'll both be very happy. And tell Nigel to look after every precious hair on my daughter's head.'

'Are you threatening my fiancé? If so I'll have the police on you and issue a Restraining Order. Do you understand?'

'Good-bye Annie.'

'Don't you dare hang up on me!'

'I'll see Ruby next weekend.'

'No you won't. We're going house shopping and we want her with us. You had your opportunity for access this weekend, but you chose not to take it. You'll just have to wait another two weeks.'

'Great. So in effect, by that point, I won't have properly seen my daughter for three weeks. That's not very kind, Annie.'

'Your fault, Sam. It always has been.' And with that Annie hung up.

Sam stared at the quietly whirring handset. The woman could never let up on point scoring. Right down to who hung up first. Quietly, he replaced the handset. Sam felt beyond miserable that he had to wait another two weeks before he could see Ruby. But what was making him even more depressed was the thought of Josie leaving him and never seeing her again. He couldn't get through the rest of his life without her by his side. He just couldn't. Nor did he want to. It was time to change things around. Prove to Josie that he could be depended on. All the time. Starting right now.

Sam hurried across the kitchen and into the hall. He grabbed the banister rail and took the stairs two at a time.

Chapter Thirty-Two
A few months later

Josie was flat on her back, staring at one of the bluest skies she'd ever seen. Her fingers trailed in warm water. Bliss. She closed her eyes and let a Jamaican sun kiss her body. Seconds later she was flailing about. Josie surfaced and spat out chlorinated water.

'You sod!' she spluttered at Sam.

'That's not a very nice thing to call your new husband,' Sam laughed and grabbed the lilo that Josie had toppled from. 'Sorry, couldn't resist. Here, let me give you a leg-up and you can climb back on.'

Josie flicked back a sheet of wet hair and wiped her eyes. 'No thanks. I was thinking about getting a banana daiquiri anyway. All this honeymooning is thirsty work.'

'It is indeed, Mrs Worthington,' Sam grabbed her playfully, drew her to him and kissed her on the nose. 'Do you realise you are the sexiest woman on this island.'

Josie laughed. 'Silly.' She leaned in and kissed him on the mouth.

'It's true. In fact, it's a good thing I'm in this swimming pool with a lilo covering my modesty because you're having an embarrassing effect on me in a public place.'

'Disgraceful,' Josie pulled back and waggled a finger in Sam's face. 'And I'm sorry to leave you alone with your...er...embarrassment, but I really can't wait another second for my daiquiri.' Josie swam the short distance to the side of the swimming pool and hauled herself out.

'Get one for me!' Sam called after her.

He watched his new wife, slim, long legged and tanned, as she strode off to the poolside bar for refreshment. Josie looked so relaxed and happy. Thank God. He just wanted to make everything up to her. Love her forever. Without stresses or upsets or interference by his ex-wife. He just wanted peace. They both did. And it seemed as though, finally, they had it.

Annie was engaged to Nigel, and whilst she was still uncivil at every given opportunity, at least access difficulties had reduced somewhat. Ruby, whilst always quiet on her visits, did at least seem to enjoy participating in family activities and playing with Lucy.

Sam had had a tough time winning Josie back. Trying to convince her that he would never let Annie control or dictate to him again, had required a lot of spade work. But at the end of the day, they'd both agreed they still loved each other, and that if there was love, then there was something to build upon. Josie certainly hadn't wanted Lucy to suffer the devastating effect of a split, nor had Sam wanted another relationship breakdown affecting Ruby. Both kids had had enough to cope with in their short lives so far. Gradually, bit by bit, Josie had forgiven Sam over the baby business. Sam had even asked her if she wanted to try for a baby, but Josie had been adamant about focussing their energies on their daughters, and unless they happened to have another *accident*, then becoming parents again was not on the agenda. Sam hadn't wasted a moment in getting married either. Once Josie's engagement ring had been back on her finger, he'd wanted to prove to her once and for all that he was right by her side. To be her husband. And, by God, her rock.

The wedding had been beautiful. A small, very personal affair with only immediate family. Annie had initially kicked up and refused to co-operate about Ruby being a bridesmaid, but Sam had stood up to her. 'Fine,' he'd said. 'So if my daughter isn't allowed to dress up in a pretty frock for my day, you'll have no problem with my opposing her dressing up on *your* big day?'

'Oh go fuck yourself, Sam,' Annie had said. But she hadn't objected again, and the wedding had gone ahead without a hitch. Sam just hoped that Annie's own wedding would happen very soon. A small part of him felt as though he were still walking a tightrope of tension every time Annie opened the door to him on access days. But other than giving him looks that would curdle milk, an uneasy sort of truce prevailed.

Sam swam to the water's edge and climbed out. Dripping, he went to join Josie. He loved his wife. Deeply. The two of them had endured testing times, but survived. The last six months had been about rediscovery, reconnection, fresh promises and new starts. And long may it last.

Chapter Thirty-Three
Six years later

Annie sat in her office at The Pilkington Medical Practice. She stared at the computer screen before her, but was unable to concentrate. She'd not long come off the phone to her estate agent who had advised the market to be sluggish, but he was doing his best for her. Huh! She hadn't had a viewing in nearly three weeks. Ludicrous!

Annie twiddled the engagement ring on her finger. She'd been wearing it for six years and there was still no sign of the wedding band to go with it. To say she was pissed off was an understatement. In the last few years she'd watched Sam marry his trollop and seemingly travel down the road of Happy Ever After. Well it was high time she had some of that. Either that, or put a stop to Sam's happiness. She'd already laid down provisional plans in that area pending the outcome on her own grand strategy. Meanwhile Nigel had remained adamant that he wasn't marrying Annie until both their houses were sold and they'd found a joint property together for their fresh start.

'But the ruddy conveyancing chains keep breaking,' Annie had ranted. 'How the heck are we ever going to achieve this move when we can't get a synchronised exchange of contracts?'

Sometimes Annie felt their buying a house together was jinxed. Six years ago she'd accepted an offer on her house by a pair of young professionals. Nigel's property, being much bigger and more expensive, wasn't so quick to shift. A recession had bitten and property prices had nose-dived, but Nigel was flatly refusing to drop below a certain price.

'I'm not *giving* my house away,' he'd protested, 'so stop ranting and raving. Sooner or later it will happen.'

By the time Nigel had a buyer, the young professional couple who'd wanted Annie's house had grown impatient and withdrawn their offer. And then, just as Annie had found another buyer, the couple who'd wanted Nigel's house had split up. This set the pace for the next two years until Annie, ready to tear her hair out in frustration, had announced she would sell her house to the next buyer irrespective of Nigel having a purchaser, and move in with him.

'No.' Nigel had been adamant. 'In my house the boys and I have our own space. It just wouldn't work having you and Ruby on a full-time basis. We need a bigger property for us all to be living in together.'

'Well in that case I'll move into rented accommodation while you await a purchaser. At least that way we'll only have one house in the property chain.'

'Don't be ridiculous,' Nigel had raised his voice. 'If you step off the property ladder, you'll pay an astronomical amount of rent in contrast to the small mortgage payments you currently make. Renting would be like flushing money down the toilet.'

And then – hurrah! They had found a property *and* had two complete chains on their own houses. For the next three weeks Annie had been beside herself with excitement. Until they were gazumped on the property they were after. Annie had marched round to the vendor's house and cursed him from here to eternity.

It didn't help that their search radius was within such a small area. Annie was all for packing up, yanking Ruby out of school and moving to the coast, but Nigel was having none of it.

'What about Sam seeing Ruby?'

'What about Sam seeing Ruby! He's got a car. He can still drive to wherever and pick her up.'

Nigel had frowned. 'That's not very fair.'

'Oh so what,' Annie had grumbled. In front of Nigel she had to be careful regarding treatment of Sam. Nigel wasn't up for Annie dissing her ex-husband, especially as she'd been the one to leave Sam and Nigel had effectively been *the other man*.

'Apart from anything else,' said Nigel, 'my sons won't come and visit me if I'm living somewhere like Brighton or Eastbourne. Their mates are here. Their school is here. And so is Ruby's. You're also forgetting that my work is here – as is yours.'

'So we join another practice,' Annie had rolled her eyes. 'Believe it or not, Nigel, there are doctors' surgeries all over the UK.'

'No, Annie.' Nigel had been resolute. 'When we move, we stay in the borough. Patience. It will happen eventually.'

But it hadn't happened. And Annie was starting to despair it ever would. Six years ago they'd coveted a large family home. But quite frankly such a big house was starting to raise question marks to Annie. Ruby was now fourteen years old. Nigel's boys were fourteen and seventeen. Ben was studying for A Levels. Another year and he'd be off to university and living in the Halls of Residence. No, it simply wasn't on. Nigel had told Annie to be tolerant. Well she had. For six long years. Tonight Nigel was coming over. He was staying the whole weekend. Annie decided that as soon as Sam had collected Ruby tomorrow morning, she would have it out with Nigel. She wanted marriage and the two of them living together. And she didn't give a toss about whether they had a new family home. At the end of the day, if you loved somebody, you wanted to be with them all the time. Nigel professed he loved her. Well he could jolly well start proving it. Enough was enough.

Ruby jumped off the bus and began the short walk home. She fished in her blazer pocket for her house key. She'd been a *latch key kid* ever since starting secondary school. But that was fine by her. Most of her classmates were in the same boat as her due to having both parents working. A few other kids, like Lucy, still had Mummy ferrying them to and fro. Although in Lucy's case it was because she'd passed her Eleven Plus and gone to the local grammar where Josie, having long since qualified as a teacher, now taught.

Ruby let herself into the house. She dumped her school bag and PE kit in the hall, kicked off her shoes and thumped moodily up the stairs to her bedroom. It hadn't been a good day. Her secret crush, Jackson, had jeeringly pointed out that Ruby's face resembled a Dominoes pizza. Ruby stood before the full-length mirror in her bedroom and scowled at her reflection. Angry red lumps smattered across her otherwise chalk white complexion. Sometimes the lumps developed pus and Ruby would squeeze them, splattering muck across the mirror, leaving her skin an oozing mess that threatened to scar. She already had two craters on her chin. She'd tried every spot treatment on the supermarket shelves, all to no avail.

'I want antibiotics,' she'd demanded to her mother.

'Don't be ridiculous. You'll outgrow a few spots.'

'It's making my life a misery.'

'*You're* making *my* life a misery,' her mother had snapped back, 'so shut up or I'll ground you.'

Ruby had flounced off to her bedroom banging the door after her. There wasn't a day that didn't pass without her door slamming.

Ruby turned this way and that in front of the mirror, passing a critical eye over herself. Long hair hung like unwashed curtains around her face, which was another cause of angst. She washed her hair every morning before school, but by the end of the day it was greasy again. Her figure was good though. Almost overnight she'd sprouted a generous bosom which was accentuated by a tiny waist. Jackson had once pressed Ruby up against the corridor wall at break time. Ruby had felt a frisson of fear and excitement.

'Shame about the face, babe,' he'd mocked, 'because you have a hot bod.'

And then he'd laughed and swaggered off, hands stuffed in pockets, leaving Ruby in a confused state about whether she'd been complimented or insulted. At night Ruby dreamt about Jackson pushing her up against the corridor wall again, but this time snogging her. She wondered what it would be like to have him kiss her. His big mouth on her lips. Those dark brown eyes gazing into hers. She longed to touch his dark springy hair. Her mother would go ballistic if she knew Ruby was hankering after a black boy.

'I don't agree with mixed marriages,' Annie had once commented, after observing a white man and a black woman pushing a buggy down the road with a mixed-race child.

'Why?' Ruby had asked.

'It causes problems.'

'What problems?'

'It just does, Ruby. Don't you ever bring a black boy home.'

'So what if I do?' Ruby had glared at her mother. 'It's *my* life.'

'Don't answer me back or I'll ground you.'

'Oh that's great isn't it,' Ruby had snarled, 'my mother is a racist.'

'No I'm not, and don't answer me back. Go to your room.'

'Don't worry,' Ruby had spun on her heel, 'I'm going.'

Seconds later the house had shook to its foundations as Ruby's bedroom door had executed its familiar slam.

Ruby stripped off her uniform and dumped it on the floor. She'd hang it up later – two minutes before her mother came home. She opened her wardrobe door and selected a pair of jeans and a loose top, then slumped down on the bed with her laptop. Homework could wait. Right now it was far more important to get on Facebook and Twitter. She wanted to check out some classmates – see which bitch was slagging off what tart for going out with which bad boy and behaving like a slapper. Sex was a hot topic amongst her girlfriends. Daisy Pritchard had already done it and said it was so painful she never wanted to do it again. Emily Clark had also done it and said it was great and she couldn't get enough of it. This had come to Jackson's attention who had recently been circling Emily like a bird of prey. Ruby was beside herself with jealousy. She wanted to lose her virginity and more than anything to Jackson.

Downstairs there was the sound of the front door opening and closing. Ruby jumped. Bugger. Where had the last hour gone?

'Ruby?' Annie yelled from the hallway. 'Put your school stuff away – now! Nigel will be around soon and I don't want him seeing this place in a tip.'

Ruby exhaled in annoyance. Bugger Nigel. She couldn't stand the guy. Arrogant bloody doctor swanning about like he was God's gift to women just because he accessorised his suit tie with a stethoscope. And what was he doing coming over tonight? Usually Nigel stayed over when she was at her Dad's, so that she didn't have to listen to her mother and Nigel grunting and groaning as they had dinosaur sex.

Ruby shut her laptop and slid off the bed. 'Coming.'

Downstairs in the kitchen Annie was emptying the tumble drier from an earlier cycle. 'Here,' she thrust a pile of towels, socks and pants at Ruby, 'put them away for me while I start getting a meal together.'

Ruby chucked the towels in the airing cupboard, dumped half the underwear on her bed, then went into her mother's room. She'd better put her mother's stuff away neatly or else she'd never hear the end of it. Ruby tugged at the handles on the chest of drawers. And then she froze. She'd not seen that before. Inside the drawer was a large A4 notepad headed *My Years of Hell with Sam Worthington*. Neatly, Ruby layered her mother's underwear within the drawer's depths. But not before pocketing the pad.

Chapter Thirty-Four

Dear Ruby. I hope you never read this. But in case anything happens to me, I don't want you living with your father. Live with your Nan. She'll look after you. Properly. Unlike your father, who quite frankly isn't fit to raise a dog. I know you've had moments of sadness about not having your dad living with us. All those drawings you used to leave around – 'Mummy, Daddy and Ruby'. Remember? And your letters to Father Christmas. 'Dear Daddy Christmas, please can you get back with Mummy and make me the happiest girl in the world.' There are things you need to know about your dad, Ruby, like why we split up. Let me start at the beginning.

'Ruby?' Annie called up the stairs. 'Dinner's ready. And you haven't said hello to Nigel. Come down now please.'

Ruby slid the notepad under her pillow. 'Can I have dinner in my room?'

'No.'

Ruby scowled. Heaving herself off her bed, she drooped across her bedroom, along the landing and down the stairs. Nigel was already seated at the dinner table, tie loosened.

'Hi, Roobs. Good day at school?'

Ruby shrugged. She wished Nigel wouldn't call her *Roobs* or ask about her day. His interest sounded so fake. She resisted the urge to retort, 'Hi, Niggle. Killed any patients today?' Instead she pulled out a chair and slumped down opposite him.

'I've seen a lovely wedding dress for sale,' said Annie as she set plates before them. 'I thought it might be nice to take a trip into town tomorrow and try it on.'

'If you like,' Nigel shrugged. 'Although it's a bit pointless buying anything until we've sorted out the house business.'

'I've been thinking about that,' said Annie picking up her knife and fork. To hell with waiting to talk to Nigel about this until tomorrow. 'I think we need to review the type of house we need. Ben will be off to uni in the not-so-distant future. Aiden is only visiting at weekends. Ruby is the one who is a full-time occupier. Quite frankly the type of house we needed six years ago is no longer relevant. The goal posts have changed.'

Nigel put his fork down. 'So what sort of house are you proposing?'

'Well, in all honesty, what's wrong with yours?'

Nigel sighed. 'Annie, I've already told you, we all have our own areas. There isn't room for you and Ruby at my place on a permanent basis.'

'What you really mean is that you don't want us invading your space.'

'Well, I wouldn't have worded it quite like that, but in essence yes! The boys have their own rooms, and I think that's important.'

'But they're not there half the time!'

'That's not the point. For their emotional security it's key for them to know they have their own bolthole. Just as Ruby should have her own sanctuary too. Kids need it. Eh, Roobs?'

Ruby pulled a face by way of answer. As far as she was concerned, she had her own space. It was here. In *this* house thank you very much.

'If Aiden and Ben doubled up, Ruby *would* have her own space.'

'But then Aiden and Ben wouldn't have theirs.'

'Course they would! When Ben is at uni, Aiden will have *space* all to himself.'

'That's another year away. I'm not compromising the boys.' Nigel picked up his fork again. 'Sorry, Annie, but the answer is no.'

'I've had enough of this. We've been engaged for six years. At this rate I'm going to be the oldest bride in history.'

'Now you're being a Drama Queen.'

'If you loved me, you'd want to be with me all the time.'

'Shall we discuss this when we're on our own?'

'No. I want to talk about it now. And it's not a problem discussing it in front of Ruby. She's quite used to adult conversation.'

'That's as may be. But I'd prefer not to chat about it in front of Ruby.'

Ruby shovelled the last of her meal in her mouth and put her knife and fork together. 'You go ahead and thrash it out. I've finished my dinner and have homework to do.'

'Good. You may be excused,' said Annie before turning her attention back to Nigel. 'If you're so adamant about your boys having their own space, then I'm going to present you with Plan B.'

'Which is?'

'We go ahead and get married. You live with me and Ruby during the week, but go back to your place on the weekends when the boys are with you.' Annie was quite pleased with this suggestion. It meant she wouldn't have to suffer Aiden and Ben at all.

'Well, okay. That's quite a sensible idea,' Nigel ticked off pointers on his fingers as he spoke, 'because we won't be wasting money, won't be stepping off the property ladder, won't be–'

Ruby left them to it. She wasn't interested in who lived where or how long for, so long as Nigel's moving in didn't mess up her life, or stop her being able to hop on a bus to see friends, or be within striking distance of the main town for shopping, or go to the cinema, or take a trip to Mackey-D's when the whim took her.

Shutting the door of her bedroom, Ruby retrieved the notepad from under her pillow. To hell with homework. This was far more interesting.

When I first met your dad, I was naive and swept away by his good looks. I didn't take the time to examine the inside of the packaging, instead letting myself become enthralled with the outer layer. Never make the same mistake, Ruby. Always get to know the young man of your dreams. A man who looks like God's gift to a woman is rarely anything but – as I eventually found out.

Your dad was clever. He kept his dark side hidden. All his mates were hooked up with girlfriends, and your dad didn't want to feel left out. He pursued me relentlessly until I agreed to be his girl. When his pals had moved their girlfriends in with them, your dad wanted me to do the same thing. So I agreed. I'd barely unpacked my suitcases when he was insisting we get engaged – just like his friends who almost overnight had suddenly obtained fiancées. After much persuasion, I accepted your father's proposal of marriage. I was expecting a long engagement, but your dad had other ideas. He was in a huge hurry to march me down the aisle and make me truly his.

We'd barely settled down to married life when more pressure followed. He wanted a baby – and right now! I was hoping we'd have two or three years of married life together before giving in to sleepless nights and dirty nappies, but when I suggested this I was met with endless sulking. He would hardly speak to me unless we were out shopping, where I'd find myself being marched into Mothercare to check out the price of a pushchair or cot. He'd hold up little outfits in blue and say, 'Can't you just imagine our little prince wearing this?'

By this point I should have realised I'd married a bully, but the optimistic part of me thought he'd change. Wrong! His mate Stu was the first to announce he was going to be a father. Within weeks all the other lads were buying rounds of drinks and puffing on celebratory cigars. All but your dad. Being with him at this point was a living nightmare. Eventually I gave in to the pressure. By doing this I thought he'd finally cheer up and stop giving me such a hard time. Wrong again! Every month, when my period came, he'd moan and complain. He kept having a go at me, as if it was my fault I wasn't pregnant. 'What's wrong with you Annie?' he'd cry. 'Are you barren?' Such cruel remarks. He even sent me off to a gynaecologist to see if my fallopian tubes needed blowing. The consultant was really cross and told him to be patient. I left the surgery in tears.

And then, just when I thought I couldn't take another month of being subjected to black looks and complaints, I was pregnant! I was overjoyed, as was your dad. The following six weeks were harmonious and peaceful. Until the morning sickness kicked in. I had a difficult pregnancy Ruby. My back hurt. My legs ached. I was tremendously tired, and constantly nauseous. Was your dad supportive? No.

I'd barely reached the second month of pregnancy when your dad refused to share the same bed as me. He would look at my little bump, shake his head and declare my changing figure repulsive. I can't tell you how much this upset me. My self-esteem plummeted to zero. At weekends your father would disappear for hours on end. He said he was playing football with the lads and then going out for a beer and a curry *afterwards. Sometimes he'd opt to stay the night at Stu's – or so he said anyway. I never questioned it. Despite the emotional bullying, black moods and lack of intimacy, I trusted him. Foolishly as it transpired.*

One day, by now heavily pregnant, I was struggling to bend down and load the washing machine. I always checked pockets for tissues or loose change. That day was no exception. I can remember checking the front pocket of one of your dad's shirts. My fingers poked inside the fabric. There was a rustling sound as I touched a piece of paper. I pulled the paper out and stared at it in shock. It had a woman's name on it followed by a phone number. I began to shake. Trembling violently, I rang the number. And that was when my world fell apart. Your father was having an affair.

Ruby stared at the diary in shock. She couldn't take any of this in. Dad had behaved like this to Mum? No wonder her mother never had a good word to say about him. Was it any surprise she was always so disparaging of Dad? The bastard! The bloody bastard! How *dare* he have treated her mother like a piece of shit and–

'Ruby?' Annie's voice floated up the stairs. 'Have you done your homework?'

Ruby slid the diary under her pillow. 'Nearly finished,' she called out. She rolled off her bed and pulled out the chair by her desk. She'd better make a half-hearted effort to get History out the way.

'Well hurry up, and then have your shower.'

'Yes, Mum.' God her mother was so annoying. She wished she'd stop treating her like a little kid all the time. Still, she wouldn't be here at the weekend. She'd be with her father, step-mother and step-sister. Whoopee-do. Not. Ruby was fed up with Lucy's company. Or rather, lack of company. These days Miss Swot could barely stop for a decent conversation lest her grade results slip from A* to B. But then again, it wasn't entirely Lucy's fault. When it came to education, Josie was so up herself she'd lost sight of her own arsehole.

A few hours later Ruby was tucked up in bed. Mum had been in to kiss her goodnight ages ago. But sleep had evaded Ruby. She'd lain awake staring at the ceiling, thinking about the contents of her mother's diary, and what she'd read so far. Her poor mum. Ruby felt so sorry for her. She'd had such a rotten life. First a selfish and mentally abusive husband. Then divorce. Finally she'd had to bring up a child on her own. And she wasn't having any better luck with the doctor. What sort of man refused to let you live in his house? What sort of man put a ring on your finger but didn't follow it up with a wedding? For six years her mother had been wearing that ring – almost half Ruby's life. Ridiculous! The doctor was nothing but a time wasting berk.

Ruby could now hear her mother and Nigel in the room next door. Low voices. The occasional giggle by her mother. And then silence. She wondered if they were kissing. Bleurgh! Ruby sat up, plumped her pillow with balled fists, and then flopped back down again. She wasn't aware of nodding off. The moment between wakefulness and sleep had blended seamlessly.

Ruby was floating over the earth. Far below, something caught her eye. She set her intention at it and zoomed down, down, down. Now she was hovering over a rooftop. And then the very roof tiles seemed to be sucking at her formless body, until she was finally consumed, absorbed by rafters and loft space and spat out into a living room below. Ruby was invisible to the man and woman before her. They were clearly in the middle of a big row. The woman was heavily pregnant and cowering, and the man was berating the woman for being fat and repulsive. With a sudden sense of shock, Ruby realised she was looking at her mother and father, and that the woman's swollen stomach housed the body that would become Ruby.

Ruby felt a sudden sense of panic. She didn't want the man to be her father. He was horrible. And now he was raising an arm to the woman. And the woman was letting out a scream. A horrible, unearthly wailing. Ruby tried to block her ears, but she had no arms to do so. Instead she was being lifted out of the scenario before her at such an almighty speed she could hardly breathe. Her heart was galloping at a zillion miles per hour as she hurtled through space. Ruby came to the conclusion that she'd fallen into a black hole and would surely fall forever. But suddenly, from nowhere, a huge wall sprang up. It was so vast it stretched to infinity in both directions. Was this the end of the universe? Ruby braced herself for impact. A second later she experienced a sensation of crashing into her mattress and jolted wide awake. Oh my God. A nightmare. She sat up gasping for breath, heart racing. She wanted Mum – and right now.

Tossing back the duvet, Ruby leapt out of bed and fled the short distance from her room to her mother's.

'Mum!' Ruby cried as she dived into her mother's bed.

'Oof,' came a man's voice.

Shit. Nigel.

'Wassup?' said Annie groggily. She flicked the bedside light on. For a moment everybody squinted.

'I've had a nightmare,' Ruby gasped, 'it was awful...terrifying...oh, Mum!' And with that she promptly burst into tears.

'For God's sake, Ruby,' Nigel shoved her sideways, 'get out of the bed!'

'Don't do that to her,' Annie scolded.

'Well she's a bit bloody big to get into bed with us,' Nigel protested.

'I can't sleep on my own, Mum,' Ruby bleated. 'Don't make me go back to my bed.'

'Don't be ridiculous, Ruby, you're fourteen years old,' Nigel snapped.

'Don't speak to my daughter like that,' Annie growled. 'Get out of my bed, Nigel.'

'What?'

'You heard. Get in Ruby's bed. Let her sleep with me.'

'Are you joking?'

'I want my Mum,' Ruby howled. She didn't care that she was behaving like a three-year-old. She wanted this man out of her mother's bed. Preferably out of the house.

'Oh for God's sake,' Nigel huffed as he flung back the bed covers.

'Pants!' Annie yelled.

'Fucking hell!' Nigel swore as realisation dawned.

Ruby had a fleeting vision of one white buttock and a shrivelled up sausage before Nigel sank to the floor, groping for his underwear. Ruby stopped bawling and curled her lip at Nigel. How pukey. Although to be fair, when he stood up again Nigel's own expression wasn't far off mirroring Ruby's. He stomped off to Ruby's bedroom muttering under his breath. Seconds later her door banged shut.

Annie flopped back down on her pillows. 'Lay down, love,' she said to Ruby.

'I can't sleep.'

'Course you can.'

'Don't marry Nigel, Mum.'

'What?'

'I said don't–'

'I heard what you said. Why? Why are you saying that?'

'I don't like him.'

'Don't be bloody daft!'

'I don't.'

'Why?'

'I just don't. I want it to be us, Mum. You and me. I don't want Nigel and Aiden and Ben in our lives. And I don't want Dad and Josie and Lucy either.'

There was a resounding silence. Annie wasn't particularly chuffed by Ruby's suggestion of eliminating Nigel, Aiden and Ben from their lives. But it was music to her ears to hear that Ruby didn't want to be with her dad, his trollop and the trollop's daughter.

'What's brought all this on?' Annie said eventually. When she didn't get an answer, she turned to look at Ruby. But her daughter's eyelids were closed, lashes fanning her pale cheeks. Sighing, Annie flipped off the bedside light.

Chapter Thirty-Five

Ruby climbed into the passenger seat of her father's car.

'Morning,' Sam grinned, 'how's my princess?'

Ruby shrugged by way of answer.

'What's up?'

Ruby shrugged again.

Sam's smile faded. He cast a look back at Annie's house. His ex-wife was framed in the lounge window, watching their departure. Sam couldn't be sure, but Annie's expression looked...what was the word? Triumphant. Yes, that was it. So what was that all about? He indicated and pulled out. Perhaps Ruby would unbutton on the journey home. After a couple of minutes Sam tried again.

'So, how was school this week?'

Shrug.

'As good as that, eh!' Sam laughed. He gave Ruby a sidelong look. His daughter was staring, stony-faced, out of the passenger window. 'Can I ask you something, Ruby?'

Silence.

'Have you and your mum had a row?'

Ruby's head swivelled one hundred and eighty degrees. 'Don't be ridiculous,' she spat.

Sam was taken aback. What on earth was the matter with his daughter? 'Um, good. That's good. I just wondered. Because...well, you don't seem yourself, darling. I'm just concerned, that's all.'

Ruby gave him a murderous look before resuming staring out of the window. Sam decided to let his daughter just be for the rest of the ride home. Perhaps she had PMT. She *was* fourteen years old after all. Although he'd never discussed *women's matters* with his daughter, he was aware that Ruby had started her periods. He knew that Lucy had too, last summer. Not that he'd discussed it with Lucy either. But judging from the packs of sanitary towels that Josie now bought along with her own boxes of tampons, you didn't have to be Einstein to work it out.

Sam pulled up on the driveway just as Lucy opened the front door. She waved to Ruby and smiled. Ruby lifted one arm and gave a lethargic wave back.

'Ooooh, I love your dress,' Lucy said as Ruby walked into the hallway.

'Thanks.' Ruby followed her step-sister into the kitchen where Josie was making a picnic for later. Ruby inwardly sighed. She was fourteen. A bit long in the tooth for picnics. She'd much rather be out with her girlfriends from school. They were catching a bus into town this afternoon to see the latest Mission Impossible film. Ruby was pretty sure Jackson and his mates were going too. She had a sudden acute feeling of missing out.

'Where did you get your dress from?' Lucy was asking.

'Top Shop.'

'I wish I could wear that style.'

'What's stopping you?'

'This.' Lucy patted her tummy. 'I wish my belly was as flat as yours, and my waist as tiny.'

'There's nothing wrong with your figure, Lucy,' said Josie as she transferred a mound of sandwiches into a Tupperware.

'I'm fat.'

'Now you're being silly,' Josie tutted.

'No I'm not.' Lucy's shoulders sagged. 'How much do you weigh, Ruby?'

Ruby shrugged. 'Dunno. About seven and a half stone I think.'

'Seven and a half–?' Lucy shut up. She'd been nine stone six pounds when she'd stood on her mother's scales that morning. Dear Lord. That was pretty much two whole stones heavier than Ruby.

'You're the perfect weight for your height,' Josie assured as she transferred the Tupperware to a cooler bag. She began adding bags of crisps and a packet of chocolate Digestives. 'Remember you're a couple of inches taller than Ruby.'

'Where are we going today, Josie?' Sam picked up an apple from the fruit bowl and bit into it.

'I thought it would be nice to go to Greenwich Park,' Josie replied. 'Perhaps we can take in a boat ride on the Thames after our picnic.'

Ruby rolled her eyes. God Almighty. Josie treated her and Lucy as if they were still little kids. 'I'd rather see Mission Impossible actually.'

'Would you now?' Sam gave his daughter an amused look. 'Fancy Mr Cruise, eh!' he joked.

'I'd have to be a pervert to fancy him,' Ruby sneered. 'He's old enough to be my father.'

'Okay, keep your hair on,' Sam put a friendly arm around his daughter.

Ruby instantly shrugged Sam off. 'And stop hugging me. I'm not a kid you know.'

There was a moment of highly charged silence where everybody experienced mixed emotions. Ruby was feeling furiously angry with her father and wanted nothing to do with him. Sam felt a sting of humiliation at his public rejection. Josie was taken aback at her step-daughter's apparent anger, not to mention surprised that the previously silent Ruby with the blank expression was actually showing emotion. Lucy resisted the temptation to gawp, instead trying to ignore a feeling of envy washing over her. What she'd give to have Sam cuddle her spontaneously and playfully, instead of duty hugs that lacked warmth. Josie was the first to speak.

'Well perhaps we'll go to the cinema this evening. After dinner.'

'It will be too late then,' said Ruby moodily.

'Too late for what?' asked Lucy.

'You wouldn't understand,' Ruby muttered. All her friends would have long gone from the cinema by this evening. As would Jackson and his mates. Ruby couldn't gossip to Lucy about boys. She wasn't interested. Lucy was still happy doing kiddie stuff – peddling her bike up and down Sycamore Drive or curling up on the sofa with a book. She had yet to discover make-up, or experiment with hairstyles or even develop fashion sense. Ruby stared at Lucy's non-descript top and jeans by George. Jesus! She'd bet Josie still chose Lucy's clothes too. The only thing Ruby coveted about Lucy was her flawless complexion. Teenage spots had never troubled her, the lucky cow.

'Come on,' said Sam, desperately trying to win back his daughter's favour. 'Let's get this picnic out to the car and if you play your cards right, we'll have an ice-cream later.'

Ruby gritted her teeth and willed Saturday to quickly become Sunday. She couldn't wait to go home. Her proper home.

When Sam dropped Ruby off, Annie greeted him coldly.

'What sort of time do you call this?'

'Five o'clock,' Sam replied mildly. If Annie was in one of her moods, he wasn't going to give her any verbal ammunition.

'It's five past five, Sam. You're late.'

'I'm sorry.'

'Oh fuck off,' Annie snarled. 'You can put your apology where the sun doesn't shine.'

Ruby gave her mother a curious look. Why was she in such a foul mood?

'Bye, princess,' Sam turned to give his daughter a kiss, but Ruby had already pushed past him and was now firmly over Annie's threshold. One second later and the front door had slammed in his face. Sam gave a deep sigh. Things hadn't exactly been peachy between him and Annie over the last few years, but he'd rather hoped his ex-wife's days of picking a fight were over.

'What's the matter with you?' Ruby asked her mother.

'What's the matter with me?'

'Is there an echo in here?'

'Don't be rude or I'll ground you.'

Ruby instantly switched tactics. The last thing she needed was a ban on her freedom.

'I'm sorry. What's wrong, Mum?' Ruby caught sight of her mother's left hand. Where was her engagement ring?

Annie followed Ruby's gaze. 'Nigel and I are finished.'

'Oh don't be silly.' Ruby wandered into the kitchen in search of a snack. 'You two are always squabbling and then making up.'

Annie followed Ruby. 'Not this time.'

'Why?' Ruby peered into the fridge looking for chocolate. No doubt it would aggravate her spots, but she didn't care. Right now her sugar craving needed addressing.

'Well your comment had something to do with it.'

'Eh?'

'The other night. You said you didn't want Nigel, Ben and Aiden in our lives. That you just wanted it to be the two of us.'

'I didn't mean it. Not literally anyway.'

Annie's shoulders drooped. 'It wasn't just what you said Ruby. There were other factors too.'

'Like?'

'Like how long is a piece of string? I mean, come on. A woman with an engagement ring on her finger for six years and not even a wedding invitation in the post to anyone.'

'But I thought Nigel was going to move in with us. You were talking about *Plan B*. Wouldn't the wedding have followed on from that?'

'No. That was the last straw for me. Nigel said he didn't want to get married until you'd left home.'

'I see,' said Ruby. So the doctor hadn't cared for her after all. Never mind. The feeling had been mutual. And Ruby knew that her mother hadn't been fond of Aiden and Ben. Was that what was known as a *quid pro quo*?

'I'm sure you'll get back together in a few months.'

'No. This time it really is over.'

'Sure?'

'Oh absolutely. And after insisting we stay in this area, Nigel dropped the bombshell that he's moving to another GP practice. And in a totally different area. More money, perks, kudos. I mean, fancy not telling me about it. I was meant to be his fiancée!'

Ruby put her arms around her mother. 'His loss Mum. I think you're fab.'

For a moment Annie's eyes watered. 'Yeah. I'm fab.'

'Just you and me Mum. The way we like it.'

A few hours later and Ruby was curled up in her bed. Her heart felt heavy in her chest. Like it was full of black stuff. Depression? Anger? Hatred? Maybe a bit of everything. Ruby was livid about Nigel's treatment of her mother culminating in their split. Well fuck Nigel. If she ever bumped into him, she'd have some choice words to impart. And as for her father! Ruby pulled the notepad from under her duvet. She was starting to feel real loathing about him. The diary was giving a whole new insight into what sort of man her father really was. Ruby leafed through the pages and found the place where she'd left off.

After finding out your father was having an affair, I went into shock. The discovery of infidelity had a terrible effect on my body. Within minutes I was experiencing contractions. In all fairness to your dad, he did immediately come home from work. And for the first time in ages, your dad was all smiles.

We had chosen not to be told the sex of our baby. We wanted it to be a surprise. However, your father was convinced you were going to be a boy. 'I'm going to have a son,' he proudly told staff at the hospital, 'and he's going to be my little prince.'

The midwife helped me into a gown. I saw your dad's expression when he briefly saw me naked. His face was filled with revulsion. I'd put on five stone during my pregnancy. My ankles were so swollen from fluid retention that I could only wear flip-flops. I remember your dad looking at my ankles folding over my insteps. He looked incredulous. When the midwife momentarily left the room he turned to me and said, 'You look like a whale. You've really let yourself go, Annie.' I immediately burst into tears. When the midwife returned, she assumed I was crying from labour pain.

Your father stayed throughout the labour, but he was no help. It was the midwife who allowed me to crush her hand, the midwife who massaged my back, the midwife who gave words of encouragement. Your father sat on a chair throughout my eighteen-hour labour, occasionally rubbing his eyes, mostly yawning with boredom and periodically sleeping. Sleeping! When the most momentous event of his life was unfolding in the same room!

Finally you were born. The midwife asked your dad if he'd like to cut the umbilical cord. Your father looked like he was going to throw up. 'Absolutely not,' he told the midwife. She made no comment, but pursed her lips. I could tell she thought his refusal bang out of order. 'Congratulations,' she said, 'you have a beautiful bonny girl.' For a moment your dad couldn't speak. I thought he was deliriously happy. It transpired he was pissed off! 'A girl?' he spluttered.

I was checked over by a doctor in case I needed stitches, and then the midwife told your father to take me to the bathroom and help me shower. Your dad refused. The midwife couldn't hide her feelings anymore at your father's lack of care, consideration and support. 'Why ever not?' she snapped. 'Because I can't bear to look at her,' your father replied. The mid-wife gasped and said, 'Who? Your daughter or your wife?' 'My wife,' your father replied. Then he said, 'Sorry, but I'm knackered. I'm going home for some sleep.' And with that he upped and left. Just like that! He hadn't even held you, Ruby. I was so embarrassed at his behaviour in front of the midwife. I burst into tears again. For the next few weeks I spent every waking moment crying.

I made a huge effort to shed my baby weight in a bid to win back your father's affection. This included dieting and gentle exercise. One day I was standing in front of the mirror trying on a pale pink dress that I hadn't been able to wear for ages. It slithered over my head and, although it was a bit tight, it fitted! I was overjoyed – really chuffed that the calorie counting was paying off. At that moment your dad walked into the bedroom. He caught sight of me looking at myself in front of the mirror and began to make pig noises. Snorting and snuffling. The sounds pigs might make when at a feeding trough. Yet again I was reduced to tears.

Eventually my GP put me on anti-depressants. He thought I had the baby blues. But the simple truth was this: I was stuck in a marriage with a cold husband who mentally abused me.

Your father didn't support me financially. He insisted we divide the bills and mortgage between us, despite him earning a tidy income. You will never find a poor dentist, Ruby, but your father kept me penniless. Three months after your birth, I had no choice but to return to work. Your grandmother was a Godsend. She looked after you while I ran The Pilkington Medical Practice. You were the one light in my miserable life Ruby. You were my reason for living.

And then a new doctor joined the practice. He saw how sad I was. How lonely and unloved. I was so vulnerable Ruby – like a *parched flower suddenly being given water. And just when I was least prepared, the doctor swept me right off my feet. His name was Nigel.*

And what a bloody let down he'd turned out to be. Ruby put down the pad. She couldn't do anything about Nigel. He was gone. But she could do plenty about her father. He had to pay for what he'd done to her mother. And Ruby would see that he did.

Chapter Thirty-Six

Sam struggled to understand why his relationship with Ruby was disintegrating. Nor did he know how to stop it, other than to keep telling his daughter how much he loved her – usually when speaking on the telephone. This was because these days Ruby rarely visited 2 Sycamore Drive. She trotted out one excuse after another in order to absent herself. Reasons to stay away included flu, an asthma attack and wanting to be near Mum, a special aunt's birthday, and finally a friend sleeping over.

'No problem,' Sam had said upon hearing the latest pretext. 'I'll pick you up Sunday morning when your friend has gone home.'

'No, Dad,' Ruby had said. 'We'll be going shopping.'

Then there had been excuses about exam revision. Sam had been disappointed at Ruby's next spate of absence, but pleased his daughter at least had her head down. So it had come as a shock when she flunked all her exams. On the odd occasion Ruby did deign to come over, she was frosty to Sam and distant with Josie and Lucy. Sam began to despair.

'She's growing up,' Josie had soothed. 'Give her a bit of space.'

'But I never see her,' Sam had said. 'I miss my daughter. You don't understand, Josie. You see Lucy all the time. I don't have that luxury with Ruby. I feel as if this huge chasm has opened up between us, but for the life of me I don't know why.'

'It's just her age. She's a teenager.'

'She treats me so coldly.'

'I'm sure it's just a phase that will pass.'

But it didn't. More weeks went by. The annual summer holiday loomed.

Annie telephoned. 'Ruby doesn't want to go to Spain with you this year.'

'Why ever not?'

'She doesn't have to give a reason, Sam. You're like some fusty headmaster demanding an excuse note.'

Sam took a deep breath, aware that he needed to keep calm and not antagonise Annie. 'Look, I'm sorry. I didn't mean to act that way. It's just that things haven't been good between Ruby and me for, well, a little while now. And I have no idea why.'

'Of course you don't. That's because you have a sensitivity chip missing.'

Sam ignored Annie's attempt to bait him. 'I would really appreciate having a fortnight with Ruby and getting things back on track between us – a bit of bonding.'

'Bit late for that.'

'What the devil is it that I'm meant to have done?'

'Such a short memory, Sam.'

'What the heck's that meant to mean?'

'I'm bored with this conversation. Bottom line – Ruby's not coming on holiday with you. And don't go quoting your Court Order at me about your rights, because you're no longer dealing with a child who has to bend to your will. In case you hadn't noticed, Ruby is a young woman. She's perfectly able to stand up in Court and speak for herself. She'll tell the judge that going away with you for a fortnight is not top of her list. It's not even bottom of her list. It's a total non-event.' And with that Annie hung up.

Sam immediately tried calling Ruby on her mobile, but his call went to voicemail. Despairing, he sent a text. *Hi, Princess. Your mum said you're not keen to come away with us. I'd really love for you to join us. I've had an idea. What about you choose where we go? Anywhere you fancy...no expense spared. I want us to have a really great summer holiday together. Miss you and love you loads, Dad xx*

Sam's text went unanswered.

'When are we going to book the holiday?' Josie asked a few days later. She was standing at the ironing board, steadfastly working her way through a backlog of creased clothing while Sam peered inside the fridge looking for a snack. Outside it was raining so hard it sounded like buckets of gravel were being chucked at the window panes. Josie couldn't wait to exchange dreary England for a golden beach.

'We're not.' Sam reversed out of the fridge with a selection of cheeses before rootling through the larder for crackers.

'Pardon?'

'We're not going on holiday this year.'

Josie put the iron down and stared at Sam. 'Why not?'

'Because Ruby doesn't want to come.'

'Okay,' Josie said carefully, 'I'm sorry Ruby's opting out. But why do the rest of us have to forfeit our holiday?'

'Because it wouldn't be right to go without my daughter.'

'Why ever not?'

'Because one member of the family will be missing,' Sam said through gritted teeth, 'and I'm not going without her.'

'Don't you think you're over-reacting?'

'Will you drop the subject please, Josie. I don't wish to talk about it. There will be no holiday this year.'

'But that's not fair on Lucy and me!'

Sam instantly abandoned his cheese and crackers and stalked out of the kitchen. Despite numerous attempts to reason with Sam over the ensuing days, he remained adamant. Josie had been furious. Lucy had been gutted. Lucy had even resorted to unashamed pleading with Sam, but he was having none of it. The atmosphere at 2 Sycamore Drive became so tense you could practically cut the air with a knife. Finally Josie assured Lucy that they'd have fun on an English beach and enjoy days out in places like Whitstable and Brighton. But in fact Britain had the wettest summer on record that year, and trips to the beach didn't happen. Even outings to the park were iffy.

On the rare weekends Ruby did visit, she treated Sam as if he was a piece of dog turd on her shoe. He continued trying to reason with her but it was like talking to a wall. Ruby simply stared at him, silent and aloof. On one occasion Sam became emotional at Ruby's lack of love and warmth. Ruby had been horrified by Sam's welling eyes, and instantly demanded to be taken home to her mother. Upon arriving at Annie's, Ruby's own waterworks began to flow.

'What the fuck have you done to her?' Annie snarled.

'Nothing!' Sam attempted to placate both mother and daughter.

'I'll tell you why she's upset,' Annie prodded Sam in the chest. 'It's because you're a crap father.'

'Well tell me how I can make it up to her!' Sam howled. 'I want to be a good father. I *am* a good father.'

'You don't know the first thing about it, Sam,' Annie spat before slamming the front door in his face.

A lengthy period went by where Ruby again stayed away. She finally agreed to see Sam, but only after he'd virtually harassed his daughter for a piece of her time.

'Let's have a coffee together,' Sam suggested.

'I have a lot of essays to write.'

'Just for an hour.'

Ruby huffed and puffed but finally relented. 'Okay,' she agreed reluctantly.

In Costa's, they sat opposite each other in a window seat. 'Ruby,' Sam began, 'you're my precious daughter, and I can't tell you how much I love you. Something's gone wrong between us, but I don't know what it is. Please talk to me. If I've done something wrong, tell me.'

Ruby's eyes flashed. Done something wrong! Was her father really so thick-skinned? She couldn't be bothered to articulate the disgust she felt for him. He wasn't worthy of her taking the time and effort to do so. So she simply stared at him. Contemptuously.

Sam allowed frustration to get to him. He began to get annoyed. And then angry. 'Your behaviour is out of order, young lady. I haven't brought you up to behave like this.'

Suddenly Ruby was unable to contain herself. 'Come again? You haven't brought me up, Dad! It's my mum who's done that – and absolutely no thanks to you.'

'What are you talking about?' Sam cried. 'Of course I've had a hand in your upbringing!'

'I've had enough of this conversation.' Ruby stood up. 'Take me home please.'

'No! Look, Ruby,' Sam raked his hair, aware of people staring, 'sit back down. Can we just talk please – civilly?'

'I don't want to talk to you.' Ruby remained standing, shrugging herself into her coat and then picking up her little handbag.

'How can I put things right if you don't tell me what I've done wrong?'

'You really are unbelievable. And forget taking me home, I'll get the bus.'

'No! Ruby, please – come back here!'

But Ruby had gone. Sam charged after her, but his daughter had disappeared within the crowded shopping mall. He stared this way and that, turning three hundred and sixty degrees as he sought his daughter's head bobbing amongst the throng of shoppers.

Summer rolled into autumn and finally winter. Months passed. Ruby turned fifteen but Sam didn't even have the pleasure of seeing his daughter on her birthday. He transferred two hundred pounds into Ruby's bank account, but didn't receive any acknowledgement. The relationship breakdown took its toll on Sam. He sank into a deep depression. Josie did everything she could to jolly up her husband, but it was hard going.

'Why don't you talk to somebody?' she suggested.

'Like who?' Sam asked bleakly.

'Well,' Josie hesitated, 'a professional. You know – somebody to offload to.'

Sam's eyes narrowed. 'You mean a shrink?'

'No! I mean...well...a family mediator for example. Somebody who has experience of teenagers and everything they go through. It's hard for fifteen-year-olds Sam. Ruby's probably got a lot on her plate.'

'So why doesn't she share it with me? Why doesn't she tell me what's wrong?'

'Because...because sometimes teenagers feel they can't share things with their parents. I mean, what if it was boyfriend trouble? Ruby's hardly going to tell you about it! She'd find it embarrassing.'

'She hasn't got a boyfriend,' Sam said dismissively.

'How do you know?'

'Josie, I know you mean well. But I don't think Ruby's potential romantic life is anything to do with her contempt for me.'

'So suggest mediation to her.'

'As if Annie will agree to that!'

'This isn't about Annie. It's about Ruby. Just talk to her – gently. Plant the seed.'

'No. My daughter and I are fine. We don't need mediators to sort us out for God's sake.'

'Well you need somebody,' Josie could feel her voice going up an octave, 'because I for one am fed up with the atmosphere in this house. And quite frankly I'm getting damned resentful of Ruby.'

'How dare you,' hissed Sam.

'Sam, I love Ruby, but by golly she's causing some major problems in this family. For years we've had Annie impacting on us. Now Ruby's joined in. It's not fair, Sam.'

'I don't grumble about Lucy,' Sam began to shout, 'so don't you *dare* complain about my daughter.'

'Lucy doesn't cause problems, Sam!' Josie flung her hands up in the air. 'Quite frankly if my daughter treated me the way Ruby has treated you, I'd give her a bloody good slap!'

'Oh, so that's the answer is it? I need to beat up my child? What sort of crap advice is that?'

'Oh for God's sake, Sam, I was speaking metaphorically so *don't* manipulate my words. I'm talking about laying the law down and demanding respect, instead of being walked all over. All you do is chase after Ruby, begging and grovelling and pleading, and utterly demeaning yourself. How the hell do you expect to have any respect from the girl when you set yourself up to be trampled upon and–'

'SHUT UP!'

The two of them stared at each other. The air fairly crackled with resentment and anger. Josie stood there, eyes blazing, cheeks pink. Sam stared at his wife, his face pale and mouth set in a grim line.

Josie was the first to speak. 'Look, I'm sorry, I just–'

'I'm going out.' Sam picked up his car keys.

'Sam, don't. Come back. Please–'

The front door slammed. Seconds later Josie heard her husband's car roar into life. The engine revved hard. Then tyres squealed as he accelerated away.

'Why were you two rowing?'

Josie spun round to see Lucy standing in the doorway. For a moment she was shocked at how her daughter looked. Washed out. And very thin. Why hadn't Josie noticed this before? Well the answer was obvious. She'd been so wrapped up in Sam's well-being – the constant attempts to cheer him up, support him, nurse his depression, crack jokes to lighten the atmosphere, gabble brightly to fill dark silences and just rah-rah-rah along. And in so doing, Josie realised with a jolt that she'd completely neglected keeping an eye on her own daughter's needs.

'Have you been dieting?'

'Mum, answer my question. I heard you and Sam shouting at each other.'

'It's nothing,' Josie sighed.

'Oh for God's sake,' Lucy clutched the doorframe, 'why don't you just spit it out. It's Ruby isn't it?'

'Not really, it's just–'

'Stop trying to pretend, Mum. All I ever remember in my life is Ruby's mother causing problems. And then, just when she goes off the radar for a bit, Ruby picks up the baton and carries on with it.'

'Ruby is a teenager, Lucy. It's hard for her.'

'Yeah, and *I'm* a teenager too. Or hadn't you noticed?'

'It's different for Ruby. She's had a difficult time.'

'Eh?'

'Her mum and dad split up when she was tiny. She's been caught in the cross-fire all her life. Used by her mother as a pawn. Tugged this way and that. Fought over.'

'Well isn't Ruby the lucky one,' Lucy sneered. 'Nobody's ever fought over me. Nobody gives a *shit* about me.'

'Lucy!' Josie stared at her daughter, aghast. 'Don't speak like that. And that's simply not true.'

'Yes it is,' Lucy's eyes welled. 'You're so wrapped up in Sam all the time. And in turn he's wrapped up in chasing after his bitch of a daughter. What about ME?' Lucy jabbed a finger at her chest. 'What about the miserable life *I've* had?' Tears were rolling down her cheeks now.

'Darling, please,' Josie stumbled towards her daughter, arms open. 'Your life hasn't been miserable. I've worked so hard to give you all the things you've ever needed.' Josie went to fold her daughter into her chest. To hug her tight. But Lucy pushed her mother away.

'I'm not talking about material things,' Lucy sobbed, 'I'm talking about *emotional* things. You say Ruby's had it hard. Well haven't I? My father died when I was little. Ruby's father is still here.'

'But not living with her.'

'BUT HE'S HERE!' Lucy shrieked. Rage turned her cheeks pink. 'He's here on earth and wanting to be part of Ruby's life. My God, his focus isn't ever on anything else. Are you blind?'

'Lucy, darling, calm down. One of the reasons I married again was to give you another father.'

'Don't make me laugh!' Lucy snorted causing snot to fly out of her nose. Angrily she wiped a sleeve across her face. 'Sam's not been a father to me. Not since that holiday all those years ago. Is your memory so short? I can still remember the pain Ruby used to inflict on me – slapping me, pulling my hair, pinching me. All because I called Sam *Daddy* for...ooh...a whole five minutes.'

Josie looked stricken. 'Yes, I do remember, Lucy. Of course I remember. It was hard for all of us. Annie was causing so many problems...telling Ruby so many terrible lies. We were just trying to ease Ruby's pain.'

'AND WHAT ABOUT MY PAIN?' Lucy yelled. 'Have you ever stopped to think about the effect of everything on me over the years?'

Josie was bewildered. 'But I thought you were happy, darling. You've always appeared to be cheerful enough. I know missing out on a holiday this year got you down, but it got me down too, and Sam of course and–'

'I'M NOT TALKING ABOUT THE HOLIDAY,' Lucy screeched. She was so angry and upset she could feel herself on the verge of hyperventilating. She made herself take a couple of deep breaths. 'I'm talking about MY pain. Here!' She made a fist and beat it against her heart. 'Endless pain. Never ending pain. "Hands off Sam, Lucy",' she mimicked, '"Don't cuddle Sam, Lucy. Don't call him Daddy, Lucy." Having to make do with the occasional hug from Sam – like him patting a stray dog he's not particularly bothered about.'

'That's not–'

'Having to be grateful for the occasional kiss goodnight.'

'Sam's always–'

'NO HE HAS NOT!' Lucy bellowed. 'And you know why?' Lucy ploughed on without waiting for Josie to answer the question. 'I'll tell you why he's not always remembered to kiss me goodnight. It's because my name isn't RUBY!'

'Darling, I'm sure if you tell Sam how you feel he'll–'

'He'll what? He'll tell me not to be daft? That I'm imagining it all! I don't think so, Mum. I finally understood how little I meant to Sam when he refused to go on holiday with the two of us. I begged him. I told him I loved him and wanted us to go away all together. And do you know what he said?'

'What?' Josie asked in a small voice.

'He said we weren't a family without Ruby. Did you hear what I just said? *We are not a family without Ruby.* In other words, I'm not like a daughter to him.'

'Lucy, you've interpreted it the wrong way and–'

'No I haven't, Mum.' Lucy took a deep, shuddering breath. 'Do you know how rejected I feel? How hard it's been trying to cope, simply because I'm not the person Sam wants me to be? It hurts, Mum. It hurts so much. And do you know how much Ruby infuriates me constantly shoving away the very thing I so want to have? I love Ruby, but by God she's an ungrateful bloody cow.'

Josie shook her head. She was appalled at everything that had tumbled out of her daughter's mouth. And she felt so guilty. So awful for failing to notice her daughter's angst.

'Darling, I'm so sorry,' Josie whispered. 'We'll talk to Sam. Together. We'll make it better. *He'll* make it better.'

'Mum,' Lucy shook her head, 'I think Sam and I have lost our way. We both need help.'

'Yes,' Josie nodded, 'we'll talk.'

'No, Mum. You're not understanding me. Sam needs to sort his head out. But not with me or you. And I need to sort my head out too. With somebody impartial.'

Josie's brow knitted. 'What are you talking about? Do you mean a counsellor?'

'Yes. A counsellor,' Lucy said in a flat voice. 'And I'm also talking about this.' She rolled up her left sleeve and held out her arm, turning it to reveal the underside. It was a mass of scribbled scratches. Some were pale mauve scars. Some were scabby. And some were so fresh they were still bleeding.

'What on earth–?'

Lucy followed her mother's gaze and stared at the damaged skin. She felt calmer now. Like a huge weight had been lifted from her shoulders. 'I'm sorry, Mum,' her eyes watered again, 'but I've been self-harming for months. And that's not all I have to tell you. I'm also bulimic.'

Chapter Thirty-Seven

Josie couldn't take Lucy's words in. Bulimic? Self harming? Princess Diana had once famously confessed on television that she'd done the very same things. Diana had also said that the Royal Family thought her a basket case – in other words somebody with mental health issues. Josie had sympathised with Diana. But the princess had been a woman reviled by her husband. Cheated on. Shunned by her in-laws, and generally made to feel like a pariah. Was it any wonder that she'd gone half round the bend with grief? Whereas Lucy was *so so so* loved – Josie said those words to Lucy every single day. And she cuddled Lucy endlessly, and always encouraged and praised her school work and achievements. Josie had believed her daughter to be emotionally secure. Safe. Happy. How could she have got it so wrong? Worse, how could she not have even noticed? To say she felt a failure was an understatement.

Josie wanted to rush over and cuddle her daughter, but having been pushed away once, she was wary about approaching Lucy again. Her daughter was now sitting on the sofa, her legs curled to one side. She'd stopped crying and even seemed composed.

'Can I...can I hug you?' Josie ventured.

'Yes,' Lucy replied in a small voice.

And suddenly the two of them were clinging to each other as if their very lives depended on it.

'I love you,' Josie whispered into Lucy's hair. 'I love you more than words can say.'

'I love you too, Mum,' Lucy whispered back.

'I've let you down.'

'No you haven't.'

Josie released her daughter, and the two of them sank down on the sofa together. 'Do you...do you feel able to talk to me? A bit?'

'What do you want to know?'

Josie allowed her gaze to fall on Lucy's arm. Gently, she took it. Lucy initially resisted, but then allowed Josie to turn the wrist so the soft white skin was fully revealed. Josie mentally winced and felt her tummy flip as she looked at the angry marks. 'Do you want to kill yourself?'

'No,' Lucy gave a small smile. 'Definitely not.'

'So...what exactly do you get out of hurting yourself?'

Lucy closed her eyes for a moment. How could she explain? 'Sometimes I get all this anger in me. I see Sam looking dejected, I mean *really* dejected. All because of Ruby treating him like pooh. But also he's been behaving oddly at times. Almost...irrationally. Haven't you noticed?'

Josie nodded. The thought had occurred to her on more than one occasion too, but she'd batted it away. It was easier to cope if you brushed things under the carpet. Well, for a while anyway. 'Yes,' she sighed. 'Recently I had a clear out of your wardrobe. I made a pile of clothes that you'd outgrown, and put them in a big bin bag for the charity shop. Then I went into Ruby's wardrobe and did the same thing. Some of the clothes hanging on her rail hadn't been worn in three years – jeans that would have been up to her knees they were so short. I pulled them out along with some tiny t-shirts, and Sam caught me. He asked me what I was doing. When I told him, he went ballistic. He made me put everything back. And then he said that Ruby's room was not to be disturbed other than for vacuuming or dusting.'

'It's like her bedroom is a shrine,' Lucy nodded. 'And I heard him in her room earlier on in the week. He didn't realise I knew he was in there. And Mum, do you know what he was doing?'

'Go on.'

'He was talking to Ruby.'

'Eh? She's not been over in God knows how long.'

'Exactly. But he was pretending, Mum. How sad is that? "Hello, princess! Are you all right? Do you want to come outside and play on your bicycle? I'll take you to the park." I was freaked out.'

'Oh God.' Josie felt almost consumed with despair. 'Even if Ruby had been in her room, going to the park on her bicycle is the last thing she'd have agreed to doing.'

'I know. It's like he can't accept that his daughter isn't a little girl any more. That he can't come to terms with the fact that she's a teenager. And I don't think this is the first time he's gone in her room talking to nobody. It's unnerving. Creepy even.'

'I think it's his way of coping.'

'Like this is my way of coping,' Lucy pointed at her arm. 'Sam's last fantasy chat with Ruby made me feel so angry and, well, *isolated*, that before I knew what I was doing I was reaching for my compass and scratching my arm to pieces.'

Josie closed her eyes for a moment. She swallowed. How was she meant to react hearing her daughter saying these words oh so casually? A part of her wanted to scream and shout at Lucy – to make her promise never to do it again. But the sensible part of her knew it was important to keep calm and listen. 'But why self harm? Why not get hold of your pillow, for example, and bash the hell out of it?'

'It's not the same, Mum. It's...it's like the inside of you is aching *so* much – all this dreadful emotional hurt – that by actually inflicting pain *on* your body it distracts you from feeling the pain *inside* your body. Does that make sense?'

Josie exhaled slowly. 'Well, yes and no. I hear what you're saying, and it does make some sort of sense, it's just that I can't identify with it because I've never dealt with my own emotional difficulties in the same way. And what about the bulimia? Is that tied in with anger and self-harming?'

'Not as such, no. It's me wanting to be thinner. I enjoy my food too much to diet, so if I binge I make sure it all comes up again afterwards.'

'Darling, you've never been fat. Ever.'

'Not fat but–' Lucy hesitated.

'What?'

'I wanted to have Ruby's figure.'

Josie shook her head. Ruby again. 'Ruby is very slender, but you've always had a lovely figure Lucy. Why try and be like her? Why can't you just *be?* A rose doesn't try to be a daffodil. A rose just *is.*'

'I know,' Lucy said in a small voice. 'And I want to take control back. Over the bulimia and the self-harming. I'm going to stop watching all those stupid reality programmes on the television. Model programmes. Make-over programmes. I'm truly going to stop throwing up. I'm one hundred per cent sure I can do it. But I'm not so sure I can stop the self-harming.'

'Why?'

'It's addictive Mum. You get, like, an adrenalin rush. I've been on some forums on the internet and talked to other kids who self-harm and who are also trying to stop. From what I can gather, the body releases endorphins which makes you feel better, and that's why you get this sense of relief. In the short term,' Lucy added.

Josie nodded. 'So, while we're having this very open and honest conversation, can I make a suggestion?'

'Yes.'

'It may or may not help but...what about we take up running together? You talked about endorphins just now. I know exercise releases endorphins. If we run every day, hopefully you'll get endorphins whizzing about on a regular basis and that might help lower the urge to self-harm. And running is a good way to let off steam, including anger, and has the added benefit of keeping you in shape and nicely toned.'

'Okay. I'll give it a go. But I still want to see a counsellor.'

'Sure. But I also think Sam should know. Can I tell him?'

Lucy shrugged. 'That's up to you Mum. But I personally don't want to talk to Sam. Frankly, the way I feel about Sam right now is...don't be angry at me Mum...but I don't want anything to do with him. I've tried and tried and tried to be the daughter he wants but can't have. And he's not interested. I realise now that nothing on this earth can turn me into Ruby. I'm that rose Mum. Not the daffodil. And finally I've got my head around that.'

When Sam eventually returned home, it was gone midnight and Lucy had long gone to bed. Josie was sitting alone in the lounge, a stack of completed marking by her side, when she heard Sam's key in the front door.

Sam came into the hallway. He pushed open the living room door. Lamplight haloed around Josie's hair. Her face was in semi-darkness, but even so Sam could see his wife had been crying. He perched next to her on the sofa.

'I'm sorry.'

Josie gazed at him silently.

'Look,' Sam reached out and took Josie's hand, 'I'm aware that I've been hell to live with lately.'

'There's no denying that,' Josie murmured.

'Can you just bear with me? For a bit longer? I'm...I'm sorting my head out.'

'Sam, you're my husband, and I love you. I like to think – and hope you'll agree – that I've always been there for you. That you can lean on me.'

'I need you to be patient with me, Josie.'

'The thing is, I'm floundering a bit myself now.'

'I'll get there.'

'No, you don't understand, Sam. I've tried supporting you throughout all your challenges with Annie, and now all the difficulties with Ruby.'

'Look, I've said I'm sorry. I'll–'

'Hang on a minute. Let me finish talking. I'm struggling now, but not because of you. While you were out, I had a long chat with Lucy. She's in a bad way, Sam. All this Ruby business–'

'You talk like Ruby is a *thing*. She's my *daughter* Josie.'

'Yes,' Josie could feel fire kindling in her belly and desperately tried to push it down. The last thing she wanted was to raise her voice or incite Sam into going on the defensive about Ruby and slamming out of the house again. 'And Lucy is *my* daughter Sam. And I've let her down. Badly.'

Sam shook his head. 'What are you talking about?'

'Everything that's gone on between you and Annie, and now between you and Ruby, along with all the years of Lucy being denied a proper father-daughter relationship because of your ex-wife lying to Ruby and feeding her insecurities, well it's impacted on Lucy.'

'Lucy's fine,' Sam said dismissively.

'No, Sam. No she's not. My daughter gave me a confession tonight. Not only is she bulimic, but she's self-harming.'

Sam looked at his wife as if she'd suddenly sprouted four arms. 'Self-harming? What the devil are you talking about?'

'She's finding family life very difficult. It's a coping mechanism.'

'I don't know what to say. I can't get my head around it.'

'I'm struggling with it myself. But one thing is for sure Sam, from now on my focus is on Lucy. I'm sorry for all the problems you've had with Annie, and I'm desperately sorry that you're now having such a terrible time with Ruby. It's grossly unfair. But the stress that Annie and Ruby have caused, and are continuing to cause, is something I'm no longer getting suckered into.'

'What are you saying here?'

'I'm saying that I strongly advise you to talk to somebody in a professional capacity, ideally with Ruby too. But if Ruby won't go along, then go by yourself. But I'm now stepping out of this situation. It's *my* coping mechanism. I don't want to talk about Annie and Ruby anymore, nor do I want to hear how the pair of them treat you. As far as I'm concerned, they are no longer part of my world. My only priority is my daughter, and making sure she gets better. We have private medical insurance, so first thing tomorrow I'm going to get on the phone to the Mental Health Division.'

'You mean counselling?'

'Yes. It's what Lucy wants. And from now on my daughter is going to get exactly that. What *she* wants.' Josie stood up. 'If you'll excuse me, I'm going to bed. I'll be in the spare room.'

Sam held on to his wife's hand. 'There's no need for that Josie.'

'Yes there is, Sam. I need to be on my own. My brain is so overloaded it feels like it could explode.'

'Please don't go in the spare room. Let's go to bed and spoon into each other. Hold each other. I love you.'

Josie nodded. 'I love you too. But I really do need to be on my own. Just for now.'

Moments later Sam was sitting by himself in the lounge. He put his head in his hands. What on earth was happening? He felt like his world was falling apart. His daughter didn't give a toss. His step-daughter was apparently a mixed-up bunny. And his wife was at her wits end with them all. And Sam didn't blame her. He felt lonely, rejected, and above all guilty for the misery he had caused Josie and Lucy.

For the first time, Sam wondered if it wouldn't just be better to cop out of it all – take a packet of sleeping pills and snore, soporifically, from this world into the next. Nothing would hurt then. He'd be at peace. And everybody else would be at peace too. Annie would be deliriously happy to know Sam was six feet under. Ruby would be thrilled to bits to no longer have a father she couldn't abide forever chasing to see her. Lucy would no longer have a miserable step-father upsetting her mental wellbeing. And Josie would be able to have a happy life without all Sam's issues sending her doollally. Problem solved all round.

Sam stood up. He wondered how many paracetamols were in the upstairs bathroom cabinet.

Chapter Thirty-Eight

As it turned out, there were only two painkillers in the bathroom cabinet along with an ancient packet of Lemsip and a tube of Bonjela. Sam left the paracetamols untouched and leant on the bathroom sink. He shook his head and wondered how he'd even entertained such dark thoughts. Straightening up, he squeezed some toothpaste onto a toothbrush. As he began the nightly ritual of teeth cleaning, Sam decided – once and for all – to get to the bottom of why his daughter so reviled him. He wanted to make peace. God, how he craved peace.

And as for Lucy, he couldn't take in the bombshell that Josie had dropped. Why was Lucy finding family life so difficult? Hadn't he been a good step-father? He'd always helped her with Chemistry homework, listened about her day at school, paid for lovely holidays and been the main breadwinner. She didn't want for anything! He'd have to talk to his step-daughter. Tell her to stop all this self-harming and bulimia nonsense. Just as soon as he'd seen his own daughter and healed the yawning chasm between them.

For Sam, the situation with Ruby was beyond intolerable. He felt continually tired. Constantly upset. The despair he felt over the breakdown of the relationship with his precious daughter consumed him. Where had he gone wrong? He flopped into bed but sleep evaded him. When he did finally nod off, it was to wake three hours later. Sam lay in the darkness combing over the past, looking for hidden clues. Across the years, Annie's words repeatedly floated back to torment him. *I'm going to use Ruby to destroy you.* Those words had always chased Sam, snapping at his heels. He'd done everything in his power to ensure Annie's prophecy would never happen. He'd made sure Ruby had grown up knowing she was loved and cherished. From the moment he'd returned to being a singleton, his daughter had been his first priority. Hadn't he made sure Ruby had known that? He'd lavished her with love and cuddles, and spoilt her rotten with material things. He'd fought Annie tooth and nail through the Family Court to have regular uninterrupted access. So why was his daughter punishing him?

Josie fell into the spare bed like a rock. Her body physically ached with a tiredness that, these days, never seemed to go away. Lucy's confession had just about finished her off. Josie recognised that in order to support her daughter, she probably needed support herself. Right now she felt engulfed with depression. Perhaps she should go to her GP? Get some happy pills? God knows she needed something. Josie turned over and curled into the foetal position. Five minutes later she switched sides. Half an hour later she kicked the covers off. An hour later and she had a blistering headache. Tossing back the duvet, she padded off to the bathroom in search of painkillers. She reached for the packet of paracetamol and swallowed the last two. And then Josie had an idea. She would write to Ruby. Plead with her. But she had to do it in such a way so as not to upset her step-daughter, or cause repercussions with Annie. The last thing Josie wanted was for the written word to act like a match and ignite a bonfire of emotions.

Quietly, Josie padded downstairs. She went into the study and switched on the computer. Moments later she was on Facebook and sending her step-daughter a direct message.

Dear Ruby

I hope you don't mind me contacting you like this, but there are some things I need you to know. Your dad is very distressed. So is Lucy. And so am I.

I know you haven't stayed over for such a long time, but I'm at a loss to know why. I suspect you have a lot of things going through your head. Can we not all get together and have a chat? I'm desperate to reassure you, and I know your dad is too.

When you are a parent your children are so important you would happily die for them. Your dad and I always wanted our girls to have a family unit. It was one of the reasons we married...to give our daughters a that family unit. Families are important. Your dad and I wanted our girls to know the 'traditional' unit was there...and it's still there if you want it.

I appreciate that as you have grown older, friends and other interests have probably diverted you. But the family unit is still here, and the door has never closed. You still have your bedroom in this house – with the soft furnishings you chose, the paint of your choice on the wall, your pictures, and a computer that was top of the range when bought.

Your dad still thinks of you as his little girl. You probably find that rather annoying, and I appreciate that when you are a teenager parents can seem terribly irritating, but your dad means well Ruby. He misses you terribly. We all do. We love you.

Hoping to see you soon.

Hugs xx

Josie hit the send button. She felt marginally better. She'd appealed to Ruby's better nature to get in touch, especially with her father. Hopefully her letter would work. Sighing, she switched off the computer and went back to bed.

Lucy was sitting in her Mum's car. She was on the way to school. Josie was listening to Capital Radio as they crawled through heavy traffic. Lucy contented herself with Twitter via her mobile phone. She was feeling a bit more positive this morning. Telling Mum about the bulimia and self-harming had definitely been a starting point. She'd be even happier once the first counselling appointment was lined up.

Lucy scrolled through the tweets on her mobile. She spotted some tweets by Ruby. Her step-sister was sending out a string of cryptic messages.

'Looks like Ruby is mad with someone,' Lucy said idly.

'How do you know that?'

'I'm on Twitter. She's tweeting a barrage of abuse to somebody.'

'Who?'

'God, I don't know. Who knows what makes that girl tick.'

Josie silently agreed. 'So what's she tweeting?'

'Hang on. Let me scroll back up. *No mate, go away.* Swiftly followed by *No thanks, don't want to be part of your clan.* And then there are loads of other tweets that are just single words but clearly aimed at somebody.'

Josie clenched the steering wheel. 'What are the single words?'

'Just crap.'

'Tell me.'

Lucy gave her mother a curious look. 'Why are you so interested?'

Josie came to a halt at some red traffic lights. She gave Lucy a sidelong glance and took a deep breath. 'Okay, don't tell Sam, but last night I messaged Ruby via Facebook.'

Lucy's eyes widened. 'And said what?'

'Basically it was a plea to get in touch with her dad and to come and see us all – that we missed her being a part of our family.'

Lucy's mouth formed a perfect O as she turned back to the Twitter feed. 'So *No thanks, don't want to be part of your clan* is a direct reference to your letter!'

'Clearly.'

Lucy scrolled through the remainder of tweets. 'What a charmless bitch.'

Josie shrugged. 'I tried.'

'I don't know why you bothered.'

The lights changed to green. Josie put the car in gear and pulled away. 'I did it for Sam. It was a last ditch attempt to get his daughter back on track with him.'

'Does he know you wrote to Ruby?'

'No. And I'd rather you didn't tell him. He's not in the right frame of mind to discuss it.'

'None of us are Mum. We're all messed up. All because of Annie and Ruby. They deserve each other.'

'They do,' Josie nodded, 'but let's not say that they've messed us up. It's a negative comment, and I'm fed up with negativity. From now on I want us being positive and putting it all behind us. For me, Annie and Ruby no longer matter. The only thing that's important for me... is you.'

'Does Sam not matter to you too?'

'Yes. Of course he does. But he's not my priority. I've reached a point where I need to take a big step back. I've suggested Sam talks to somebody in a professional capacity. I've tried helping him – and Ruby – in the only way I know how. And my attempts have failed. For my own sanity I need to draw a line under Sam, Annie and Ruby.'

'Do you think you'll leave Sam?'

Josie inhaled sharply. This wasn't the first time in her years of marriage to Sam that their relationship had hit the rocks. Hadn't all their arguments and disagreements fundamentally stemmed from his wretched ex-wife and now the *mini me* daughter? 'I'm not sure I should answer a question like that Lucy. I think your world has been rocked enough. You have a lot on your plate right now.'

'I don't want you to leave Sam.'

'Really?' Josie was surprised. After Lucy's blistering criticisms of Sam, Josie would have thought Lucy would have quite welcomed his departure from her life. 'I thought you said he'd been a rubbish dad – or words to that effect.'

'His fathering has lacked warmth and affection. But at the end of the day I still regard him as my father figure. And I know I'm a poor daughter substitute, but I'd rather have a bit of him than none of him.'

Josie felt her eyes well. Hastily she blinked back the tears. 'Sam doesn't think of you as a poor daughter substitute,' she assured. Even to her ears, the words sounded like hypocrisy. 'And rest assured, I have no plans to leave Sam.' If her daughter wanted her to stay in the marriage, then Josie would. What Lucy wanted was the only thing Josie now cared about.

When Sam came home from work, Lucy was sitting at the dining room table, homework spread about.

'Hey, Luce, how's it going?' Sam tweaked his step-daughter's ponytail.

'So so.' Lucy put down her pen. 'You look how I feel.'

Sam grimaced. 'Let me go and say hello to your mum, then – if it's all right with you – I'd like to have,' Sam hesitated for a moment, 'well, a chat about...things.'

Lucy's shoulders drooped. She knew what was coming. 'Okay.'

Sam turned and went into the kitchen. Josie was standing at the sink draining boiled potatoes.

'Hi.'

'Hello,' Josie looked sideways and regarded Sam through a cloud of steam. 'Good day at the surgery?'

'Yeah. Busy. As always.'

'Dinner won't be long.'

'I want to talk to Lucy about, you know, the bulimia business.'

'And self harming,' Josie murmured sotto voce.

'That too. Can you join us?'

'I need to mash these potatoes for the shepherd's pie.'

'Well I think this is more important than shepherd's pie.'

Josie put the colander down. 'Look Sam. My presence isn't going to make any difference. This is between you and Lucy. I'm not the one with issues about a step-father or believing there is a lack of warmth and affection. I'm not the one sticking fingers down my throat to emulate a figure like your daughter's. Nor am I the one taking a compass to my arm because of hankering for the father that your daughter so thoroughly rejects. Lucy needs to talk to *you*. She needs answers from *you*. So *you* talk to her.' Josie turned back to the potatoes and shook the contents of the colander into a bowl.

'Right.' Sam found himself gazing at Josie's back. 'If that's what you think, I'll talk to Lucy on my own.'

Sam went into the dining room. He pulled out a chair and sat down beside Lucy. For a moment, step-daughter and step-father quietly regarded each other.

Lucy was the first to speak. 'Mum's told you, hasn't she?'

Sam nodded his head. 'Yes.' He looked down at Lucy's hands, one neatly folded over the other. He deliberated whether to take one of them. If it were Ruby, she'd snatch it away. Would Lucy whisk her hand away? There was only one way to find out. Slowly, he reached out and laid his hand on both of Lucy's. She didn't reject his touch. Instead Sam found his step-daughter's fingers curling into his. It was such a simple gesture, but communicated a myriad of emotions. Affection. Calmness. Comfort. Security. Trust. 'I owe you an apology, Lucy.' He looked from their hands up to her face and saw the start of tears rolling down her cheeks. 'I'm so sorry you lost your dad when you were a little girl.' Lucy didn't say anything. Instead the tears sped up. They were plopping now, silently, onto the table and across his own hand. 'Your mum has told me about the bulimia and,' Sam swallowed, 'the self harming. Lucy, I can't tell you how horrified I am to know you've been doing this to yourself. Why didn't you tell me?'

'You've not been,' Lucy gulped, 'in the right frame of mind. You've been...unreachable, Sam. It's like me and Mum both ceased to exist to you.'

'God no,' Sam shook his head, 'no, no, that's not true. I love your mum so much. And I love you too, Lucy.'

'Do you?'

'Yes, of course.'

'But you've never shown it. Not really. Not properly.'

'Of course I have!'

'No you haven't. Not like you do to Ruby.' Lucy pulled her hands away from Sam's, but only to delve into her sleeve and pull out a crumpled tissue. She blew her nose noisily. 'I know Ruby's your flesh and blood, Sam, and I'm not. I'm just a poor second best.'

'Lucy, don't talk like that. I've tried to be a good dad to you. Haven't I made sure you've never gone without anything?'

'You're not including a *father* Sam. I go without a *father*. All the time. And I always have done. Because I'm not Ruby.'

Sam looked ashamed. 'If that's how I've come across, I can only apologise. The word *sorry* is so useless, but at the same time it's the only one there is to convey just how much regret I have in my heart over how you've had to take a back seat when it comes to my own daughter.'

'I'm so jealous of Ruby,' Lucy's voice cracked as a fresh bout of weeping took hold of her. Suddenly her whole body was wracked with long overdue sobs. 'I know I shouldn't say this,' she spluttered, 'but I think your daughter is a prize bitch.'

'Yes,' Sam nodded, 'as much as it pains me to say this, I agree with you.' Suddenly Sam felt a rush of emotion whoosh up from his stomach and into his throat. It gagged him. Choked him. He could hardly breathe. Before he could stop himself, his eyes were streaming, his nose running and he was bawling his head off. Lucy looked appalled. She stood up and awkwardly put her arms around his shoulders, but she was in full flow herself. The din was terrible.

Out in the kitchen, Josie had finished making the shepherd's pie and was now cleaning a saucepan. She paused as the noise from the dining room assaulted her eardrums. Dear God. It sounded like two animals in terrible pain. And then she attacked the saucepan she'd been scrubbing with fresh vigour. The gunge within had long been removed. But Josie couldn't stop scrubbing. She was aware that the frenzied scouring was odd behaviour. Manic even. But it made her feel better. As if the harder she mashed the wire wool against the saucepan, the greater release from the angst in her heart. The scrubbing action was almost akin to emotional self-cleansing. It was cleaning away all her buried pain, upset and tears.

Chapter Thirty-Nine

Yet another weekend loomed. Ruby was sitting at the desk in her bedroom, scrolling through Facebook. She was in a foul mood. She'd read Josie's message for the umpteenth time but still not replied. She had no intention of spending Saturday and Sunday at 2 Sycamore Drive. She wanted to be available for Jackson. Ruby had spent the entire week at school batting her eyelids at him and was convinced a call was imminent inviting her to hang out with him. Meanwhile Josie's message was distracting her.

So her father was distressed. Well, good! He deserved all the misery in the world for what he'd put her mother through. And how dare that so-called step-mother of hers try and make her feel guilty for spurning her father. Josie wanted a chat? Oh Ruby would chat all right. She had *plenty* to say, like informing Josie about the sort of man she'd married. As for the *family unit* that Josie spoke of – ha bloody ha! That particular family unit was nothing to do with Ruby, and she would make sure Josie understood why. It was time to enlighten her father. Ruby was going to give it to him with both barrels!

Ruby swung round on her swivel chair, and reached down to the bag on the floor. Locating her mobile phone, she checked to see if Jackson had texted her. Nothing. Bastard. Ruby raised her eyes to the ceiling and contemplated. So Josie wanted Ruby to see her dad. Okay, she would. But on her terms. It was time to set the record straight. She tapped out a message. *Hi, Dad. I think we need to talk. Coffee in Starbucks tomorrow afternoon.*

Sam was overjoyed at his daughter's text message. Ruby wanted to see him! Thank goodness. Everything was going to be all right – even though his guts twisted with nerves at the prospect of the meeting. Sam told himself not to be ridiculous. This was his *daughter* – his precious flesh and blood! So why did his bowels lurch with fear at what Ruby wanted to talk about? Lucy appeared by his side, scattering his thoughts like a kaleidoscope.

'Sam? Mum and I are going to go for a run.'

'That's nice, sweetheart. The fresh air will do you good.'

'I thought it would be nice if you came too.'

'Really?'

'Yeah. It would be good to do something,' Lucy gave Sam a level look, 'as a family.'

Lucy's last three words echoed around Sam's head. *As a family.* 'Sure. That would be great. I'll just go and fetch my trainers.'

Lucy smiled gratefully. Since their talk, she'd been feeling a bit better. More hopeful. Optimistic even. Maybe, just maybe, she could now have the relationship with Sam that she'd always craved. It was far too late in the day to call him *Dad*. Even though he felt like a dad, it no longer felt right to call him anything other than *Sam*.

She waited in the hallway for her step-father. Mum was already outside, laced into her trainers and looking faintly ridiculous in an ancient pair of Spandex leggings. A long t-shirt covered her bottom. Lucy could see her mother's outline through the frosted panes of the door as Josie performed a series of stretches by way of warming up.

There was a creak on the landing and Sam came down the stairs. 'Come on then,' he grinned at Lucy before pushing past her to where Josie was standing. 'Ah, there's my gorgeous wife.' Sam kissed Josie on the cheek. 'Knees bent, arms stretched,' he joked. 'You look quite the part, darling.' Sam began jogging on the spot. 'Ready? Let's go!'

Lucy pulled the front door shut after them and together they set off. They'd barely gone a hundred yards downhill when Sam stopped.

'Come on,' Lucy laughed as she jogged past him, 'you can't be out of puff already.' She pounded off.

'Slowcoach,' Josie giggled as she too jogged past Sam.

'Tell you what, girls,' Sam called after them, 'you go that way, and I'll go this way.' He turned and began to jog back up the tree lined hill towards the main road.

'Wait!' Josie called.

Sam stopped and turned round. 'What?'

'Where are you going?'

'Up the road.' He paused while Josie conferred with Lucy.

'But we're jogging this way,' Lucy shouted.

Sam hesitated. He looked up and regarded the sky for a second or two before glancing back at his wife and stepdaughter. They were walking towards him now, retracing their steps up the hill. 'I want to run alone,' he finally called out.

A few more seconds and Josie and Lucy had reached him. They stopped and regarded him curiously.

'Why do you want to run alone?' Lucy frowned.

'I...I just do.'

'But why?' Josie persisted. She shifted her body, planting her feet wide, and placed her hands on her hips. The body language told Sam she was pissed off. 'I thought we were doing this all together. As a family.' She gazed at her husband who, for some reason, was once again apparently fascinated by the sky. Josie found herself looking up too. A few rufty tufty clouds had gathered. Their dirty grey colour heightened a sense of foreboding within the pit of her stomach. When Josie looked back at Sam, she realised his eyes were welling. He was looking upwards in an attempt to contain the tears.

'I just...I just want to run up the hill,' Sam mumbled.

'As opposed to running down it?' Lucy asked.

'Yeah.'

'Okay,' Lucy nodded, 'then we'll run up the hill all together.'

'No, I can't do that. If you would rather run up the hill, I'll run down it.'

'Sam,' Lucy's eyes suddenly flashed, 'do you have any idea how ridiculous you are sounding? You're making no sense. Why won't you run with me and Mum?'

'Because...because I can't.'

'It's because I'm not Ruby isn't it?' Lucy's voice began to rise. 'I'm not good enough for you to run with. That's it, isn't it? Why don't you just admit it?'

'Sam, for God's sake,' Josie implored.

'I can't cope with him anymore, Mum,' Lucy threw her hands up in the air. 'He's round the bend,' she turned to fully face her mother. 'Mum, I've never wanted to interfere in your marriage. I've kept my nose out, and I've always told myself that having a bit of Sam is better than not having anything of him. But I can't deal with this anymore. He's doing my head in.'

Josie rounded on Sam furiously. 'Can't you see how your behaviour is affecting Lucy?'

'Yes, and I'm sorry. But I can't jog with you,' Sam shook his head, blinking back the tears that still threatened.

'Why not?' Josie demanded angrily.

'Because...because you've both said we're doing this as a family.'

'And your point is?' Lucy demanded.

'We're not a family. Not without Ruby.'

'Yes, we are a family!' Josie shouted.

'No, my daughter isn't with us.'

'We're still your family!' Lucy screamed. 'Do you hear me? MUM AND I ARE STILL YOUR FAMILY!'

Josie regarded Sam coldly. 'I'm done with you, Sam. By God I've said it enough times in the past when your ex wife has pushed all my buttons, but this time I have your daughter impacting on all of us too. The bloody pair of them – a double whammy! It's quite obvious that your behaviour is totally irrational and you are in need of professional help. I've asked you before. Begged you. But now I'm not interested. You can go to bloody hell. And take Annie and Ruby with you. My daughter has been reduced to a self-harming wreck because of the screwy way you three interact.' Josie took a step away from Sam, as if he were suddenly radio-active. 'Come on, Lucy,' she took her daughter's arm, 'let's jog. Let's pound all this upset out of us.'

Lucy wiped the back of her hand across her face before taking off after her mother. All she really wanted to do was go home, take the stairs two at a time, find her compass and scratch her arm to blazes. She crossed her arms in front of her as she ran, gripping her forearms with her fingers, squeezing and releasing, squeezing ever harder before again releasing. She tried to dig her nails into her flesh as she jogged, but the fleecy material of her hoodie's sleeves wouldn't permit the release she craved. Suddenly she was aware of heavy steps pounding behind her. Panting, she glanced over her shoulder. Sam was catching them up. Oh no.

'Josie! Lucy!' Sam called out. 'I'm sorry. It's okay. I'm fine now. You're right. We're a family. We'll run together.'

Lucy and Josie glanced at each other and sped up. 'Go away, Sam,' Josie shouted.

But Sam's legs were longer and stronger and he caught them up in no time. Reaching out he grabbed their arms and yanked them both to a standstill. For a moment the three of them stood there, staring at each other and panting from exertion. Then Josie shook Sam off. 'We're not interested.'

Sam caught her arm again. 'Josie, listen. Please. I'm sorry. I'm really sorry.'

'Let go of me,' Josie attempted to pull away again but Sam held on tight.

'I'm okay now. Really.'

'Bully for you. Unfortunately Lucy and I are *not* okay. Comprendez? Now let go of us.'

Lucy attempted to wriggle away. 'You're hurting me, Sam.'

'Please don't jog without me. Please.'

'You're WEIRD!' Lucy yelled.

'No,' Sam released their wrists, 'I'm not weird. I'm just...struggling...can't deal–'

His hands flew up to his face, fingers splayed across his eyes to stem another fresh crop of tears. Josie and Lucy looked from Sam to each other.

'I think he's having a nervous breakdown,' Josie murmured to Lucy.

Lucy contemplated her trainers for a moment. Then she looked back up at her mother. 'Let's go home,' she said in a flat voice.

The three of them turned and headed back towards the house. The broken man, the angry wife and the frustrated teenager. As they walked, Lucy fumbled in her hoodie pocket for her mobile phone. She fell in step behind her mother and step-father, and as she walked she tapped out a long overdue text. *Congratulations, Ruby. You and your mum have done a great job on your dad. Hope you're proud of yourselves, because you've finally destroyed him.*

Lucy trailed Sam and Josie back to the house. By the time they were inside, Sam was blubbing like a baby. Josie led Sam into the kitchen. Before closing the door, she gave Lucy a meaningful look. The message was clear. Make yourself scarce for a bit. Well Lucy was more than happy to do that. She'd been envisioning this moment with every step of the walk home.

Upstairs in her room, she found her pencil case. She was just hastening off to the bathroom where she could lock herself in and cut her arm without interruption, when Sam's ringing mobile phone had her pausing. She stood on the landing and listened. The merry tinkling was coming from the master bedroom. Downstairs she could hear Sam sobbing. It sounded dreadful. There was something about a man crying that made Lucy cringe. A man was meant to be the strong one! And once upon a time Sam had been just that. But now look at him! Eroded over the years to a blubbering baby. These days it was Josie who was the strong one. She'd been Sam's rock for such a long time and now Lucy was leaning on her heavily too due to her own psychological issues. Sometimes Lucy wondered how her mum coped with all the anger Annie and Ruby directed at her, and all the grief Sam and Lucy put upon her.

The mobile phone stopped ringing. Lucy wondered if it had been Ruby wanting to complain to her father about Lucy's text message. Having sent the text in a moment of white hot anger, Lucy was already regretting it. Her message would have been a red rag to a bull. More than anything, Lucy hadn't wanted to stoop to Annie's and Ruby's level and join in their crusade of bitterness with a war of words. But she'd fallen into the trap and done precisely that. Although, another part of Lucy reasoned that she'd also felt an urge to protect Sam. He might be the father figure, but right now he was vulnerable and emotionally in bits. Whilst that didn't excuse her message to Ruby, it did give good reason for what she'd done.

Lucy decided to take a quick peek at the call log on Sam's phone. She crept into the master bedroom and picked the phone up from the bedside table. Six missed calls, and every single one from Ruby! She was just contemplating whether to delete the log record when the phone lit up and began another bout of shrill ringing. The sound caused Lucy to jump. On reflex she threw the phone as if it were a hot coal. It smacked against the bedside table before clattering onto the floor. Lucy's heart was pounding so hard she could hear it beating in her ears. She froze, half expecting her mother to erupt out of the kitchen and yell up the stairs by way of complaint at the thumps Lucy was making. But nobody disturbed her. Shaking slightly, Lucy gingerly picked up the ringing phone. Ruby's name was once again in the caller display.

'Hello?'

'Put me on to my dad.'

Lucy's palms had broken out into a muck sweat, so much so the mobile nearly slipped from her grasp. 'Don't you think it's me you need to talk to, Ruby?'

'Put me on to my dad,' Ruby repeated.

'No.'

'Lucy, I don't want to talk to you. I want to speak to my dad.'

'Well you can't. Right now he's being comforted by my mum. He's in a terrible state, Ruby. All because of you and the horrible way you've treated him.'

'It's none of your business.'

'Oh yes it is! He's my step-dad. You might not want him, but I do. Well, I did. But not anymore. He's wrecked. Completely ruined. And you and your mum are the ones who've destroyed him. You should be grateful for the dad you have. You don't know how lucky–'

But Lucy was talking to thin air. Ruby had hung up. Seconds later the phone chirruped the arrival of a text message. Lucy peeked at the text. Oh God, it was from Annie. Lucy was now shaking like an aspen. She felt nauseous too. Presumably it was from the huge rush of adrenalin that was now whooshing around her body. With trembling fingers, she touched the mobile's screen and read the message.

You've got a lot of explaining to do Sam. And keep your trollop's brat under control. Our daughter is bawling her eyes out because of her.

Lucy's hand fluttered to her mouth. Oh God. She was going to be portrayed as a troublemaker. Sam would hate her. The little bit of precious relationship that she had with her step-father would take a final nosedive down the toilet. Lucy burst into tears. The last thing she wanted to do was badger her mother with yet another sobbing family member, but she didn't know what else to do. She'd have to come clean and own up about the text to Ruby. She picked up the mobile phone and, with jelly legs, made her way downstairs.

Chapter Forty

Lucy stood outside the kitchen door. Sam's sobs had quietened. She could hear her mother talking in a low voice to her husband, but was unable to work out what she was saying. Lucy took a deep breath and tapped on the kitchen door.

'Can you give us five minutes, Luce?' Josie called.

'No. It's urgent.'

Sam said something indiscernible to Josie before replying to Lucy. 'It's okay, sweetheart. You can come in.'

Lucy pushed the door open. She stood, anxiously, in the doorway and regarded her step-father and mother. Sam's eyes were red and swollen. Her mother looked worn out and older than her years. Lucy didn't suppose she looked much better. 'I've done something terrible.'

Josie stiffened. 'Have you hurt yourself?'

'Not that,' Lucy replied quickly. 'Something else. But you'll both be mad at me. Especially you, Sam.'

Sam rubbed a hand across his face wearily. 'I won't.'

'You will.'

'Lucy, whatever it is, it can't be that bad. Really. I promise I won't be cross.'

'I texted Ruby.'

Sam's brow furrowed. 'What's so awful about that?'

'Maybe it's best you read my message for yourself.'

Lucy held out her mobile phone. Sam stared at it for a moment, before wordlessly taking it. He touched the screen and read. Josie gave her daughter a quizzical look. Lucy gave the smallest shake of her head before chewing her lip. There was a highly charged silence, and then Sam put the phone down on the kitchen table.

'I'm not cross,' he assured Lucy.

Lucy immediately burst into fresh tears. 'I'm sorry.'

'What did you write?' asked Josie.

Sam picked up the phone and gave it to Josie, then turned to Lucy and patted his lap. She walked over and sat on his knee, aware that she was miles too big and heavy to be doing such a childlike thing, but as Sam hugged her to him Lucy couldn't help relishing the security and reassurance of the parental hug. For a moment she could cherish the father/daughter relationship that she so yearned for and which Ruby so thoroughly rejected.

Josie lay the phone back down on the kitchen table. 'Oh,' she said. 'Oh dear.'

'Listen,' Sam spoke to Lucy, 'all you did was fight my corner, and for that I'm immensely grateful. I wish my own daughter felt as fiercely protective of me as you clearly do, Lucy. I know I keep apologising all the time, and the two of you stick by me until the next load of crap comes along and upsets us all, but truly I am sorry. Sorry that my ex-wife is so foul mouthed and my daughter so cold and aloof. Sorry that, between the two of them, they are causing this family such pain. And I'm also sorry that in struggling to deal with their treatment, I've allowed my own despair to additionally impact on you both. All I can say is that I desperately hope Ruby will one day grow up and be free from her mother's poison, and see for herself that the only so-called terrible thing I've ever done is to love her.'

'She's a lucky girl to have a dad like you,' Lucy mumbled.

'Sam, I think you'd better go and see Ruby. You're meant to be meeting in Starbucks for that coffee. Perhaps you can sort things out once and for all. For your sake I really hope so. But what I said earlier still stands. You're my husband and I love you. But I loathe this situation. I don't think Lucy and I can deal with it anymore. Truly.'

Sam nodded. 'For what it's worth, I totally understand. And whether you go ahead and leave me, or change your mind and stay put, I've decided that I will be seeking counselling. I need support, and you're right about getting support from somebody who is impartial. You've been ace letting me lean on you to the extent that I have. But it's not fair on you, Josie.' He gently tipped Lucy off his knee and stood up. 'Let me go and see my daughter. Who knows. Maybe, just maybe, things will come good again. But either way, I'll be sorting my head out first thing Monday morning.'

Josie nodded sadly. 'Good. Well, for what it's worth, give Ruby our love.'

'I will,' Sam said softly. He walked over to the messy drawer where all the keys were kept and extracted his car keys. 'See you both later.' And then he was gone.

Josie and Lucy looked at each other. Josie was the first to speak. 'I just want to say that I thought your text was absolutely cracking.' She gave a wan smile.

'I hope I haven't made things even more difficult for Sam.'

'Darling, things have been shitty for him for so long, they couldn't possibly get any worse.'

Ruby sat opposite her father in Starbucks. She'd never felt so angry in all her life.

'Why are you defending Lucy?' Ruby asked incredulously. 'She was bang out of order texting me a message like that.'

Sam regarded his daughter wearily. 'Ruby, I don't think you have any idea what's been going on in our home.'

'Your *family unit*,' Ruby spat, 'is nothing to do with me.'

'All I've ever wanted, Ruby, is to have a relationship with you, be a dad, and love and support you in everything you do. Josie and Lucy are your step-mother and step-sister–'

'I never asked for that.'

'No, I know you didn't. But sometimes relationships go wrong. Like my relationship with your mum. We split up. People move on, Ruby. Your mum moved on and in with Nigel and, in time, I met Josie.'

'You abandoned me.'

'What are you talking about?' Sam asked incredulously.

'You've never been there for me.'

'Of course I have!'

'Really? So why aren't you living in my house?'

'Because your mum didn't want me – we split up!'

'She *did* want you. She asked to get back together with you but you abandoned us.'

'Ruby, that's not quite the way it happened.' Sam paused, choosing his words carefully. If he bad-mouthed Annie, he had no doubt that Ruby would just up and walk out and he'd never see her again. 'Listen, I don't want to say detrimental things about your mum, but I think you need to know that *she* is the one who left *me*. I didn't abandon either of you.'

Ruby sat back in her seat and eyed her father coldly. 'Yes, I know she was the one who left you. And I know she went off with Nigel.'

Sam looked surprised. 'In which case you can hardly point the finger of blame at me.'

'I think you need to ask yourself, Dad, exactly why Mum left you. I suggest you take your head out of your backside and face up to reality.'

'Whatever are you talking about?'

'The way you treated my mum. The years of abuse you put her through.'

'Ruby, I haven't the faintest idea what you're saying here.'

Ruby's lip curled with contempt. 'She kept a diary, Dad. Oh don't look so startled. I happened to come across it and I read it from cover to cover. It catalogues her entire relationship with you, including my birth and the breakdown of your marriage.'

Sam stared at Ruby in bewilderment. 'Darling, I have no idea what this diary contains but–'

'Don't you *darling* me. My God, when I read about your reaction to my arrival in this world and what a disappointment I was for not being a boy–'

Sam's eyebrows nearly shot off his forehead. 'What the devil are you talking about? I was overjoyed when you were born. I didn't care about anything other than whether our baby had all its fingers and toes and was healthy.'

'Oh, if you say so,' Ruby's voice was scathing in its sarcasm, 'but what about refusing to assist Mum with a shower after the birth?'

'The midwife took her for a shower!'

Ruby leaned forward in her seat. 'BECAUSE YOU REFUSED!' Her raised tone caught the attention of several nearby customers.

Sam squirmed in his seat. 'Ruby, please don't shout.'

'Shout? I'd like to holler out loud and tell the whole world what you're like. And my poor mother had to listen to you making pig noises in the delivery room and ridiculing her body shape. She'd just given birth for Christ's sake!'

'Ruby, this is ridiculous. I can't believe what you're coming out with here. I have no idea what this diary says, but I can assure you I was with your mother throughout the entirety of your birth, held her hand, and encouraged her all the way. When you were born I was overcome with an emotion I've never experienced before or since in my entire life. I was weeping tears of joy! The midwife let me cut the umbilical cord and then, when your mum was helped into the shower, I sat there holding you, unable to tear my gaze away from this perfect tiny human being that your mum and I had made.'

'I don't believe you.'

Sam put up his hands and held them, palms outward, in a gesture of helplessness.

'Ruby, all I can say is if you ever have children yourself one day, you will understand what I'm saying. Believe me, I would walk through fire for my child. I would go to the ends of the earth for my child. I would die for my child.'

'Yeah, right. You just won't be there for your child.'

Sam shook his head in disbelief. 'Do you know how hard I've had to fight to see you, Ruby? Tooth and nail? Through the Courts? How can you accuse me of such a thing?'

'Because when I have kids I'll be there *with* them. Under the same roof! Always. In other words not an absent parent – unlike you!' Ruby stood up. 'I'm done with this conversation. And I never want to see you again.'

Sam watched his daughter move out of the coffee shop. He didn't run after her. He couldn't if he'd tried. He was so stunned at Ruby's revelations, all he could do was sit there, immobilised, as the after effects of his daughter's words shook the very centre of his being.

When Sam did finally manage to move and go home, he spent the remainder of the weekend sleeping. Suddenly it was a major effort to keep his eyes open. Josie found him kipping in front of a football match and presented him with a sandwich. Before he knew it, he'd fallen asleep again and was being awoken for dinner. Sam crawled into bed that night thinking he'd never sleep after napping so extensively throughout the remainder of Saturday and the entirety of Sunday, but Morpheus was leading him down the corridors of sleep no sooner had his head touched the pillow. Sam's last thought was that he must be coming down with something. But a deeper part, an element that he barely wanted to acknowledge, knew the excessive sleep was a way of coping. By retreating into a dark womblike place, it cut off all pain. Being suspended in a silent nothingness stopped him from acknowledging he had a daughter who despised him, a step-daughter who was screwed up because of him, and a wife who was about to leave him.

On Monday morning Sam made an appointment to see his GP. By Tuesday evening he was in possession of a letter to his private health cover's Mental Health Team. He'd declined a prescription for sleeping tablets – that was the last thing he needed. When Friday rolled around, Sam found himself nervously awaiting the last appointment of the day with a psychotherapist. As he stood up to go into her room, the prospect of discussing his problems emanating from Annie and Ruby put his guts into their familiar twist.

The counsellor talked about a relationship of trust and safety. She wanted Sam to talk about his life – who he was, what he did, how he felt – and that each session would be completely focussed on the individual. She pointed out that there was no magic wand, but he would be assisted in becoming the person he wanted to be or felt he really could be. Sam experienced such a sense of relief that, as he opened his mouth to speak, he burst into tears.

'There's a box of tissues on the table to your left,' the counsellor said gently.

'Thank you,' Sam pulled a couple of Kleenex from the cardboard opening. He couldn't help noticing a stack of boxed tissues to one side of the table.

The counsellor caught his look. 'I swear my business keeps companies like that afloat,' she said before giving him an encouraging smile.

Sam gave a watery smile back. 'I'm so sorry.'

'Please don't be. Your reaction is perfectly normal.'

Sam nodded gratefully and took a deep breath. 'Where do you want me to start?'

'Right at the very beginning.'

The following week Lucy began her own counselling. Not with the same therapist because that would have been a conflict of interest, but she attended the same centre as Sam. Josie would spend an hour in the waiting room, marking students' work, while Lucy poured her heart out to a stranger. Josie never asked her daughter about the sessions. Likewise, she didn't ask Sam about his. Emotionally she was still in a very precarious place herself. At times she longed to offload to somebody, just like Sam and Lucy. But a part of her didn't feel comfortable with the idea. She'd already worked through so many difficulties in life off her own steam – like early widowhood and being left to raise a tiny child singlehandedly – that a stubborn part of her felt unable to permit herself to sit opposite a stranger and divest herself of the grief one human being had caused everybody. For Josie, such an admission smacked of failure. And also, if she was absolutely honest with herself, she felt it would be a victory to Annie. And under no circumstances would Josie permit that woman the smallest triumph where her own mental well-being was concerned. Instead, she wrote Annie a long letter. She had no intention of sending it. Thousands of words flowed from her pen and the exercise gave Josie a sense of therapy. Josie almost filled an entire notepad with words of anger and despair. She concluded with an attempt at forgiveness, although had to admit she found that bit hard. But the writing exercise itself proved cathartic enough. When the writing was done, Josie set fire to the notepad. And then she soldiered on, thanked God for her good friend Kerry who frequently offered broad shoulders to lean upon, and just generally got on with it.

Prior to counselling, Sam and Josie discussed splitting up. But once counselling was underway, there was such a noticeable difference in both Sam's and Lucy's mental well-being, that the impending separation was put on hold. And although Sam and Lucy always left the clinic emotionally drained and red-eyed, it was as if they'd dumped their struggles at the centre. Emotionally speaking, problems in the main no longer came home to 2 Sycamore Drive. Consequently the tension within the family home reduced considerably.

Sam still checked his phone for messages from Ruby in the hope that his daughter would make contact. Once a week he'd try ringing Ruby but his calls went unanswered. Instead, he'd tap out texts wishing her a good week at school, or to have a nice weekend, and always sign off with lots of love. From time to time Annie would ring him to fire off a stream of abuse about him being a crap father. Sam no longer tried to reason with the woman, or beg for the crumbs of a relationship with his daughter. Instead he'd simply press the disconnect button on Annie's call and cut off her diatribe. The counsellor had helped Sam see so much. For years Annie had pulled his strings and made him dance to her tune. He'd been like a marionette, driven by fear. Fear of losing touch with his daughter. But then Ruby had picked up the baton where Annie had left off, and the very thing he'd been so scared of had happened anyway. But now he'd stopped begging for a relationship. And in doing so, he'd taken away their power. But by God it hurt. The counsellor had assured Sam that one day Ruby would come back to him. Sam could only hope she was right.

Within three months Lucy felt she'd beaten her bulimia demons. The urge to self-harm was improving but a little more difficult to master. It was an addiction. And like all bad habits, it needed willpower and determination to beat it. Lucy kept a mood diary and learnt to recognise her triggers. A couple of times a week she'd jog with her mum to the park and back, and at weekends Sam would join them and they'd run all together. It was a good stress buster and helped fight the doldrums. Lucy had made peace over her relationship issues with Sam. He might not be her biological dad, and she might not call him Dad, but he was still *her dad* and nobody could change that. Not Annie. Not Ruby. Sam was the man who'd raised her and the man she lived with. He'd had a huge influence on her life – and in the main it was a good influence. Lucy had come to terms with the fact that she wasn't Ruby, never had been and never would be, but that didn't mean Sam didn't love her. Because he did. He loved her as any father would love a daughter. And now that she was talking to somebody impartial, she could see all this and understand it. It was about overcoming obstacles, living in the here and now, and enjoying life in a more fulfilling way. These days Lucy's step was lighter. Finally she was learning to be happy.

Chapter Forty-One
Eight months later

Sam put an arm around Josie. She snuggled into his chest. They were lying in bed and enjoying a lazy Sunday morning.

'Have you remembered that there's a very special day coming up?' Sam gave his wife a squeeze.

'Oh?'

'You mean you don't know!' Sam pretended to be outraged.

'Ah,' Josie smiled. 'Would you be referring to our wedding anniversary?'

'Of course! So, to celebrate, what would you like me to buy you?'

'Well,' Josie considered, 'I wouldn't mind a new hairdryer.'

'A *hairdryer*? That's not very romantic!'

Josie sat up and looked at Sam. 'Ooh, I'm allowed to have something romantic am I? In that case, what about a candlelit dinner somewhere *fritefly porsh*.'

Sam laughed. 'No problem, you can have your posh nosh. I was thinking more along the line of,' he took her left hand, 'a piece of jewellery. A ring more specifically. An eternity ring.'

'Oh my God,' Josie gasped, 'ohmigod, ohmigod, ohmigod – yes please!'

Sam pushed Josie onto her back. Leaning over, he kissed her thoroughly on the mouth. 'We've been through a great deal together. I love you so much, Josie. Second time around isn't easy, and at times our relationship has been no bed of roses. But we're still together. Love is a beautiful thing. Love is also painful. It's entanglement with reality, which isn't always very kind – as we both know so well. I want to buy you a full diamond eternity ring.'

'A diamond for every quarrel,' Josie teased.

'On the contrary. A diamond to symbolise the number of difficulties that have tested, but not defeated, us.'

Josie reached up and cupped her husband's face in her hands. 'Have I told you that I love you?'

'Not for about twenty-four hours.'

'Then I think I'd better say it one more time.'

'You can do better than that,' Sam threaded his fingers through Josie's hair, 'you can prove it.'

And for the next half an hour, Josie did just that.

Lucy was propped up against her pillows. She loved Sundays and not having to get up to rush off somewhere. Right now she was relaxing with her iPad and chatting via Facebook with Tom, one of the hottest lads in the boys' grammar directly opposite Lucy's school. Lucy liked Tom enormously. Despite being good-looking, he wasn't full of himself. He'd been chatting with Lucy on the bus home for the last two or three weeks. And now he was asking her if she'd like to see a film with him! Lucy didn't think her mum or Sam would mind her having a boyfriend. Lucy's self-esteem had gone from strength to strength recently. Having a boy like Tom ask her out was the icing on the cake.

'So what do you say?' Tom had typed.

And now Lucy typed back. 'I say that would be fab!'

Annie had just had a huge row with Ruby. They'd ended up screaming at each other and were now in their respective bedrooms. There had been much door slamming by both of them. Rows with Ruby were becoming more and more prolific. Indeed, Annie was struggling to control Ruby. These days her influence held less sway. Their argument had been about university of all things. Ruby still had a couple of years to go before that was even a reality, but when her daughter had so casually announced she was hoping to apply to Oxford to study English Language and Literature, Annie had been horrified.

'What the heck do you want to go to uni for?' she'd demanded. 'You hate school. What makes you think you'll like university?'

'I don't hate *school*,' Ruby had countered, 'it was all the irrelevant subjects that I had to do for my GCSEs that got me down. Just soooo twatty.'

'Don't use that word.'

'Oh get *over* it,' Ruby had rolled her eyes.

'I thought you hated studying full stop.'

'No. I hated wasting my time swotting subjects like physics and chemistry which were irrelevant for my chosen career.'

Chosen career? This had been news to Annie. 'I thought you could get a job with me at the doctors' practice. Play your cards right and you'll be running the place by the time I retire.'

'No thanks,' Ruby had screwed up her nose disdainfully. 'I want a bit of fun. I want to meet people. Do the freshers' fortnight. Live in digs with friends.'

'Live in digs? Don't be ridiculous. You're dependent on me.'

'Well I won't be when I'm eighteen.'

Annie had pursed her lips. 'You're not going to uni. And as for leaving home – that's something that I don't want you to do until you're thirty.'

'Thirty?' Ruby had screeched. 'I don't think so. Have you any idea how bloody ridiculous you sound?'

'I don't want to hear another word about university.'

'What's wrong with you, Mum? Why can't you be ambitious for me? Why don't you encourage me to follow my dreams?'

'Because your so-called ambitions are nothing more than pipedreams, Ruby. You'd be homesick within two minutes of unpacking your suitcase. You've never been independent in your life.'

'That's because you haven't let me.'

'How dare you speak to me like this?' Annie had felt fury rising within her. 'Go to your room – now!'

'Don't worry – I'm bloody going!' Ruby had spat back.

The truth of the matter was – much as Ruby loved her mother – she was starting to find Annie's stranglehold stifling. Annie didn't even know her daughter was dating Jackson. Her mother would go mad, not just because Jackson was black but because Ruby now realised her mother was possessive about her. Years ago Ruby had been dependent on her mother. These days the roles had reversed. Annie had made Ruby the centre of her universe. She had hardly any friends and absolutely no romance in her life. During the week she worked at the medical practice. At weekends Annie looked to Ruby for her social life. Whether it was out at the local shopping mall doing a bit of retail therapy, going out for a pizza, taking in a movie, or even going off to Brighton on a jolly. Not that long ago Ruby had been up for such events. But not anymore. Now she wanted to be available for an impromptu sleepover with her girlfriends, or disappear to watch a video at Jackson's house, or take off on a giggly girly outing to London and lark about in Trafalgar Square.

Annie sat down on the edge of her bed. In the distant corners of her mind she'd been aware that one day Ruby would leave home. But that had seemed so far away. Annie herself had been in her twenties before she'd felt brave enough to leave her mother's side. Almost immediately she'd met Sam. Annie had never properly been alone in her entire life. And now Ruby had sprung some madcap idea about going to university in less than two years time. Annie couldn't imagine living in her house all on her own. Suddenly a future without Ruby loomed horribly close, and Annie didn't like what she saw. A yawning and lonely chasm. The thought terrified her. Softly, she began to cry.

Ruby threw herself onto her bed. She felt frustrated and pissed off. Why wasn't her mother proud of her desire to one day get a degree and do something with her life? How could Mum possibly even begin to imagine that Ruby would be happy glued to her side twenty-four-seven. They lived together, and often went out together. To work together too was nothing short of smothering. Ruby longed to have somebody else to talk to about it. She picked up her mobile phone and considered ringing some friends. But in all truth, they wouldn't understand. They'd be sympathetic naturally, but they couldn't help her realise her dream. That was something a parent did for you. Well that ruled out her mum, because she was so anti. But...Ruby fingered her mobile phone...it didn't rule out her dad. Did it?

Ruby chewed her lip. These past few weeks she'd thought about her dad a lot. So many times she'd gone to call him, and then abandoned the idea. Initially, she'd curled her lip at his regular texts and messages of love. But as the months had gone by, she'd come to cherish them. And a part of her felt ashamed. She didn't know who to believe about her parents' marriage. Mum had written a detailed and utterly convincing diary. But Dad had looked so flabbergasted at the so-called revelations and sounded so genuine when talking about the joy of her birth. And lately, in still moments, a small voice in Ruby's head had spoken up: *whatever happened between your parents was their business – it was their relationship and nothing to do with you!*

Ruby turned the phone over and over in her hands. She loved her dad. And she missed him. And if she was really honest, she missed her step-mum and step-sister too. Ruby knew that Josie would encourage her desire to go to university, and doubtless assist with application forms. And Lucy would probably shout, 'Yay, let's go to the same university and share digs.'

Ruby's eyes welled. She wanted to see them – her family. Above all she wanted to see her dad. It was Sunday. He'd be at home. Ruby knew her father would be over the moon to hear from her. He'd *always* been there and never turned his back on her, despite her accusing him otherwise. It was time to make peace.

Trembling slightly, Ruby pressed her mobile's touch screen.

ALSO BY DEBBIE VIGGIANO

Stockings and Cellulite

As the clock strikes midnight on New Year's Eve, Cassandra Cherry's life takes a turn for the worse when she stumbles upon husband Stevie lying naked, except for his socks, on a coat-strewn bed with a 45-year-old divorcee called Cynthia. Suddenly single, Cass throws herself into the business of getting over Stevie with gusto. Her main problems now are making her nine-year-old twins happy, juggling a new social life with a return to work and avoiding being arrested by an infuriating policeman who always seems to turn up at the most inopportune moments. Then, just when Cass is least prepared, and much to Stevie's chagrin, she crashes head over heels in love with the last person she'd ever expected.

AVAILABLE NOW AS AN E-BOOK AND PAPERBACK

ALSO BY DEBBIE VIGGIANO

Flings and Arrows

Steph Garvey has been married to husband Si for 24 years. Steph thought they were soulmates. Until recently. Surely one's soulmate shouldn't put Chelsea FC before her? Or boycott caressing her to fondle the remote control? Fed up, Steph uses her Tesco staff discount to buy a laptop. Her friends all talk about Facebook. It's time to get networking.

Si is worried about middle-age spread and money. Being a self-employed plumber isn't easy in recession. He's also aware things aren't right with Steph. But Si has forgotten the art of romance. Although these days Steph prefers cuddling her laptop to him. Then Si's luck changes work wise. A mate invites Si to partner up on a pub refurbishment contract.

Son Tom has finished Sixth Form. Tom knows where he's going regarding a career. He's not quite so sure where he's going regarding women and lurches from one frantic love affair to the next.

Widowed neighbour June adores the Garveys as if her own kin. And although 70, she's still up for romance. June thinks she's struck gold when she meets salsa squeeze Harry. He has a big house and bigger pension – key factors when you've survived a winter using your dog as a hot water bottle. June is vaguely aware that she's attracted the attention of fellow dog walker Arnold, but her eyes are firmly on Harry as 'the catch'.

But then Cupid's arrow misfires causing madness and mayhem. Steph rekindles a childhood crush with Barry Hastings; Si unwittingly finds himself being seduced by barmaid Dawn; June discovers Harry is more than hot to trot; and Tom's latest strumpet impacts on all of them. Will Cupid's arrow strike again and, more importantly, strike correctly? There's only one way to find out....

AVAILABLE NOW AS AN E-BOOK AND PAPERBACK

ALSO BY DEBBIE VIGGIANO

Lipstick and Lies

41-year old Cassandra Mackerel is loved up and happily re-married to new husband Jamie. Together they have a ready-made family and a six month old baby boy. Juggling her own children with step-children and an infant is both hectic and stressful, especially with a mother-in-law who seems to have taken up permanent residence.

Cass has a strong support system in good friend and new mum Morag – who is the fourth Mrs Harding with more step-children she can keep up with – and also old neighbour and great pal Nell who has a baby girl.

Rising to the challenge of a second marriage and the emotional baggage that comes with it is tough. The last thing Cass needs is the reappearance of husband Jamie's ex-girlfriend Selina. Gorgeous and glamorous but utterly unstable, Selina once stalked Cass and contrived to split her and Jamie up. And now Selina is engaged to Jamie's business partner, Ethan Fareham. Seemingly it is appalling coincidence.

Cass can't shake the feeling that Selina is up to her old tricks. And she's right to be worried. For if Selina has her way, she'll split Cass and Jamie up permanently. Because this time it's murder...

AVAILABLE NOW AS AN EBOOK AND PAPERBACK

ALSO BY DEBBIE VIGGIANO

Mixed Emotions

Life is a funny old thing. There are times when we love it, relish every moment and can't get enough of it. Equally there are other times when life is jail sentence. Something comes along that knocks us right off our feet. The sun ceases to shine and our smiles vanish.

As we walk through life we fall in love, out of love, and in love again - sometimes many times over. We forge long and rewarding friendships - but sometimes are betrayed. We deal with tricky ex partners, and picky neighbours. We get pregnant, give birth and some of us experience stillbirth. And just when we think we can't take any more, something happens to cause our hearts to expand with love.

We are left feeling warm and fuzzy inside.

Life is full of mixed emotions. And that's what this little book is about.

AVAILABLE NOW AS AN EBOOK AND PAPERBACK

ABOUT THE AUTHOR

Prior to turning her attention to writing, Debbie Viggiano was, for more years than she cares to remember, a legal secretary. She lives with her husband, children, a food-obsessed beagle and a cat that thinks it's a dog.

Follow her blog: www.debbieviggiano.blogspot.com

Tweet @DebbieViggiano or look her up on Facebook!

Printed in Great Britain
by Amazon

A story
Excels

living history.

THE
Excelsior
TRUST

Edited by Jamie Campbell

http://www.excelsiortrust.co.uk

cover photograph. archives

First published in this edition in 2001

by

Hamilton Publications Ltd.,
9 Marine Parade,
Gorleston on sea,
Norfolk. NR 31 6DU.
http://www.hamiltonpublications.com

for The Excelsior Trust,
Harbour Road,
Oulton Broad,
Lowestoft
Suffolk. NR32 3LY
Telephone: 01502 - 580507
Facsimile: 01502 - 585302
email: sales@excelsiortrust.co.uk
http://www.excelsiortrust.co.uk

British Library cataloguing in publication data. A catalogue record of this title is available from the British Library.

ISBN 0 903094 09 6

With the exception of outside copyrights, The Excelsior Trust has no objection to the reproduction of anything contained in this booklet, with the sole proviso that the source is acknowledged.

Printed in Great Britain by Micropress Ltd., 27 Norwich Road, Halesworth, Suffolk. IP 19 8BX.

Excelsior LT472. Vital Statistics.

Port of Registry: Lowestoft, Suffolk, UK.

Length overall: 77 feet (23.2m)

Length between perpendiculars: 68' 6" (20.6m)

Waterline Length: 66' 9" (20.1m)

Total length over spars: 108' 6" (32.7m)

Max. Beam: 19'3" (5.8 m)

Draught aft: 9'3" (2.8m)

Draught forward: 4'6" (1.4m)

Displacement: 100 tons

Gross Registered tons: 55.36

Net Registered tons: 29.86

Air draft. 78' (23.5m)

Rig: Dandy or Gaff Ketch.

Working sail area: 2,700 square feet.

Maximum sail area 3,400 square feet, set on 1 1/2 miles of rigging.

Auxiliary engine: Lister JK 6W

Generator: air cooled Lister

Crew: originally five

Crew: now 17 including twelve guests; more in sheltered waters.

Construction: oak on oak, iron fastened.

Built by John Chambers & Co., Laundry Lane, Lowestoft, Suffolk.

Foreword by The Right Honourable Lord Somerleyton GCVO. Chairman, Excelsior Trust.

This short booklet has no ending. It is the story of *Excelsior*, but a story that continues with every new trainee that sets foot on deck. *Excelsior* is an historic ship and recognised by the National Maritime Museum as one of the nation's "core list" of fifty most important vessels, alongside household names such as HMS *Victory*, the *Cutty Sark* and the *SS Great Britain*. Her restoration and seaworthiness is testimony to a huge amount of work and generosity by and from a very large number of people. She has proved to be a triumph of optimism over realism.

Excelsior represents the once great fleets of sailing trawlers that landed fresh fish from the unkind waters of the North Sea. *Excelsior* was extensively and painstakingly restored. Apart from the addition of modern safety equipment, no effort has been spared to maintain her authenticity. She is the only sailing trawler in the UK that can still trawl for fish. If a fisherman from the late nineteenth century were able to walk her deck today, he would find things very much as he expected.

Excelsior sails; therefore she lives. In stark contrast to current museum practice, it is central to the ethos of our Trust, that ships are best preserved by use. There is pure pleasure in pushing a hundred tons of English oak through the water, using only the power of the wind. *Excelsior's* sheerline serves to show off her elegant, eliptical counter, so typical of the Lowestoft boats. She is preserved for all to share. Come on board, have a look over *Excelsior*, possibly take a trip. If you like what you see, and feel able to support the Trust's work, please have a look at the last page of this booklet.

Somerleyton Hall, Suffolk.

Excelsior was built by Chambers & Co. of Lowestoft and first registered in 1921. She was one of the last sailing trawlers to be built and although a new vessel, she was essentially built to a design that had been perfected and hardly altered since the 1880's. She exemplifies the zenith of the evolution of sailing trawlers.

Two Lowestoft sailing trawlers have borne both the name *Excelsior* and the registration number LT472. The first was built in 1885 by Samuel Allerton. Unlike many of her contemporaries, she survived the First World War but was badly damaged when a Dutch fishing vessel rammed her in thick fog, early in 1919. She managed to limp back to Lowestoft but the damage was such that the hull was condemned. Her owners immediately ordered a new smack from Chambers, to carry the same name and registration number.

The first *Excelsior*, leaving Lowestoft harbour with a couple of steam drifters and lug rigged, Scottish Zulus.   *photo: Ford Jenkins.*

John Chambers had taken over or merged with several other Lowestoft ship yards, making them one of the largest builders of fishing boats in the country. They owned three yards in the town; No 3 yard was at Oulton Broad, about where the Green Jack Brewery is today. No 2 yard was on the south bank of Lake Lothing and eventually incorporated into Richards Shipbuilders, whilst the No 1 yard was at Laundry Lane. Laundry Lane was at the end of Commercial Road and the facilities of the yard were divided by the railway line. It was there that the current *Excelsior* was built. She was was one of five sister ships built after the first world war. Harry Wren was an apprentice at the yard at that time and reported in 1986, that the boat had been built on spec. by mainly apprentice labour. The accident with the Dutch boat must have almost come to order. Harry's father, E.J.Wren, at the time working from

Belvedere Road, rigged the new *Excelsior* from gear salvaged from the old boat, which was subsequently broken up.

This Chambers family photograph was presented to the Trust by Shirley Pidgeon, grand-daughter of John Chambers. John Chambers is in the centre of the photograph holding the child, with his wife on his right hand side. Immediately behind is his son, Ernest who designed *Excelsior*. In total four of his sons and two daughters are included in this family grouping.

Chambers shipyard at Laundry Lane, Lowestoft.

photo. H. Jenkins

Sir Samuel Morton Peto was a high rolling Victorian entrepreneur. He had been building contractor for the new House of Commons and pursued ventures in Denmark. As part of the war effort, he built a railway in the Crimea, for which he was knighted. Closer to home, he developed much of South Lowestoft into a highly fashionable health resort. Crucially, he also extended the harbour, built a fish market and provided a rail link to vital markets inland. In 1831, Lowestoft's population was just 2,000 souls and fish had traditionally been eaten as a penance on Fridays and fast days. The options for those inland consisted of dried cod or salted herring. Peto stood up in the Town Hall in 1843 and promised a meeting of the Lowestoft Commissioners that he would deliver Lowestoft fish to Manchester on the same day it was landed. The inland markets exploded.

At that time, the Acts of Inclosure were forcing people off the land. Norfolk and Suffolk lead the Agricultural Revolution but the Industrial Revolution largely by-passed East Anglia and provided little alternative employment in the towns. By contrast, Lowestoft must have had a "Klondyke" feel. The town was transformed into a vital, thriving centre of the fishing industry and by 1893, the population had risen to 26,000. Sir Samuel Morton Peto provided the catalyst for change. Along the way, he found time to develop Somerleyton Hall for himself.

The sailing fishermen were divided by two differing methods of fishing. "Luggers" drifted for the migratory, surface shoals of herring or mackerel. Mackerel were more of a gamble than herring but very profitable when successful. The drifters crews were often local agricultural workers during the spring and summer; going to sea after harvest festival. The Scots would follow the fish south, in their distinctively rigged "Zulus" and "Fifies". The early Scots boats were open and far more spartan than their English equivalents. In spite of a great deal of official advice, they suffered appalling losses. When there was no wind, they would row around the coastline. (*Excelsior* is still fitted with "sweeps" for the energetic.) The Scots brought their women with them, to gut and cure the herring and the "Scots girls" became a familiar sight along the east coast. 1913 was the record year for drifters, when 1,776 vessels had landed 1,359,213 crans at the east coast ports. A cran comprised roughly 1,000 herring. Landings are even more impressive when account is taken of a season lasting only from October to December. The fishing fraternity thought the harvest would go on for ever but even in 1893, fears of over fishing brought about a House of Commons Select Committee Enquiry.

Smacks, unlike drifters, fished the bottom, mainly for plaice and sole, with a beam trawl or sometimes "longlined" for cod with very long lengths of baited hooks. The smacks brought home better fish, in better condition. Smack design was descended from fast revenue and pilot cutters, as they needed power to drag their net along the bottom. Although commercial sailing boats were eventually developed to carry out both types of fishing (called "converters"), the Lowestoft fleet of nearly seven hundred first class vessels, was divided roughly equally between drifters and trawlers. The trawling fleet caught more fish during the winter months but fished all year round. Lowestoft became the largest centre in England for sailing trawlers.

Fishing trips would normally be about four days for a single trawler, which had to be fast enough to race back to market before ice melted. Drifters fished for a much shorter period, hoping to fill their holds overnight.

It was obviously more profitable to keep the smacks away for longer periods and an unpopular "fleeting" system of unloading each days catch into fish carriers became prevalent elsewhere. "Fleeting" trips could be eight to ten weeks long and much more dangerous, as the catch had to be transferred whilst at sea. The prospect of hauling 150 fathoms of six inch circumference hemp warp, complete with all the attached nets and gear, every five or six hours, in all weathers for two months on end, must have been truly daunting.

A significant fleet of shrimpers and inshore vessels completed the picture. Thus it was once possible to walk across Lowestoft harbour on a thousand fishing boats during the season.

The fleet in harbour. *photo. Ford Jenkins*

The thriving industry attracted some colourful characters, including Edward Fitzgerald, who had earlier translated The Rubaiyat of Omar Khayyam. "Old Fitz" was a noted eccentric and a keen east coast yachtsman; he was sometimes seen on the deck of his yacht, *Scandal* wearing a silk top hat and a feather boa. Fitzgerald part owned a Lowestoft fishing boat, the *Meum & Tuum* (locally known as the MumTum). The boat was not particularly successful but Fitzgerald wished to sponsor his fisherman friend, "Posh" Fletcher.

photo. H. Jenkins

Trawlermen were often illiterate and many went to sea at twelve years of age after the most rudimentary education. Most had no formal navigational training and there were no shipping forecasts, radio, GPS or radar. Electronic fish finders and graph plotters had not even entered the imagination. These men navigated hundreds of miles with a compass, a traverse board and a lead line. The lead would not only provide the depth of the sea but tallow set in the bottom, gave a sample of the sea bed. Most contemporary reports note never seeing a skipper using a chart. They shared an intimate knowledge of the changing colour of the water, set courses from memory and intuitively made allowances for tide and leeway. They were ship handlers that will never be matched.

Ted Grint's brother is the boy in the photograph holding the halibut, his school uniform may have been his only clothes. Today *Excelsior* continues to give young men their first taste of the sea. *photo. Bill Nobbs.*

Fishing by shares was the most common system for payment of the crew. The usual arrangement was for net earnings (after deduction of running expenses) to be divided on a basis of nine shares for the the owner(s) and seven to the crew.

Ships in shares usually amount to sixty four; useful as a highly divisible number. When *Excelsior* was launched in 1921, her owners shares were:
Wood Greaves (fish merchant) 16 shares.
Frederick Burton (Runner or Ship's husband) 16 shares.
Arthur Gouldby (described as a boat owner.) 16 shares.
Reginald Gouldby 8 shares
Clifford A. Gouldby (fish merchant) 8 shares.
In 1934, Arthur Gouldby acquired Frederick Burton's shares. There were no further changes to registered ownership until the register closed in 1936.

photo: Ford Jenkins

The steam tug *Despatch* towing sailing trawlers out of the harbour. The charge for a tow was 5/- out and 7/6d back into the harbour. (Trainees should enquire of their parents for a current equivalent). In November 1877, the tug *Messenger* towed a smack out of North Shields and in flat calm weather, continued to tow her after she had shot her trawl. The tugmaster, William Pandy reasoned he probably didn't need the trawler and went home and had his tug fitted out for fishing. His was the first successful experiment into steam fishing. This photograph shows a yacht waiting to leave the harbour, presumably waiting for a race. The Norfolk & Suffolk Yacht Club moved its base to Lowestoft in 1885 at the height of the "Klondyke" years. Now described as the Royal Norfolk and Suffolk Yacht Club, it has long been associated with a small but competent yachting fraternity.

On the 25th of November 1925, Lowestoft experienced its worst gale since November 1897. Wind and driving rain came with terrific force from the NNW. It then veered to the NE and threw up a very heavy sea. *Excelsior* was fishing forty miles, east a half north of Lowestoft. At 11.30 skipper Jimmy Strong ordered a third reef in the mainsail. Suddenly, the third hand shouted: "Look out, water!" A tremendous sea swept the vessel and when the decks had cleared, the skipper shouted: "Are you all there?" The mate Henry Bydle was standing in the small boat holding on to the deckhand, J. Whitlam, who had been swept off his feet and fetched up against the boats transom, injuring his right arm and shoulder. Somebody shouted "Jimmy's gone!" and James Lockett, the cook, aged 50, was in the sea some 30 yards astern, on the lee quarter. The skipper threw a lifebuoy but it fell twenty yards short. The cook, dressed in oilies and seaboots could only just keep himself afloat and couldn't reach the lifebuoy. The skipper put the boat around on the starboard tack and got within ten yards of him, with the boathook at the ready, but he sank and never appeared again. They hove to for an hour, hoping to catch sight of him and then sailed for Lowestoft with the gale still blowing.

A lad known as "Smokey" Lewis joined Excelsior in place of poor old Jimmy Lockett. It was his first trip to sea and at that time, boys were supposed to be seen but never heard. He was dipping the bucket for water to peel some potatoes when, as so often happens if you are not shown how, the sea took charge of the bucket and wrenched the lanyard out of his hands. He was too frightened to tell anyone but a couple of hours later, when the trawl was hauled and the catch shot on deck, there was the bucket for all to see. He said: "the skipper just looked at me, I felt two inches tall."

Skipper Jimmy Strong (second from the left) with his crew on the stern of a smack, sometime between 1907 and 1914. *photo. Mrs. Eva Spindler*

James William Hoppins Strong was something of a character himself, who worked at sea for forty-two years. Born into an old fishing family at Brixham in 1875, he moved with his family to the expanding port of Lowestoft. Jimmy Strong first went to sea at the age of eleven as a cook in a smack. At twenty-five, he changed tacks, to sail in mail and troop ships to the Cape of Good Hope and India. After a spell crewing yachts on the east coast of the United States, he returned to England to crew Lord Iveagh's yacht *Cetonia*. He was part of the crew, when according to Jimmy they took "the King's prize" at Cowes. His next ship was the *Valhalla*, owned by the Earl of Crawford. The earl was a keen ornithologist, a trustee of the British Museum and a Fellow of the Zoological Society. In 1900, *Valhalla* sailed to Trinidad, Tristan da Cunha, Cape Town, the Seychelles via the Mozambique Channel, Aden and the Red Sea. In 1907, Jimmy married and returned to fishing out of Lowestoft. For several years he skippered a smack for George Hume. During the First World War, skipper Strong had command of armed smacks and saw action. He fought five German submarines and on March 16th 1916, managed to sink two in one day. Jimmy Strong became *Excelsior's* first skipper. He stayed with the boat until 1928, when his son, Jack Strong was born. Conscious of his responsibilities, the new father gave up his sea-going career and took a job ashore. Jimmy lived in Bevan Street, Lowestoft until he died in 1958, aged 83.

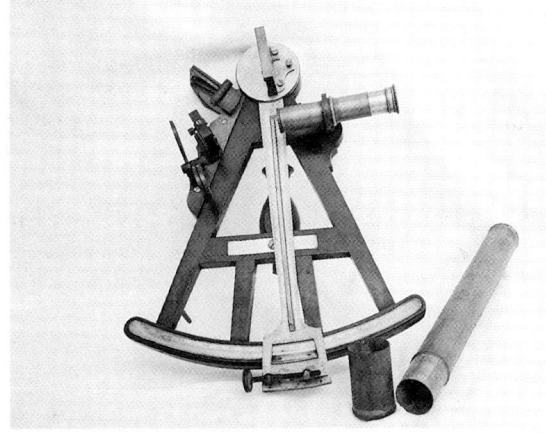

photo. editor

Jimmy Strong's octant and his waterproof document case. These tin document cases were issued to trawler skippers during the First World War. Both were donated to the Trust by his daughter, Mrs. Eva Spindler.

Bob Evans joined *Excelsior* in 1927 as boy/cook. His brother did a trip in his school holidays, which was the way in which many boys were introduced to fishing. In 1986, Bob recalled a narrow escape he had one day, when a strop on the top block of the for'ard fish tackle parted with the weight trawl head and the block narrowly missed him as it crashed onto the deck. He said "You should have heard the skipper (still Jimmy Strong) tearing a strip off the mate for that. It was the mate's responsibility to check that sort of thing."

Bob recalled, that after a trip on *Excelsior*, he went as usual for a trim and a shave. The barber asked, as barbers do, what sort of a trip it had been:
"Pretty fair"
"What was the weather like?"
"Not too bad."
"Did you make much money?"
"I did all right"
"Which smack?"
"*Excelsior*"
"What's she like?"
"Oh pretty good" replied Bob. At this point a big old chap in the next chair said: "I should think I own most part o' her." Bob said: " It was Wood Greaves, who I knew was one of the owners but I'd never met him before. Well, I obviously said the right things because he paid for my haircut."

The nineteen twenties saw the rise of steam but *Excelsior* continued to fish until 1936, when she was laid up on the beach in the Hamilton Dock. East coast boats found a ready market in Scandinavia, whilst the Ramsgate boats were usually sold to Belgium. Brixham sailing trawlers had no obvious commercial market but most found homes with Englishmen for conversion to yachts. As several are still seen around our coast, there is a popular misconception that Brixham was home to the largest fleet of sailing trawlers, whereas it was one of the smallest.

Excelsior was sold to Bjørn Stensland of Norway. She sailed across the North Sea with a cargo of steaming coal as ballast. In 1937, her conversion to auxiliary motor coaster was taken in hand. The hull was gutted and a 60 hp single cylinder Grenaa semi-diesel was installed. The sail locker became a two berth crew mess and the rest of the hull devoted to cargo, with two hatches cut into the deck. A wheel house was built over the engine and a new two berth cabin for master and mate was constructed on the counter. The mizzen mast was somewhat precariously stepped on top of the new cabin whilst topmast and bowsprit were removed. She was re-registered in Mandal under the name of Svinør; her home port being the island of Svinøy, just east of Linderness. She traded from Svinøy but was destined to become the last trading vessel to be operate from that port. Fortunately her hull and bulwarks were unaltered and clear evidence remained of her various sailing fittings. This was to become important, as no original, detailed drawings of Lowestoft built smacks survived - Survived as her eventual rebuild was to be as close as possible to the original.

In 1954, she was sold to two other islanders, Sverre and Ole Börufsen. They eventually took down the mizzen and removed all sails apart from the foresail.

The Börufsens traded mainly cement cargoes until their retirement in 1971. In that year, she was purchased by John Wylson of Rye and two partners, concluding a lengthy search for a sea going, commercial sailing vessel in restorable condition. The following year, they set a course sail for Lowestoft and *Excelsior* arrived home on August 10th 1972. They were not allowed to leave Norway without a sample of the original coal ballast cargo of 1936.

The brothers Börufsen   *photo Wylson.*

Excelsior on her return to Lowestoft, disguised as a Norwegian motor coaster.
photo. Peter Waller

1972 saw a change of partnership and left the boat jointly owned by John Wylson and Mark Trevitt of Beccles. By 1981, they had stripped away the Norwegian alterations, replaced a third of the framing, fitted new stringers and renewed half a dozen deck beams. Significant progress for two individuals but clearly the project was not going to be completed within an acceptable timescale. The following year, the pair decided to create a Charitable Trust to enlist wider support; donating to the new trust both the vessel and the accumulated stockpile of material. Via no less than three government departments, The Excelsior Trust was finally incorporated on 2nd February 1983.

The publicity of the day added an optimistic target of £75,000 to make the vessel seaworthy, although the real key to the completion of the restoration of *Excelsior* was George Prior's generosity in making one of his slipways available on Lake Lothing.

Excelsior on George Prior's slip in 1985   *photo. archives*

Here, with labour provided by the government's Manpower Services Commission, work could progress much faster. The project provided work, initially for seventeen craftsmen and labourers, taken on in early 1985 but expanded to thirty one the following year. Unemployed persons gained work experience and picked up skills their grandfathers would have recognised. There were many personal success stories from this scheme, although it must often have been sapping work. A seven thirty start on a February morning with an east wind driving through flogging polythene sheeting is great training for the work ethic. John Wylson completed the research and supervised the project. Smacksman Bill Nobbs provided a series of fifty photographs that he took with a Brownie box camera between the wars. The information these photographs provided was to prove invaluable.

Both Lowestoft and Great Yarmouth businesses helped with cash and kind, George Darling chaired the fund rasing committee and provided a considerable lead in Great Yarmouth. Grant giving Trusts provided generous donations to help with local unemployment, whilst assistance from the community varied from supporting large fundraising events to donating grandfather's tools.

One of the largest tasks was replanking; each plank was cut from a rough sawn, oak tree trunk. A hundred trees might be used in the building of a smack. The planks vary in length to ensure that the butts (vertical joints) are staggered. From cutting to fixing could take three days and each plank required four people to lift it - more to carry it from the steam chest. The rest of the deck beams were replaced - they were up to seven inches square and nineteen feet long and took eight "young gentlemen" to manhandle them into position.

The hull took to the water again on 24th July 1986. The amount of work achieved becomes apparent from a list of items replaced:-

A completely new stern.
Rebuilt bows.
All timber heads. (top sections of frames)
New rudder and rudder trunk.
New propeller, shaft and stern gland.
Beds for new engine.
Installation of rebuilt 6 cyl. Lister engine.
Fifteen deck beams.
Full set of 4" oak lodging knees for deck beams.
Twelve new starkes - planks of up to 3" x 8" x up to 35' of oak.)
Fairing of 1,000 square feet of hull and 1/3 mile of caulking.

The Trust were given use of the CPS Fuels Quay on Lake Lothing for fitting out and space for temporary workshops was made available by Seabed Scour Control Systems. Fitting out work, including new deck planking, bulwarks, accommodation and deck fittings took place at the CPS Fuels quay.

Excelsior at the CPS Fuels quay on Lake Lothing undergoing redecking.

photo. David Standley

In 1884, William Garood of Beccles invented a steam capstan that was to have a significant impact on the design of fishing vessels. His company were to sell six thousand to the fishing fleets of the world. Initially the new capstans were not popular with crews, as the owners tried to charge them for using the mechanical assistance! In some ports, this lead to local disagreements known as the capstan riots. Sailing trawlers of the day were predominantly cutter rigged, with large areas of canvas that took a lot of manpower to handle. Garood's new capstan made four capstan hands redundant and with fewer hands available, a rationalisation of the rig was required. The ketch or dandy rig, became popular - its larger number of smaller sails were more easily managed by fewer crew. These trawlers were a good example of transitional technology; they used steam for their equipment but still relied on the wind for their motive power. The steam capstan made handling larger nets possible and encouraged larger smacks. In Great Yarmouth particularly, vessels were often cut across the point of maximum beam and lengthened by ten or fifteen feet. Steam motive power was not to become prevalent until the 1920's.

In 1976, Mark Trevitt discovered a small steam capstan lying derelict at George Overy's yard on Harbour Road (by coincidence, now the Excelsior yard) and persuaded Mr Overy, who was about to retire, to sell the capstan. It was duly carted away in sorry state. The age of the capstan is uncertain but it probably dates from about 1922. It had been removed from the Fifie *Onway* that Overys had refitted and altered in 1952. *Onway w*as built in 1922 and if the capstan was not original equipment, it was certainly on board by the 1930's. The capstan had remained at Overy's "just in case", until Mark stumbled across it. The unit was similar, although smaller, than *Excelsior's* original equipment.

"B" Size STEAM CAPSTAN & BOILER.

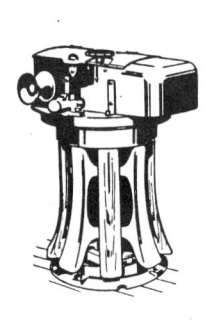

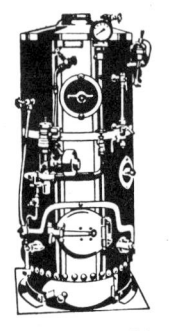

The "B" size Steam Capstan and Boiler are smaller than any set supplied to the Fishing Industry and are intended for use on the smaller Motor Vessels of about 50 ft. in length, where saving in weight and space is essential. The Capstan only weighs 5 cwt., but will pull 3 cwt., and the weight of the whole equipment is only 16½ cwt.

CAPSTAN CYLINDERS :	BORE	2½"	DIAMETER OF BARREL		1' 3"
" "	STROKE	3½"	HEIGHT	" "	1' 6"
TOTAL HEIGHT		3' 0"	WEIGHT		5 cwt.
DIAMETER OF BOILER (OVER SHELL)		2' 0"			
HEIGHT " "		...	4' 11"		

Total Weight of the Set - 16½ cwt.

John Buchanan of Beccles, for many years secretary to the Trust, undertook its restoration. Whilst Elliott and Garood were no longer trading, invaluable helped was provided by a former foreman, Clary Kerridge. In 1989, John Buchanan was awarded the Dorothea Award for Industrial Archaeology for the high standard of his restoration work. Although the restoration was completed right down to the puffing steam engine; when the unit was fitted to *Excelsior*, it was decided to operate the capstan with a compressor, rather than steam.

Gary Brown made the new spar single handed, but with advice from his father, Arthur Brown, who was Richard's Shipbuilders sparmaker. There was a lot of advice from elders and betters around during the rebuild! It must have been fifty years since a spar of such size had been made in Lowestoft. *Excelsior's* new mast was hewn by hand from a fifty seven foot (17.8 metres to trainee seamen) Douglas fir tree, nearly three feet (.9m) in diameter at the butt. The finished length was 53' (16.5m) and generally 1'3" in diameter. It is octagonal below decks, round to the hounds, and "D" shaped at the cap to accommodate the topmast. Over two hundredweight (100kg) of fittings had to be fixed. The mizzen was only slightly smaller at 49'6" (15.5m). Both masts were lowered

The mainmast taking shape in March 1987. *photo David Standley* into position on 25th June 1987, when the opportunity was taken to lower the water tank into the main cabin.

Traditionally smack masts had been made from pitch pine, which is no longer available in the required lengths. As if to prove that work on an old wooden boat is never finished, the new mast broke on the way to Copenhagen during the 1996 Tall Ships Race, after less than ten years. The Douglas fir may have rotted but at least it got her sailing again. A replacement was fashioned out of larch, after a suitable tree was found in Scotland and delivered to Lowestoft via Hull, where Barchards carried out the rough sawing.

One day in April 1987, a retired Canadian gentleman came to visit the re-emerging *Excelsior*. He introduced himself as Captain Strong, of St. John's, Newfoundland. Jimmy's boy! Captain Strong was staying with his sister, Mrs. Eva Spindler of Lowestoft. A seafarer himself, he was introduced to the team, shown over the boat and had a look at the new mast in production. He later wrote - " I can appreciate the work, problems and satisfaction - involved, solved and achieved in your project. My congratulations to the Trust on the work to date and continued success in the future"

The windlass and some original ironwork had been recovered from beneath a hut in Norway, where it had lain since her conversion to a motor coaster. This too was painstakingly rebuilt. It's apparently simple structure belied it's sixty nine components.

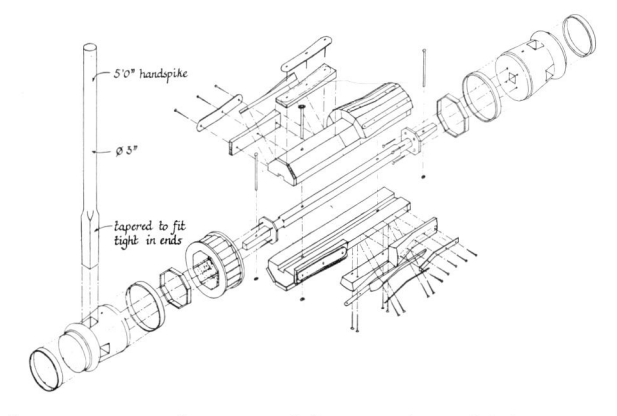

The Windlass. an extract from one of the many beautiful drawings executed by trainee, Mike Vining

Excelsior's first sea trial took place on Friday 29th July 1988. No-one on board was entirely sure what to expect but most were impressed by her steadiness and relieved that all their hard work had been to good effect. Two accompanying boats of photographers had to struggle to keep up as she reached eight knots.

photo. John Mummery

HRH the Princess Anne recommissioning *Excelsior* at Lowestoft on August 5th 1988 with Lord Somerleyton, Bishop Hugh Blackburne and a very proud John Wylson.

At the recommissioning, Lord Somerleyton welcomed the Princess with the following words:

"It is with great pleasure that we welcome you on board *Excelsior* today. It hardly seems possible that six years ago, two young men gave up the unequal struggle of restoring *Excelsior* on their own and set about forming a Trust to help them in their endeavours. The Trust was formed by several starry eyed individuals, some of whom, including myself, suffered from bouts of very cold feet at the enormity of the task we had set ourselves!"

"There we were, (about ten individuals), with what can at best be described as a hulk with a sound bottom, no money and mooring fees to pay."

"Within two years, we had built up sufficient interest for Waveney District Council to give us a generous grant from their Charitable Lottery. At the same time, there was a downturn in activity in the shipping and fishing industries in Lowestoft which meant that unemployment became very serious. The Manpower Services Commission, much to their credit and our good fortune, agreed that the restoration of *Excelsior* would make a good community programme, as Lowestoft had a long tradition of building wooden vessels and was one of the last ports to have a sizeable sailing contingent within their fishing fleet."

"The skills were all here - it was just a matter of dusting off some cobwebs and getting fathers to show their sons how jobs were done."

"*Excelsior* is a classic example of a specialised industrial sailing craft at the peak of its development. - she also typifies the history of her age. Built by Chambers of Lowestoft in 1921, to replace an earlier vessel, she fished out of Lowestoft until 1936, when she was sold away .. ."

"A vessel like *Excelsior,* however well restored, cannot remain just a thing of beauty to be looked at and admired from afar - she needs to be regularly used and maintained to keep her in good heart and to keep alive the knowledge and feel of sailing vessels very different from their modern counterparts ... "

The Princess unveiled the plaque on the bulkhead in the main cabin.

Despite the fine words, *Excelsior* was still not finished. Basic equipment was required and accommodation still had to be fitted below decks. Work had progressed ahead of the fund raising. By Easter of 1989, the Trust were obliged to lay off the workforce for a fortnight. Funding the restoration process had been far from easy and a great deal of energy was expended by a large number of people. The same year, the Trust was a finalist in the Scania Transport Trust

Award for preserving the nation's transport heritage, but were unfortunately pipped at the post by the Windermere Steamboat Museum.

On the second of July 1989, John Wylson handed the restored *Excelsior* over to Mick Hart, who was to become her first skipper in her new existence as a sail training ship. Under Mick's command, she made her way to London with a film crew on board, to take part in her first Tall Ships Race. She managed a satisfactory third in her class, amongst a fleet of 120 competitors.

Mick Hart with John Wylson. This photograph was published on the front page of a Norwegian daily news paper on *Excelsiors* return under sail.

Excelsior off Pakefield. Photographed by John Mummery the shot was published by the Trust as a card.

Cutty Sark Tall Ships Race 1989, from *Excelsior* entering Hamburg. *photo. archives*

Excelsior entering Plymouth during the 1991 Tall Ships Race.
photo. Peter Dawes

If raising the money to complete the restoration had been difficult, then her new occupation as a sail training vessel provided a whole new series of challenges. Shell Expro (UK) stepped in with a donation of £10,000 in 1990 to celebrate the opening of their Clipper Platform in the Sole Pit gas field; waters that were and still are used by *Excelsior*. Shell continued to support sail training for local schools for several years. The Foundation for Sport and the Arts most generously gave £50,000 in 1992. The Trust has been extremely fortunate in its gifts both large and small. £5.00 from a pensioner may be proportionately greater than any corporate gift the Trust could receive. Waveney District Council have over the years contributed mightily, not least allowing the Trust use of a quay, blighted by road proposals. Norfolk, Essex and Suffolk Training Services donated new sails, the largest single item required to finish the boat and costing in the region of £14,000. All were extremely gratefully received and whilst a list crediting each benefactor would be proper, today's reader may be less than enthralled.

Excelsior never ceases to pull the crowds and carries out a fine job as a silent ambassador for Lowestoft. Since her rebuild, she has sailed the equivalent of twice around the world and given over five thousand, sometimes disadvantaged young people a chance to go to sea. She is all that remains of an era of fishing without hydrocarbons; but the heritage is saved and there to be shared. Adults, families, even management training groups sail aboard. The famous LT registration marks have been carried to the Arctic Circle, St. Petersburg and Corunna, far farther than her traditional fishing grounds.

A wise visitor. This long eared owl stopped for a rest when *Excelsior* was en route to Bergen. *photo. archives*

Excelsior must be one of the most photogenic boats afloat. Wherever she goes she excites interest and spectators. Clicking lenses don't pay bills but her alternative role as a film star has helped.

***Excelsior* with a reefed mainsail, about to shoot her trawl.** *Photo. Wylson*

On Monday 21st April 1997, *Excelsior* slipped out of Lowestoft harbour on her first fishing expedition for fifty eight years. The Trust had been asked to participate in a Television programme for Channel 4's Real History series. The task was to authentically recreate conditions for trawling under sail in the 1880's. Even the crew had to be dressed as nineteenth century fishermen. Preparation and research required was substantial and skipper Stewart White went as far as Fleetwood to seek help from a Lowestoft smacksman. Many of the modern deck fittings for her new existence as a sail training ship were reoved and the capstan was replaced with an hydraulic powered replica of a full-sized smack's capstan. A forty-five foot (14m) trawl beam was stowed along the port side of her hull. The cameras failed to show Victor Vigo di Gallidoro below decks with his electronics! *Excelsior's* restoration as a fishing smack was completed and she caught a kit of fish. She is now the only surviving British sailing trawler capable of trawling in the traditional manner.

When *Excelsior* trawled for a living, the area currently used as a for'ard cabin held the nets and the fishing gear. The main cabin was the fish hold, the engine compartment held a steam boiler and the crews quarters were in the stern, precisely as at present.

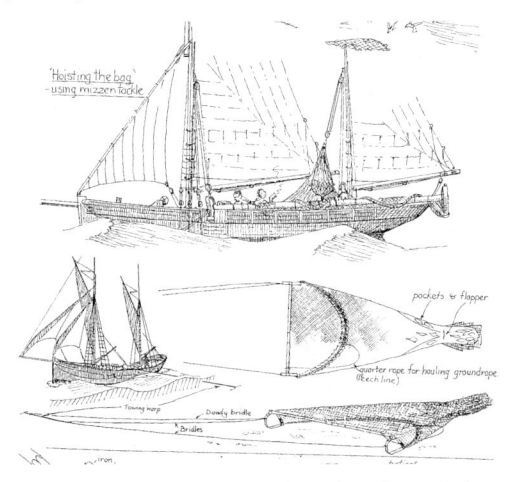

Diagram of trawling from a sailing smack. Taken from "The Trawlermen," by courtesy of David Butcher

Safety has always been a prime consideration in operating *Excelsior* and her skippers have received two awards for seamanship. In 1997, thanks to the work of Stewart White and his crew, *Excelsior* was awarded the seamanship prize of the Honourable Company of Master Mariners, for the manner in which they coped with their broken mast between Turku and Copenhagen. It was a prize she had received several years earlier, when skipper Mick Hart had to cope with a broken bowsprit during the Tall Ships Race in 1990, on the way to Corunna.

None of the skippers would object to the observation that their job requires the patience of Job, combined with quite remarkable depths of resourcefulness.

Stewart White (left) and Bill Ewen. After several years as mate, Bill took over as skipper for the 2000 season.

Excelsior anchored in a Norwegian fjord en route to Bergen.   *photo. archives*

A scale model of *Excelsior* made by D.R. Castle Smith of Lowestoft and presented to the Excelsior Trust. A full set of drawings suitable for model makers are available from the Trust. *photo. editor*

The newsletters that the Trust published during *Excelsior*'s rebuild, show the massive weight of enthusiasm behind the project and include several anecdotes from "good old boys" who wanted to be a part of it. They can't tell us any more of their stories and many of their considerable skills passed away with them. No longer is it possible for fathers to tell sons how it was done. Whilst the stories gave the boat a sense of history and belonging, the skills were and are essential to maintaining a traditional sailing trawler. By 1998, crew costs were spiralling, smaller shipyards closing fast and maintenance costs rising inexorably. Should facilities became unavailable in Lowestoft, the next yard was on the Humber. The Trust needed to take a brave step forward to ensure it's survival. If income from sail training never quite seemed to cover costs, then commercial rates of maintenance would be prohibitive.

After two years of fund raising, greatly assisted by the European Regional Development Fund and the East of England Development Agency, the Excelsior Trust acquired a disused shipyard, as a secure maintenance and operating base for the future. Here, the required skills can be kept alive for the future. Coincidentally, this was the very same shipyard where Mark Trevitt had found the original steam capstan, a quarter of century earlier and where George Prior had allowed *Excelsior* to be slipped fifteen years before, to have most of her planking replaced. The yard has two slipways and the Trust has developed extensive woodworking and metalworking facilities for those who need to develop their skills in a genuine industrial environment. Skilled men are retained to pass on their knowledge. Long term restoration projects include H1394 *City of Edinboro'*, the only surviving Hull sailing trawler, now into her second century, and RX8 *Estralita*, an original and possibly unique East

Channel Punt. The slipways are rarely idle and many local firms make use of the facilities. The Trust hopes to help bring this part of Lake Lothing back to life, with the community actively enjoying its rich maritime heritage.

Excelsior on her own slipway. Compare this photograph with that on page 15. *photo. Editor*

Acknowledgments.

All our thanks are due to John Wylson. Despite an earlier incarnation in the Merchant Navy and a career in architecture, *Excelsior* has occupied much of his life. She is very largely a story of one man's struggle; ranging from hard, dirty, work, to begging, cajoling, scrounging and pleading. The dream is realised. He will probably be embarrassed by the accolade and the first to point out the considerable help given by an army of others. Nevertheless it remains true that without John Wylson's continued drive and enthusiasm, the project to rebuild and preserve a Lowestoft smack for the future would never have come to fruition.

Acknowledgments and fullest thanks are due to so many, not the least to Micropress Ltd., of Halesworth for their understanding in producing this booklet. Over the years, the Excelsior Trust has received so many gifts of money, in kind, of enthusiasm, information and professional help. It has been a huge effort against all the odds but she survives for all to admire and share. *Excelsior* today is a fine tribute to Lowestoft men. To the many thousands that earned their living in the fishing industry and a fitting memorial to the very large numbers of sailing fishermen that died at sea.

The Trust seek a true and accurate record and pictorial history of the boat. Inevitably there will be unintentional omissions and inaccuracies in this booklet. If you should find fault, please do not hesitate to advise the Trust.

photo. Andrew Wolstenholme

Glossary of nautical terms based on words encountered within this leaflet and in the sense implied within the leaflet.

Aft. Rear section of a vessel
Beam. Width of a ship's hull
Berth. A "parking space" for a ship or person.
Bilge. The inside of the bottom part of a ship.
Bow. Fore part of a vessel.
Bowsprit. (pronounced bo'sprit) Spar projecting over the bow for setting foresails.
Bulkhead. "Wall", divisions of a ship at right angles to the centreline.
Bulwark. That part of the ship's side that is above the deck.
Butts. Square ended joints.
Capstan. Hauling device with a vertical drum.
Caulking. Material driven into joints to make them watertight.
Coaster. Small vessel carrying coastal cargoes.
Counter. Overhanging part of the stern.
Cutter. Fore and aft rigged sailing boat with one mast and usually more than one headsail.
Drifter. Fishing vessel for surface feeding fish.
Framing. The ribs of a ship.
Fifie. Scots fishing boat. Several were built in the yard of William Fife, father of the famous yacht designer.
Gaff. Spar with one at the mast and the other holding out the head of the sail.
Ketch. Two masted rig with the mizzen mast for'ard of the steering position.
Kit. 10 stones of fish.
Knot. A nautical mile per hour.
Mizzen. After mast, usually shorter than the mainmast.
Octant. Navigational instrument - similar to a sextant.
Port. Left hand side of a boat looking forwards.
Shrouds. Wire or rope supports for the mast, usually from the point of maximum beam of a hull.
Starboard. The right hand side of a vessel, looking forwards.
Stern. rear of a vessel
Strake. A continuous run of planks for from stem to stern
Sweep. Large oar used singly.
Tussie (also known as baggywrinkle.) Furry looking addition to rigging to prevent chafe. Usually made from old rope.
Warp. Rope, traditionally made from hemp.
Windlass. a winch for retrieving the anchor cable.
Zulu. Around 1878, William Campbell of Lossiemouth built the first Zulu. It was a bigger, faster version of the Fifie and gained its name as the Zulu wars were in progress at the time.

Excelsior needs Friends!

The Excelsior Trust welcomes your support and has two membership categories: Friend of The Excelsior Trust or Governor of the Excelsior Trust. The latter category includes a free days sail on *Excelsior* in your first year of Governorship.

- Both categories of membership enjoy the benefits of The Excelsior Trust which include:

- A newsletter, published several times a year to keep you up to date with the Trust's activities.

- Invitations to social events in East Anglia.

- The sailing programme, showing dates and voyages in which you may wish to participate.

- Excelsior Trust merchandise for sale, including ties, postcards, videos, mugs, pens, car stickers etc..

- The opportunity to step aboard Excelsior in Lowestoft and meet the crew.

- A certificate of your membership.

For an application to become either a Friend or a Governor of the Excelsior Trust, please either telephone 01502 - 580507 or write to:

The Excelsior Trust,
Harbour Road,
Oulton Broad,
Lowestoft. NR32 3LY

Registered Charity Number 285899.